John Pendleton Farrow

**History of Islesborough, Maine**

John Pendleton Farrow

**History of Islesborough, Maine**

ISBN/EAN: 9783337406776

Printed in Europe, USA, Canada, Australia, Japan

Cover: Foto ©Andreas Hilbeck / pixelio.de

More available books at **www.hansebooks.com**

John S. Farrow

# HISTORY

OF

# ISLESBOROUGH,
## MAINE.

BY

## JOHN PENDLETON FARROW,
### MASTER MARINER.

BANGOR:
THOMAS W. BURR, PRINTER.
1893.

FROM THE PRESS OF THOMAS W. BURR, BANGOR, ME.

# PREFACE.

In the performance of this work I have availed myself of the records of the Massachusetts archives, and by the kindness of the town clerk I have had the records of the town, many books, magazines, and papers of early settlers, and the traditionary information from aged persons that have passed away, and from many still living. It affords me great pleasure to acknowledge the generous aid received from kind friends, and to them I tender my sincere thanks.

I have tried to avoid the error of conflicting statements. If mistakes are detected, they are such as would naturally occur in a cento of so many authors. The genealogies of the families are not complete, as they do not extend in the records in full up to this date. The family records that are complete have been obtained, for the last ten years, by personal knowledge, and prior to this by the town records, and in other ways to which I have made reference. I hope the perusal of its pages may be of interest to the native born, and also to the stranger who may spend his summers on this beautiful island.

In writing this History I have received great assistance from Hon. Joseph Williamson, of Belfast, and Hon. Joseph W. Porter, of Bangor, members of the Maine Historical Society, and of the New England Historic-Genealogical Society. These gentlemen are acknowledged authorities in all matters relating to the early settlers of this town and their descendants. Without their assistance I should not have been able to put this in print. I feel old age coming on, and if in 'after years any historical value is gathered from the annals of Islesborough, I shall be amply rewarded for my labor.

I am also under great obligations to Mr. L. H. Murch, of Belfast, for valuable assistance, and to Messrs. Winsor and Dixon, of the Islesborough Land and Improvement Company, for favors. It has required a great deal more time and labor to perform this work than was first anticipated. The information could not be obtained without expense and trouble. It was not done for a mercenary motive, and I do not expect to realize any pecuniary benefit. After the materials were accumulated I was undecided whether to put this in print, but by the advice of friends I have concluded to do so, for the benefit of the inhabitants and their descendants. The manuscript has been read by competent authority, and the work must stand or fall on its own merits.

I now submit the History of Islesborough to my fellow townsmen, with its errors, hoping it may be accepted, in lieu of a better one that may be written in after years.

JOHN P. FARROW.

ISLESBOROUGH, April, 1893.

# ABSTRACT OF CONTENTS.

# INDEX OF ILLUSTRATIONS.

# INDEX OF NAMES.

—

## A

## B

## C

## H

## J

## K

## L

## M

# History of Islesborough.

## CHAPTER I.

### DESCRIPTION OF ISLESBOROUGH.

THE town of Islesborough is beautifully situated on Penobscot Bay. Its extreme length is nearly thirteen miles, and it varies in width from three rods to two miles, without any very high hills or deep valleys. Its area is six thousand acres. It was formerly named Longue Island, being so designated on the map of Eman Bowen, geographer to King William III of England, 1747.

Capt. Benjamin Church* made his third expedition to Maine in 1692, and arrived in Penobscot Bay in August. He landed on Seven-Hundred-Acre Island, where he found a few French and Indians. They fled over to Long Island in fair sight of Church, and got away from him, as he had no boats suitable for the chase. He followed over to Long Island, where he found more French and Indians, who also fled. His boats were no match for their canoes. He seized considerable plunder here, mostly beaver and moose skins. He soon after sailed away for the westward.

### THE WALDO PATENT.

As this patent is the foundation for all the land titles in Islesborough, a brief description of it is here given.

---

* Church's Narratives, by Rev. Henry M. Dexter, D. D., LL.D., edition of 1867, and Bangor Historical Magazine, vol. VI, page 252.

In 1620 King James I of England* granted about all of
the continent of North America to forty noblemen,
knights and gentlemen, who were styled "The Council of
Plymouth, in Devon, England." This Council surren-
dered its charter in 1635, (having been outgeneraled by
the Massachusetts settlers). Before surrendering it they
made several grants of land within the State of Maine,
which held good. One of these grants was known as
the Muscongus Patent, now known as the Waldo Patent,
which had in it, by estimation, nearly one thousand square
miles. It included the whole of Knox County except Fox
Islands, and of Waldo County except some towns in the
western part, Long Island, now Islesborough, which,
being within three miles of the main land, was claimed
and held as in the grant, and a part of Penobscot County.
In the course of time the grant came into the hands of
General Samuel Waldo, who died near Bangor, on the
east side of Penobscot river, May 23, 1759, aged 63
years. From General Waldo the grant descended to his
heirs.

In the year 1789, George Washington, President of the
United States, appointed Henry Knox, Esq., Secretary
for the Department of War, which office he filled for over
five years. He then obtained the reluctant consent of
Washington to retire. In consequence of his marriage
with Lucy Flucker, she having her inheritance of a portion of the Waldo Patent, Brigadier Waldo's estate was
divided in five portions ; and, his son Ralph having previously deceased without issue, it was shared as follows :
viz., Col. Samuel Waldo (2), by right of primogeniture,
two shares ; Francis Waldo, Mrs. Hannah Flucker, and
Mrs. Lucy Winslow, one share each. Thomas Flucker,
the husband of Hannah Waldo, having in 1765 purchased
of her brother Samuel his two shares of said estate, and

* Joseph Williamson's History of Belfast, page 36.

having since, in consequence of his having joined the
British, been declared an outlaw, and his estate confis-
cated, Mrs. Knox, the only loyal member of his family, became seized in right of her mother of one-fifth part of the
Waldo Patent ; and the two other fifths belonging to her
father remained to be disposed of by an agent or admin-
istrator appointed by the Judge of Probate for the County
of Suffolk, the late residence of said Flucker. Joseph
Pierce, the agent first appointed, seems to have confined
his doings to the property in Boston, or other parts of
Massachusetts proper, and, having resigned his office,
was succeeded by Gen. Knox, in accordance with a resolve of the General Court of June 28, 1784. His bond
was given to Oliver Wendell, Judge of Probate for Suffolk
county, for 20,000 pounds, with Benjamin Hitchborn and
Henry Jackson, Esqs., as sureties ; at which time Flucker
was styled an absentee, lately deceased. In October, 1790,
Knox obtained license of the Supreme Judicial Court to
sell all the real estate of Thomas Flucker, and, May 27,
1791, gave bonds faithfully to account for the same to
the State treasurer. Having been duly sworn before
Judge Iredell, of Philadelphia, and having caused adver-
tisements, dated March 21, 1791, to be posted up in
Boston, Charlestown, and Roxbury, as also at Pownal-
borough, Newcastle, Nobleborough, Waldoborough, Warren, Cushing, Megunticook, Thomaston, Camden, Meduncook, Ducktrap, Frankfort, Belfast, Penobscot, Union,
and Hope, he made sale, at the Bunch of Grapes tavern,
in State street, Boston, July 2, 1791, to Oliver Smith, of
Boston, of the two-fifths of the Waldo Patent belonging
to said Flucker's estate, estimated at sixty-five thousand
or seventy thousand acres, with the exception of what had
been sold prior to April 19, 1775, and subject to the conditions of the resolves of 1785 and 1788. This purchase
Smith conveyed to Henry Jackson, of Boston, who, Octo-

ber 1, 1792, transferred it to Gen. Knox, still of Philadelphia, for the sum of $5,200. In the following year, 1793, Knox purchased of Samuel Waldo (3d) and others, the two remaining fifths; and thus, in his own right and that inherited by his wife, became sole proprietor of the Waldo estate, with the exception of what had been previously alienated.

Knox having now become the owner of the extensive domain, lost no time in taking possession, occupying, and improving the same. As the quitclaim deed from the heirs of Francis Waldo and Lucy Winslow could legally transfer only such estate as they were in actual possession of, and as large portions of it had been taken up and were in the actual possession of those who had settled upon it during and since the war of the Revolution, it was necessary to put the grantee in possession by actual entry on these lots, and by "livery and seizin made by sod and twig." This legal ceremony was gone through with by Ebenezer Vesey, attorney to the said heirs, and John S. Tyler, attorney to Gen. Knox, in the autumn of 1793, upon the lots of eighty-seven settlers in Thomaston, eighteen of Thomaston Marsh, sixty-one in Warren, seventy-five in Cushing, twelve in Camden, five in Canaan, seventy-two in Ducktrap, ten in Meduncook, one hundred and one in Waldoborough, one on Brigadier Island, eighteen in Islesborough, eight on the pond back of Ducktrap, and forty-seven in Frankfort.—[*Eaton's History of Thomaston and Rockland, page 207.*

### STATEMENT FROM THE KNOX PAPERS.

An estimate of land within the Waldo Patent belonging to the Winslow family, which they derive title to from a deed of division made by Brigadier Waldo's heirs, March 19th, 1768, and from a deed of Belcher Noyes, viz.:

First pr. divisional deed is assigned to I. Winslow, Esq.,

and Lucy his wife in her right, four islands. Contents:
Long Island, No. 92, 5,883 acres; No. 80, 655 acres; No.
81, 77 acres; No. 42, 6,657 acres.

## AGREEMENT BETWEEN HENRY KNOX AND LONG ISLAND

### SETTLERS, 3D AUG., 1799.

Memorandum of an agreement made at the house of Major
Philip Ulmer, in Ducktrap, this 3d day of August, 1799,
between Henry Knox on the one part, and the following
settlers on Long Island on the other.

1. That the following surveyors are hereby appointed to
make a survey, so far as to ascertain the distance from the
nearest part of the main to the centre of Long Island, and
that the said surveyors shall ascertain the centre of said
island : To wit, John Peters, of Bluehill Bay, to be notified
by the inhabitants of Long Island ; John Harkness, of
Cambden, to be notified by Henry Knox ; James Malcom,
Esq., of Cushing ; and if by any circumstances that one of
the said persons shall not accept the appointment, the other
two of said surveyors shall appoint a third.

The said surveyors shall be notified of this appointment as
soon as possible, and be desired to meet together for this
business on or before the tenth of September next ensuing,
and they shall as soon after proceed to the execution of the
trust reposed as they shall find it practicable.

2. The said surveyors and chainmen are to be sworn
to the faithful discharge of their duties ; and it is further
agreed that if the centre of said island shall be determined
to be less than three miles off the main, that Henry Knox
shall pay the entire expenses of said survey ; but if the
centre of said island shall be further than three miles, the
inhabitants of said island shall pay the expenses of the
survey.

3. And it is further agreed that if the centre of said
island shall be found within three miles of the main, that
John Harkness shall immediately proceed to the running out

of the lots referred to the commissioners, appointed by the Legislature of the Commonwealth.

*Witness to all the signers :*

PHILIP ULMER,
CHARLES ULMER.

H. KNOX, first part,
MIGHILL PARKER,
PRINCE HOLBROOK,
HOSEA COOMBS,
ELLISON LASSELLE,
NOAH DODGE,
NEHEMIAH (?) COOMBS,
THOMAS GILKEY,
JOHN GILKEY,
JOSEPH WILLIAMS,
GODFREY TRIM,
SAMUEL WILLIAMS,
SAMUEL VEAZIE,
FIELDS COOMBS,
JOSIAH FARROW,
JEREMIAH HATCH,
ROBERT SHERMAN,
JONATHAN PARKER.

1.   Capt. William Pendleton, 100 acres.
2.   Jonathan Pendleton, 100 acres.
3.   John Pendleton, 300 acres.
4.   Oliver Pendleton, 100 acres.
5.   Henry Pendleton, 100 acres.
6.   Capt. Shubael Williams, about 200 or 300 acres.
7.   Capt. John Gilkey, 100 acres.
8.   Thomas Gilkey derived his title from the heirs of Joshua Cheesbrook, who died about 1794. Admitted by Capt. William Pendleton in the year 1774, in May. 100 acres.
9.   William Elwell derived his title from Benj. Thomas originally, who conveyed to Nathaniel Pendleton, who conveyed it to Samuel Morse, who conveyed it to said Elwell. About 100 acres.
10.   Joseph Boardman, 1775. Taken up by himself. About 100 acres.

11. Joseph Pendleton derived his title from Thomas Pendleton, who took it up in the year 1769—an acknowledgment. About 100 acres. (Thomas Pendleton, Junior, was probably a minor before the war. Moved to an island in Passamaquoddy.)

12. Josiah Farrow derived from Nathaniel Pendleton, who conveyed to John Gilkey, who conveyed it to the present possessor. This lot was taken up in 1774. 100 acres.

13. Paoli Hewes, William Griffin, originally, who convey it to Silvester Cottrell in 1772, who conveyed it to Paoli Hewes, present possessor.

1. On Seven-Hundred-Acre Island. William Griffin. Taken up by Poll in 1774, and conveyed to said Griffin 118 acres.

2. David Thomas. Taken up by Samuel Turner and conveyed to said Thomas. Said lot was taken up in 1772. 10 acres.

3. Joseph Phillbrook, who derived his title from Elihu Cheesbrook, who took up said lot in 1774. 100 acres.

### LONG ISLAND DESCRIBED, ALSO AN ISLAND NEAR, OF SEVEN HUNDRED ACRES.

Long Island, in Penobscot Bay, is a superb island of about six thousand acres of excellent land. Said island is about twelve miles in length, possessing excellent harbours, and about two miles from the western shore of the bay. Excellent fisheries of cod, halibut and salmon are in its waters. It is all high land, that is favors (?) are on the main from, has upwards of sixty families thereon, all without title excepting agreements for about two thousand acres. This island is an incorporated township by the name of Islesborough.

The title perfect : Isaac Winslow, Esq., in the right of his wife, having had this as a divided portion in the year 1768, and was then and afterwards in the undisputed possession thereof. At the latter end of the war the settlers or usurpers went on the island. Before the war there were several tenants on lease, all of whom have expired. The heirs of

Isaac Winslow and wife conveyed to the subscriber in the year 1793. References to a committee of the General Court for the price which should be given. A bond given by the settlers and the subscriber; but when the surveyors went upon the business of the surveyors, some of the settlers declined having their lands surveyed. This can only occasion an enhancement of price. The agreements which have been made were at two hundred and twenty-five cents per acre in the year 1797, with interest from the date. If the references shall not be carried into effect, it is probable that the release form of compromise sale of three dollars would leave the island without inhabitants, under state of nature. The subscriber has solid reasons to believe that he could obtain at the rate from ten to twelve dollars per acre. At present it abounds with excellent farms and many good houses, and some with no buildings thereon, may be averaged at an higher rate than twelve dollars. There are many vessels belonging to the inhabitants, used on the coast, and every flat of wood is so circumstanced that it may command ready market at one dollar per cord.

There is an island in the neighborhood called Seven Hundred Acres, which also probably belongs to the subscriber, although some doubts have been entertained by the inhabitants. Mr. Winslow possessed it completely before the war, and the centre of it is, I have no doubt, within three miles of the main, which is the criterion of its belonging to the subscriber.

After having given this description the estimation is made that it will net the subscriber from fifteen hundred to eighteen hundred dollars, the payment of which will be secured by the possessions, buildings and farms of the inhabitants, and better security cannot well be imagined, as the property will amount to four times that sum.

This island may be conveyed for security of the following notes:

One note of $3,752.98-100
One ditto of   5,000
One ditto of   6,000
————
$14,752.98-100

GILKEY'S HARBOR AND CAMDEN MOUNTAINS.

GULF POINT, FROM ISLESBOROUGH INN.

If this security should be accepted by the note-holders in the above farms, payable in five or six years with interest annually, the joint bond of Knox and Jackson* will be given for the first sum, and the name of B. Lincoln† thereto added for the two others.

In this case it would be desired that the sum for three thousand eight hundred dollars should be suspended, and two notes taken, payable with interest in eighteen months, given by Knox and endorsed by H. Jackson, and with security if desired ; but the money shall be punctually paid at the time stipulated.

## THE FIRST SETTLERS.

Mighill Parker, Esq., of Islesborough, wrote Governor Williamson in 1821 that Benjamin Thomas, from Cape Elizabeth, was the first settler, in 1768, bringing his family here in 1769. But from the most thorough investigation, I am satisfied that Shubael Williams was the first settler. He came in 1764, and cleared land on the east side, at what is now known as Bounty Cove, near the center of the island. Here he built a log house. With him were his sons Samuel, Amos, Joseph and Benjamin. His lot extended from the east to the west bay, and contained about three hundred acres. In 1786 he conveyed his home to his son Benjamin (unmarried), from whom it descended to the other members of the family. These facts are well authenticated by the descendants of Shubael now living on the island, being handed down from father to son, and are fully substantiated by an old gentleman, now living, and over seventy years of age. Without doubt Samuel Pendleton came with Shubael and settled on the east side, on what is known as Little Island, in the month of September, 1764, and his descendants live there yet. When Shubael Williams came

---

* Gen. Henry Jackson.

† Gen. Benjamin Lincoln.

2

to Long Island, his son Amos was ten years old. Amos was the grandfather of Thomas and Emery Williams.

William Pendleton, from Stonington, Conn., came in September, 1769, with his sons, John, Job, Harry, Jonathan and Oliver. All settled at the extreme southern part of Islesborough, except Job, who settled on an island adjacent, which now bears his name. All this property is now owned by Mr. Jeffrey R. Brackett. It includes the extreme end of Islesborough, formerly the Thomas Boardman lot, and contains a total of five hundred acres. On the main island Mr. Brackett has built a summer residence, the outlook from which is not surpassed on the coast of New England. The property of John and Oliver is now owned by the Islesborough Land and Improvement Company, of Philadelphia. On Oliver's lot is situated the splendid hotel known as the "Islesborough Inn." This company has improved the land, and what was formerly Oliver's lot has been sold at great prices to wealthy people, who are now (1892) erecting costly cottages.

Thomas Pendleton, from Stonington, Conn., came in 1775, with his sons Thomas, Samuel, Gideon, Joshua, Nathaniel and Stephen. He settled on the east side, below what is now known as Hewes' Point. Most of this land is now owned by his great-great-grandchildren, who are wealthy and enterprising. Thomas Pendleton, senior, was a cousin to William Pendleton, senior. It is said that Hon. George H. Pendleton, late United States Minister to Berlin, was a grandson of Thomas Pendleton, senior.

Elder Thomas Ames came from Marshfield in 1770, with his son Jabez. They settled on a beautiful point of land on the east side of what is now known as Gilkey's Harbor, to the west of Ames' Cove. Elder Ames was the first settled minister. When he moved off the island Mr.

The editor throws in a query here.

Ames conveyed his land to Joseph Woodard. Joseph Woodard conveyed to James Sherman, who lived here and raised a large family. At his death Sherman's heirs conveyed to John Pendleton Farrow, who sold to J. D. Winsor, of Philadelphia, President of the Islesborough Land and Improvement Company, who now holds the estate of one hundred and twenty-six acres.

Captain John Gilkey came in 1772, probably from Cape Cod. He settled on the west side of Gilkey's Harbor, and it is from him that this harbor derived its name.

Valentine Sherman and his son Robert came about 1791, probably from Connecticut. Both settled at Gilkey's Harbor, near Elder Thomas Ames. Valentine sold his land to his son on Aug. 1, 1792.

Capt. Anthony Coombs senior came about 1782, from New Meadows, with his sons Anthony, Jesse, Robert and Ephraim. He settled on the lot next north of Shubael Williams, where the meeting house now stands. His descendants still own and live on part of the estate. His sons settled on the north-east side of the island, above Sabbath-Day Harbor, where they built a saw and grist mill.

Capt. Peter Coombs, senior, came in 1784 or 1785 from Brunswick. He settled at Sabbath-Day Harbor, on the lot now occupied by "The Islesborough" hotel and other buildings, summer cottages, steamboat wharves, stores, etc. He sold his land to Mighill Parker in 1791, Aug. 1, and returned to Brunswick. Mr. Parker sold to Joseph Ryder, whose grandson, Jason Roscoe Ryder, still lives on and owns part of the estate. Mr. Ryder, senior, had a grist mill on his land and a tide mill, where the early settlers carried their grist to be ground.

Hosea and Fields Coombs, brothers, came about 1782. Hosea settled northerly of Capt. Anthony Coombs, on the

lot known as that of the late Capt. Solomon P. Coombs, a
grandson of Hosea.  On this lot are the cottages of Hon.
Joseph W. Porter, Sanborn, Bragg, Garland, Burr, Spratt
and Milliken.  Fields Coombs settled at the head of Sabbath-Day Harbor.  Philip Coombs, a grandson of Anthony Coombs, and now 84 years old, says that there is no
relation between his family and the descendants of Hosea
and Fields.*

Joseph and Peter Woodard came in 1784 from Hingham, Mass., and first settled on the north-easterly side of
the island.  Joseph afterwards bought Elder Ames' lot at
Gilkey's Harbor, and also the lot now owned by John P.
Farrow, which had been sold to Derby Academy, of Hingham, Mass., by Joseph Woodard.  Joseph was drowned
in Belfast Bay.  Peter probably moved away.

Sylvester Cottrell came about 1786, and settled on or
near Hewes' Point.  He sold his lot July 1, 1790, to Samuel Jackson, of Boston.  This deed was the first recorded
in Hancock County Records.  Mr. Cottrel is said to
have died in Miramichi.

Elihu Hewes came about the same time, and settled on
the Cottrell lot on Hewes' Point, which was named for
him.

Joseph Boardman came in 1774, from Boston.  He
married here the same year, and settled on the extreme
southerly point of the island.  His descendants say he
was one of the innumerable number who threw the tea
overboard in Boston Harbor.

Benjamin Marshall was here early.  The town records
say, "Old Mr. Ben. Marshall came to town meeting July
5, 1793.  He was probably the father of Thomas Marshall, who settled on the northerly end of the island."

Simon Dodge, senior, came about 1784, from Block
Island, R. I., with sons Simon, Noah, Rathburn, Mark,

---

* Query by the editor.

SAMUEL WARREN, SEN.

A First Settler.

Israel, Solomon, and Joshua. He settled on the east side, below Mr. Thomas Pendleton, on what is now known as the Bonnet. His sons settled on various parts of the island, some at the north-west side. Joshua lived and died on the home estate. Walter F. Dodge, son of Joshua, was a man of note in Islesborough, and was buried on the home lot.

William Burns came before 1794, from Bristol, Me. There are none of his name on the island at the present time.

Joseph Pendleton, son of Peleg, came about 1790 from Stonington. He settled on the southern part of the island, above Dark Harbor. The estate extended from the east bay to Gilkey Harbor on the west. It remained in the family more than ninety years. Then it was sold to the Islesborough Land and Improvement Company, of Philadelphia. They have improved the land by building roads. It is at present occupied by J. Murray Howe and family, of Boston, Mass.

Samuel Warren came before 1790, probably from Bristol. His oldest son John was a Quaker preacher, and at one time visited England.

Charles Newell was here in 1789.

Samuel Veazie came from Harpswell or Brunswick, about 1790. He was son of Rev. Samuel Veazie of Harpswell, and also of Hull and Duxbury, Massachusetts, and who graduated from Harvard College 1757. Samuel, Jr., settled on the northerly part of the island, east side, where his descendants now live.

Ellison Lasselle first settled on Lasselle Island, and afterwards on the extreme northern end of the island. His lot included Turtle Head. In all over one hundred acres. This property went into the hands of a relation, the founder of Lasell Female Seminary, who at his death willed it to three nephews, William, Edward and Zenas

Laury, who sold the property to J. P. Farrow, who sold
it to James Dodge. Dodge in turn sold it to Dr. A. S.
Davis, of Chelsea, Mass., who built him a cottage on the
head, and was the pioneer to build summer cottages in
Islesborough.

Rev. Charles Turner Thomas was here in 1788, and
married Mary Gilkey. He may have been a son of Benjamin Thomas, senior.

William Grinnell came before 1791, from Block Island,
R. I. He was selectman that year. He settled on the
west side, below Sprague's Cove. He sold out to Joshua
Moody, and moved to Belfast, where he died Dec. 5, 1842.
Moody's grandson, John Moody, who is eighty-seven
years old, now lives on the same lot.

Josiah Farrow came about 1790 from Bristol. He was
a Revolutionary soldier.

John Farrow came in 1785 from Bristol. He was a
nephew of Josiah Farrow, and he purchased the land of
Benjamin Thomas. He built the schooners Rebecca,
Mayflower, Specia, Rialto, and Mary Jane. His great-
great-grandson, John O. Farrow, still lives on the estate.

Jonathan Parker came before 1795, from Groton, Mass.
He settled on the northerly end, east side, next north of
Samuel Veazie.

Godfrey Trim came about 1792, or before, with his sons
Godfrey, James and Robert. He settled on the north end
and east side.

Simon Parker was here 1791. He bought the lots of
Benjamin Coombs and John Sprague.

Mighill Parker came about 1790. He bought out Capt.
Peter Coombs at Sabbath-Day Harbor. The lot was
afterwards owned by Joseph Ryder.

Prince Holbrook, from Brunswick, came here about
1790.

Joseph Jones here in 1791. He married Betsey Ames, daughter of Elder Thomas Ames. They had no children.

William Elwell came in 1789, from Burton's Island, St. George. He removed to Northport.

David Thomas came before 1786. He settled on the north end of Acre Island. The names of the children have an "Old Colony flavor."

Adam Turner was one of the early settlers.

John Sprague came before 1794. His lot was near Sprague's Cove, west side. Lydia Sprague, widow of Jonathan, brother of John, came about 1800, with her sons, Simon, Solomon and Rathburn, and settled on the west side near Sprague's Cove.

Elisha Nash, from Weymouth, Mass., came in 1791, and bought a lot August 1st.

Jeremiah Hatch, Jr., came here about 1780, from Marshfield, Massachusetts, settled on the south-west side. His descendants live on this lot.

Benjamin Thomas, Jr., came in 1790, from Marshfield, Massachusetts. He settled on the north end of Seven-Hundred-Acre Island. This property remained in the family one hundred years. Then sold to Islesborough Land and Improvement Company.

# CHAPTER II.

## GENERAL KNOX AND THE SETTLERS.

IN 1788 the inhabitants sent a petition to the General Court asking for examination of the claim of General Knox to the ownership of the island, and for incorporation as a town. For some reason action on the petition relating to the claim was deferred for several years. In the meantime many of the settlers took deeds from General Knox, while others, the most of whom lived above the Narrows, declined to do so. After further petitions the General Court, March 9, 1797, appointed a commission to "settle and declare their rights." I give a copy of reference and agreement:

Whereas the Legislature of this Commonwealth, by a resolve passed on the ninth day of March last, appointed Nathan Dane, John Sprague, and Enoch Titcomb, Esquires, commissioners, they, or the major part of them, to settle and declare the terms on which any settler on the lands held under the late Brigadier General Samuel Waldo (and not heretofore alienated) shall be quieted in the possession of one hundred acres of land, that may best include his improvements, and who hath not made any agreement in writing concerning the lands with Henry Knox, Esquire, representative of the heirs of the said Waldo, as by the same resolve may appear ;

And whereas, since the war with Great Britain, to wit, in the year of our Lord one thousand seven hundred and eighty-seven, William Burns was a settler on a lot of one hundred acres of land situated in Islesborough, the bounds

ISLESBOROUGH SKETCH.

whereof shall be ascertained and settled by the said commissioners in their report hereon—the same lot being part of the land held under the said Waldo and said William Burns, a claimant now in possession thereof ;

Now, in pursuance of the said resolve and appointment, we the said Henry Knox, representative as aforesaid, and the said William Burns, do refer and submit it to the said commissioners, they or the major part of them, to settle and declare the terms aforesaid on which the said William Burns, his heirs and assigns, shall be quieted in the possession of the said lot, holding ourselves, our heirs, executors, administrators and assigns respectively, bound by their report in the premises, when made into the Secretary's office of said Commonwealth, as directed by the said resolve.

In witness whereof we hereto set our hands this twenty-fourth day of August, in the year of our Lord one thousand seven hundred and ninety-seven.

HENRY KNOX,
By David Fales, his Attorney.

*Signed in presence of*                WILLIAM BURNS.
Fields Coombs,
John Harkness.

COMMONWEALTH OF MASSACHUSETTS.

This twenty-fourth day of May, in the year of our Lord one thousand and eight hundred.

On the foregoing reference between Henry Knox, Esquire, and William Burns, for quieting the said William Burns agreeably to the before-mentioned resolve, in the possession of said lot of land, bounded as follows : Beginning at a stake and stones standing on Penobscot west bay, thence running south thirteen degrees east adjoining on Samuel Warren's land two hundred and thirty-two rods to a spruce tree for a corner; thence south fifty-four degrees west forty-six rods to a stake and stones ; thence north fifteen degrees west adjoining on Amos Williams' land two hundred and thirty-two rods to a stake and stones at shore; thence easterly as said Penobscot runs forty-nine and a half rods at right

angles to the first mentioned bounds, containing sixty-seven
and a half acres of land, as by the plan and description
signed by John Harkness, surveyor, hereto annexed, will
appear, reference thereto being had.

We the commissioners before named, having met and
heard the parties, do settle, declare and report that the said
William Burns be quieted in the possession of the above
bounded premises, to have and to hold the same to him the
said William Burns, his heirs and assigns forever, to his and
their use forever, on the terms following, namely : the said
William Burns, his heirs, executors or administrators, shall,
on or before the first day of October, which will be in the
year of our Lord one thousand eight hundred and one, pay
to the said Knox, his heirs, executors or administrators, the
sum of eighty-one dollars with interest from the first day of
June, one thousand eight hundred. And on the payment of
the same, the said Knox or his heirs shall make, or cause to
be made to the said William Burns, his heirs or assigns, a
deed of the above described premises, whereby he and they
may hold the same in fee simple forever.

Given under our hands and seals.

NATHAN DANE.      [Seal.]
JOHN SPRAGUE.      [Seal.]
ENOCH TITCOMB.      [Seal.]

WILLIAM BURNS' LOT IN ISLESBOROUGH, NOV. 4, 1799.

Surveyed for William Burns a lot in south-west division on Long Island, Islesborough, in the county of Hancock, bounded as follows, viz.: Beginning at a stake and stones standing on the bank of Penobscot west bay, thence running south thirteen degrees east adjoining on Samuel Warren's land, two hundred and thirty-two rods to a spruce tree for a corner; thence south fifty-four degrees west forty-six rods to a stake and stones; thence north fifteen degrees west adjoining on Amos Williams' land two hundred and thirty-two rods to a stake and stones at shore; thence easterly as said Penobscot runs forty-nine and a half rods at right angles to the first-mentioned bound, containing sixty-seven and a half acres of land.

JOHN HARKNESS, Surveyor.

N. B. Twenty acres middling; thirty acres swamp, poor cold land; ten acres barren ledges; seventeen broken with ledges; upland broken with ledges so that there is not more than one and a half acres of plowing in a piece. No water in a dry time except one spring.

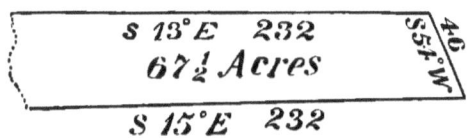

BENJAMIN WILLIAMS' CLAIM AS A SETTLER, IN 1787,
UNDER THE SAME REFERENCE.

*Benjamin Williams' Lot in Islesborough, Nov. 5, 1799.*

Surveyed for Benjamin Williams a lot of land in north-east division on Long Island, in Islesborough, in the county of Hancock, bounded as follows, viz.: Beginning at a spruce tree on the west bank of said island, thence running south twenty-seven degrees east adjoining on William Grinnell's land, ninety-four rods to a spruce tree standing on the bank at the head of Seal Harbor; thence south-westerly as said harbor runs, bounded thereon to Seal Harbor Point; thence northerly and easterly as Penobscot west bay runs, bounded thereby to the first-mentioned corner, containing one hundred acres of land.

JOHN HARKNESS, Surveyor.

N. B.  Twenty acres good land; twenty swamp, cold poor land; thirty acres barren ledges; thirty broken land.  Said lot very much broken with ledges.  Not more than one acre in a piece fit for plowing.

* Perhaps 94 should be 27.

## JOSEPH WILLIAMS' CLAIM AS A SETTLER, 1786.

*Joseph Williams' Lot, Islesborough, October 30, 1799.*

Surveyed for Joseph Williams a lot of land in north-east division on Long Island, in Islesborough, in the county of Hancock, bounded as follows, viz.: Beginning at a cedar standing on the bank at the head of Seal Harbor; thence running south seventy-three degrees east one hundred and thirty rods to a stake and stones; thence south nineteen degrees east adjoining on Captain Anthony Coombs' land, eighty-four rods to a stake and stones; thence south forty-five degrees east adjoining on said Coombs' land to a stake and stones standing on the east bank of said island; thence south-westerly as Penobscot east bay runs, bounded thereby ninety rods on a straight line to a stake and stones standing on the bank at shore; thence north seventy-four degrees west adjoining on Shubael Williams' land, forty-seven rods across said island to a stake and stones on the west bank at Seal Harbor; thence northerly as said Seal Harbor runs, bounded thereby to the first-mentioned bounds, containing one hundred acres of land. JOHN HARKNESS, Surveyor.

N. B. About thirty acres good land—hard wood; thirty acres swamp, cold, poor—spruce wood; forty acres ledgy, broken.

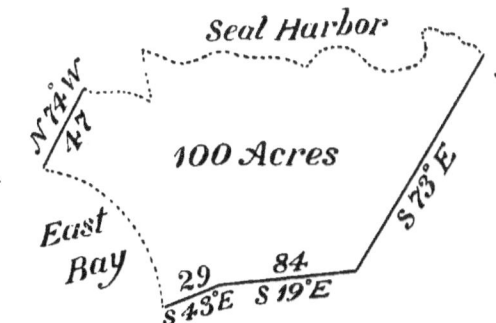

### Noah Dodge's Claim as a Settler, 1784.

*Noah Dodge's Lot in Islesborough, October 23, 1799.*

Surveyed for Noah Dodge a lot of land in north-east division on Long Island, in Islesborough, in the county of Hancock, bounded as follows, viz. : Beginning at a stake standing on the bank of Penobscot west bay, thence running south eighty degrees east adjoining on Nathaniel Toothaker's lot, one hundred and four rods to a stake and stones ; thence south thirty-one degrees west adjoining on Joseph Woodard's lot, seventy-one rods to a stake and stones ; thence south forty-two degrees west adjoining on Mighill Parker's land, forty-four rods to a stake and stones ; thence south twenty-eight degrees west adjoining on said Parker's lot, eighty rods to a stake and stones; thence south seventy degrees west adjoining on Hosea Coombs' lot, thirty rods to a stake and stones ; thence north twenty-six degrees west one hundred and twelve rods to a stake and stones on the bank of said Penobscot west bay ; thence north-easterly as said bay runs to the first-mentioned corner; containing one hundred acres of land.        JOHN HARKNESS, Surveyor.

N. B.   About fifty acres good land ; twenty-acre swamp, mossy, poor spruce ; thirty acres shoal soil.   No water in a dry time.   Six miles to mill by water.

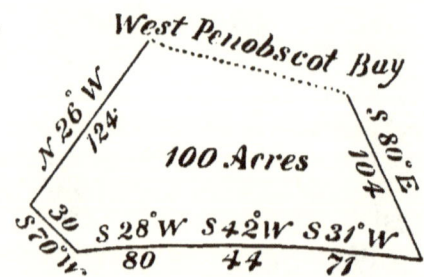

## NATHANIEL TOOTHAKER'S CLAIM AS A SETTLER, 1793.

### *Nathaniel Toothaker's Lot in Islesborough, October 24, 1799.*

Surveyed for Nathaniel Toothaker a lot of land in north-east division on Long Island, in Islesborough, in the county of Hancock, bounded as follows, viz.: Beginning at a stake and stones standing on the west bank of said island, thence running north forty-two degrees east one hundred and ten rods to a stake and stones; thence south forty-seven degrees east two hundred and forty-seven rods to a stake and stones; thence south forty-seven degrees west to a stake and stones standing at shore at Sabbath-Day Harbour; thence westerly as the shore runs, sixteen rods to a stake and stones; thence north forty-seven degrees west adjoining on Joseph Woodard's lot, one hundred and sixty rods to a stake and stones; thence north eighty degrees west adjoining on Noah Dodge's lot, one hundred and four rods to a stake on the bank of the west bay; thence across the cove to the first-mentioned corner; containing one hundred acres of land.             JOHN HARKNESS, Surveyor.

N. B.  About fifty acres good land; fifty acres swamp, poor spruce wood.  Five miles to mill by water.

Understood to be Thomas Toothaker.

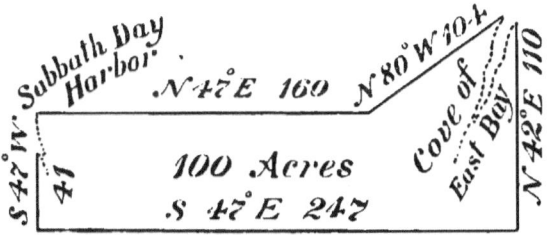

## SAMUEL WILLIAMS' CLAIM.

That during the war with Great Britain, in 1776, he left his lot when the Britons came to Biguaduce, and did not return until after the war. Said Williams stated that the reason of his leaving his lot was because he would not take the oath of allegiance to the king of Great Britain.

*Samuel Williams' Lot in Islesborough, October 26, 1799.*

Surveyed for Samuel Williams a lot of land in north-east division on Long Island, in the county of Hancock, bounded as follows: Beginning at a white birch tree on the west bank of said island, thence running south forty-nine degrees east adjoining on Rathburn Dodge's land, one hundred and two rods to a stake and stones; thence north forty-two degrees east one hundred and forty-seven rods to a stake and stones standing on the bank at Lassell Cove; thence westerly and southerly as said cove and Penobscot west bay runs to the first-mentioned bounds; containing one hundred acres of land.

JOHN HARKNESS, Surveyor.

N. B. About twenty acres, swampy, spruce and hemlock, poor; eighty acres beech, birch, maple, middling; good land, but rocky, hard land. No water in a dry time except one spring.

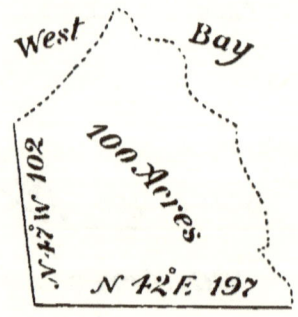

## ELLISON LASSELLE JR.'S CLAIM AS A SETTLER, 1786.

*Ellison Lasselle's Lot in Islesborough, Oct. 12, 1799.*

Surveyed for Ellison Lasselle a lot of land in north-east division of Long Island, in Islesborough, in the county of Hancock, bounded as follows : Beginning at a white birch tree standing on the west bank of said island, thence running south forty-seven degrees east sixty-five rods adjoining on Samuel Williams' lot, to a stake and stones ; thence north twenty-nine degrees east, two hundred rods to a stake and stones standing at shore of east bay ; thence northerly as Penobscot east bay runs, bounded thereby to Turtle Head ; thence westerly and southerly as the Penobscot west bay runs, bounded thereby to the first-mentioned bounds ; containing one hundred acres of land. JOHN HARKNESS, Surveyor.

N. B. Thirty acres good land ; twenty about half middling ; thirty swampy, spruce wood, cold, poor ; three acres salt marsh ; the rest dry, poor. Five miles to mill by water.

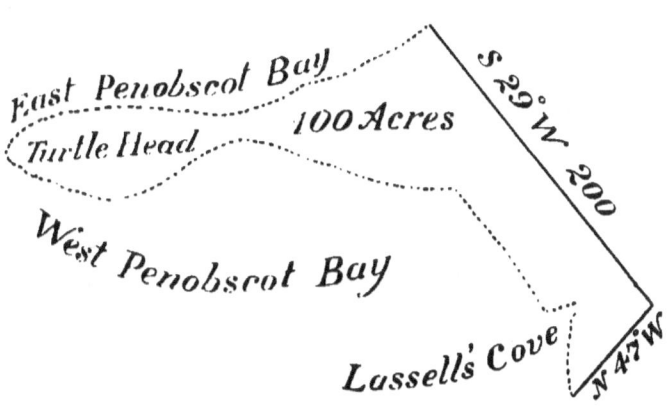

JONATHAN HOLBROOK'S CLAIM AS A SETTLER, 1783.
(Assigned to Prince Holbrook.)

*Prince Holbrook's Lot in Islesborough, Oct. 24, 1799.*

Surveyed for Prince Holbrook a lot of land in north-east division on Long Island, in the county of Hancock, bounded as follows, viz.:   Beginning at a stake and stones standing on the east bank of said island, thence running north forty-seven degrees west adjoining on James Trim's land, two hundred and fifty-nine rods to a stake and stones; thence north forty-two degrees east seventy-eight rods to a stake and stones; thence south forty-seven degrees east adjoining Samuel Warren, Jr.'s, land, one hundred and forty-eight rods to a stake and stones standing on the bank at shore; thence southerly as Penobscot east bay runs, bounded thereby to the first-mentioned corner; containing one hundred acres of land.

JOHN HARKNESS, Surveyor.

N. B.   About twenty-five acres middling good land; the rest swampy, cold, mossy, poor wood; about ten acres hard wood, the rest spruce; no good timber.   Six miles to mill by water.   No good harbor for a boat.

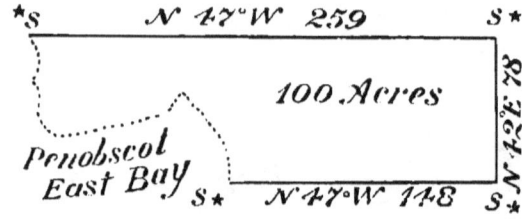

## JAMES TRIM'S CLAIM AS A SETTLER, 1784.

*James Trim's Lot in Islesborough, October 23, 1799.*

Surveyed for James Trim a lot in north-east division on Long Island, in Islesborough, in the county of Hancock, bounded as follows, viz.: Beginning at a stake and stones standing on the east bank of said island, thence running north forty-seven degrees west adjoining on Jonathan Parker's land, two hundred and fifty-three rods to a stake and stones; thence north forty-two degrees east sixty-one rods to a stake and stones; thence south forty-seven degrees east adjoining on Prince Holbrook's land, two hundred and seventy rods to a stake and stones standing on the bank at shore; thence southerly as Penobscot east bay runs, bounded thereby sixty-one rods at right angles to the first-mentioned bounds; containing one hundred acres of land.

JOHN HARKNESS, Surveyor.

N. B. About twenty-five acres middling, the rest swampy, cold, poor land; about fifteen acres hard wood, the rest spruce; no good timber. No landing for a boat. Six miles to mill by water. No water in a dry time.

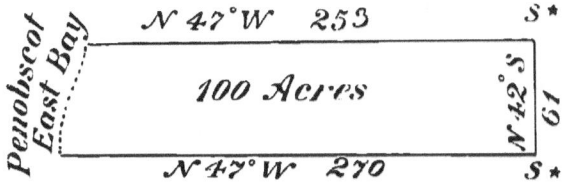

## JONATHAN PARKER'S CLAIM AS A SETTLER, 1784.

*Jonathan Parker's Lot in Islesborough, County of Hancock.*

Surveyed for Jonathan Parker a lot of land in north-east division on Long Island, in Islesborough, bounded as follows, viz.: Beginning at a stake and stones standing on the east bank of said island, thence running north forty-seven degrees west adjoining on Samuel Veazie's land, one hundred and sixty-three rods to a stake and stones; thence north forty-two degrees east seventy-eight rods to a stake and stones; thence south forty-seven degrees east adjoining on James Trim's land, two hundred and fifty-eight rods to a stake and stones standing on the bank at the shore; thence south-westerly as Penobscot east bay runs, bounded thereby to the first-mentioned bounds; containing one hundred acres of land.

JOHN HARKNESS, Surveyor.

N. B.  Thirty acres middling good land; fifty acres swamp, mossy, cold, spruce wood, poor land; twenty acres about one half middling, very little hard wood, chiefly spruce, greatest part dead; no good timber. Seven miles to mill by water.

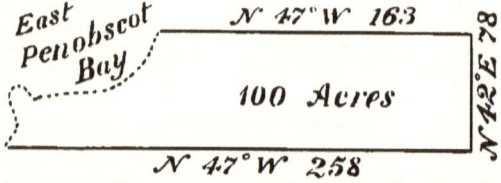

### JONATHAN COOMBS' CLAIM AS A SETTLER, 1784.

*Jonathan Coombs' Lot in Islesborough, County of Hancock, October 25, 1799.*

Surveyed for Jonathan Coombs a lot of land in north-east division, on land bounded as follows, viz.: Beginning at a stake and stones standing on the east bank of said island, thence running north forty-seven degrees west adjoining on Samuel Warren, Jr.'s, land, one hundred and twenty rods to a stake and stones; thence north seven degrees east one hundred and fifty rods to a yellow birch tree; thence south fifty-seven degrees east, ninety rods to a stake and stones standing on the bank at shore; thence southerly as Penobscot east bay runs, bounded thereon to the first-mentioned corner; containing one hundred acres of land.          JOHN HARKNESS, Surveyor.

N. B.  Thirty acres middling good land; twenty about half middling; fifty swamp, cold, poor land; spruce wood; no good timber.  Six miles to mill by water.

Penobscot East Bay

100 Acres

S. 57° E 90

N 7° E 150

120 N 47° W

## MIGHILL PARKER'S CLAIM AS A SETTLER, 1784.

*Mighill Parker's Lot in Islesborough, in the County of Hancock, October 19, 1799.*

Surveyed for Mighill Parker a lot of land in north-east division on Long Island, in Islesborough, bounded as follows, viz.: Beginning at a stake and stones standing on the east bank of said island, thence running north forty-seven degrees west adjoining on Hosea Coombs' land, one hundred and sixty rods to a stake and stones; thence north twenty-two degrees east one hundred and thirty rods to a stake and stones; thence south forty-seven degrees east adjoining on Joseph Woodard's land, one hundred rods to a stake and stones standing on the bank at Sabbath-Day Harbor; thence easterly and southerly as the said harbor and Penobscot east bay runs, to the first-mentioned corner; containing one hundred acres of land.

JOHN HARKNESS, Surveyor.

N. B. About twenty-five acres middling good land, hard wood; the rest swampy, cold, mossy, poor, broken with gullies; spruce wood, chiefly dead. Seven miles to mill by water.

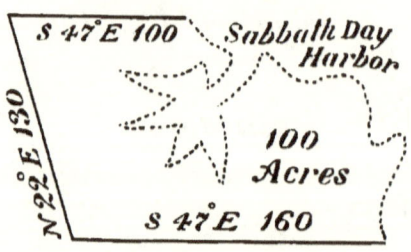

## HOSEA COOMBS' CLAIM AS A SETTLER, 1784.

*Hosea Coombs' Lot on Long Island, in Islesborough, in the County of Hancock, Oct. 19, 1799.*

Beginning at a cedar tree marked for a corner, thence running north forty-seven degrees east adjoining on Noah Dodge's land, nineteen rods to a stake and stones; thence north seventy degrees east adjoining on said Noah's land, thirty rods to a stake and stones; thence south forty-seven degrees east adjoining on Mighill Parker's land, one hundred and eighty-six rods to a stake and stones standing on the bank of Penobscot east bay; thence south-westerly as said bay runs, bound thereon seventy-two rods at right angles to a white birch tree; thence north forty-seven degrees west adjoining on Capt. Anthony Coombs' lot, one hundred and ninety-six rods to a stake and stones; thence adjoining on William Grinnell's land to the first-mentioned corner; containing eighty-seven acres of land.

JOHN HARKNESS, Surveyor.

N. B. About one half good land; one half swampy, cold, poor land; one fourth hard wood, birch and maple; three fourths of wood spruce. No water in a dry time.

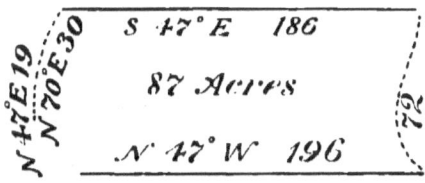

S 47° E 186
87 Acres
N 47° W 196
N 47° E 19
N 70° E 30
72

## ANTHONY COOMBS' CLAIM AS A SETTLER, 1784.

*Capt. Anthony Coombs' and Ephraim Coombs' Lots, in
Islesborough, Oct. 30, 1799.*

Surveyed for Capt. Anthony Coombs and Ephraim
Coombs a lot of land in common and undivided in north-
east division on Long Island, in Islesborough, in the
county of Hancock, bounded as follows, viz.:   Beginning
at a white rock on the east shore of said island, thence
running north forty-three degrees west adjoining on
Joseph Williams' lot, twenty-nine rods to a spring; thence
north nineteen degrees west adjoining on said Williams'
lot, eighty-four rods to a stake and stones; thence north
forty-seven degrees west adjoining on said Williams' lot,
one hundred and sixteen rods to a stake and stones;
thence north thirty-one degrees east twenty-six rods to a
stake; thence north forty-four degrees east seventeen rods
to a stake; thence north thirty-six degrees east adjoining
on William Grinnell's lot, thirty-four rods to a stake;
thence south forty-seven degrees east adjoining on Hosea
Coombs' lot, one hundred and ninety-six rods to a white
birch tree standing on the bank at shore; thence southerly and westerly as Penobscot east bay runs, bounded
thereby to the first-mentioned corner; containing one
hundred and sixteen acres of land.

JOHN HARKNESS, Surveyor.

N. B.   Thirty acres good land; thirty acres swamp,
cold, poor land, spruce wood; the rest broken, ledgy
land.   No water in a dry time except one spring.   Eight
miles to mill by water.   About an acre fit for plowing in
a piece.

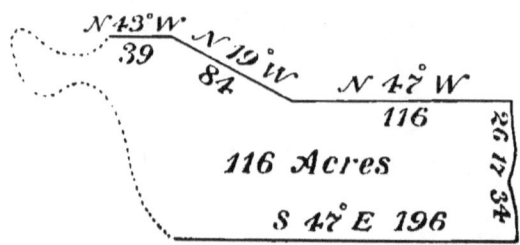

## THOMAS GILKEY'S CLAIM AS A SETTLER, PRIOR TO 1783.

*Thomas Gilkey's Lot on Long Island, in Islesborough,*
*November 6, 1799.*

Surveyed for Thomas Gilkey a lot of land in Isles-borough, in the county of Hancock, bounded as follows, viz.: Beginning at a stake and stones standing on the northerly bank of Long Island harbor, thence north sixty-five degrees east adjoining on Charles Thomas' land, two hundred and twenty-one rods to a stake and stones; thence south seventeen degrees east sixty-one and one half rods to a stake and stones; thence south sixty-five degrees west adjoining on John Gilkey's land, one hundred and thirty-seven rods to a spruce tree standing on the west bank of Mill Cove; thence south-westerly and northerly as the said cove and Long Island harbor runs, bounded thereon to the first-mentioned bounds; containing one hundred acres of land.

JOHN HARKNESS, Surveyor.

N. B. About thirty-three acres good land, wood birch and maple; thirty-three acres swamp, wood spruce; thirty-four acres cold, flat land, wood spruce.

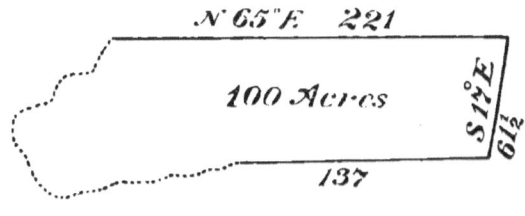

### ROBERT SHERMAN'S CLAIM AS A SETTLER, 1784.

*Robert Sherman's Lot in Islesborough, November 3, 1799.*

Surveyed for Robert Sherman a lot of land in south-west division on Long Island, in Islesborough, in the county of Hancock, bounded as follows, viz.: Beginning at a stake and stones on the bank, thence running south seventeen degrees east adjoining on Robert Coombs' land, twenty-eight rods to a stake and stones; thence south sixty-seven degrees east adjoining on said Coombs' land, thirty-nine rods to white birch stumps; thence south seventeen degrees east adjoining on said Coombs' land, ten rods to a maple tree; thence south sixty degrees west adjoining on Jeremiah Hatch's land, two hundred and twelve rods to a stake and stones; thence north forty-eight degrees west adjoining on said Hatch's land, three rods to a stake at the shore of Penobscot west bay; thence north-easterly as said bay runs, bounded thereon to the first - mentioned corner; containing seventy - two acres of land.          JOHN HARKNESS, Surveyor.

N. B.  One third good land; one third swamp, cold, poor land; one third half-middling, broken with ledges. No water in a dry time. No good harbor for a boat. The wood now on the land chiefly spruce, and no good timber.

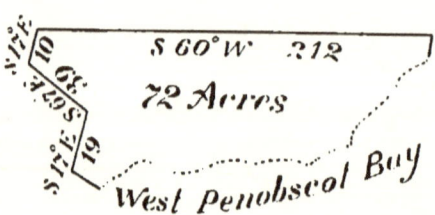

## JEREMIAH HATCH'S CLAIM AS A SETTLER, 1784.

*Islesborough, November 4, 1799.*

Surveyed for Jeremiah Hatch a lot of land on Long Island, in south-west division, bounded as follows, viz.: Beginning at a stake and stones standing on the bank of Penobscot west bay, thence running south forty-eight degrees east adjoining on Robert Sherman's land, three rods to a stake and stones; thence north sixty degrees east adjoining on said Sherman's land, two hundred and twelve rods to a maple tree marked for a corner; thence south seventeen degrees east adjoining on Robert Coombs' land, sixty-six rods to a hemlock tree, south sixty degrees west adjoining on Joseph Farrow's land, two hundred and seventy rods to a birch stump for a corner, standing on the bank of said bay; thence north-easterly as said Penobscot west bay runs, to the first-mentioned corner; containing ninety-six acres of land.

JOHN HARKNESS, Surveyor.

N. B. Thirty acres middling good land; forty acres swamp, cold, spruce, poor land; twenty-six about half-middling; the upland broken with ledges. No water in a dry time. No good harbor for a boat.

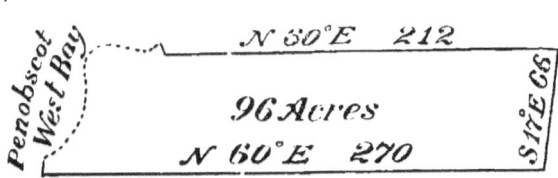

# CHAPTER III.

## THE INCORPORATION OF THE TOWN.

IN 1788 the subjoined petition was sent to the General Court, asking for incorporation as a town, by the name of Winchester:

To the Honorable the Senate and the Honorable the House of Representatives of the Commonwealth of Massachusetts, in General Court assembled:

Humbly shews the committee appointed by the inhabitants of Long Island Plantation, in the county of Lincoln, that there has been several surveys of the said island, from the report of which we have always understood that no part of the centre of said island lay within three miles of the main, except from the report of Capt. Stone, who made the last survey, who says that the said island was within three miles of the main; but your petitioners humbly beg leave to observe that they conceive Capt. Stone may be mistaken, as they have understood that in his calculations he governed himself by Grant's survey and plan, which survey by said Grant is deemed very erroneous. It appears by the resolve of the Honorable General Court, confirming the grant of thirty miles to the heirs of Brigadier General Waldo, that all islands whose centre is within three miles of the main shall be considered and included within this grant. Your petitioners conceive that the true meaning of the word centre is by a line running through the centre of said island, and not confined to any point or neck of land jutting out of the body of said island.

LILY POND, HEAD OF SPRAGUE'S COVE.

Since the survey and report made by Capt. Stone, your petitioners have had an accurate survey of the distance of said island from the main, by an able surveyor, who assures your petitioners that no part of said island is within three miles of the main, and chainmen were duly sworn to faithfully and truly execute the duty of their several stations. Your petitioners therefore humbly entreat the Honorable General Court that some disinterested principal inhabitant in the vicinity may be empowered as well in behalf of the inhabitants as of the Commonwealth, to employ and inspect such persons as he may think capable of taking an accurate survey of the true distance of said island from the main, and make report thereof to the Honorable the General Court for their determination, and your petitioners will defray the expense attending such survey.

Your petitioners also entreat the Honorable General Court that all tax bills forwarded to be assessed on said plantation and its inhabitants may be stayed, and the assessing and collecting the same may be suspended until the lands are meted out and confirmed to the settlers, and a legal valuation can be presented. And as the different plantations in this part of the county of Lincoln are to be incorporated, your petitioners pray that Long Island Plantation, with the islands contiguous, may be incorporated into a town by the name of Winchester, that the inhabitants may be in the enjoyment of those privileges which are annexed to towns corporate, there being more than sixty families settled and residing therein, and as in duty bound will ever pray.

SHUBAEL WILLIAMS, } Committee.
JOHN GILKEY, }

Long Island, Oct. 22, 1788.

January 28, 1789, the act was passed, but the name was changed.

An act for incorporating Long Island Plantation, with islands adjacent, in the county of Lincoln, into a town by the name of Islesborough.

Section 1. Be it enacted, etc., that the tracts of land

described as follows, viz.: Long Island, Seven-Hundred-Acre Island, Job's Island and Lime Island, situated in Penobscot bay, in the county of Lincoln, with the inhabitants thereon, be and they are incorporated into a town by the name of Islesborough.

### First Town Meeting in Islesborough, 1789.

*Commonwealth of Massachusetts.*

To Shubael Williams, one of the principal inhabitants of Long Island Plantation, in said county, yeoman:

Whereas by an act of greeting the General Court passed the twelfth day of January, in the year of our Lord one thousand seven hundred and eighty-nine, it is provided that the land described as follows, viz., Long Island, Seven-Hundred-Acre Island, Job's Island, and the Lime Islands, situated in Penobscot bay, in the county of Lincoln, with the inhabitants, be and they are hereby incorporated into a town by the name of Islesborough; and whereas by the same act the subscriber, one of the Justices of the Peace for the said county, is directed to issue his warrant to one of the principal inhabitants of the said plantation, to call a meeting of the inhabitants thereof in the name of the Commonwealth, directed to notify the meeting of the inhabitants next at nine of the clock in the forenoon, at the dwelling house of you, the said Shubael Williams, for the following purpose, viz.: To choose all such officers as towns are by law requested to choose at their annual meeting, in the month of March or April annually, and to act on all such other business as may be necessary to be done.

Given under my hand and seal at Penobscot, this seventeenth day of March, in the year of our Lord one thousand seven hundred and eighty-nine.

GABRIEL JOHONNOT, Esq.

Islesborough, April 6, 1789.

April 6, 1789. A record of the first meeting after the incorporation of the town.

Agreeable to the above warrant, we met at the time and place appointed.

1. Voted Thomas Ames moderator.
2. Voted Fields Coombs town clerk.
3. Voted Capt. William Pendleton, Valentine Sherman and Fields Coombs, selectmen.
4. Voted Capt. John Pendleton for town treasurer.
5. Voted Hosea Coombs and John Gilkey, constables.
6. Voted Harry Pendleton and Capt. Peter Coombs, tythingmen.
7. Voted Capt. Anthony Coombs surveyor of wood and other lumber.
8. Voted Capt. Thomas Pendleton and Noah Dodge, surveyors of highways.
9. Voted Noah Dodge and Joshua Pendleton, for hog-reeves and fence-viewers.
10. Voted Gabriel Johonnot seven votes for register of deeds. Voted Richard Hunnewell seven votes for register of deeds.

April 15, 1789, same year, they called a town meeting. Voted to raise taxes.

Town meeting June 9, 1789. Voted John Gilkey and Samuel Pendleton to lay out town roads.

Town meeting April 19, 1790. William Pendleton, Shubael Williams and John Gilkey, selectmen.

Voted hogs run at large, but yoked, according to law, from 10th May to last of October.

Town meeting Nov. 25, 1790. Voted for a representative to send to Congress. George Thatcher, Esq., had sixteen votes.

Town meeting April 24, 1791.   William Elwell, Samuel Warren and William Grindle, selectmen.

Town meeting Sept. 4, 1794.   Voted that the town be divided into districts for schooling, and every district have his part of the money now assessed for that purpose and put to that use.

Town meeting April 6, 1795.   Samuel Warren, William Philbrook and Godfrey Trim, selectmen.

Voted that the whole sum of money as assessed for building the meeting-house, the bills shall be returned to the selectmen again, and they that have paid shall receive their money again from the constable.

Town meeting April 4, 1796.   Samuel Warren, Shubael Williams and William Philbrook, selectmen.

Town meeting April 3, 1797.   Samuel Warren, Mighill Parker and Thomas Gilkey, selectmen.

Town meeting April 4, 1798.   Samuel Warren, John Gilkey and Mighill Parker, selectmen.

Town meeting Nov. 5, 1798.   Agreed to build a meeting-house, and voted John Gilkey, Joseph Boardman and Mighill Parker' for committeemen to purchase a spot of land and cultivate the same at the best and cheapest rates.

Voted to leave it with the said committee to build said meeting-house at the best advantage for the town.

Voted four hundred dollars to be laid out upon building the said meeting-house, &c., &c.

Town meeting April 1, 1799.   Samuel Warren, John Gilkey and Jeremiah Hatch, selectmen.

Voted to do nothing about the meeting-house.

Town meeting October 7, 1800.   Voted to select a minister.   Voted Charles Thomas for the minister.

At the town meeting April 23, 1792, Samuel Warren, William Grindle and William Elwell, selectmen.

Town meeting, May 1, 1792.
Voted for a separation, fifteen votes; voted against it, nine votes.

Voted every man must work one day on the highway.

Voted to choose a committee to fix a place where to set up a meeting-house. William Elwell, Anthony Coombs and Samuel Pendleton for the committee.

Voted hogs run at large if properly yoked.

That the constables shall have one shilling on the pound for collecting of rates.

Town meeting, January 14, 1793.
Voted to build a meeting-house.

Voted to choose two men to appoint a plan to build a meeting-house.

Voted Capt. Job Pendleton and Capt. Godfrey Trim for said men, and appoint the place.

Voted Capt. Shubael Williams and Mighill Parker for committeemen to agree with carpenters to build the meeting-house, the work part thirty by forty, one story high.

Voted fifty pounds be raised to build said house and other charges.

At the regular town meeting, April 1, 1793, Samuel Warren, Shubael Williams and William Elwell, selectmen.

Town meeting May 30.

Town meeting, Sept. 5, 1793. Voted liberty to keep bars across the highway, if so minded.

At the town meeting, April, 1794, Shubael Williams and John Pendleton were selectmen.

Voted that fifty pounds, that is now assessed for building a meeting-house, shall be collected for building two

6

meeting-houses, and each end of the town have their part, what they paid for building said house.

Voted to settle Mr. Thomas Ames a minister, under salary of twenty pounds a year.

Town meeting, April 7, 1800. Samuel Warren, John Gilkey and Jeremiah Hatch, selectmen.

Voted gates, and across the road.

Town meeting, Aug. 25, 1800. Voted to have a town school-master.

Voted one hundred and twenty dollars to support a town school.

Town meeting, April 6, 1801. Samuel Warren, Jeremiah Hatch and Fields Coombs, selectmen.

Town meeting, April 5, 1803. Mighill Parker, Jeremiah Hatch and Benjamin Williams, selectmen.

Voted Ephraim Coombs rates-gatherer, three cents per dollar.

Town meeting, April 7, 1803. Samuel Warren, John Gilkey and Mighill Parker, selectmen.

Town meeting, April 2, 1804. Samuel Warren, John Gilkey and Mighill Parker, selectmen.

Town meeting, Nov. 5, 1804. Voted fifty dollars for weights and measures.

Voted no money for the meeting-house.

Town meeting, April 1, 1805. Noah Dodge, John Gilkey and Samuel Warren, selectmen.

Town meeting, April 7, 1806. Noah Dodge, John Gilkey and Samuel Warren, selectmen.

Voted to build one pound to Mr. Jones' field, driven this year, and one to Mr. Noah Dodge this year.

Voted Joseph Jones and Joseph Pendleton to build one, and Noah Dodge and Mighill Parker to build the other. They are to be built — feet square.

Town meeting, April 6, 1807. Samuel Warren, John Warren and John Gilkey, selectmen.

Town meeting, April 16, 1807. Voted chose Mighill Parker and John Warren with the meeting-house committee, the time that Sat. is on or before the first day of July next.

Town meeting, April 4, 1808. John Gilkey, Thomas Boardman and Mighill Parker, selectmen.

Voted twelve cents a head for crows.

Voted two dollars on him that kills the most crows.

Voted that Philip Sylvester shall take William Getchell six months for nothing, and return him clothed as well as he takes him.

Voted that the surveyors of roads have power to distress, if people will not work on the roads.

Voted Mighill Parker and John Warren committeemen to finish the business and settle the accounts against the meeting-house.

They held these meetings the first time in the meeting-house, 1804.

We, the subscribers, do hereby request the inhabitants of the upper end of this island to meet Saturday, at the house of Hancock Rose, for the purpose of consulting with each other respecting a school, and, if they shall see fit to appoint a committee, establish the same. We do furthermore request the inhabitants, of both classes, to meet or consult whether it would not be beneficial for them to form themselves into one body or class.

*Signers:*          RATHBURN DODGE,
STEPHEN VEAZIE,
JONATHAN PARKER,
FIELDS COOMBS,
JOHN VEAZIE.

Town meeting, Oct. 29, 1808. Town met at time and place appointed, for the purpose of settling that execution brought against the town by Doctor Webster, of Castine.

Voted to choose an agent to settle with Webster.

Voted Mighill Parker for agent.

Voted to board William Getchell from house to house— every house according to what they are worth—till next April meeting.

Town meeting, April 3, 1809. John Gilkey, Jr., Thomas Boardman and Mighill Parker, selectmen.

Town meeting, April 2, 1810. Mighill Parker, Thomas Boardman and John Farrow, selectmen.

Voted that the road that goes across the northern corner of Mighill Parker's land may be moved close to the line between himself and Joseph Woodard, only Mr. Parker is to make it as good as it now is, on his own expense.

Town meeting, Dec. 5, 1810. Met at the time and place appointed, agreeable to law, for the purpose of raising money to support of William Getchell.

Voted one hundred and seventy dollars for that purpose.

Town meeting, April 1, 1811. Thomas Boardman, William Philbrook and Jabez Ames, selectmen.

Town meeting. Voted that they should build gates across the roads ten feet wide in the clear. Should have but two gates to one farm.

Voted that the bounty upon crows' heads be twelve cents per head.

Town meeting, April 6, 1812. Thomas Boardman, Jabez Ames and William Philbrook, selectmen.

Voted Benjamin Williams, Noah Dodge and Paoli Hewes are the committee to judge between Jabez Ames and Elisha Nash where the road should be, so that Jabez Ames should clear the road and make it good passing.

Voted twelve cents for old crows' heads, and six cents for young crows' heads.

Voted good gates to be on the roads.

Town meeting, March 20, 1813. Thomas Boardman, Jabez Ames and Mighill Parker, selectmen.

Voted Mighill Parker and Thomas Boardman should be a committee to settle all bills on the meeting-house with John Gilkey, Esq.

Voted that Paoli Hewes be allowed three dollars per year for keeping the town treasury.

## COPY OF WARRANT, 1814.

To Joseph Pendleton, one of the constables of the town of Islesborough, greeting.

You are hereby required, in the name of the Commonwealth of Massachusetts, to warn the male inhabitants of said town of Islesborough of twenty-one years of age and upwards, having a freehold estate within the Commonwealth, or the annual income of three pounds, or any estate to the value of sixty pounds, to meet at the meeting-house on Monday, the fourth day of April next, at ten of the clock in the forenoon, to give in their votes for Governor, &c., &c. A true copy.   By me,

WILLIAM BOARDMAN,

Town Clerk.

Pursuant to the within warrant I have warned the inhabitants of said town qualified as by therein expressed, to meet at the time and place, and for the purpose therein mentioned.

JOSEPH PENDLETON, Constable.

Town meeting, April 4, 1814.   Mighill Parker, Henry Rose and John Farrow, selectmen.

Voted that the town pound should be brought down to the meeting-house, if fit to move.

Voted Jesse Coombs should bring down the above to the meeting-house, and set it up in as good order as it was before, and that Jesse Coombs should have the privilege of repairing the same, if he would do it as cheap as anybody.   Jesse Coombs to have fourteen dollars for bringing down the above and setting it up again.

Voted that Benjamin Williams and Thomas Boardman should trade with Mr. Still for his house, providing they can get it for fifty dollars.

Town meeting, April 3, 1815.   Thomas Boardman, Jabez Ames and Benjamin Williams, selectmen.

Voted widow Calton bid to John Gilkey, Esq., for four shillings per week.

Voted Mr. Hardy and his wife to Joshua Dodge for four dollars and seventy-five cents per month, at public vendue.

Town meeting, March 16, 1816.   Benjamin. Williams, Jabez Ames and Paoli Hewes, selectmen.

Voted no school money this year.

Voted Mrs. Hardy should remain as she was last year.

Town meeting, May 20, 1816. Holden for the purpose of giving in their votes for or against dividing the State of Massachusetts from the District of Maine.

For division, none ; against the division, seventeen.

Town meeting, Sept. 2, 1816. Voted against the separation, thirty-four votes ; for the separation, none.

Town meeting, April 7, 1817. Benjamin Williams, Jabez Ames and Paoli Hewes, selectmen.

Town meeting, March 18, 1818. Elisha Eames, Henry Rose and John Farrow, selectmen.

Town meeting, March 18, 1819. Josiah Farrow, Thos. Gilkey and Josiah Eames, selectmen.

Town meeting, July 17, 1819. Voted in favor of separation, two ; voted against it, twenty-five.

Town meeting, Sept. 11, 1819. For the purpose of electing one delegate on the second Monday of October, for the purpose of forming a Constitution for the District of Maine. Elected Josiah Farrow.

Town meeting, Nov. 17, 1819. To give in your votes in writing, expressing your approbation or disapprobation of the Constitution agreed on by the convention at Portland, October 29, 1819.

Voted in favor of Constitution, ten ; against it, one.

Town meeting, March 18, 1820. N. B. The Constitution of the State of Maine, under which we now assemble, provides that every male citizen of the United States of the age of twenty-one years and upwards, excepting paupers, persons under guardianship, and Indians not taxed, having his residence established in this State for the term of three months next preceding any election, shall be an elector of Governor, Senator and representative, in the town or plantation where his residence is so located.

Town meeting, Oct. 18, 1820. Josiah Farrow, Henry Rose and Jonathan Parker, selectmen.

Town meeting, April 2, 1821. Josiah Farrow, Jonathan Parker and Thomas Gilkey, selectmen.

Voted to raise no school money.

Voted Samuel Pendleton take Joseph Hardy for a year, and give twenty-five cents per week.

Town meeting, March 25, 1822. Josiah Farrow, Jonathan Parker and Henry Rose, selectmen.

Mighill Parker, Esq., had votes for a representative, twenty-nine.

Town meeting, Sept. 9, 1822. Voted fourpence halfpenny as a premium on crows' heads.

Town meeting, March, 1823. John Gilkey, Samuel Warren and Simon Sprague, selectmen.

Mighill Parker was the first representative.

Town meeting, April 15, 1824. Josiah Farrow, Simon Sprague and Thomas Gilkey, selectmen.

Voted gates on the road to have posts near them convenient to fasten horses to when passing the road, and also something to set the gate back with, when horses are passing through.

### LICENSE.

Sept. 13, 1824. Mr. Philip Gilkey having applied for license to sell liquors, the selectmen and town clerk, after said Philip Gilkey having complied with the requirements of the law made and provided in such case, do license him, Philip Gilkey, to sell wine, beer, ale, cider, brandy, rum, and other strong liquor by retail, in said town of Islesborough, for one year next ensuing, at his dwelling house in said town.

Town meeting, April 4, 1825. Josiah Farrow, Thomas Boardman and Thomas Gilkey, selectmen.

Voted no money to defray town charges.

Josiah Farrow had eleven votes for representative.

Town meeting, March 25, 1826. Josiah Farrow, Henry Rose and Thomas Gilkey, selectmen.

Town meeting, April 2, 1827. Josiah Farrow, Thomas Boardman and Thomas Gilkey, selectmen.

Voted to accept a road laid out from Capt. Philip Gilkey's wharf or landing to the road named in the petition, where laid out by the selectmen, provided the cost to the town do not overrun or exceed five dollars.

Town meeting, March 31, 1828. Josiah Farrow, Henry Rose and Thomas Gilkey, selectmen.

Town meeting, April 13, 1829. Simon Sprague, Thos. Boardman and Benjamin Williams, selectmen.

1830. Simon Sprague, Samuel Warren and Henry Boardman, selectmen.

Voted to sell the pews in the gallery, and have the house underpinned.

1831. Simon Sprague, Samuel Warren and Samuel Pendleton, selectmen.

1832. Henry Rose, Jonathan Parker and Thomas Gilkey, selectmen.

1833. William Farrow, Thomas Gilkey and Jonathan Parker, selectmen.

A charge was brought against Josiah Farrow, by the town treasurer, in 1829. A committee was appointed by the town. The following is a report of the committee:

7

That we have carefully and impartially examined and compared the clerk's, treasurer's, and said Farrow's accounts with the town, commencing with the year 1819, the year that said Farrow was first chosen one of the selectmen, and proceeding through said books to March 20, 1829, and to the satisfaction of your committee, have found the accounts of said Farrow substantially correct; and in every instance where an order had been drawn in favor of said Farrow, he has proved to the satisfaction of your committee that he has observed a scrupulous exactness, not varying one cent in ten years, which we should have thought almost impossible for him to have shown, considering the imperfect manner in which the clerk and treasurer's books have been kept. Accounts that had been credited and settled once a year and vouchers mislaid, thrown by, or destroyed as useless. It further appeared to your committee that in all contracts and expenditures of the public money, that he has proceeded openly, the strictest principles of economy and honesty, and in the most satisfactory manner exonerated himself from the false impression cast upon him by the town treasurer.

JOSEPH PENDLETON,  
ELISHA EAMES,          Committee.  
THOMAS BOARDMAN,

1834. Henry Rose, Rathburn D. Sprague and Joshua Farrow, selectmen.

1835. Thomas Boardman, William Farrow and Andrew P. Gilkey, selectmen.

1836. Rathburn D. Sprague, Jonathan Parker and Peleg Pendleton, selectmen.

1837. Rathburn D. Sprague, Thomas Boardman and Samuel Marshall, selectmen.

Voted to have the selectmen number the lots in the town.

Voted the gates should stand as formerly.

Also voted to loan the public money, with security on real estate, not less than one hundred dollars, nor more than five hundred dollars; for not less than six months, nor more than one year. Left with the selectmen and treasurer.

1838. Joshua Farrow, James B. Williams and Dexter Farrow, selectmen.

1839. Joshua Farrow, James B. Williams and Henry Boardman, selectmen.

The selectmen bound out William G. Thomas, son of Wealthy Thomas, to James Skinner, until he shall come to the age of twenty-one.

1840. James B. Williams, Dexter Farrow and Thomas H. Parker, selectmen.

1841. James B. Williams, Andrew P. Gilkey and Thomas H. Parker, selectmen.

1842. James B. Williams, Thomas H. Parker and William Farrow, selectmen.

1843. James B. Williams, Nelson Gilkey and Joseph Boardman, selectmen.

1844. Nelson Gilkey, Andrew P. Gilkey and William Farrow, selectmen.

1845. Thomas H. Parker, Henry Boardman and Chas. Nash, selectmen.

1846. James B. Williams, Charles Nash and Philip F. Coombs, selectmen.

1847. James B. Williams, Charles Nash and Othniel Coombs, selectmen.

1848. James B. Williams, Charles Nash and Othniel Coombs, selectmen.

1849. James B. Williams, Charles Nash and Simon D. Sprague, selectmen.

1850. Charles Nash, Nelson Gilkey and Andrew P. Gilkey, selectmen.

1851. Charles Nash, Nelson Gilkey and Simon D. Sprague, selectmen.

1852. Charles Nash, Simon D. Sprague and Walter F. Dodge, selectmen.

1853. Nelson Gilkey, Thomas H. Parker and Silas Bunker, selectmen.

1854. Nelson Gilkey, Thomas H. Parker and Silas Bunker, selectmen.

1855. Nelson Gilkey, Thomas H. Parker and Silas Bunker, selectmen.

1856. Nelson Gilkey, Thomas H. Parker and Silas Bunker, selectmen.
Voted to have the old meeting-house converted into a town-house.

1857. Nelson Gilkey, Silas Bunker and Benjamin Ryder, selectmen.

In 1855 and 1856 there was a political society known as Know-Nothings, or Native Americans. They held private meetings in the school-houses. They created considerable excitement, and had a strong opposition, with a kind of hostile resistance. When the decisive vote was declared, the Know-Nothings having the most votes, elected their town officers.

1858. Silas Bunker, Benjamin Ryder and Elisha K. Pendleton, selectmen.

1859. Silas Bunker, Calvin Eames and Lorenzo Pendleton, selectmen.

1860. Silas Bunker, Benjamin Ryder and Lorenzo Pendleton, selectmen.

1861. Nelson Gilkey, Lorenzo Pendleton and William P. Boardman, selectmen.

1862. Silas Bunker, Benjamin Ryder and Daniel Hatch, selectmen.

At a meeting of the inhabitants in 1863, voted to raise three hundred and twenty-five dollars, to be paid to each man that would volunteer to fill the town quota of twenty men, for the call of the President of the United States, October 17, 1863.

Voted Finley B. Keller a recruiting officer of the town, and the recruiting officer shall not pay over three hundred and twenty-five dollars out of the town, and to get them as cheap as possible.

Voted that the town treasurer be authorized to hire money to pay volunteers as fast as needed.

Voted that if the town fail to get their quota of volunteers, and should a draft be made, that the town pay three hundred and twenty-five dollars to each man that is drafted and accepted and mustered into the service of the United States.

1863. James B. Williams, Benjamin Ryder and William Farrow, selectmen.

1864. James B. Williams, Benjamin Ryder and William Farrow, selectmen.

1865.   James B. Williams, Henry B. Coombs and William Farrow, selectmen.

1866.   James B. Williams, Henry B. Coombs and William Farrow, selectmen.

1867.   James B. Williams, Thomas H. Parker and William Farrow, selectmen.

1868.   James B. Williams, Thomas H. Parker and William Farrow, selectmen.

1869.   James B. Williams, Charles Nash and Henry B. Coombs, selectmen.

1870.   James B. Williams, Charles Nash and Finley B. Keller, selectmen.

1871.   Nelson Gilkey, Calvin W. Sherman and Silas Bunker, selectmen.

1872.   Nelson Gilkey, Calvin W. Sherman and Silas Bunker, selectmen.

1873.   Charles Nash, Finley B. Keller and Dodge Pendleton, selectmen.

Voted that the tax bills committed to William P. Sprague, Ephraim Coombs, James B. Williams and E. K. Pendleton, be put in the hands of the selectmen, and for them to appoint some person to collect the amount due on them.

Voted to recall and take out of the Supreme Judicial Court in this county, in favor of the inhabitants of Islesborough, and against William P. Sprague, the suit now pending.

1874.   Charles Nash, Finley B. Keller and Dodge Pendleton, selectmen.

Voted to accept the proposals of William P. Sprague in relation to tax bills committed to him for collection, for the years 1865 and 1866, as follows :

If the town will relinquish their claims against William P. Sprague and his bondsmen for uncollected taxes for the years 1865 and 1866, he will agree to deliver the bills for said years to the selectmen, without any claims for his commissions, for money he has collected, which commissions would amount to two hundred and one dollars. Voted to accept the above offer.

Voted to choose a committee of three. Chose Mark Pendleton, Benjamin Ryder and Henry B. Coombs to take William P. Sprague's tax bills, and examine them and report to the town.

1875. Charles Nash, Finley B. Keller and James H. Ryder, selectmen.

Voted this year to raise seven hundred dollars to pay L. A. Knowlton for interest.

Voted that the selectmen appoint a man to collect the balance due on the tax bills of Ephraim Coombs, E. K. Pendleton, James B. Williams and William P. Sprague.

1876. Charles Nash, Calvin W. Sherman and James H. Ryder, selectmen.

Ninth article in the warrant :   To see if the town will vote to exempt from tax money furnished by parties in town, to pay in part or the whole of what the town owes L. A. Knowlton, providing they will let money to the town for six per cent. annual interest.

Voted to adopt article ninth in the warrant, as it reads, providing it can be done legally.

1877. Charles Nash, Calvin W. Sherman and James H. Ryder, selectmen.

Voted to pay the taxes in to the treasurer, and after six months expire, the bills to be put into the hands of the high sheriff of the county for collection.

At a town meeting December 17, 1877, voted to pass the article to rescind the vote in relation to putting the tax bills into the high sheriff's hands for collection.

1878. Charles Nash, Daniel A. Hatch and James H. Ryder, selectmen.

1879. Charles Nash, Daniel A. Hatch and George M. Dix, selectmen.

1880. Nelson Gilkey, Daniel A. Hatch and Watson H. Coombs, selectmen.

1881. Nelson Gilkey, Daniel A. Hatch and Watson H. Coombs, selectmen.

1882. Nelson Gilkey, George M. Dix and James H. Ryder, selectmen.

1883. Nelson Gilkey, Daniel A. Hatch and Samuel T. Keller, selectmen.

1884. George M. Dix, James B. Williams and Samuel T. Keller, selectmen.

1885. George M. Dix, James B. Williams and E. A. Eames, selectmen.

1886. Amariah Trim, Samuel T. Keller and Walter E. Haynes, selectmen.
Voted a discount of ten per cent. on those who pay their taxes on or before the first day of November.

1887. Amariah Trim, Samuel T. Keller and Walter E. Haynes, selectmen.

1888. Amariah Trim, Samuel T. Keller and Austin Trim, selectmen.

1889. Amariah Trim, Samuel T. Keller and Austin Trim, selectmen.

1890. Austin Trim, Samuel T. Keller and Winfield S. Pendleton, selectmen.

1891. Austin Trim, Samuel T. Keller and Winfield S. Pendleton, selectmen.

1892. Austin Trim, Winfield S. Pendleton and Benjamin F. Heal, selectmen.

Voted to raise three thousand dollars to build town hall and high school.

## Town Clerks.

| | |
|---|---|
| Fields Coombs, | 1789 to 1801, 1807 to 1810 |
| Joseph Pendleton, | 1801–1807 |
| Jeremiah Hatch, | 1810–1812 |
| William Boardman, | 1812–1817 |
| Elisha Eames, | 1817–1824 and 1827 |
| Josiah Farrow, | 1825–1827 |
| Luther Coombs, | 1828 |
| Elisha Parker, | 1829–'32 |
| Andrew P. Gilkey, | 1832 |
| Anderson Parker, | 1833 |
| Rathburn D. Sprague, | 1834–1837 |
| James B. Williams, | 1837 to 1854 and 1866–'68 |
| Silas Bunker, | 1854 and 1862 |
| Otis F. Coombs, 1855–'57, '58–'62, '63–'65 & '79 | |
| Peleg Pendleton, | 1857 |
| Charles Nash, | 1868–1879 |
| Benjamin Ryder, | 1865 |
| Nelson Gilkey, | 1880–1885 |
| Jason R. Ryder, | 1885 and 1892 |
| Lincoln L. Gilkey, | 1886–1892 |

8

## The Finances of the Town of Islesborough.

The town, as shown by the reports of the selectmen, has never been in an embarrassing condition, the reports showing that their assets were more than their liabilities. The town frequently voted to pay the taxes in to the treasurer, and in many cases where the tax payers failed to do so, the treasurer or the constable became the collector. There was a residue remaining uncollected year after year; moneyed men out of town holding the orders and receiving great usury. In the year 1875 the town paid to one man seven hundred dollars for interest. One of the principal causes was unsettled taxes, and the town having a lawsuit about that time, was a sufferer to quite an amount.

In early Islesborough days the taxes were promptly collected, the town loaning money to the inhabitants, having a surplus in the treasury, the collector often paying into the treasurer the whole amount, on or before the annual March meeting. History repeats itself, and the halcyon days of our fathers have come back. In the years of 1888 and 1889 the taxes were all paid in to the treasurer, also in 1890 and 1891, to Amariah Trim and John P. Bragg, collectors. In 1891 the town was out of debt, with a small surplus in the treasury.

# CHAPTER IV.

## Schools and School-Houses.

ABOUT the year 1823 the Legislature made a law requiring the taxing of real estate for the building of school-houses, and repairing the same, in the districts where they are situated, and the town then defined the districts by limits, not by families or houses. Among the first transactions of the town after the organization was to divide the town into school districts.

At the commencement of the present century the first settlers were limited in books, and it is surprising that so few grew up without learning to read or write. All the books that they had were the Bible, Watts' hymn book and the Almanac, which were resorted to on all occasions. Many who never had but a few months' schooling became good readers and writers, and spelled correctly in after life. The first schools were kept in rooms in some house in the district, the teacher boarding around from house to house in the district where he taught school. This practice was kept up for more than fifty years. Each family would contribute and haul their proportion of the fuel, which was used in an open fire-place that burned half a cord a day. The ferule and birch were often made use of, and at times with great severity, whenever the teacher thought necessary, and were remembered by the scholars as long as they lived. The first school books were the American Preceptor, English Reader, Webster's Spelling Book,

Walsh's Arithmetic, Greenleaf's Grammar and Webster's Dictionary.

A transient visit was occasionally made by some traveling preacher, who would be hired to teach the winter school, among whom were Lemuel Rich, Elder Macomber, and Elder Ephraim Emery. The summer school was often kept by some of the inhabitants' daughters. Among the first teachers were Masters Powers, Abbott, Hall, Witham, Williams, Luce, Trueworthy, Andrew and George Pendleton and Josiah Eames; Mrs. Christina Thompson, Lydia Phillips, Eliza Farrow, Betsey and Sally Eames and Henry Rose; and at that time there was a plan made of the town, dividing it into seven school districts. I have made diligent search, but have not been able to find the plan. After a number of years they added a new district known as the Bluff, or No. 8. These school-houses remain on or near the same places where they were first located more than sixty years ago. That of district No. 1, situated on Seven-Hundred-Acre Island, remains the same as originally built. It has been kept in repair, and while not ornamental it is comfortable.

In district No. 2, a new school-house was built a few years ago, and is called by the inhabitants Dark Harbor school-house.

In district No. 3 the original school-house is to be taken down this year and a new one built. The school is known as the Creek school.

In district No. 4 a new school-house was built a few years ago. It is of good size with modern seats, is painted white, and has green blinds. It is built on or near the same place where the old school-house stood. This district is the largest in Islesborough, and has the most scholars. The school-house is known as the East Side school-house.

In district No. 5 the school-house was built in 1864, twenty eight years ago, and this year, 1892, has had extensive repairs. It is second in size in regard to scholars. The school-house is known as the Ryder school-house.

District No. 6, called the Sprague or West district, is a small one, having but a few scholars. The original school-house is still standing, but is kept in good repair.

District No. 7, known as the Parker district, has one of the best school-houses in town, having been recently repaired. A high school is being taught in it the present year. At present all the children in town have good schools and competent teachers, and many are sent to seminaries, high schools and commercial colleges, with but little thought on their part of the hardships those who preceded them sustained in order to acquire an education. It remains to be seen whether with their education they can fulfil their duties of life and make the record of their fathers.

I wish each school could be supplied with a copy of the town history, not as a special study, but for reference. How many good compositions could be written from it; and the rising generation would better know what it cost the first settlers to establish the town.


## NEW TOWN-HOUSE.


In 1892 the town made a handsome appropriation for building a new town-house, with accommodations for the high school. It is built on the commanding eminence between Crow Cove and Bounty Cove, being the site of the first meeting-house and town-house. A plan of the building is herein given.

## REPRESENTATIVES TO THE LEGISLATURE FROM ISLESBOROUGH.

Josiah Farrow was a member of the convention for framing a Constitution, 1819–20.

| 1823, 1826 and 1829, | Josiah Farrow. |
|---|---|
| 1832 and 1836, | Thomas Boardman. |
| 1842, .......... .... | Varnum Rose. |
| 1839 and 1845, Dexter Farrow. | Senator, 1847 |
| 1848, 1851 and 1852, | Joseph Boardman. |
| 1855,..................... | Calvin Eames. |
| 1858, | Nelson Gilkey. |
| 1862, | Andrew P. Gilkey. |
| 1864, | ....Otis F. Coombs. |
| 1867 and 1869, | Thomas H. Parker. |
| 1870 and '74, Calvin W. Sherman. Senator, 1881 | |
| 1877, | Lorenzo Pendleton. |
| 1880, | Winfield S. Pendleton. |
| 1889, | Mark P. Pendleton. |

1820. Thomas Waterman was the Representative from North Haven and Vinal Haven, originally Fox Islands; not of Islesborough, as given by the Maine Register, Islesborough being in the same class.

### JUSTICES OF THE PEACE,

and the years their names appear on the records.

| John Gilkey, | 1805 to 1809 |
|---|---|
| Mighill Parker, | 1818–1824 |
| Josiah Farrow, ... .......... | 1825–1836 |
| John Payne, | 1834–1840 |
| Henry Rose, | 1835 |
| Francis Grindle, | 1838 |
| R. D. Sprague, | 1842–1866 |
| Simon D. Sprague, | 1844–1875 |

Joshua Farrow, 1846–1866
Charles Nash, 1853–1879
Nelson Gilkey, 1861–1879
Rodolphus Pendleton, 1865
Thomas H. Parker, 1867–1875

William P. Sprague, 1874, last commission dated March 15, 1888.

Joseph A. Sprague, 1878, last commission dated May 15, 1890.

Alonzo Coombs, last commission dated April 27, 1886.

John P. Farrow, commission dated Feb. 6, 1889.

## PHYSICIANS.

One of the worst troubles the first settlers had to contend with was the want of a physician. There was no regular doctor here until 1830. When sickness was in any of the families they would man a boat and cross the bay, the people of the lower end going to Lincolnville, there get a team, and one of the party go to Camden after Dr. Estabrook, he being very popular with the first settlers, and was employed by them as long as he would come. He probably was their principal physician for more than thirty years. The people of the upper end of the town generally sent to Castine after Dr. Oliver Mann. He has crossed the bay a good many times for the Islesborough families, never refusing to come, no matter how bad the weather. The town was indebted to the late Dr. Joseph L. Stevens, of Castine, who was called there often for a large number of years. The old people speak of him with great respect. Mrs. Lydia Pendleton was called when there was no doctor (while the boat was gone to Camden). She had acquired some practical knowledge, and became very useful; was known by the inhabitants as Aunt Lydia Jonathan.

The earliest physician of whom we have knowledge, that practiced in Islesborough, was Dr. John Payne. He was here from 1830 to 1840.

The next physician was Dr. Fairfield, who married Thankful Phillips. She was a daughter of Elder Thomas Ames. He came about 1840, practicing for several years. He was a surgeon in the war of 1812; served on board the private armed brigantine called the "Scourge."

Dr. S. D. Buzzell came here about 1852, practicing here a number of years. He was well advanced in years. He moved away. The date of his death and his age are unknown.

Dr. John DeLaski came here from Fox Island about 1857. He was a man of good education, and a skillful physician. He stayed only two or three years, then moved back to Fox Island.

Dr. Moses Dakin came here, about 1860, from Hope. He was well advanced in years when he commenced practicing here. He was here a number of years, and was respected, but somewhat eccentric.

Dr. Nathaniel Davis was here for a short time, and though a regular practitioner, was not popular.

Dr. L. W. Hammons moved here in 1885, meeting with fair success. Having a large family, he thought he could do better, and moved to Belfast in 1891.

## Churches and Meeting-Houses.

Prior to 1790 the religious privileges of the town were few. Occasionally a minister came on to the island and preached a few Sabbaths. That year Rev. Isaac Case, Baptist pastor at Thomaston, came here and preached, and in 1791 he organized the first Baptist church. The inhabitants were for many years Baptists of the old school.

In 1794 the town voted £20 a year to Thomas Ames as minister. In 1800 the town employed the Rev. Charles Thomas to preach. Mr. Thomas married Rachel Gilkey, Jan. 30, 1788, and lived on the island many years. Rev. Charles G. Porter in his memorial address at Winthrop, 1874, says that Mr. Case came here and settled, but I doubt if he brought his family here. In 1804 Mr. Case baptised forty-three persons, who were admitted to the church. The same year Thomas Ames was ordained pastor of the church, continuing until 1809, when he removed to Hope.

In 1809 Rev. Lemuel Rich was ordained pastor of the church. He was born at East Machias, Jan. 10, 1780. He married, while here, Grace, daughter of John Gilkey. Published Feb. 16, 1810. He was dismissed in 1819, and removed to Union or Hope, where he died in 1864.

About 1832 Rev. Ephraim W. Emery came. He married here Temperance, widow of Stephen Pruden. Published March 10, 1832. She was daughter of Benjamin Williams. He continued here until after 1834.

Rev. William J. Durgin was ordained pastor of the church in March, 1843. He died here Dec. 19, 1868.

In 1845 the church membership was one hundred and twenty-eight. Since this time many other Baptist ministers have preached here.

Many of the inhabitants came to meeting in their boats. They brought their dinners with them, and would remain till the afternoon service. Some came on horseback, their wives riding on behind, the children walking with their shoes in their hands, and when they got to church putting them on. The men were dressed with long-tailed coats made of blue broadcloth, with bright brass buttons, with a ruffled shirt and a buff vest, a red handkerchief, part of which would hang out of their coat pocket. The

9

ladies were dressed with short waists and short skirts; their feet covered with shoes, with a black silk bow or a buckle on top; a ruffle round the neck, and a head dress called a calash.

The first meeting-house was built wholly or in part by the town. It was occupied by the Baptists, and by the town for town meetings. It was begun soon after 1794, and completed in 1804. The building was thirty-seven by forty, two stories high, and but a single door. It was neatly finished inside and out. There were sixteen large windows. The porch was about sixteen feet square on the ground and sixteen feet high, divided into two rooms, and a stairway to go up into the galleries. The house was twenty feet posts, with a hip roof. It was placed nearly north and south, and the pulpit was in the north end, with winding stairs leading up to it. In front of the pulpit on the ground floor, was what was called the deacon's seat. The galleries ran around three sides of the house. Across the south side were the singing seats opposite the altar. The galleries were nine feet wide, with four rows of seats rising one above the other. The under part was plastered. It was finished with heavy mouldings. The galleries were supported with heavy columns and finished with capitals. The work was done in a thorough and workmanlike manner. In 1794 the town raised fifty pounds to build the house, but it was not completed till 1804, when they had their first meeting. Mr. Mark Dodge did the stone work, and laid the underpinning. Simon, his brother, worked with him. Capt. Stephen Pendleton and Noah Dodge loaned money to the town for the house. There was no steeple or chimney, and no means of warming the house were provided.

Tithing-men were chosen by the town, whose special duty was to enforce regulations for observing the Sabbath.

OLD TOWN HOUSE AND MEETING HOUSE.

NEW TOWN HOUSE—1892.

## First Baptist Meeting-House, 1794-1804.

[*The following is a copy of the original ground plan, with the names of pew-owners.*]

| Jonathan Parker | Minister | | Pulpit | Joshua Dodge | Simon Pendleton | Simon Sprague | |
|---|---|---|---|---|---|---|---|
| Simon Dodge | | | Deacon Seat | | | | Thomas Williams |

| Mighill Parker | David Thomas | Rathburn D. Sprague | Benjamin Williams | Amos Williams | Thomas Williams |
|---|---|---|---|---|---|
| Robert Pendleton | Jeremiah Hatch | Rathburn Dodge | Noah Dodge | Joseph Pendleton | Isaac Coombs |
| James Sherman | William Pendleton | Paoli Hewes | John Farrow | John Pendleton | Mark Dodge |
| Elisha Nash | Robert Coombs | Ellison Lassell | Joseph Williams | Thomas Gilkey | Joseph Pendleton |
| Mark Pendleton | | | | | Anthony Coombs |
| Elisha Eames | Robert Sherman | Josiah Farrow | Fields Coombs | Robert Farnsworth | Joseph Boardman |

Stairs to Gallery

This meeting-house was occupied until 1845, when the Baptists built a new church.

[*Ground plan of the Second Baptist Meeting-House, built in 1815, with the names of the pew-holders.*

| Daniel Hatch | Prudence Williams | James Sherman | Minister | Pulpit | | Church | Lorenzo Pendleton | Catherine Sherman | Joseph Boardman |
|---|---|---|---|---|---|---|---|---|---|
| 13 | 14 | 15 | 16 | | | 42 | 41 | 40 | 39 |
| Daniel Hatch | 12 | | Dea. John Pendleton | Dea. Thomas Gilkey | | | | Elisha Pendleton | |
| John Gilkey | 11 | | Dea. James Hatch | Roscoe Gilkey | | | | Nelson Gilkey | |
| Robert Trim | 10 | 19 | Avery Gilkey | Elsie Pendleton | | | | Thomas Williams | |
| George Hatch | 9 | 20 | Eben Babbidge | Winsor Williams | | | | Charles Pendleton | |
| Emma Farrow | 8 | 21 | James Hatch | Edwin Eames | | | | O. F. Scott | |
| Catherine Pendleton | 7 | 22 | Amasa Hatch | Benjamin Hatch | | | | F. C. Pendleton | |
| Emily Pendleton | 6 | 23 | Nathaniel Hatch | William Dodge | | | | Judson Philbrook | |
| Calvin Sherman | 5 | 24 | Luther Farnsworth | Charles Dodge | | | | Justina Thomas | |
| Joseph Pendleton | 4 | 25 | Simon Sprague | David H. Rose | | | | Anna Pendleton | |
| Richmond Pendleton | 3 | | Dolly W. Farrow | William Farrow | | | | James F. Grindle | |
| James B. Adams | 2 | | Henry Boardman | Noah Dodge | | | | Emery Williams | |
| Isaac Warren | 1 | | | | | | | Pyam Hatch | |

Door     Door

Door     Door

FREE BAPTIST CHURCH.

FIRST BAPTIST CHURCH.

The Free Baptists built a meeting-house at the northerly end of the town in 1843. Elder Ephraim Coombs was the first preacher there the same year.

[*Ground plan of the Free Baptist Meeting-House, built in 1843, with the names of pew-holders.*]

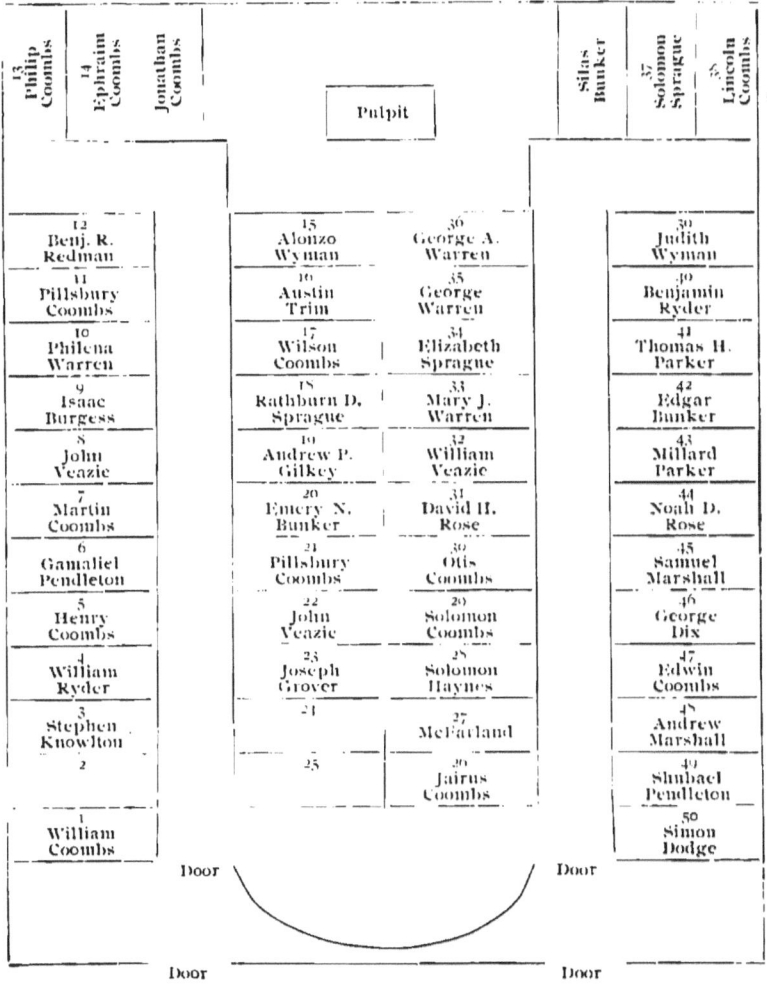

The following is a list of ministers or preachers in Islesborough, with the year in which their names appear on the records :

Rev. Thomas Ames, 1789-1807.
Rev. Charles Thomas, 1800.
Rev. Lemuel Rich, 1810.
Rev. John Still, about 1810.
Rev. Enoch Stedman, 1817.
Rev. Samuel Macomber, 1825.
Rev. Ephraim H. Emery, 1831-'42, here again 1873-'76.
Rev. Varnum S. Rose, 1844-'65, born in Islesborough.
Rev. William J. Durgin, 1844-'67, died Dec. 19, 1868.
Rev. John Clark, 1849-'56.
Rev. A. Ross, 1850.
Rev. D. Small, 1855-'56.
Rev. William Small, 1856.
Rev. Aaron Clark, 1857.
Rev. Edward Turner, 1858-'60.
Rev. James Small, 1861.
Rev. J. R. Bowler, 1861-'62.
Rev. C. M. Roades, 1866-'69, again 1872-'75.
Rev. N. E. Everett, 1870.
Rev. Jabez Fletcher, 1875.
Rev. N. A. Avery, 1879.
Rev. Ephraim Coombs, born in Islesborough, died 1872.
Rev. Joshua Pendleton, of Islesborough, died at Islesborough.
Rev. Hugh R. Hatch, born in Islesborough May 20, 1865.
Rev. J. K. West, 1886, Free Baptist.
Rev. William A. Atchley.
Rev. David Haggett, 1877.
Rev. ―――― MacMaster, 1865.

## FRAGMENTARY HISTORY AND INCIDENTS.

In the war of 1812, when the English ships were in Castine, there was a neutrality established between the settlers on the island, on account of its situation. The inhabitants found a ready market for their produce. Everything that they had to sell brought good prices, and to a certain extent they reaped a harvest. They had but little land under cultivation, and their supply was limited. Their money being scarce, they would get together all that was possible to obtain, and carry it to Castine, and sell to the English ships. The neighboring towns hearing of this, would bring their produce over to the island, the island people carrying it to Castine as their own production; the English thinking Islesborough the garden of Eden. Their action on this occasion was not patriotic, but considering the hard times they had to get along, they were excusable in a manner; and in those days, as well as the present, they sacrificed principle for money. The neutrality was not carried out to the letter, in the case of Mr. Henry Boardman. He had a yoke of oxen, which the English wished to purchase for beef. On his refusing to sell the oxen they told him they would take them without paying for them. Discretion being better than valor the oxen were sold.

Upwards of seventy families were here in 1812 and 1813. Great hardships were endured in consequence of the high cost of the necessaries of life. Some, without doubt, would have entered the military or naval service, but on account of their insular situation they were not permitted to join either side. The inhabitants were not hostile to the United States government. The harsh and frigid realities of war were sensibly felt. Commerce was at an end, and hardly a coaster dared venture out of the harbor. The price of provisions was fabulous: flour twenty dollars per barrel; molasses one dollar and a half per gallon;

tea from two to three dollars per pound; coffee forty cents
per pound.*

Scarcely half a century has passed since the inhabitants
would carefully rake up the ashes over the coals in their
fire places, when retiring for the night, as they had no
means of lighting their fires excepting by a flint and steel,
which was kept in a tinder box. This process of getting
fire was obtained with considerable trouble, so if their fire
went out they would often go to their nearest neighbor
and get a fire-brand or some live coals (in a box with a
handle, which was made for that purpose). The first
matches were of lucifer or sulphur, ignited by drawing
through sand paper. They were introduced here about
1839. Afterwards a match called locofoco became universal, and at the present time when a person goes very early
to a neighbor's house, he will often be greeted with "Did
you come after fire?"

The first inhabitants, after clearing a part of their land
and building their log cabin, next provided themselves
with a boat, which was indispensable to them. It was
used for fishing, going to mill, to cross to the main land,
to sell their produce and get their stores, and was used on
Sunday to go to meeting; not to attend divine worship or
go to church, but simply to go to meeting. Some of the
more wealthy, about the year 1815, purchased horses, and
the first six that were in Islesborough were owned by
Rathburn Dodge, Jonathan Parker, Mighill Parker, William Pendleton, John Pendleton and Joseph Boardman.
They would ride on horseback, their wives sitting behind
them on a pillion, when going to meeting or visiting some
of the neighbors. The first carriage was owned by Rathburn Dodge, and was called a "chaise."

* Williamson's History of Belfast, page 435.

When the first settlers came here the island was mostly covered with spruce, with a scattering of beech, birch and maple. All that had ever been here to stop were the Tarratine Indians, who would visit the island in the summer. The waters abounded in fish and the shores in clams. The wild ducks were plenty in the coves, and on the shore hatched their young. The wild fox dug his hole unscared. The mink was plenty on the rocky shores, with none to molest but the Indian, who paddled his birch canoe along the shores a few weeks in summer. Tradition informs us that the salmon were so plenty that the first town poor protested against being served with salmon more than twice a week.

The island was taken up mostly in lots of one hundred acres. After felling the trees not more than one-third of the land was fit to cultivate, the residue being ledgy and swampy. The land that they could cultivate produced bountifully. One of their principal crops was potatoes, which they would ship to Boston, where they would get nine pence (12½ cents) per bushel. The average price paid·for their land to the proprietors was about one hundred and twenty-five dollars for each farm. They built their houses one story, with three rooms, bedroom and buttery on the ground floor. They had one chimney in the centre of the house, which would take ten thousand bricks to build. The fire-place in the kitchen would burn cord wood six feet long. The kitchen was ornamented with a pole hung from the ceiling used for drying pumpkins, herbs, clothes, etc., with a gun hung up on the partition. They used sand on the floors and cedar boughs for a broom.

The people were united, and would often club together and build a coaster, which their sons would often take charge of at the age of twenty years. Their money was principally Spanish milled dollars. Their hospitality was

10

unlimited, and the stranger found a welcome at their
table. Honesty and plain dealing were characteristic of
them. The children were brought up to respect the aged,
always using the title "sir" to the men, and would take
off their hats or make a courtesy. Their carriages were
supported by thorough-braces for springs, and were so
well made that they would last for half a century. The
first sleigh had but one thill, with tugs hitched to a
whiffle-tree. Now the supposed millionaire. summer
guest, with his span of horses and his barouche, rides the
streets, while those who are native here, and "to the
manor born," look on with an amused surprise which he
hardly appreciates.

Mr. Mark Dodge owned an island in east Penobscot bay
by the name of Beach Island, which he deeded to his son
Joseph. He got Esquire Nash to make out the conveyance. When he signed the deed he wrote his name in
capital letters. "Why did you sign your name all in
capitals, Mr. Dodge?" asked the justice. "Did you not
know that Mark Dodge was a capital man, sir?"

Jack Farrow was a dog that was a friend to every-
body, and every one was friendly to Jack. He would go
to church early Sunday morning with the man who had
charge of the house, and lay by the stove through the
service, and after meeting come home. One Sunday
another dog came into church, and Jack pitched in for a
fight. The deacon got up to put the dogs out, when an
old lady rose and said, "Don't you put Jack Farrow out.
He is all the one of the family that goes to meeting."

Jack Richardson was a Frenchman. He lived on an
island known as Frenchman's Island. He was a very
short and thick-set man. He would get a little too much
of strong drink, though in this respect he was only following the example of many of the settlers. There was a
minister by the name of Pullen, who went to visit Jack,

and after showing him the evil of his ways he (Jack) promised to do better. So the minister left him on probation, and would return and baptize him. When he came back to the island, and was ready to perform the services, Jack said, "Brother Pullen, let us take a drop of grog before we go into the water." "Oh, no, brother Richardson." "You refuse to drink with Jack? Go to hell, then." There lived on the same island a man and his wife named Nichols. There was born to them a boy and a girl. This being Jack's paradise, he insisted and had them named Adam and Eve.

Joshua Dodge was a salmon fisherman. He came from his nets one day and had twelve salmon in his boat. John Bowden, who was a town pauper, was on the shore when Mr. Dodge landed. "Them are nice fish, Mr. Dodge." "Johnny, I will give you one," said Mr. Dodge. "Oh, no! I shall dirty my clothes if I take one home."

The hardships of some of the first settlers, in the Revolutionary war, were severe. The case of Esq. John Gilkey was peculiarly hard. He settled on the point where the light-house now stands, and from him the harbor derives its name. He had five small children, and but one cow. He was at work in the field, when a privateer boat came on shore and by force made him go with them in the boat, leaving everything just as it was. He was gone nearly three years from home, all of this time never hearing from his family, his wife having a hard time with her small children. One day a boat came, full of men, and took her cow and butchered it, she begging them with tears running down her cheeks; saying that it was all she had, and if they took her cow her children would starve. He was at last released, and landed on White Head, an island on the coast of Maine in the Mussel Ridge channel, where he started on foot and walked home, hiding in the daytime and walking nights. At Lincolnville he found an Indian canoe, in which he crossed the bay, and at last got home. He received a pension from the United States government towards the last of his life.

One of our young men in charge of a coasting vessel, coming home from a trip, anchored in Sabbath-Day harbor on a foggy night, paid out forty fathoms of chain, furled the sails, manned the boat and permitted the crew to go home. The captain went to see his sweetheart. There was very little wind in the night, but in the morning the schooner was ashore on the beach at the head of the harbor. With some surprise the captain went to the schooner. Sure enough there were forty fathoms of chain in the hawse, but the anchor was on the bobstay.

There is a story of one of the old persons, who did not agree with his nearest neighbor; but when there was any stone work to do—laying cellar wall or building stone wall—they always worked together. One of them died suddenly, and the other began to lay up wall alone. He was laying up a cellar wall, when a passer-by said to him, "Don't you wish that uncle (mentioning his name) was here to help you complete the wall?" "Well, yes, if he would go straight back to Tophet as quick as the wall was laid up."

The use of ardent spirits was a source of more or less dissatisfaction among the people in early days. On one occasion a member of the church, who was in the habit of making too free with intoxicating liquor, was dealt with by the church. The charge was proved against him, and he was to be suspended. The presiding minister said, "Brother, what have you got to say why you should not be expelled?" "Well, I confess that I have done wrong, but the last time that I drank any liquor, you and I drank it together when we were in Providence."

ISLESBOROUGH SKETCH.

SHORE RAVINE, NORTH ISLESBOROUGH.

## DESCRIPTIVE.

The points of interest on the island of Islesborough are numerous and varied. A great diversity of scenery greets the stranger when driving from Turtle Head to the southern end of the island. The scenery along the east and west bays is especially striking. Jutting promontories and headlands, stern ledges and boulders, beautiful beaches covered with sand and pebbles, and numerous coves, are observable on either side and along the entire length of the island. The east and west bays are dotted with sails of every description; schooners, yachts and steamboats lend enchantment to the view. The roads are fringed on either side with evergreens, and the houses are neat and modest. The landscape is one of fields and pastures. Away in the west are seen the mountains of Camden and Northport, and in the east Cape Rosier, Blue Hill, and Isle au Haut. No scenery, to my mind, is superior to that of the grand Penobscot bay from some of the points overlooking its eastern and western branches.

Being surrounded by water, the thermometer does not rise so high nor fall so low by several degrees as on the main shore. There is a difference, in very cold weather, between the east and the west side, of two and three degrees; the north-west winds sweeping the westerly shore, and driving the snow in heaps, while the east side remains comparatively level. The southerly and easterly winds are mild in comparison with the northerly and westerly winds in the winter. Violent north-west winds were frequent in the winter months, lasting two or three days, with a change of temperature. The thermometer would often go below zero. For the last ten or twelve years the north-west winds have not blown with the same severity that they did formerly, and there has been a noticeable change in the climate in this respect.

In 1780 the winter was particularly severe. Travelers went on foot across the ice. The celebrated dark day occurred May 19.

1786-'87. Intense cold. Ice was formed in the bay so thick that when the water rose, rocks of large size were lifted from their beds.

1793. October 31, snow fell six or eight inches.

1798. Snow fell Nov. 16 and remained until April. The spring was early.

1810. January 19, cold Friday; violent storm; change of temperature, forty-six degrees in fifteen hours.

1816. For the first time during a period of thirty-five years the bay was frozen over. The coldest summer on record in Europe and America. June 11, ice froze one-fourth of an inch thick. July 5, ice froze the thickness of window glass. Corn was frozen in August so that it was cut for fodder. There was frost and ice every month in the year, and the farmer was discouraged. Some built brush fires around their corn-fields, and succeeded in raising corn for seed. The inhabitants generally feared a famine, so great was the scarcity of food. They lived principally on fish, as there were no vegetables grown excepting potatoes, in sheltered localities.

1818. The bay frozen, and the people going to Castine and Belfast on the ice until March 23.

1821. Snow-storm October 19, snowing the whole day.

1823. June 9, heavy frost. Ice formed the thickness of window glass. Nothing in the history equal to the drought of that year, before or since. Rivers dried up, vegetation withered; cattle were driven for miles to water, and September 29 there was a considerable fall of snow.

1826. The thermometer in this locality twenty-four degrees below zero.

1828. The winter was the mildest ever known.

1829. Roads obstructed by heavy drifts. May 25, the thermometer in this vicinity indicated ninety-five in the shade.

1830. June 7, heavy frost. July 16, the thermometer ninety-two in the shade in the vicinity. July 18 and 19 it was ninety-six.

1832. April 28, a snow-storm which continued thirty-six hours.

1833. March 14, snow very deep. Nearly all the harbors east of Cape Cod closed by ice.

1835. February 8, the bay frozen to the outer islands. Horses and sleighs crossed the bay until March. The longest continuation of severe cold perhaps ever known in the State by the white inhabitants. A great scarcity of hay. Mr. Benjamin Ryder went on the ice to Isle au Haut, from Fox islands.

1837. January 1 a snow-storm commenced, snowing five days that week. The drifts were very deep, and there was no traveling by teams for four or five days.

1839. April 18 (Fast Day) there was a heavy fall of snow.

1840. April 27, rain and snow, and frost the first day of June.

1843. January 4, the coldest day for three years.

1844. January 27, coldest day for the winter. Thermometer twenty-five degrees below zero in Belfast. The bay frozen to the outer islands.

1845. April 26, a snow-storm. A total failure of the potato crop, on account of the potato rot.

1848. An open winter.

1849. Extremely cold on February 16. Bay frozen, and so remained for ten days. Persons crossing the bay on ice-boats.

1850. April 13, a snow-storm. Heavy fall of snow for the season of the year.

1853. February 13, the most severe storm of the season. It is said that no storm had occurred on that date before for one hundred and two years.

1854. January 1, severe snow-storm, and no mail for a week. May 7, ice made one-half inch thick.

1855. February 8, thermometer twenty degrees or more below.

1856. The snow the deepest for years. Roads impassable for two or three days.

1857. January 18 to 25 the week intensely cold, and almost unceasing storm; known as the cold term of 1857, and undoubtedly the most remarkable of this century. The mercury in the thermometers at Bangor and other places congealed. In Belfast it was thirty-four degrees below; this being the coldest day since the cold Friday of 1810. The inhabitants went to Belfast from Castine on the ice, and all the harbors closed as far south as the Potomac.

1859. February 14 was a very cold day.

1861. February 8, one of the coldest days ever known. Between February 7 and 8 the thermometer showed a change of more than fifty degrees in twelve hours.

1870. Ice was formed one-half inch thick on May 2. The hottest day ever known in the latitude was July 24.

1874. The Colorado beetle (potato bug) made its first appearance.

BENJAMIN AMES HOUSE—LATER JOHN P. FARROW.

1875. In January the bay froze over, and remained frozen until April, teams crossing to Belfast all that time. April 2, Mr. Hooper, of Castine, crossed with his team to Belfast. There was a regular conveyance running daily, carrying passengers to and from Belfast, besides the private teams, which crossed for more than two months. The only accident which happened to the island people was in the case of Capt. George Keller, who lost his horse through a hole in the ice, between Spruce Island and Seal Harbor Point.

## OLD HOUSES OF ISLESBOROUGH.

The old house of the Rev. Thomas Ames is still standing. It has been a feature of the town for more than a century, with its huge frame of hewn ash timbers. The house was covered with pine shingles split out by hand, which were .perfectly sound on the walls, nailed on with wrought nails. The roof was covered with these shingles, and was re-shingled in 1890. The architecture was cosmopolitan, at the time it was built, and all the old houses were run in very much the same mold. It was one story, and only eight feet posts. According to the most reliable information that can be obtained, it is the oldest dwelling house remaining in Islesborough. It was

NOTES.—In 1865 the drought was very severe in September. The wells and springs failed entirely. The inhabitants of the upper end of the town hauled their water from the meadow pond, and carried their clothes there to be washed.

It is said of an old man in the town that he refused water to one of his neighbors whom he did not like, and he was taken dry, and remained dry until his death ; that water would not satisfy his thirst. It was probably his complaint or disease.

The authorities consulted in obtaining these records of the weather were Hon. Joseph Williamson, Dr. George A. Wheeler, of Castine, Mr. Lucius H. Murch, Robert B. Thomas' Almanac, and by oral transmitting of the old inhabitants.

11

modified somewhat in 1890, in its exterior, by the addition of an ell on the south end, and dormer windows set in the roof, by the Islesborough Land and Improvement Company, who own the property and make use of the land for raising vegetables to supply their hotel at Dark Harbor.

The accompanying view shows the house as it was originally built. The chimney still remains in the centre of the house, with the three fire-places somewhat modified. It is covered with plank treenailed to the sill and plate. It stands as firm as when built, and if left to remain, with proper care would last another century.

The first framed house was built on the lower end, and known as the Boardman house. Not being kept in repair it became dilapidated. It was taken down a few years ago, and the old material used for other purposes. The situation of the house was on the land now owned by Jeffrey R. Brackett.

The old house of Deacon John Pendleton is one hundred and fourteen years old. It is owned by the Islesborough Land and Improvement Company, and is to be taken down. The walls are covered with plank treenailed to the sill and plate. It was shingled a few years ago, but with this exception there have been but very few repairs on its exterior since it was built, and it is in a remarkable state of preservation, considering its age.

Captain J. Francis Grindle's house has passed its centennial year. Always being kept in repair, it hardly shows its age, excepting in its architecture. It was built by John Gilkey, Esq., a man prominent among the first settlers. It is held with a kind of veneration by Captain Grindle and his relatives. It is situated near the entrance of Gilkey's harbor, and has been a landmark for the mariner for more than one hundred years.

Mr. Abner Marshall's house is situated on the south side of Crow Cove. A part of this house is among the first built in Islesborough. The house was repaired, with additions, painted, and to a certain extent modernized, in 1891.

The old house of the late Henry Boardman, situated on the east side, being among the first built, was repaired a few years since, it being very conspicuous when sailing up or down the east Penobscot bay.

A few of the old settlers' houses are still standing, among which are Mrs. Catherine Sherman's, Mr. Edson Sherman's, Capt. D. A. Warren's, Amasa Hatch's, Luther Farnsworth's, Nelson Gilkey's, and the old Farrow house. These houses are situated on the lower end, or below the Narrows.

At the upper end of the town, the old Coombs house is standing, and in good condition. It is now occupied by the third generation.

The old Warren house has been repaired, and is now used by the Lime Kiln Company.

The Jacob Moody house, situated on the west side, near Seal Harbor, at present occupied by Mr. J. B. Adams, is one of the old houses still remaining. It will probably be replaced by a new and more modern house.

There are some of the original frames of these old houses that remain, but they have a modern appearance, with no similarity of the original.

The writer of these sketches was born in one of those old houses, and has seen them disappear one by one until the present time, when but few remain. In their stead the moneyed men now build their costly cottages, while the natives are obliged to seek other homes. There is a decrease of our inhabitants (as shown by the census), who are gradually leaving the old homes of their fathers, and their children's children will not know the place, excepting by history.

After the log house was built at Henry Boardman's, the timber was hewed from the trees that were felled near the place where the barn was erected, and the old people say that this was the first framed building in Islesborough. The tradition is somewhat contradictory in regard to the first framed building, and I quote authority. Mrs. Charlotte Boardman, a lady of seventy-one years, now living, says that she has often heard her father and the old people make mention of this fact. There is on this estate a double damask rose bush, that was transplanted when they built the log house. At the present time it is flourishing, and this year (1892) it bore more than three hundred roses.

In this barn they held their first meeting, and there was where the first church was organized. Elder Thomas Ames was the minister. They used this barn for a meeting-house until 1804, when the new meeting-house was completed.

### NAMES AND DESCRIPTION OF LOCALITIES.

1. The town landing, at the southern end of the island, on the land of Jeffrey R. Brackett, in Gilkey's Harbor. Near this landing was the first cemetery, and here is the oldest gravestone in Islesborough.

2. Dark Harbor, on the east side, near the Islesborough Inn. The proprietors, when the land was first taken, were Oliver and John Pendleton; at present, Islesborough Land Company.

3. Boardman's Bluff, on the east side, above Dark Harbor. The cove that makes in from the bluff, at pres-

ent, tradition says, was a straight shore when the Board-mans first settled there. This shore has been used for baptisms for more than a century.

4. Capt. Joe's Rock, on the east side, on the shore of the late Capt. Joseph Pendleton estate. There was a salmon berth there, which was used for many years.

5. The Bonnet, on the east side, on the land of the late Joshua Dodge; owned at present by his son, William S. Dodge.

6. Little Island, on the east side, off the land of Mark Pendleton, below Hewes' Point, in Pendleton Cove.

7. Abram's Mountain, near Hewes' Point, on the east side. Elevation one hundred and thirty feet.

8. Hewes' Point, below the Narrows, on the east side, a summer resort, with steamboat wharf, hotel, and summer cottages.

9. Ice-House Hill, near the Narrows. The town road went over this hill. Mrs. Lucy Pendleton was thrown out of a carriage on this hill, breaking her arm. She claimed damages of the town, and entered into litigation, and the case was finally settled in her favor. After a time the road was shifted around the hill.

10. The Narrows, or Carrying Place. At extreme high tide, and heavy wind, the water flows across from west to east Penobscot bay.

11. Bounty Cove, on the east side, near and above the Narrows. Here the first settler built his log cabin, and the place was known as Williams' Cove, Bounty Cove being a modern name.

12. Sabbath-Day Harbor (or Ryder's Cove), on the east side, about a third of the way from the Narrows to Turtle Head. Sabbath-Day Harbor derives its name from the fishermen. In early days the fishermen in east Penobscot bay would come in here and remain over the Sabbath

day. A road is in contemplation, running around the head of the harbor to the Bluff.

13. The Bluff, on the north-eastern side of Sabbath-Day Harbor. The elevation is one hundred and forty feet.

14. Coombs' Cove and Parker's Cove, on the east side, above the Bluff.

15. Hutchins' Island, a small island of about fifteen acres, with a sand bar to the main land. Off this island, in east Penobscot bay, is a ledge called by the inhabitants Old Frank Ledge. Its name is derived from Capt. W. Franklin Dodge, who got his vessel ashore on this ledge more than once.

16. Philip Coombs' Point and Beach. The first steamboat wharf was built off this beach for the T. F. Secor, which commenced running in 1846. The wharf was about half-way from Turtle Head to Sabbath-Day Harbor.

17. Lime Kiln. There was a lime kiln here that was used by the first settlers, but it went to decay. The quarry is now owned by a New York company, who are manufacturing lime at the present time. They built a wharf, and the steamboat regularly makes her landing at this wharf, to and from Belfast.

18. Turtle Head, the northern extremity of Islesborough.

19. Lasell Beach, on the west shore, in Turtle Head Cove; the sea wall making the town road.

20. Kidder's Hill. The high land rising from Turtle Head Cove on the west side, so called, probably, from a family that lived there when the island was first settled. None of their descendants are in town at the present time.

21. Dailey's Cove, on the west shore, to the northward of Sprague's Cove. It is thus designated by a man of that name who once lived there.

HEAD OF SEAL HARBOR

SEAL HARBOR POINT

22.   The Meadow Pond contains about ten acres when there is no freshet, or heavy fall of rain.   Its outlet is in Sprague's Cove.   The pond furnishes the supply of ice for the town.

23.   Sprague's Cove, on the west side.   At the head of the cove there was a shingle mill.   The power was obtained from the Meadow Pond.   A part of the old dam remains.   Mr. Noah Dodge had a tannery here, and the old holes or vats can still be seen.   The ledges that lay off the cove are called Sprague's Ledges.   One of these ledges is designated the Barley Ledge.   A vessel loaded with barley ran on to the ledge and filled with water. The inhabitants got more or less of the damaged barley for their hogs.

24.   Seal Harbor, on the west side, is used for a winter harbor to haul up coasting vessels.   At the head of the harbor there is a lime quarry, where lime was burnt for a number of years, but it has now gone out of use.

25.   The Burying Point, on the south side of Seal Harbor, and the north side of Crow Cove.   The elevation is sixty feet.   It was used as a burying ground by the first settlers.

26.   Crow Cove, on the west side.   The head of the cove makes the Narrows.

27.   Stone's Hill, south of Crow Cove, and on the west side.   Elevation one hundred and twenty feet.   It took the name from Stone, who lived there seventy years ago.

28.   Gooseberry Nubble.   The point which makes out into the bay, on the west shore, above Grindle's Point.

29.   Grindle's Point.   The entrance to Gilkey's Harbor, west Penobscot bay.

30.   Sherman's Point, in Gilkey's Harbor, on the east side.

31. Warren Mountain, on the east side of Gilkey's Harbor. Elevation one hundred and forty feet.

32. Richmond's wharf, in Gilkey's Harbor, near Warren Mountain.

33. Shipyard in Gilkey's Harbor, to the southward of Warren Mountain.

34. Eames' Cove, in Gilkey's Harbor, opposite Dark Harbor.

Turtle Head derives its name from Governor Pownal. At the same time Owl's Head, at the entrance of the Mussel Ridge channel, was named by him. He says: "About opposite the ridge called Megunticoog begins the south point of an island, which lies lengthwise in the middle of Penobscot bay. It is about twelve miles long, and is called Long Island. The north point, from the shape which it makes from sea, exactly resembling a turtle, we called Turtle Head."[*]

During the war of 1812 the Penobscot bay was infested with vessels of the enemy, and particularly privateers, cutting off the principal support of the inhabitants of Islesborough, who followed the sea in their coasting vessels. They were often under the necessity of risking their lives for the necessaries of life. In the year 1813 Capt. Hosea Bates was taken by a British privateer, and he and his crew were set on shore near Camden. The vessel was put in charge of a prize master. A few of the island people manned their boats, went off and recaptured her; and in about four hours from the time she was first captured they carried her to Camden. In a short time after this [†] the schooner Fly, a British privateer, was in the roadstead of Owl's Head flying the American ensign,

---

*Williamson's History of Belfast.

† Locke's History of Camden.

and by this means succeeded in capturing one of our island vessels, and at the same time captured a vessel belonging to Thomaston.

## THE ECLIPSE OF 1780.

The total eclipse of 1780 was visible on Long Island. Upon petition of many distinguished and learned men the General Court, by a resolve, Sept. 12, 1780, approved of an expedition to Long Island, and gave assistance. Joseph Williamson, Esq., of Belfast, read a paper giving an account of it, before the Maine Historical Society, which is here given :

Resolve directing the Board of War to fit out the State galley for the conveyance of Rev. Samuel Williams, Hollisian professor of Mathematics, &c., to Penobscot, to make observations on the eclipse of the sun, to be on the 27th of October next. Passed September 12th, 1780.

Whereas representation has been made to this court by the Hon. James Bowdoin, Esq., and others, lovers of learning and mankind, that on the 27th day of October next there will happen in the neighborhood of Penobscot a central and total eclipse of the sun, a phenomenon never apparent in these States since their settlement : and as observations thereof may be of much consequence in science, particularly in geography and navigation ; and that the Rev. Samuel Williams, Hollisian professor of Mathematics in this State, will be ready to give his aid, with such assistance as may be proper, to make the necessary observations at the most convenient place near Penobscot : therefore

Resolved, That the Board be and they hereby are ordered and directed to fit out the State galley, with proper stores and accommodation, for the conveyance of the Rev. Samuel Williams, Hollisian professor of Mathematics and Natural Philosophy at the University of Cambridge, and such attendants as he may think proper to take with him, to make the

12

aforesaid observation on the central and total eclipse of the
sun, which will happen on the said 27th day of October, at
or near Penobscot, and that the Council be and they are
hereby requested to write proper letters to the British com-
mander of the garrison at Penobscot, that the important
designs of the said observations may not be frustrated.

[*From Memoirs of the American Academy of Arts and Sciences.*]

Observations of a solar eclipse, October 27, 1780, made on
the east side of Long Island, in Penobscot bay. By Rev.
Samuel Williams, Hollis professor of Mathematics at
Harvard College.

A total eclipse of the sun is a curious phenomenon. From
the principles of astronomy it is certain that a central eclipse
will occur in some part of the earth in the course of every
year; but it is but seldom that a total eclipse of the sun is
seen in any particular place. A favorable opportunity pre-
senting itself for viewing one of these eclipses on October
27, 1780, the American Academy of Arts and Sciences and
the University at Cambridge were desirous to have it properly observed in the eastern parts of the State, where, by
calculation, it was expected it would be total. With this
view they solicited the government of the Commonwealth
that a vessel might be prepared to convey proper observers
to Penobscot bay, and that application might be made to the
officer who commanded the British garrison there, for leave
to take a situation convenient for this purpose. Though in-
volved in all the calamities and distresses of a severe war,
the government discovered all the attention and readiness to
promote the cause of science which could have been expected in the most peaceable and prosperous times, and passed a
resolve directing the Board of War to fit out the Lincoln
galley to convey me to Penobscot, or any other part at the
eastward, with such assistants as I should judge necessary.

Accordingly I embarked, October 9, with Mr. Stephen
Sewall, Professor of the Oriental Languages, James Winthrop, Esq., librarian, Fortesque Vernon, A. B., and Messrs.

Atkins, Davis, Hall, Dawson, Rensselaer, and King, students in the University. We took with us an excellent clock, an astronomical quadrant of two and one-half feet radius, made by Sissons, several telescopes, and such other apparatus as was necessary. On the 17th we arrived in Penobscot bay. The vessel was directed to come to anchor in a cove on the east side of Long Island. After several attempts to find a better situation for observation, we fixed on this place as the most convenient we had reason to expect, and on the 19th we put our instruments on shore, set up the clock and quadrant in a building facing towards the south, near the house of Mr. Shubael Williams, where the following observations were made: [Here follows a minute account of observations from October 20 to October 27, inclusive, from p. 87 to p. 103, inclusive.]

The greatest obscuration was at twelve hours, thirty degrees twelve minutes, at which time the sun's limb was reduced to so fine a thread, and so much broken, as to be incapable of mensuration. There was little wind while we were making the observations, and no clouds to be seen; but the air was not perfectly clear, being a little thick or hazy.

From the beginning of the eclipse unto the time of the greatest obscuration, the color and appearance of the sky was gradually changing from an azure blue to a more dark or dusky color, until it bore the appearance and gloom of night. As the darkness increased, a chill and dampness was very sensibly felt. In one hour and nineteen minutes, when the light and heat of the sun were rapidly decreasing, there fell two-thirds as much dew as fell the night before or the night after the eclipse. To this we may add, so unusual a darkness, dampness and chill, in the midst of day, seemed to spread a general amazement among all sorts of animals. Nor could we ourselves observe such unusual phenomena without some disagreeable feelings.

As the officer who commanded at Penobscot, in his answer to the application of the government, had limited us to a time wholly inadequate to our purpose—from the 25th to the

30th of October,—we were obliged to make a second application to enter Penobscot bay. Leave was granted, but with
a positive order to have no communication with any of the
inhabitants, and to depart on the 28th, on the day after the
eclipse. Being thus retarded and embarrassed by military
orders, and allowed no time after the eclipse to make any
observations, it became necessary to set up our apparatus
and begin our observations without any further loss of time;
in the course of which we received every kind of assistance
from Capt. Henry Mowatt, of the Albany, which it was in
his power to give.

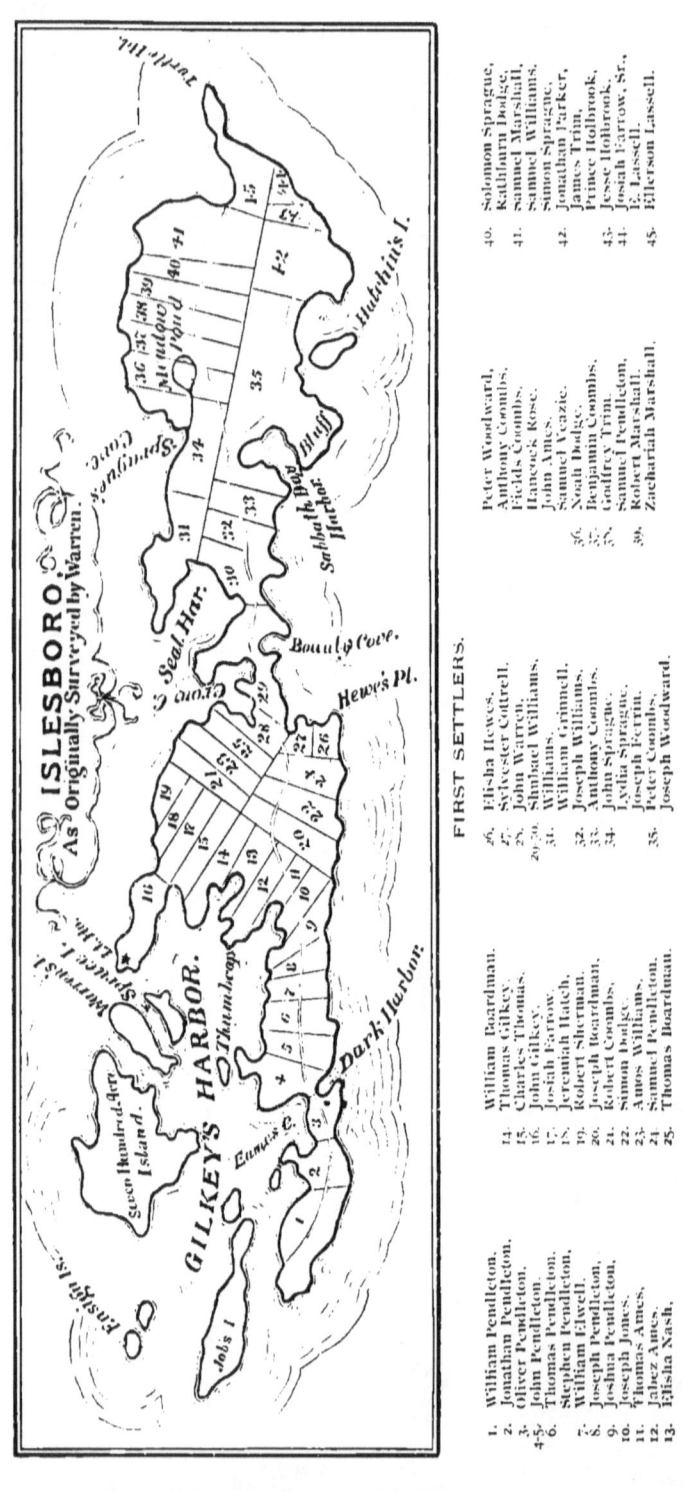

# CHAPTER V.

## DOCUMENTARY.

*Lease from Isaac Winslow to William Pendleton, 1771.*

THIS Indenture of Lease, made the twenty-second day of May, one thousand seven hundred and seventy-one, and in the eleventh year of his Majesty's reign, between Isaac Winslow, of Roxbury, in the county of Suffolk, Esq., on the one part, and William Pendleton, of an island in Penobscot bay, in the county of Lincoln and province aforesaid, known by the name of Winslow's Island, or Long Island :

That the said Isaac Winslow, for the consideration hereafter mentioned, hath demised, leased, and farm let, and by these presents doth lease unto said Pendleton a certain tract of land on Winslow's Island aforesaid, where the said Pendleton now resides, containing six hundred and twenty acres more or less, for and during the term of twenty-five years from the date hereof. And the said William Pendleton, for himself, his heirs and assigns, doth hereby covenant and agree with the said Isaac Winslow that he will cut, clear up and keep down yearly, and every year during said term, ten acres of said land, and subdue the same, so that the whole shall be cleared during said term, and shall be brought to good mowing or tillage. That he will make no strip or waste, or cut any wood off any other part of the land than what he subdues in the manner aforesaid. That he will pay all taxes the premises may be subject to during said lease. That he will in every respect manage and improve the said land in an husbandlike manner, and at the expiration of said lease will deliver up the herein-leased premises to the said

Winslow, his heirs or assigns, with what buildings there may be thereon, and with all the improvements which shall be made, and under proper fencing. And the said Pendleton also engages that he will reserve such lots of wood in proper places, as may be needful for the use of such farm or farms, as shall be on the premises, and that he (be) careful not to plow the same piece of land too often, and such as he doth plow he will dung, and after proper plowing he will sow the same with grass seed.

And the said Winslow on his part, and for his heirs, executors and assigns, doth hereby covenant and agree with the said Pendleton that he or his heirs or assigns shall quietly possess and enjoy the premises hereby leased during the term of twenty-five years, and that at the expiration thereof, and on his compliance on his part with the covenant hereby entered into, he the said Pendleton, his heirs, etc., shall be entitled to a deed of fifty acres of the land hereby leased, such as shall be equal in quality to the rest, taking into consideration the value of the leased premises as they lay, and which shall be accordingly granted to him and his heirs forever.

In witness whereof we have hereunto interchangeably set our hands and seals, this twentieth day of November, 1771.

*Signed, sealed and delivered in presence of*

　　　　　　　　ISAAC WINSLOW. [Seal.]

The three lines in the margin on the other side being first written.

　　　　　　　　WILLIAM PENDLETON. [Seal.]

LOTT WHITE.

HANNAH WINSLOW.

(On the back.) Lease to Capt. Pendleton, Dated November, 1771; but it ought to have commenced in July, 1769, the time when he went on. Lime rocks to be excepted.

May 22, 1771.

LAW RELATING TO GATES.

CHAPTER CCCXLVII. An act granting certain privileges to the town of Islesborough.

Be it enacted by the Senate and House of Representatives in Legislature assembled, that the inhabitants of the town of Islesborough, upon Long Island, in Penobscot bay, in the County of Hancock be, and they hereby are authorized to erect permanent gates across the principal road leading lengthwise of said island, through said town, at such places and under such directions as shall be considered by the said inhabitants, at their annual meeting in March or April, most expedient for the safe keeping of their cattle and the further improvement of their respective farms.

Section 2. Be it further enacted, that the said inhabitants shall keep said gates in good repair, and shall provide convenient and secure fastenings for the same during all parts of the year, in which they shall require the same to be kept shut ; and it shall be the duty of each and every person passing through any of said gates, at any such time or times, to shut after him or them, and to leave shut and secure, with such fastenings provided therefor, such gate or gates : and if any person or persons shall open, and carelessly or with evil intent leave open or injure, or destroy, any or all of said gates, he or they shall be liable to pay all damages of every kind which may thereby accrue to said gate, and to any of said inhabitants, from the breaking loose of cattle through the same : to be recovered by said inhabitant or by any individual suffering such damages, in an action of the case, before any court of competent jurisdiction to try the same.

This act passed February 25, 1835.


This may certify that black woman by the name of Janey has come to John Gilkey. She belongs to Sandwich, and he has ——————— and notify the town of the same. She came there in August, tenth day, one thousand eight hundred.

ISLESBOROUGH, September 27, 1800.

This is to notify the inhabitants of the town to meet at house of Capt. Anthony Coombs, on Tuesday, the seventh day of October next. It is the request of the church for to give in their votes and minds concerning the Gospel being settled in the town, either for or against it, both old and young, male and female. And all that cannot attend on the said day send in their votes on the said day.

JOHN GILKEY.
DAVID THOMAS.

ISLESBOROUGH, August 18, 1800.

Have warned the said Polly out of this town, and likewise her children according to law.

ELISHA NASH, Constable.

And recorded by me.

FIELDS COOMBS, Town Clerk.

## LETTER FROM JOB PENDLETON, OF ISLESBOROUGH.

*Long Island, 29th March, 1789.*

*To the General Court of Massachusetts.*

● *Gentlemen : I, the subscriber, am possessed of an island laying in Penobscot bay, known by the name of Little Long Island, containing two hundred and four acres (likewise an island joining by a bar at low water, containing thirteen acres), which island I settled in the year 1769, together with Mr. James Matthews and Mr. Shubael Williams. On the 9th day of November, 1769, I purchased James Matthews' third part, likewise on the 23d day of September, 1772, I purchased Mr. Shubael Williams' third part, which I have their deeds to show.*

*The above written are facts that I can clearly prove ; and whereas, gentlemen, you having the power to settle and do justice to the individuals in this remote part of the State, I humbly pray that you will inform me how I may still be in quiet possession of my land, and humbly submit myself to your direction and the laws of this Commonwealth.*

*I am, gentlemen,*

*your most obedient and most humble servant,*

*JOB PENDLETON.*

*Copy of Deed dated July 19, 1790, and signed by George Miner and Anna Miner.*

*George Miner, of Islesborough, in the county of Hancock, yeoman, to Simon Dodge, of the same town and county, carpenter, "one certain tract or parcel of land lying and being in Islesborough aforesaid, containing one hundred and eighteen acres, butted and bounded as follows: Beginning at a spruce tree standing on the shore fifteen rods from the spring landing, marked with letters M. P. for a corner, running from thence north seventy-one degrees, west two hundred and two rods to a yellow birch tree marked with letters M. P. P. corner, thence running south fifty-two degrees, west one hundred and three rods to a yellow birch tree standing in the line of William Grifeth for a corner, thence running south thirty-eight degrees east along said line to a rock maple tree on the shore marked W. G., being William Grifeth's corner bound, thence easterly along the shore bounding thereon to the place first mentioned."

*Copy of Deed dated 14th September, 1790.*

Zachariah Marshall, of Islesborough, in the county of Hancock, yeoman, to Rathburn Dodge of said Islesborough,

---

* It is very hard to locate this deed, but it was probably on Seven-Hundred-Acre Island. The deed was of little value, as the land afterwards had to be bought of the proprietor to make the title good. The oldest people living have no knowledge of George Miner, nor of William Grifeth.

There is a ledge in Gilkey Harbor called Miner ledge.

a certain lot or piece of land situated in said Islesborough, bounded as follows, viz: Upon the north beginning at a birch tree at the shore, it being a boundary between Samuel Williams and Zachariah Marshall, thence running south-westerly by the shore forty rods, thence running back, keeping the same width to the head of the said Zachariah Marshall lot. Consideration fourteen pounds.

## GRINDLE POINT LIGHT-HOUSE.

The light-house is situated at the entrance of Gilkey Harbor. It was built in 1850. The first keeper was Mr. H. Dunning, second Mansfield Clark, of Islesborough, third Capt. F. Grindle, of Islesborough. Those three men served about three years. The fourth keeper was Charles Nash, fifth Nelson Gilkey, sixth Avery Gilkey, seventh S. H. Higgins, and the present keeper Isaac Hatch.

Gilkey's Harbor is one of the best on the coast of Maine. Easy of access, it is large, with plenty of water for the largest class of vessels. Entering from the west Penob-scot bay, leave the light on the port hand, and Warren Island on the starboard hand. Then steer so as to leave a point of Spruce Island on the starboard hand, giving it a berth, as it makes shoal off the island, or keep in mid bay until you have passed Spruce Island Point, when you may anchor and be secure from all winds. When the wind is to the westward and the tide is making ebb, it is hard to get out of this passage. You can go through the harbor leaving Spruce Island on the starboard hand, giving it a berth, but keeping it best aboard, to avoid a sunken rock which lies in the middle of the harbor. Also Long Ledge which you leave on the port hand. Then steer for Phil-brook's point, on Seven-Hundred-Acre Island, leaving it on the starboard hand. After passing Philbrook's Point, south-west one-fourth west for the Ensign Islands, leav-

ing them on the starboard hand, keeping then best aboard
to avoid sunken ledges that lie off from Job's Island.
There is a passage through Gilkey Harbor to the east Penobscot bay, but it would not do for a stranger. If bound
through you can always get a pilot, who will take you
through to the east Penobscot bay. This harbor ought
to be buoyed.

### ISLAND LODGE, F. AND A. M.

The first lodge of Free Masons assembled in the year
1857, in the chamber over Thomas Boardman's store. A
dispensation was granted to the following brethren, by
the Grand Lodge: * Stephen Warren, * Simon D.
Sprague, * Elisha K. Pendleton, * Rodolphus Pendleton,
Thomas Boardman, L. P. Gilkey, * Martin S. Coombs,
* Joseph S. Dodge, Charles A. Coombs, Thomas R. Wil-
liams, * Otis F. Coombs, Lorenzo Pendleton, John P.
Farrow, * James Dodge, * Joseph Boardman, and Edward
Turner.

On April 15, 1857, the following officers were appointed:

Otis F. Coombs, W. M.
John P. Farrow, S. W.
Thomas R. Williams, Treas.
Lorenzo Pendleton, S. D.
Joseph S. Dodge, S. S.
Thomas Boardman, J. W.
Simon D. Sprague, Sec.
Elisha K. Pendleton, J. D.
Stephen Warren, J. S.
Joseph Boardman, Tyler. •

November 5, 1857, they obtained their charter, and
were called Island Lodge No. 89. The next year, 1858,

---

* Deceased.

they built a Masonic Hall, which they occupy at the present time.

The following have been the principal officers since 1857 :

1858.  Otis F. Coombs, W. M.; John P. Farrow, S. W.; Thomas Boardman, J. W.; Simon D. Sprague, Sec.

1859.  Otis F. Coombs, W. M.; John P. Farrow, S. W.; Lorenzo Pendleton, J. W.; Simon D. Sprague, Sec.

1860.  John P. Farrow, W. M.; Lorenzo Pendleton, S. W.; Thomas R. Williams, J. W.; Thomas Boardman, Sec.

1861.  Lorenzo Pendleton, W. M.; E. K. Pendleton, S. W.; Thomas R. Williams, J. W.; Thomas H. Parker, Sec.

1862.  Thomas R. Williams, W. M.; E. K. Pendleton, S. W.; Rodolphus Pendleton, J. W.; Otis F. Coombs, Sec.

1863.  E. K. Pendleton, W. M. ; J. B. Coombs, S. W.; S. B. Coombs, J. W.; Wm. F. Veazie, Sec.

1864.  John P. Farrow, W. M.; E. K. Pendleton, S. W.; E. G. Babbidge, J. W.; Wm. F. Veazie, Sec.

1865.  Thomas R. Williams, W. M.; E. K. Pendleton, S. W.; Calvin W. Sherman, J. W.; Wm. F. Veazie, Sec.

1866.  Rodolphus Pendleton, W. M.; Calvin W. Sherman, S. W.; David H. Rose, J. W.; S. B. Coombs, Sec.

1867.  Thomas R. Williams, W. M.; Calvin W. Sherman, S. W.; David H. Rose, J. W.; B. R. Redman, Sec.

1868.  Thomas R. Williams, W. M.; Calvin W. Sherman, S. W.; Lorenzo Pendleton, J. W.; Wm. F. Veazie, Sec.

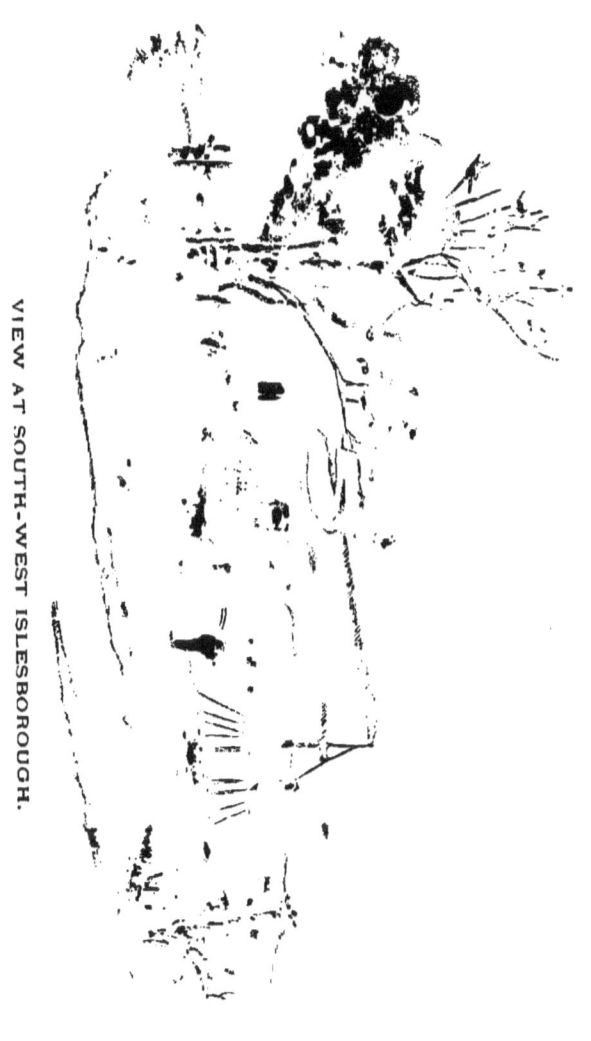

VIEW AT SOUTH-WEST ISLESBOROUGH.

1869. Thomas R. Williams, W. M.; E. K. Pendleton, S. W.; E. F. Williams, J. W.; William F. Veazie, Sec.

1870. Thomas R. Williams, W. M.; E. K. Pendleton, S. W.; E. F. Williams, J. W.; Daniel A. Hatch, Sec.

1871. Calvin W. Sherman, W. M.; E. F. Williams, S. W.; Charles H. Dodge, J. W.; Daniel A. Hatch, Sec.

1872. Calvin W. Sherman, W. M.; Lorenzo Pendleton, S. W.; C. H. Dodge, J. W.; Daniel A. Hatch, Sec.

1873. Lorenzo Pendleton, W. M.; Alonzo Coombs, S. W.; Willard M. Whitcomb, J. W.; Daniel A. Hatch, Sec.

1874. Lorenzo Pendleton, W. M.; Daniel A. Warren, S. W.; Willard M. Whitcomb, J. W.; Daniel A. Hatch, Sec.

1875. Otis F. Coombs, W. M.; Daniel A. Warren, S. W.; James F. Grindle, J. W.; Daniel A. Hatch, Sec.

1876. Otis F. Coombs, W. M.; James F. Grindle, S. W.; Edwin Coombs, J. W.; Daniel A. Hatch, Sec.

1877. James F. Grindle, W. M.; Edwin Coombs, S. W.; W. S. Pendleton, J. W.; Daniel A. Hatch, Sec.

1878. James F. Grindle, W. M.; Edwin Coombs, S. W.; G. D. Pendleton, J. W.; Daniel A. Hatch, Sec.

1879. Edwin Coombs, W. M.; J. O. Hayes, S. W.; Charles H. Dodge, J. W.; Daniel A. Hatch, Sec.

1880. Edwin Coombs, W. M.; Calvin W. Sherman, S. W.; Olney T. Scott, J. W.; Daniel A. Hatch, Sec.

1881. Thomas R. Williams, W. M.; Olney T. Scott, S. W.; Nelson Kimball, J. W.; D. A. Warren, Sec.

1882. Thomas R. Williams, W. M.; Olney T. Scott, S. W.; Nathan Pendleton, J. W.; D. A. Warren, Sec.

1883. Thomas R. Williams, W. M.; Olney T. Scott, S. W.; Willard M. Whitcomb, J. W.; Nelson Kimball, Sec.

1884. Olney T. Scott, W. M.; Willard M. Whitcomb, S. W.; J. O. Hayes, J. W.; Nelson Kimball, Sec.

1885. Olney T. Scott, W. M.; Willard M. Whitcomb, S. W.; J. O. Hayes, J. W.; Nelson Kimball, Sec.

1886. W. M. Whitcomb, W. M.; J. O. Hayes, S. W.; Charles H. Dodge, J. W.; Nelson Kimball, Sec.

1887. J. O. Hayes, W. M.; E. A. Bunker, S. W.; E. G. Coombs, J. W.; Thomas R. Williams, Sec.

1888. Edgar A. Bunker, W. M.; Emery N. Bunker, S. W.; E. G. Coombs, J. W.; Thomas R. Williams, Sec.

1889. Emery N. Bunker, W. M.; E. G. Coombs, S. W.; J. L. S. Coombs, J. W.; Thomas R. Williams, Sec.

1890. Winfield S. Pendleton, W. M.; John P. Bragg, S. W.; George A. Warren, J. W.; Thomas R. Williams, Sec.

There have been many changes by death since the Lodge was constituted. Among those who have passed away are :

Rodolphus Pendleton, drowned October 28, 1867, in Penobscot bay.

Martin S. Coombs, died September 8, 1868.

James W. Herrick, drowned January 23, 1872.

James Dodge, died March 17, 1872.

Elbridge B. Sawyer, died August 26, 1873.

Elisha K. Pendleton, P. M., died January 10, 1875.

Simon D. Sprague, died November 19, 1877.

Otis F. Coombs, P. M., died December 19, 1877.

Onslow Thomas, drowned October 13, 1878.

Matthew Ranlett, drowned December 11, 1878.

Charles A. Coombs, supposed drowned, March 31, 1879.

James Skinner, died July 27, 1879.

George A. Coombs, died in the Insane Asylum at Augusta, February 3, 1882.

Joseph L. Ryder, died September 9, 1882.

Calvin W. Sherman, P. M., died October 8, 18—.

James L. Hatch, died September 18, 1883.

Delmar Gilkey, died January 28, 1884.

John Veazie, died January 4, 1888.

Pillsbury Coombs, died January 28, 1889.

Amasa Hatch, drowned March 30, 1889.

Stephen Warren, died June 7, 1889.

David Henderson Rose, died February 21, 1890.

Andrew P. Gilkey, died February 22, 1890.

Lincoln Coombs, died 1892.

## ISLESBOROUGH IN THE WAR OF THE REBELLION.

The town of Islesborough was patriotic in the late rebellion, furnishing her quota of men as fast as called by the United States government. The following is a list of volunteers and drafted men :

Leonidas O. Boardman, in Co. B, Coast Guards. Enlisted March 30, 1864; died February 3, 1865, at Hospital, Washington, D. C. A resident of Islesborough, age 23; Corporal.

James S. Coombs, Maine Second Regiment of Infantry. Enlisted May 27, 1861; discharged October 20, 1862, by reason of disability. Promoted Corporal June 20, 1862; age 20.

Alfred Pendleton, enlisted August 14, 1862. Died at the Point of Rocks, Va., at 18th Army Corps Hospital, from wounds received at Drury's Bluff, Va.; age 31.

David Philbrook, Co. F, 11th Regiment of Infantry. Enlisted October 14, 1861; died June 13, 1862, in Hospital, New Haven, Conn., by wounds received at the battle of Fair Oaks, Va.; age 27. Buried at Islesborough.

George Farrow, Co. F, 11th Regiment of Infantry. Enlisted October 14, 1861; died May 31, 1862, near Savage's Station, Va., wounded at Battle of Fair Oaks, Va.; age 23. Buried under a peach tree.

James Bell Adams, receives a pension. In Co. H, 8th Regiment of Infantry; discharged June 11, 1865, at Richmond, Va.; age 20.

Elbridge Henderson Durgin, army, in Co. H, 4th Regiment of Infantry. Enlisted May 10, 1861.

William Wallace Thomas, death unknown; army; no records to be found.

Sylvestus Fletcher, drafted. Furnished substitute.

Thomas Moody, army. Receives a pension. Co. H, 8th Regiment of Infantry. Enlisted August 21, 1862; discharged June 11, 1865; age 35.

Eliphalet Clark, army. Receives a pension. Co. J, 8th Regiment of Infantry. Drafted September 23, 1864, discharged June 11th at Richmond, Va.; age 32.

Henry Freeman, navy. No records to be found.

Justin Herbert Pendleton, army, in Co. H, Regiment of Infantry. Enlisted September 23, 1862; discharged May 11, 1865, by reason of disability. Wounded at Cold Harbor, Va., June 4, 1864.

Joseph V. Coombs, navy.

James Watson Pendleton, army, in Co. H, 8th Regiment of Infantry. Enlisted August 20, 1862; discharged June 11, 1865, at Richmond, Va.; age 23.

Nathan Pendleton, army, in Co. H, 8th Regiment of Infantry. Enlisted September 23, 1862; discharged June 11, 1865, at Richmond, Va.; age 18.

John P. Farrow, furnished a substitute; not drafted. Substitute, John F. Bryant, United States navy; born in Liverpool.

Maximilian Pendleton, drafted. Furnished a substitute, but no record to be found of his substitute at the Adjutant General's office.

Otis F. Coombs, furnished a substitute; drafted. Substitute, Edward Rogers, United States navy; born in Belgium.

William Veazie, furnished substitute; drafted. Substitute, James McMan, United States navy; born in Ireland.

Benjamin R. Redman, drafted; paid commutation.

William P. Sprague, drafted; paid commutation.

Joseph Grover, drafted.

Avery Gilkey, furnished a substitute—George Graham, United States navy; born in Nova Scotia.

William R. Coombs, furnished a substitute — Patrick Martin, United States navy; born in Ireland.

Frank D. Libby, paid commutation.

Phillip O. Coombs, paid commutation.

George F. Keller, paid commutation.

Roscoe Pendleton, army, Co. H, 8th Regiment of Infantry. Enlisted August 20, 1862; discharged June 11, 1865, at Richmond, Va.

Eben Grover.

14

Paul Sawyer, drafted.

Alonzo Coburn.

Oliver Fletcher, army, Co. C, 17th Regiment of Infantry. Drafted September 23, 1864; never joined the regiment; age 22.

William C. Dodge, substitute—Thomas Williams, United States navy; born in Nova Scotia.

Benjamin Grover, substitute — Charles Smith, United States navy; Smith born in the Provinces.

Percy Knowles, pensioner.

Stephen H. Warren, army. Enlisted March 24, 1865, at the age of 19. Served on the quota of Belfast, but was a resident of Islesborough; received three hundred dollars bounty, and was a recruit for the 16th Maine Infantry, but never got to the front; was mustered out May 10, 1865, at Gallupe's Island, Boston Harbor.

Isaac Pendleton, navy. No record.

Calvin W. Sherman, substitute—William H. Hanson, United States navy. Hanson born in St. Stephen, New Brunswick.

Edson Sherman, substitute—Thomas Lowrey, United States navy.

Wesley A. Brown, Corporal in Company B, 2d Regiment of Infantry. Enlisted April 25, 1861; died September 23, 1862, at Baptist Church Hospital, Alexandria, Va., by reason of his wounds. Promoted Corporal, November 1, 1861; wounded at the battle of Manassas, Va., August 30, 1862; taken prisoner at Gaines' Hill, Va., June 27, 1862; exchanged August 9, 1862.

Joseph L. S. Coombs, substitute—Edward Murray, United States navy; born in Halifax, Nova Scotia.

Emery N. Bunker, substitute—John R. Quinnell, United States navy.

Lincoln Coombs, substitute—Elbridge E. Rand, United States navy.

James F. Grindle, substitute—John Anderson, United States navy; born in Sweden.

Joseph H. McFarland, substitute—James Doyle, United States navy; born in England.

William P. Marshall, substitute—John Hayes, United States navy; born in England.

Francis G. Dix, substitute—Cornelius Johnson, United States navy; Norway.

C. C. Merithew, paid commutation.

E. B. Sawyer, paid commutation.

George W. Hatch, paid commutation.

Dudley Pendleton, paid commutation.

C. M. Thomas, paid commutation.

Thomas R. Williams, drafted for one year.

Edgar A. Bunker, furnished substitute — Henry Bell, born in Jamaica; mulatto.

Hosea C. Wyman, furnished a substitute — Thomas Sweeney, born in the Provinces.

The town of Islesborough paid out for bounty twenty-three thousand and ninety-seven dollars. The lowest bounty paid was fifty dollars; the highest, eight hundred and twenty-five dollars. Sixty-six three-years men; eight one-year men; one nine-months man.

The following are the names of substitutes that filled the quota of Islesborough, with the place of birth and the State:

| NAME. | PLACE OF BIRTH. | STATE. |
| --- | --- | --- |
| Foster A. Parker, | Brewer, | Maine. |
| Thomas J. Card, | Ireland, | Great Britain. |
| Seth B. Goodwin, | Augusta, | Maine. |
| Daniel F. Sargent, | Harrington, | Maine. |
| John Tasher, | St. Mary's, | Canada. |
| James L. Wayland, | Biddeford, | Maine. |
| Abraham Grover, | Riverwell, | Canada. |
| William Johnson, | England, | |
| James W. Bray, | Brooks, | Maine. |
| John T. Cross, | Sebec, | " |
| Joseph S. Bray, | Deer Isle, | " |
| Sanford G. Parker, | Camden, | " |
| Edward W. Colson, | Frankfort, | " |
| Daniel Fitzpatrick | Bangor, | " |
| Judson G. Prescott, | Liberty, | |
| Hanson W. Young, | Glenburn, | " |
| Richard F. Pendleton, | Camden, | |
| Fred'k M. Veazie, | Camden, | " |
| Samuel T. Morgridge, | Castine, | " |
| John Chambers, | Calais, | " |
| Benson Meservey, | Liberty, | " |
| Scott Salley, | Bowdoinham, | " |
| James Sullivan, | Phillips, | " |
| John Sampson, | Islesborough, | |
| Ralph Mason, | | |
| William A. Harmon, | Liberty, | |
| Edward P. Prescott, | Williamsburg, | |
| Hanson Hutchins, | Bangor, | " |
| Wm. L. White, | Chelsea, | Massachusetts. |
| James Metcalf, | Amherst, | Nova Scotia. |
| Richard Glenn, | England, | Great Britain. |
| William Murray, | Youghal, | Ireland. |
| Patrick Kelley, | Ireland, | |

| | | |
|---|---|---|
| Hiram E. Stillman, | Nova Scotia, | |
| John Williams, | Philadelphia, | Pennsylvania. |
| James Wood, | | |
| Wm. E. Rudolph, | New York, | New York. |
| Thomas Horton, | North Troy, | Vermont. |
| Daniel Lamont, | Nova Scotia, | |
| Peter Luckie, | | |
| Dennis Leary, | Ireland, | |
| Charles McIntosh, | Nova Scotia, | |
| Richard Phillips, | England, | |
| Angus McNabb, | Pr. Edward's Island, | |
| Robert Wallace, | Lonerhanes, | Nova Scotia. |
| Robert Howell, | New Brunswick. | |

LIST OF VESSELS BUILT AT ISLESBOROUGH, MAINE. *

[*Taken from Records of Custom House, Castine.*]

Schooner William, built in 1792, Samuel Bullock, master; tonnage, 98 4-95; owners, William Pendleton, Joseph Pendleton, John Pendleton, heirs of Job Pendleton, Islesborough.

Sloop Beaver, built in 1794, Michael Small, master; tonnage, 71 75-95; owners, Michael Small, Tristam Haskell, Jonathan Haskell, Deer Isle.

Sloop Abigail, built in 1794, Job Philbrook, master; tonnage, 94 25-95; owners, Amos Williams, Joseph Williams, Samuel Williams, Benjamin Williams, Islesborough.

Schooner Thomas, built in 1795, Andrew Phillips, master; tonnage, 105 38-95; owners, Jas. Crawford, Castine; Thomas Pendleton, Prospect; Benjamin Carver, Northport; Joshua Adams, Thomaston.

Schooner Rosanna, built in 1796, Stephen Pendleton, master; tonnage, 96 77-95; owners, Simeon Dodge, Israel Dodge, Mark Dodge, Joshua Pendleton, Islesborough.

* From John F. Rea, Deputy Collector, Castine.

Schooner President, built in 1796, Jona. Holbrook, master; tonnage, 104 60-95; owners, Richard Hunnewell, Isaac Parker, and J. Hunnewell, Penobscot.

Schooner Experiment, built in 1797, Jona. Holbrook, master; tonnage, 98 40-95; owner, Samuel Rogers, Castine.

Schooner Godfrey & Mary, built in 1801, David Dunbar, master; tonnage, 131 60-95; owners, Godfrey Trim, Robert Trim, James Trim, Israel Dodge, and Thomas Marshall, Islesborough.

Schooner Harmony, built in 1803, William Boardman, master; tonnage, 105 22-95; owners, Paoli Hewes, John Warren, Ellison Lassell, Joshua Cottrell, William Boardman, Islesborough.

Schooner Five Brothers, built in 1805, Joseph Clewley, master; tonnage, 123 45-95; owners, Jonathan Coombs, Anthony Coombs, Benjamin Coombs, and others.

Schooner Good Intent, built in 1801, Josiah Berry, master; tonnage, 80; owners, Ebenezer Whitney, Prospect; John Farrow, Hosea Coombs, Thomas Eames, Elisha Nash and others, Islesborough.

Schooner Retaliation, built in 1805, Jesse Holbrook, master; tonnage, 109 61-95; owners, Fields Coombs, Hosea Coombs, Simeon Coombs, Jesse Holbrook, Samuel Veazie, Islesborough.

Schooner Rebekah, built in 1806, Andrew Phillips, master; tonnage, 117 13-95; owners, John Farrow, Thomas Ames, Andrew Phillips, John Warren and others, Islesborough.

Schooner Rising Sun, built in 1807, William Boardman, master; tonnage, 115 38-95; owners, Josiah Farrow and others, Islesborough.

Schooner Ranger, built in 1803, Josiah Farrow, Jr., master; tonnage, 85 18-95; owners, Josiah Farrow, John Farrow, Thomas Eames, Nathaniel Palmer and others, Islesborough.

Schooner Rosannah, built in 1806, William Grinnell, master; tonnage, 106 86-95; owners, William Grinnell, Belfast; Noah Dodge, Rathburn Dodge, Islesborough.

Schooner Specie, built in 1811, John Farrow, master; tonnage, 93 68-95; owners, John Farrow, Samuel Farrow, Mighill Parker, John Gilkey, Philip Gilkey, Islesborough.

Schooner Patty & Hitty, built in 1809, Fields Coombs, Jr., master; tonnage, 126 5-95; owners, Hosea Coombs, Fields Coombs, Islesborough; Samuel Keyes, Orland.

Schooner Rosannah, built in 1815, Noah Dodge, master; tonnage, 106 80-95; owners, Oliver Parker, Joshua Treat and others, Frankfort.

Schooner Edna, built in 1821, William Hewes, master; tonnage, 22 18-95; owners, Paoli Hewes, William Hewes, Islesborough.

Schooner Gold Hunter, built in 1816, Joshua Howes, master; tonnage, 138 24-95; owners, Joshua Howes and others.

Schooner Pamelia, built in 1829, James Trim, master; tonnage, 22 28-95; owners, James Trim and Godfrey Trim, Islesborough.

Schooner Orion, built in 1829, William Farrow, master; tonnage, 22 67-95; owner, Josiah Farrow, Islesborough.

Schooner Mary Jane, built in 1831, John Farrow, Jr., master; tonnage, 100 84-95; owners, John Farrow, Jr., John Farrow, Ambrose Farrow, James Farrow, John Pendleton.

Brig Melissa, built in 1837, Ambrose Farrow, master; tonnage, 175 7-95; owners, Ambrose Farrow, William Farrow, Francis Grindell, J. Sherman, Elisha Eames.

## ISLESBOROUGH CAPTAINS AND THEIR VESSELS FIFTY YEARS AGO.

Samuel Marshall,                          Alms.
Isaac Warren,                             Traveler.
John Pendleton, called Capt. Jack,   Sloop Trial.
James Sherman,                            Laurel.
Robert Farnsworth,                        Rosilla and Jane.
Albert Pendleton,                         Vistula.
Benjamin Thomas,                          Hannah.
Andrew Pendleton,                         Nantucket.
John Gilkey,                              Pierce and Citizen.
Ambrose Farrow,                           Savage.
   First three-masted schooner.  He died in Havana of yellow fever.

James Farrow,                             Morning Star.
John Farrow, Jr.,                         Mary Jane.
   Built in Islesborough.

Josiah Farrow,                            Specie.
   Taken by English in War of 1812.

Amasa Hatch,                              Champion.
James Hatch,                              Augusta.
Thomas Williams, Sr.,                     George Washington, Jr.
John Pendleton, Jr.,                      Mary Jane.
Nelson Pendleton,                         Cordelia.
Joseph Pendleton,                         Nantucket.
Ephraim Pendleton,                        Nantucket.
Thomas Cookson,                           Eugene and Jane.
William Williams,                         Oneco.
Jesse Coombs,                             Fame & Five Brothers.
Jairus Coombs,                            Boston Packet.
Elbridge Philbrook,                       Charles & Samuel.
Daniel Philbrook,                         Gazelle.
Joseph Trim,                              Megunticook.
Job Philbrook,                            Sloop Abigail.
Otis F. Coombs,                           Alert.
Henry B. Coombs,                          Susan and Phœbe.
Benj. Ryder,                              Franklin.
Henry Rose, Sr.,                          Abbiona.
James Dodge,                              Caledonia.

| | |
|---|---|
| Joseph Woodard, Jr., | Augusta. |
| Andrew Marshall, | Elizabeth. |
| Joseph Boardman, | Lucy Lydia. |
| David Warren, 40 years, | Hudson. |
| Pillsbury Coombs, | Caledonia. |
| Mark B. Dodge, | Thomas. |
| Otis Veazie, | Economy. |
| Joseph Grover, | Alfred. |
| Isaac Burgess, Fisherman. | Java. |
| Thomas Ryder, | Ranger. |
| Reuben Matthews, | Leo. |
| Elisha Trim, | St. Lucas. |
| Godfrey Trim, | Globe. |
| Henry Rose, | Albany. |
| Fields Coombs, | Sloop Packet. |
| Wm. Avery Parker, | Moro. |
| Isaac Coombs, | Nantucket. |
| Rathburn Dodge, | Merrit. |
| Simon Dodge, | Sophrona. |
| James Warren, | Maine. |
| Lewis Hatch, | Only Son. |
| Solomon Dodge, | Joseph and Willie. |
| Walter F. Dodge, | Rialto. |
| William Boardman, | Rising Sun. |
| Jeremiah Warren, | Wave. |
| Stephen Warren, | Elizabeth. |
| Mark Pendleton, | Sophrona. |
| Peleg Pendleton, | Nantucket. |
| Stephen Pendleton, | Rosanna Rose. |
| Paoli Hewes, | Ethel. |
| Luther Ames, | Good Intent. |
| John Eames, | Caledonia. |
| Benj. Warren, | Paul. |
| Sylvester Brown, | Lebanon. |
| Simon Dodge, | Sophrona. |
| Elisha Pendleton, | Return. |

Schooner Rialto and brig Daniel Webster were built in Islesborough.

15

## DISASTERS.

Captain Mathew Ranlett, of the schooner Georgia, went down loaded with coal off Wood Island, on the coast of Maine, December 10, 1878. Captain and crew were all drowned, viz.: Mathew Ranlett, Austin Warren, a son of W. S. Cookson, and a man belonging to the town of Penobscot.

Brig Gazelle, Captain Daniel Philbrook, from Boston for the Island of Cuba, 1844–'5, was wrecked at sea. The crew were twenty-four days on the wreck. They suffered great hardships from exposure and famine, and this was one of the worst shipwrecks that ever happened to Islesborough mariners. That part of the crew who belonged in Islesborough were as follows: Captain Daniel Philbrook, Mr. Haskell, Paul Sawyer, and Samuel Warren. Samuel Warren was killed at the time the brig capsized.

Schooner Remington, Captain Hosea Wyman. The schooner was lost at sea. Captain Wyman and his son Clifford were washed overboard and drowned. The remainder of the crew were taken off by a passing vessel. Captain Wyman had many warm friends and very few enemies, and his loss was severely felt by his friends and neighbors.

Schooner Anne Leland, Captain Onslow Thomas. The vessel was loaded with lumber, from Bangor for New York. She sailed from Gilkey's Harbor, and was never heard from. Mr. Amasa Williams was with the vessel as mate, and a young man from Seven-Hundred-Acre Island. The rest of his crew unknown.

Schooner Lucy and Nancy, Captain Milton Whitcomb. The schooner was loaded with lumber, and she filled with water near Cape Ann. Joel Mixer and Richard Wilson were drowned. Captain Whitcomb was the only one who was saved, and he had a narrow escape. The loss of the Lucy and Nancy was October 9, 1873.

In the year 1862 Captain Jacob Wyman, in the brig Winyaw, loaded with lumber and bricks, sailed from the port of Portland bound for Tortugas, and was never heard from. Captain Wyman and his two brothers, Jairus and Rufus, who were with him, and Josiah Maxcey, one of the crew, all from Islesborough.

Brig Zavilla Williams, Capt. W. Veazie, foundered November 17, 1875. The brig had a load of coal from New York for Bangor. There were three that belonged in Islesborough drowned, viz.: Captain William Veazie, Andrew Spinney, and William G. Coombs, all young men, who were much respected. A monument was erected in the cemetery to the memory of Captain William Veazie.

Brig Almira, Captain Tolman Pendleton, from Bangor for Boston, in October, 1876, with lumber, experienced a heavy gale of wind, and washed to pieces at sea. The crew made a raft of the lumber. They were on the raft seven days, when Captain Pendleton died from exposure, with two of his crew. Mr. Hobart Dodge and the captain's brother were rescued by a fisherman.

Schooner Henry Seavey, Captain Charles Coombs, foundered March 31, 1879. The schooner had a cargo of coal from Rondout, bound to Boston. Captain Charles Coombs, Elbridge Coombs, and Calvin Pendleton were drowned. They were all from Islesborough.

## FIRES IN ISLESBOROUGH.

A list of houses that have been burnt in Islesborough, with names of owners as far as ascertained.

Hancock Rose, dwelling house.
William Lassell, dwelling house.
1841. Samuel Marshall, dwelling house.
1857. George Dodge, dwelling house.
James R. Dodge, dwelling house.

1872.   David Warren, dwelling house.
1874.   Joseph A. Sprague, dwelling house.
1844.   Avery Parker, dwelling house.
1859.   Joseph Dodge, dwelling house.
        Mrs. Ann Hatch Warren, dwelling house.
1876.   Alonzo Coombs, dwelling house.
        Mrs. Catherine Bagley, dwelling house.
        Perez Rich, dwelling house.
1878.   Martin V. Pendleton, dwelling house.
1886.   Sewell B. Fletcher, dwelling house.
1875-'77.   P. P. Boardman had two houses burnt.
1885.   E. S. Preble, dwelling house.
1838.   Andrew Marshall, dwelling house.
1878.   Isaac Warren, dwelling house.

*Stores.*  Mansfield Clark, Hobart Dodge; Lincoln N. Gilkey, in October, 1885.

*Vessels.*  Brig Adams, Stephen Warren, master, burnt in Gilkey's Harbor; schooner Return, Elisha Pendleton, master, burnt in Gilkey's Harbor; schooner Regulator, partially burnt in Sabbath-Day Harbor.

## THE MURDER OF ANN BROWN BY HER HUSBAND, CAPT. JOSEPH J. BROWN.

As has been said elsewhere in this history, but one native of Islesborough has ever been committed to the State prison, that man being Captain Joseph J. Brown, who was tried and convicted of murder in the first degree and sentenced to be hanged.

Brown killed his wife, Ann Brown, at their house in Islesborough, April 16, 1856. The murder was a cold-blooded and unprovoked one. Brown was a sailor, and had been master of a small coaster, and was about thirty-five years of age at the time of the murder. His wife was a native of Islesborough, and about thirty years of age when killed. She was an entirely inoffensive woman. Brown, when intoxicated, is said to have treated his wife brutally, beating her on such occasions without ever alleging any provocation. The day before the murder Brown had been to Belfast, and, as usual when there, he had indulged freely in intoxicating liquor. He did not return home until the morning of the murder, arriving there just after breakfast. His family consisted of his wife, one daughter twelve years of age, and an infant of four months. Four other children had been born to them, but had all died young. Before the murder, Mrs. Brown and the two children were the only persons in the house when Brown came home; Mrs. Thomas Fletcher, Brown's sister, who had stayed there over night, having left a short time before. When Brown went into the house he gave his pocket-book to his daughter, and in a few minutes picked up a butcher knife that was lying on the floor and deliberately cut his wife's throat from ear to ear; she begging of him to spare her life, but her dying entreaties were of no avail. The young daughter tried to save her mother, but was powerless to do so. In her efforts to get the knife away from her father her fingers were badly cut.

Immediately after the murder Brown went to Thomas Fletcher's house and said to Fletcher, "Thomas, I want you to go into my house and see to them folks; there is trouble there." Mr. Fletcher at once went to Brown's house, and found Mrs. Brown lying on the floor dead. Brown also went back to the house, went in and looked at his wife's body and said, "She is dead fast enough." He then left the house again and went to an abrupt precipice overlooking the water, not far from his house, with a feigned intention of throwing himself off. He then jumped into a small boat and started in the direction of the outer islands. By this time the alarm had been spread, and Benjamin A. Warren, John Sears, James L. Michaels and Philip Pendleton followed in another boat. Seeing himself pursued, Brown rowed back into a cove, where he procured a large rock and again put to sea. He fastened a rope around the rock and to his neck, carefully securing his knife to the stone, however, so that he could easily cut the rope. He then jumped overboard. He went down, but soon came up, and was secured by the four men who were pursuing him, and was taken ashore and put into the hands of Simon D. Sprague, the constable of the town.

The next day after the murder an inquest was held by John D. Rust, of Belfast, as coroner, with the following jury: Calvin Eames, foreman; F. A. Lewis, Charles Nash, Henry Boardman, Nathaniel Hatch, James Hatch, Orris Clark, William P. Boardman, Leander Allen, Thos. Williams. The jury found the facts to be as already stated in the foregoing account, and rendered a verdict in accordance therewith. Brown was then taken to Belfast, where he was arraigned before F. A. Lewis, Esq., and after hearing the testimony of Pamelia C. Brown (Brown's daughter), who witnessed the murder, Thomas Fletcher, Benjamin A. Warren, and others, Brown was committed to jail to await trial at the May term of the Supreme Court. During the examination he manifested no feeling at all, showing no signs that he regretted the awful deed he had committed.

Brown's trial commenced at Belfast, May 19, 1856, a little over a month after the murder was committed, Judge Seth May presiding. The prosecution was conducted by Honorable George Evans, Attorney General, and James B. Murch, Esq., then of Unity, County Attorney. Honorable Nehemiah Abbott and A. T. Palmer, Esq., were counsel for the prisoner. The trial lasted about a week, and each day the court-house was crowded with an interested audience. The testimony for the State was about

the same as at the preliminary examination. The defence was insanity, and several witnesses were introduced
to prove that there had been insanity in the Brown family, and an effort was made to prove that Brown himself
had shown signs of insanity.

Doctor Henry M. Harlow, for many years superintendent of the Insane Hospital at Augusta, was a witness.
The closing arguments were very able on both sides, as
was the judge's charge. The jury were out only about an
hour, bringing in a verdict of murder in the first degree.
The verdict was received by the people present with general satisfaction. The prisoner betrayed no perceptible
emotion, and seemed as unmoved as he had all through
the trial. On his way to the jail he expressed his satisfaction at the verdict, and regretted that he attempted a
defence. The following Monday Brown was taken into
court to receive his sentence, and upon being asked if he
had anything to say why the sentence of the law should
not be pronounced against him, he arose and spoke as
follows: "What can I say? If I did the deed proved
against me, I did not know it. I am glad it was no worse.
I am glad I did not injure my children or neighbors. I
always provided for my children according to my ability.
You can do with me as you see fit. My life is in your
hands. I don't know as I have anything more to say."

Judge May then, in an affecting and deeply impressive
manner, pronounced the sentence of death by hanging,
the prisoner to be taken to State prison to await the execution of the sentence, until which time to be put to hard
labor in solitary confinement. Brown was at once taken
to Thomaston and committed to the State prison; but he
was not hanged, as within a few months he killed himself
by cutting his throat with a piece of glass. The prevail-
ing opinion at the present time is that he was insane at
the time the murder was committed, and the writer joins
in that opinion.

# CHAPTER VI.

JOSIAH Farrow was born in Bristol, Me., in 1785, and when but a few years of age moved with his parents to Islesborough, where from that time they made it their home. When but a young lad he commenced going to sea, and continued to follow it for a living for more than twenty years. His principal experiences in that line were in being once shipwrecked, and in being taken prisoner in the war of 1812. His shipwreck was in the early part of his sea-going. He was on a vessel bound to Boston, in the month of December, when they encountered a very severe gale, and were blown off the coast and dismasted. They suffered much from exposure and want of food and water, being on the wreck a number of days. They were at last rescued by a vessel on her passage to Berbice, S. A., to which port they were taken. He came back home on a vessel bound to Boston, after an absence of several months. His friends not having heard from him during all this time, had mourned him as dead. Of course his unexpected return was a joyful surprise.

His prison experience occurred when he was about twenty-eight years old. At that time he commanded a vessel, and was part owner. His business was between Boston and Alexandria, Va. At the time he was taken he was on his passage to Boston, loaded with flour (which was of more than ordinary value, owing to the embargo), having succeeded, under cover of a dense fog, in getting past the blockading squadron at the mouth of the Potomac river. All went well until they reached Cape Cod, when

JOSIAH FARROW.

January 2, 1786--August 11, 1861.

they found they were pursued, their escape being discovered when the fog lifted. It needed but a few hours to have reached their destination. This they were not able to do. They were captured, their vessel burned, and the cargo seized. They were taken to Halifax and kept in prison about six weeks, when they were sent home on parole. Thus all he had acquired in his early life was taken from him and he had to commence life anew.

Soon after this he was married to Mary Boardman, the daughter of one of the early settlers of the island. He purchased a farm, the one on which he always lived while in Islesborough. He did not however remain at home. Leaving his wife with competent help to carry on the farm, he again took a vessel and commenced running between the same ports he previously had, Boston and Alexandria. In this he continued for about three years with pretty good success, when he left going to sea and returned to his farm. Agricultural pursuits were very congenial to him, which he made both profitable and pleasant; improving on the old methods and introducing new ones. His farm became the best in the place. He took an active part in the affairs of the town, was one of the selectmen for a number of years, and one of the foremost and most zealous advocates in whatever he thought would promote the public good. Earnest in looking after the welfare of the schools, that they had comfortable school buildings and competent teachers. Always interested in the success of the young, he aided many in standing in life.

He was one of the earliest promoters of the temperance cause, starting a temperance society and holding meetings. Being a justice of the peace, many came to him to be married. He moved to Belfast in 1833, but always kept up a kindly interest in his early friends and home. There he became interested in shipping, being an owner in many

16

vessels, and making the business a remunerative one.   He
was a member of Phœnix Lodge of Free Masons, and very
earnest in the work.   His opportunities for schooling were
very limited, but his fondness for reading enabled him to
overcome very much of his early disadvantages.   He was
a zealous abolitionist, but did not live to see the success
of the cause.   His death occurred in Belfast, in August,
1861, in the seventy-sixth year of his age.

## SHUBAEL WILLIAMS.

Shubael Williams came from Stonington, Connecticut.
His father was Isaiah Williams; his mother was a
Townley.   They were originally from Wales.   Mr. Williams had suffered greatly from the English in times past.
He was taken from his vessel and put on board a man-of-
war, and had to serve three years, leaving a wife and three
small children that were expecting him home in a few
days.   At the time of the Revolutionary war a sailor was
missing from one of the men-of-war at Castine, by the
name of Jackson.   He became enamoured with a young
lady at Islesborough, so he thought he would run the risk
of paying her a visit.   He started on the ice, and was
drowned before he reached the shore.   His body was
found and buried on Hewes' Point.   They accused Mr.
Williams of helping him away.   He was arrested and
sentenced to receive sixty lashes with a cat-of-nine-tails.
They gave him forty, and found he would die, and revoked
the rest of the sentence.*

He was a man of considerable means when he came, and
took up land a year before he brought his family.   When
he brought his family he brought a year's provision,
leather and cloth enough to last them two or three years.

---

*See Williamson's History of Maine, vol. II, page 480; Bangor His-
torical Magazine, vol. IV, page 171.

This was in the year 1780.   The enemy took possession of Castine
June 12, 1779.   Williamson's History of Maine.   Dr. Geo. A. Wheeler's
History of Castine says June 17th.

OLD SETTLER'S LOG CABIN.

ISLAND INLET, SPRAGUE'S COVE.

So they did not suffer, like most of the first settlers. At one time they saw a vessel standing towards the shore. He thought it was a privateer, and hurried the women and children into a boat, and went to Belfast and stayed six weeks at James Miller's, there being but three houses in Belfast at that time, on the west side of the river. When they came back they found everything just as they had left it. He built a log house at first, and afterwards a framed house. In this house was the first window glass ever seen in the town. He took the lumber from the forest, and dug the rocks and rolled them into a crevice in the bank, and burned the lime for the chimneys and plastering. The mortar made from this lime lasted good and solid for seventy-five years. His last work was hewing the frame for the meeting-house. He was a man of integrity, honest and upright in all his dealings. His wife was Abigail Turner.

## CAPTAIN WILLIAM PENDLETON,

From Stonington, Conn., came here prior to 1769, when his family came. He settled on the lower end of the island. Mr. Jeffrey Richardson Brackett now owns the estate. He was the most prominent man on the island for many years. In the Revolutionary war he traded with the British. The Committee of Correspondence,[*] chosen at Saint George, June 6, 1775, wrote to him July 17:

·"To Capt. William Pendleton.

Sir: We can not think proper for you to contrack any traid which we supose is for the king's troops, which you no by the Congress orders is comtrary to our obligations, which we are determined to adhear to.

Per orders of the committee.

J. SHIBLES, Clerk."

---

* History of Warren, page 170.

He was the first selectman of the town at its organization, April 6, 1789, and continued to hold office for many years, retaining the respect of his fellow townsmen. He moved to Northport about 1795, and died there August 28, 1820, at the age of ninety-eight years.

### ELDER THOMAS AMES.

One of the best known settlers of Islesborough was Thomas Ames, from Marshfield, Mass., where he was born. In a petition to the General Court, in 1787, he and his son Jabez both signed their names Eames. About 1784 he settled on the south-west side of the island, at what is now known as Gilkey's Harbor. Samuel Turner was a prior settler, and July 13, 1784, he quitclaimed to Thomas Ames, for four hundred and twenty dollars (Hancock Reg., vol. 2, page 119), one certain tract or parcel of land, being on Long Island, containing three hundred and fifty acres more or less, being lots Nos. 12, 13 and 14, on a plan taken by Joseph Chadwick from the south end of said island. Subsequently he sold a part of the purchase to Joseph Jones, his son-in-law, March 26, 1793, and to his son, Jabez Ames, another part the same day. It is presumed that Mr. Ames quitted the claim of General Knox under the Waldo heirs. August 23, 1815, he sold his homestead, containing eighty-five acres, more or less, for eight hundred and fifty dollars, to Joseph Woodard (Hancock Reg., vol. 236, folio 114). Woodard was from Hingham, Mass. He moved up the island. He sold the lot to Capt. James Sherman. Woodard was drowned in West Penobscot bay. Years afterward the estate came into the hands of J. P. Farrow. The house built thereon is said to be the oldest now standing on the island. For situation it is unsurpassed on the coast of Maine, and by those qualified to know, it has been said that the view of the bay from this point is not surpassed by any view of the bay of Naples. J. P. Farrow has recently sold this property to the Islesborough Land and Improvement Company, of Philadelphia.

Thomas Ames was moderator of the first town meeting in Islesborough, in 1789. Previous to 1800 he began to preach as an itinerant Baptist preacher. He was ordained minister of the church in Islesborough in 1804, and continued as such until 1809. He was a most worthy and acceptable preacher. He sold his homestead to Joseph Woodard in 1815, and soon after moved on to the main land. He died in Appleton, February 10, 1826. His posterity are numerous and highly respected, many first-class master mariners being among them.

### SAMUEL WARREN, (JR.)

Samuel Warren (Jr.) died at the age of eighty-seven, in Islesborough. He was a man of ability and integrity, quiet and peaceful, like most men of his religious opinion, being a Quaker. He was a surveyor, and was employed by the town, laying out their roads, and by the inhabitants to survey their land. He held offices of trust in town, and was looked up to for advice by the old and young, and never betrayed his trust on any occasion. The good qualities of this old-school gentleman descended to his children, who were among the most respected of its townsmen. This family, of five boys, have all made a record and passed away, and his grand-children, now living, can look back to their forefathers with pride. The record of his family will be found among the family records of Islesborough families.

### MRS. CATHERINE SHERMAN,

Daughter of Jabez Ames and widow of Robert Sherman, now living, at ninety-one years of age. She is known as

aunt Katy by the whole town, and regarded with homage
and respect in the estimation of the old and young. All
her intimate acquaintances, companions and partner have
passed over to the banks of the dark river. Many is the
kind act she has done for her neighbors when in sickness
or distress, and she will long be remembered after she has
passed away. In the house where she now lives she has
lived ninety years, being but one year old when her father
built the house. This has always been her home, and
where she raised her family. Mrs. Thomas, her daughter,
has the care of this remarkable old lady in her declining
years. Her retentive memory is bright and clear, and her
faculties are unimpaired. The writer of this is indebted to
her for valuable information. Her family record may be
found elsewhere.

## BENJAMIN THOMAS,

Married in Falmouth, December 24, 1767, Mary, daughter
of Robert Jordan, of Brunswick.

## CAPT. ISAAC W. SHERMAN.

Capt. Isaac W. Sherman, of the ship Frederick Billings,
the largest sailing ship belonging in the United States,
when launched. He was born in Islesborough, educated
in one of the common schools, married in Islesborough,
and lived there for a time, then removed to Camden,
where he still resides.

## CAPT. WALTER F. DODGE.

Captain Walter F. Dodge took charge of one of the
coasting vessels in early life, when he amassed considerable property, owning in a large number of the coasting
vessels. He left off going to sea and went into trade, and

at the age of thirty-five was thought by many to be wealthy. He removed to Boston, and there meeting with adverse fortune, he commenced to go to sea once more. He was taken by the Confederate cruisers, his vessel burnt, and he carried to Richmond, everything taken from him, even his watch, and left to get home the best way he could. Reference to his family record in the genealogy of families.

Capt. Mark Pendleton's four sons are among the most enterprising of the Islesborough families, owning largely in navigation. They have become wealthy, and take a great interest in town affairs.

## CAPT. JOSEPH W. COLLINS.

Capt. Joseph W. Collins was born in Islesborough, August 8, 1839. His boyhood days were spent as a fisher lad, going boat-fishing with his grandfather before he was nine years old. His tenth birthday was spent at sea on board a fishing schooner. In 1862, when only twenty-three years old, young Collins was appointed to the command of a fishing vessel, and has since commanded some of the finest schooners engaged in the fishing business from Gloucester, Mass., most of the time being at sea the whole of each year.

In 1879 he became connected with the United States Fish Commission, and entered upon the work of making a statistical inquiry into the fisheries of New England, for the tenth census, under the direction of Prof. G. Brown Goode. In the spring of 1880 he was appointed on the staff of the United States Commissioner to the International Fischerei Austellung, at Berlin, and accompanied the commissioner to that city. After returning from Europe Capt. Collins resumed the inquiry he had previously

been engaged upon, but in December, 1880, he was ordered to Washington, where he took up the work of preparing reports relating to the fisheries of the country,
which were published in the Fisheries and Fishery Indus-
tries of the United States, issued by the United States
Commission of Fish and Fisheries.  He rapidly attained
distinction as a writer in this line, and also exhibited great
facility in preparing illustrations of fishing crafts and fishing scenes, with the details of which he was thoroughly
familiar.

In 1883 he was one of the staff sent by the United
States to represent this country and make a display of its
fisheries and fishery resources at the great International
Fisheries Exposition held at London in that year; and it
is largely due to his superior knowledge and familiarity
with the fisheries of this country that the United States
succeeded in obtaining such a large number of the prizes
awarded at the exposition.  Capt. Collins' intimate knowledge of the fisheries and their needs has given him many
opportunities for offering suggestions for their improvement.  He conceived the idea while abroad of a new de-
sign for vessels, and agitated the matter thoroughly in the
press of New England, where it was given wide circula-
tion in 1886.  He was given the opportunity by Professor
Spencer F. Baird, then United States Commissioner of
Fisheries, to put his ideas to practical use, which resulted
in the schooner Grampus, of the Commission, which was
the pioneer of the new type.  He has made many cruises
of investigation in the vessels of the Fish Commission.
For two years—from 1886 to 1888—he was in command
of the schooner Grampus.

In 1888 he was appointed in charge of the division of
fisheries of the United States Fish Commission, and has
since had charge of the work.  In the same year he was
appointed as representative of the Fish Commission to

prepare its exhibits at the Centennial Exposition of the Ohio Valley and Central States, held at Cincinnati. In 1884 Capt. Collins organized the section of Naval Architecture in the United States National Museum, under the direction of Prof. G. Brown Goode, and since that date has been Honorary Curator of this interesting collection.

In 1890 he was nominated by the United States Commissioner of Fish and Fisheries, Hon. Marshall McDonald, to represent that bureau on the Government Board of Management and Control at the World's Columbian Exposition, and was duly appointed to the position by President Harrison. Undoubtedly Captain Collins is the best informed man regarding fishery expositions and their conduct to be found in the country.

## GAMALIEL PENDLETON.

Gamaliel Pendleton died at his home, July 12, 1892, aged sixty-nine years and eleven months, on the same farm where he was born. In his younger days he followed the sea. The latter part of his life he was engaged in agriculture. The upright character given him by his neighbors was never contradicted, as he had no enemies. He had not only the esteem but the kindness of all who knew him. His family were present in his last sickness, and doing every thing for him that could be done, which was a consolation to him. In his business affairs his word was as good as his bond, and his promise to pay would not be outlawed as long as he lived.

> "Time, place and action may with pains be wrought,
> But Genius must be born, and never can be taught."
>
> *Dryden.*

## STEPHEN PENDLETON.

Stephen Pendleton, in 1781, when hardly nineteen years old, was taken by a number of British partisans and

17

made to go as pilot to the dwelling of Mr. Soule, a wealthy man and a staunch friend of liberty, in Waldoborough. They entered the house, seized and bound him, and told Pendleton he might have his choice, either to help plunder the house or guard Soule. Not liking the idea of plunder he chose the latter. They proceeded to ransack the house and were about to break open the desk, when Soule, unwilling to lose his treasure, made such exertions to free himself in defiance of Pendleton's threats to shoot him, that he was on the point of succeeding. Pendleton, trembling for the safety of himself, fired and shot him, severely wounding his wife at the same time. This raised an alarm, and the marauders were glad to escape to the woods, conceal themselves as they could by day and travel by night, subsisting on the bark of trees, till by a circuitous route back of the mountains they reached Penobscot and returned to Bignyduce. Pendleton after the war lived in New Brunswick.[*] He came back to Islesborough, and in after life became respected.[†]

Others equally deserving might be made mention of did our limits permit—sea captains, farmers and traders who have contributed so much to the business of the place. The reader is referred to the genealogical table of the families. I have tried to make the work thorough and exhaustive, until new facts are brought to light should be regarded as corroborating the conclusion to which I have arrived.

---

[*] Eaton's Annals of Warren.
[†] Descendants now in Islesborough.

# CHAPTER VII

## PACKETS AND BOATS.

THE insular situation of Islesborough, the communication between the island and the main land, has quite
a history. The first settlers had small boats. The inhabitants in pleasant weather would cross the bay when it became necessary, generally three or four going together, to
get their stores, or after a doctor. The main supplies
were brought in their coasting vessels, and their produce
was shipped by these vessels to Boston. After the mail
route was established between Lincolnville and Islesborough, there was a regular communication every Thursday
from Gilkey's Harbor, by the mail boat. Capt. Thomas
Gilkey built an open boat, which was called the Dove.
He found employment for her, carrying cattle to and from
the island, and she was used for that purpose for a good
many years. In the fall of the year she would carry the
grist to Camden to be ground. At the upper end of the
town they owned several small vessels, which, after they
had done fishing in the fall, they would use for packets to
go to Castine, say twice a month in the winter, with occasionally a trip to Belfast. They finally altered the mail
route to Northport, and had a mail twice a week, discon-
tinuing the lower post office and establishing the upper,
near Seal Harbor. About this time Mr. Keller bought
the old Castine packet Superior, and would go to Belfast
for freight and passengers; but had no regular days, and
only went when there was enough to go to make it an ob-
ject. Not until 1859 was a regular packet line established

from Islesborough to Belfast. The yacht Water Sprite made regular trips, leaving Islesborough for Belfast Monday, returning same night, over Tuesday, back Wednesday, over and back Thursday, over Friday, back Saturday. Using her for two years, she was found to be too small for the route, and the Planet was bought, the business increasing, and the route being a paying one.

The first packet master of the Planet was J. P. Farrow. Next was Thomas Merrithew, next W. P. Sprague, who finally sold to Capt. Wilson Coombs, who altered her over into a steamboat. The schooner Nora was built in Islesborough. She ran to Camden, with occasionally a trip to Belfast. The Spy and Nautilus were also Camden packets.

### STEAMBOATS.

About the year 1847 a steamboat wharf was built at the head of the island. The steamer T. F. Secor, Capt. Thomas B. Sanford, on her route from Belfast to Ellsworth, made a landing for several seasons. She commenced running in 1846.

In 1850 the steamer Lawrence made her landings, taking the place of the T. F. Secor. She called here for several seasons.

In 1871 the Argo, a side-wheel boat, stopped here on her way to Ellsworth and Belfast each way.

In 1874 the steamer Pioneer ran to Castine and Islesborough, making a landing at Sabbath-Day Harbor.

The next boat was the steamer May Field, Capt. Samuel H. Barbour, who ran her one winter, until the May Queen was put on. The May Queen was built in Belfast for Capt. Gilmore, expressly for the Belfast and Castine route.

The steamer Planet was an opposition boat against the May Queen one season. Both boats were sold and taken off the route. Captain Barbour built a boat at Bangor named the Florence, and put her on the Belfast and Castine route, in charge of Capt. Decker. She ran for more than four years. Then she was sold, and was followed by the Electa. She continues on the route, and runs daily, carrying the mail, and has given universal satisfaction.

Steamers Hurricane and Mabel Bird ran a short time, while the regular boats were repairing.

In 1890–'91 steamer Emmeline ran a season from Castine to Rockland, stopping at Islesborough each way.

### BANGOR & BAR HARBOR STEAMSHIP CO.

In 1875 Capt. Samuel H. Barbour built the May Field, and ran from Bangor to Bar Harbor. Stopped at Ryder's Cove each way. The boats that belonged to this line were the Bangor, Queen City, Cimbria, Henry Morrison and Sedgwick. They make a landing at Ryder's Cove and Hewes' Point daily. The Bangor and Queen City have been sold.

Steamer Castine, from Belfast to Oceanville, leaves Belfast at 10 A. M., for Islesborough, Tuesday, Thursday, and Saturday.

In 1891 a wharf was built at Dark Harbor. Steamer City of Richmond, from Portland for Machias, stops each way.

An excursion boat leaves Bangor Saturday, at 3 P. M., for Ryder's Cove and Hewes' Point, returning back Monday, through the summer season.

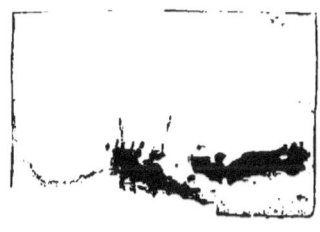

# CHAPTER VIII

## POPULATION OF ISLESBOROUGH.

THE population of the town of Islesborough, from the year 1850 to the year 1890, was as follows:

|  | INHABITANTS. | POLLS. | VALUATION. |
|---|---|---|---|
| In 1850, | 984 | | |
| " 1860, | 1276 | 266 | $148,271 |
| " 1870, | 1230 | 273 | 153,703 |
| " 1880, | 1208 | 290 | 158,033 |
| " 1890, | 1006 | 256 | 266,721 |

### DIRECTORY, 1892.

Postmasters: Islesborough, Roderick Pendleton; North Islesborough, William P. Sprague.

Selectmen: Austin Trim, Winfield S. Pendleton, Benjamin F. Heal.

Town Clerk: Jason R. Ryder.

Collector: John P. Bragg.

Constable: William P. Sprague.

School Supervisor: John P. Bragg.

Board of Health: Joseph A. Sprague, Alonzo Coombs, Dr. E. A. Williams.

Clergymen: First Baptist, vacant; Second Baptist, George Boynton; Free Baptist, William H. Fultz.

Physician: E. Williams.

Justices: Alonzo Coombs, April 27, 1886; William P. Sprague, March 15, 1888; John P. Farrow, February 6, 1889; Joseph A. Sprague, May 15, 1890.

Merchants: F. S. Pendleton & Co., Jason R. Ryder, Lincoln N. Gilkey, William Keller, meats; William P. Sprague, provisions; John P. Bragg and Miss U. J. Coombs, millinery; Amariah Trim, groceries; Thomas H. Parker, general stores.

Mechanics: L. F. Rankin, smith; Fields Coombs, smith; W. M. Whitcomb, wheelwright; E. L. Sprague, house painter; J. A. Sprague, A. A. Pendleton, George Williams, Watson H. Coombs, Edson Sherman, David Ladd, and Robert P. Coombs, carpenters.

Engineers: Fred W. Coombs, Augustus P. Coombs, Walter Decker, A. Garland.

Livery Stable: John P. Bragg.

Hotels: Islesborough Inn, N. P. Sewell; Islesborough, William Grover; Seal Harbor House, Joseph A. Sprague.

Associations: Masons, Island Lodge; meetings Thursday, on or before full moon; P. of H., No. 200, Saturday.

Islesborough has a future before it as a great summer resort, offering many attractions to the pleasure tourist. The opportunities for bathing, sailing, rowing, fishing and driving are not excelled on the seashore in Maine. Beautiful walks, level roads, variety of scene, and a place for rest and vacation for the old and young. The aged who seek rest and the young who seek exercise can spend a vacation here with pleasure, and can find accommodations suited to their tastes and means. There can be obtained an abundant supply of pure water, and the danger from contagious disease and destructive fevers is obviated. A

board of health looks carefully to the sanitary conditions,
and cleanliness is not only enjoined but enforced.

As there is no back country, no poison arising from
animal or decayed matter can exist. Competent phy-
sicians are in attendance at the hotels through the season.
Invalids visiting Islesborough can have the best attendance
the country affords. Good livery stables are connected
with the hotels. The drives are only to be seen to be
appreciated. In the township are tracts of woodland, and
groves of large spruce, beech, maple, birch, ash and cedar.
There is direct communication by steamboat from the
island to and from Rockland, Mt. Desert, Castine, Belfast,
and other points.

The Islesborough Inn is open from the last of June until
September, in charge of a thoroughly competent manager.
In addition to its large number of rooms, there are music
rooms, containing a stage for private theatricals, billiard
rooms, etc. It is one of the best appointed hotels on the
coast of Maine.

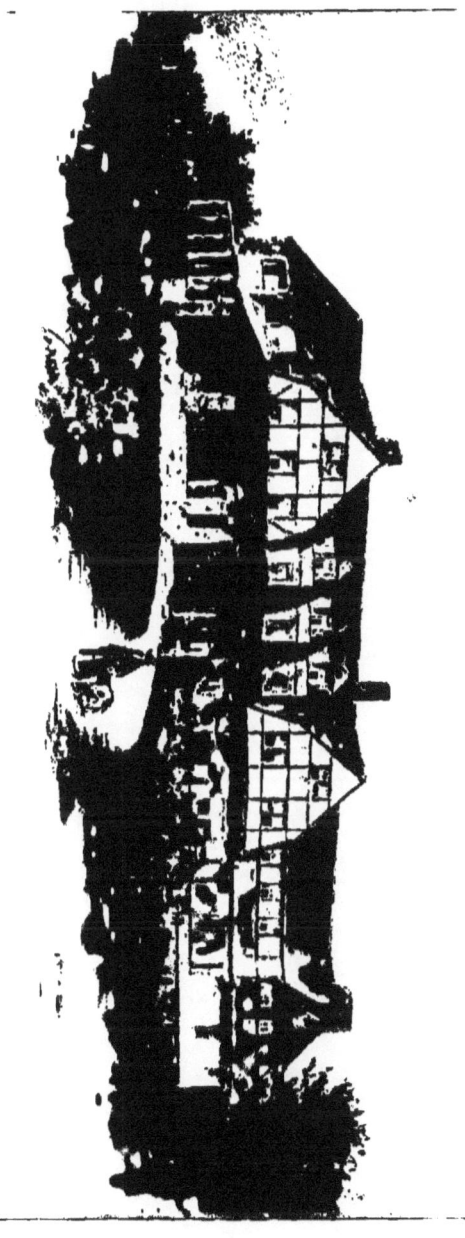

# CHAPTER IX.

## INSCRIPTIONS FROM GRAVESTONES,

In the burying grounds and cemeteries on the island.

*The old Burying Ground at the extreme lower end of the Island.*

1781. Judith, daughter of Jonathan and Jane Pendleton, died April 23, 1781. The oldest gravestone on the island.

1784. Mrs. Peggy, first wife of John Pendleton, died Feb. 21, 1784, aged 3-. The last figure obliterated on the gravestone.

1786. Sally, wife of Job Pendleton, died August 16, 1786, aged 34.

1794. Job Pendleton, died Jan. 25, 1794, aged 47. The epitaph on this old stone is not common :

"Beneath this stone I rest my head
In slumbers sweet ; Christ blest the bed."

1802. Jane, first wife of Jonathan Pendleton, died Feb. 25, 1802, aged 47.

1803. Jonathan Sprague, died in New Shoreham, R. I., Aug. 2, 1803. His wife, Lydia Dodge, died in Islesborough, June 4, 1848. Both natives of New Shoreham.

1806. Betsey, wife of Hosea Coombs, died July 16, 1806, aged 38.

1807.   Rebecca, first wife of Thomas Ames, first minister, died June 28, 1807, aged 66.   Thomas Ames, died in Appleton, Me., February 10, 1826.

1807.   Israel Dodge, drowned Feb. 17, 1807, age 35.

Deacon Joseph Boardman was born in Boston, Mass., Aug. 12, 1753; died in Islesborough, Nov. 28, 1831, aged 81 years.   Mary, his wife, was born in Stonington, Conn.; died in Islesborough, July, 1847.   Gravestones.

Joseph and Mary (Pendleton) had six sons and three daughters, who lived to womanhood and manhood's estate, and all of whom married excepting the second son. All the daughters had master mariners for husbands, and all the sons were also master mariners excepting the youngest, who in early life quit the sea to care for the folks at home.   Their names were:

 i. Thomas, born Jan. 25, 1775; died in Islesborough, Oct. 25, 1849.   Lydia, wife of Thomas, died Oct. 4, 1843, aged 67 years.

 ii. Joseph, born March 14, 1777; lost at sea, date unknown, probably from the foundering of his vessel.   He had become a resident of Swanboro, N. C., and owned and sailed the brig Polly and Betsey, in the West India trade.   The last heard of him was a marine report that he spoke another vessel just at nightfall, in heavy weather, reporting his brig as leaking badly, and asked the captain of the other vessel to lie by him until morning.   When the morning came he had disappeared forever.

 iii. William, born July 28, 1779; died in Islesborough, August 9, 1855.

 iv. Stephen, born May 24, 1782; died in Hope, June 30, 1855.

 v. Isaac, born August 27, 1792; died in Belfast, Sept. 22, 1862.

vi. Henry, born May 14, 1794; died April 17, 1872, on the old homestead in Islesborough.

vii. Mary, married Josiah Farrow; died in Belfast, Oct. 31, 1862, aged 77.

viii. Lydia, married first, Stone; second, Warren; died in Belfast.

ix. Margaret, married William Stone; died in Belfast.*

Thomas Boardman, Jr., died November 8, 1823, aged 21 years.

Captain Isaac Coombs, died Jan. 27, 1840, aged 49 yrs. 11 months.

Elizabeth Boardman, wife of Isaac Coombs, died May 4, 1835, aged 35.

Elisha Eames, died December 3, 1843, aged 81 years 11 months.

Anna, wife of Elisha Eames, died June 22, 1835.

*The Record of Gravestones on Sherman Point.*

Richmond Pendleton, born in Belfast 1811, died 1891, in Islesborough.

Lucy W., wife of Richmond Pendleton, born in Thomaston, 1817, died 1886.

Capt. Alfred Warren, died July 29, 1855, aged 24 years 5 months.

David Philbrook, died Jan. 13, 1862, aged 31 years 5 months. Soldier in the rebellion.

Sarah P., wife of David Philbrook, died Feb. 24, 1859, aged 24 years 10 months.

Eliza A., wife of Abner Marshall, died Sept. 14, 1851, aged 28 years 5 months.

* The information relating to this family was obtained from Hon. Isaac M. Boardman, of Belfast.

Susan, daughter of Rev. W. J. Durgin, died Apr. 3, 1845, aged 20 years 4 months.

Roxana, wife of Thomas Cookson, died Feb. 24, 1851. He died in California.

Calvin Eames, died Oct. 3, 1886, aged 80 years 25 days.

Mary, wife of Calvin Eames, died 1891, born 1811.

Elisha, son of Calvin Eames, drowned June 27, 1859, aged 19 years.

George Oscar, son of Calvin Eames, died Sept. 4, 1865, aged 22 years 9 months.

Capt. William Hatch, drowned in Long Island Sound, Oct. 10, 1866, aged 30 years.

Emily, wife of Wm. Hatch, daughter of William Farrow, died Apr. 3, 1863, aged 19 years 11 months.

William Farrow, died Oct. 9, 1879, aged 65 years 8 months.

Capt. John Farrow, died June 26, 1841, aged 65.

Rebecca, wife of John Farrow, died Sept. 26, 1842, aged 61.

Capt. Albert Pendleton, died June 29, 1845, aged 33.

Miss Sylvina, daughter of Robert Farnsworth, died Apr. 10, 1855, aged 12 years.

Robert Emery, son of Robert Farnsworth, died Oct. 9, 1846, aged 20 years 10 months.

Elisha Nash, died Feb. 26, 1852, aged 87 years.

Sally, wife of Elisha Nash, died Dec. 3, 1842, aged 56 years.

Mercy Ann, wife of Isaac C. Pendleton, daughter of Elisha Nash, died June 19, 1849, aged 26 years.

James Sherman, died Apr. 14, 1866, aged 75 years.

Sibyl, wife of James Sherman, daughter of Thomas Gilkey, died Nov. 10, 1873, aged 80 years.

GILKEY'S HARBOR AND CAMDEN MOUNTAINS FROM ISLESBOROUGH INN.

Betsey, wife of John F. Gilkey, daughter of James Sherman, died Oct. 2, 1873.

Elizabeth, wife of Winslow Sherman, died Sept. 22, 1851, aged 27 years.

Winslow Sherman, son of James and Sibyl Sherman, died May 25, 1849, aged 23 years 10 months.

Thomas Sherman, son of James and Sibyl Sherman, died ———, aged 21 years.

Peleg Pendleton, died Aug. 31, 1838, aged 28 years.

Wealthy Pendleton, died Nov. 12, 1869, aged 71 years 10 months.

Joseph Pendleton, died Aug. 21, 1858, aged 89 years 17 days.

Wealthy Pendleton, wife of Joseph, died Aug. 21, 1843, aged 67 years 17 days.

Georgia, wife of Lemuel Hatch, daughter of Nelson Gilkey, died July 3, 1868, aged 22 years 6 months.

Thomas Gilkey, died Oct. 10, 1847, aged 78 years 4 months. (Gravestones 87.)

Mercy Ames, wife of Thomas Gilkey, born August 12, 1772, died ———.

Robert Sherman, died July 6, 1852, aged 59 years 4 months.

Robert Sherman, Jr., died Apr. 13, 1849, aged 22 years 10 months.

Lydia Farrow, died Mar. 24, 1850, aged 66 years.

Betsey Jane, wife of Isaac Thomas and daughter of Lydia Farrow, died Jan. 21, 1857, aged 39 years 6 months.

Andrew, son of Nathaniel Hatch, drowned September 10, 1847, aged 14 years 9 months.

Thomas Pendleton, died Jan. 3, 1878, aged 26.

Eliza, wife of Joseph Harlow, died Aug. 19, 1878, aged 22 years.

Capt. Charles Pendleton, died Sept. 21 1879, aged 55 years 8 months.

Capt. Delmar Gilkey, died Jan. 26, 1885, aged 37 years.

Judson Philbrook, lost at sea Jan. 30, 1868.

Judson Philbrook, Jr., lost at sea Apr. 23, 1875.

Dea. John Pendleton, died July 18, 1863, aged 84 years 10 months.

Betsey, wife of John Pendleton, died July 18, 1881, aged 88 years.

Deborah Durgin, died Jan. 15, 1890, aged 90 years.

William Adams, died Oct. 15, 1890, aged 72 years.

Rosina, wife of Wm. Adams, died Dec. 4, 1862, aged 38 years.

Jane, wife of Judson Philbrook, daughter of Deacon John Pendleton, died Jan. 18, 1888.

*The Gravestones on Grindle Point, near the Lighthouse.*

Esquire John Gilkey, died Sept. 4, 1818, aged 74.

Sylvina, wife of John Gilkey, Esq., died Apr. 20, 1832.

Jane, wife of Philip Gilkey, died January 7, 1821, aged 32.

Capt. Frederick G. Dix, died November 19, 1863, aged 38 years 8 months.

Kate B., wife of Frederick Dix, died October 7, 1875, aged 47 years, 4 months and 25 days.

Robert Pendleton, died Aug. 30, 1839, aged 43. Here rests a man of peace.

Eliza G. Grindle, died May 10, 1891, aged 87 years.

Francis Grindle, died January 14, 1857, aged 72 years, 8 months and 5 days.

Judith Grindle, first wife of Francis Grindle, died Sept. 14, 1839, aged 38.

James F. Grindle; children, Hortense, Walter, Varnum.

Eunice Dix, died ——.

*Gravestones on the Estate of Edson Sherman, West Side.*

Capt. C. W. Sherman, died Nov. 11, 1882, aged 54 years, 2 months and 8 days.

Mary, wife of C. W. Sherman, died May 17, 1886, aged 56 years, 6 months and 29 days.

Lucy, wife of Robert Coombs, died June 21, 1835, aged 65 years.

Capt. Arthur Farnsworth, died March 15, 1865, aged 58 years, 2 months and 17 days.

Josephine J., daughter of Arthur and Louisa Farnsworth, died July 23, 1865, aged 28 years, 6 months and 18 days.

Capt. Benjamin A. Warren, died April 22, 1860, aged 32 years.

Relief, wife of Benjamin A. Warren, died March 12, 1865, aged 32 years.

Stephen V. B. Sherman, died Sept. 6, 1860, aged 22 years.

Isaac Sherman, died April 22, 1844, aged 42.

*Record of Graves on the Estate of the late Amasa Hatch, West Side.*

Jeremiah Hatch, died May 20, 1839, aged 85 years.

Lydia Porter, wife of Jeremiah Hatch, died Dec. 28, 1834, aged 76 years.

Isaac Hatch, died July 9, 1836, aged 47 years.

Capt. Amasa Hatch, born Nov. 7, 1808; died July 29, 1889.

Emeline Hatch, wife of Amasa Hatch, died Jan. 20, 1861, aged 39 years 7 months.

Sophronia, wife of Amasa Hatch, died Oct. 1, 1849, aged 41 years.

Elizabeth, wife of Isaac Hatch, died Dec. 7, 1831, aged 40 years.

*Record of the Gravestones in the Burying Ground on the east side joining the land of the late Elisha K. Pendleton.*

Lillian, wife of L. A. Farnsworth, daughter of Benjamin and Mary Hatch, died in Medfield, Mass., June 16, 1888, aged 29 years, 2 months, 11 days.

Minnie, wife of Ambrose F. Hatch, died Apr. 19, 1881, aged 25 years 7 months.

Charles E. Fields, born in Charlestown, Mass., Nov. 25, 1848; died in Islesborough, June 18, 1884.

Laura F., wife of E. D. Hatch, died May 22, 1885, aged 21 years 4 months.

Fred O. Farnsworth, drowned July 27, 1883, aged 17 years.

Edward E. Farnsworth, lost at sea, Jan. 27, 1881, aged 25 years 6 months.

Eben Otis, son of Rev. Wm. Durgin, died May 22, 1871, aged 34 years and 4 months.

Capt. James Luther Hatch, died Sept. 17, 1883, aged 63 years. Epitaph on his stone: "Storms all weathered and life's ocean crossed."

Dea. James Hatch, born in Hanover, Mass., March 3, 1796; died in Islesborough, March 13, 1878, aged 82 years.

Mary Townsend, wife of Dea. James Hatch, born in Abington, Mass., June 9, 1801; died Aug. 1, 1876, aged 75 years, 1 month 22 days.

Elbridge H. Durgin, died Feb. 15, 1886, aged 46 years 7 months. Was in the United States service.

Rev. Wm. J. Durgin, died Dec. 19, 1868.

Hannah, wife of Wm. J. Durgin, died Aug. 2, 1857, aged 58 years 2 months.

Hannah, daughter of Wm. J. Durgin, died Jan. 7, 1858, aged 21 years.

George W. Pendleton, died Aug. 29, 1883, aged 34.

Joseph Jones, died Apr. 11, 1840, aged 74.

Betsey, wife of Joseph Jones, died June 6, 1837, aged 70 years.

Mary Ames, died Oct. 27, 1838, aged 29 years.

Capt. Joseph K. Pendleton, died Jan. 22, 1890, aged 71 years, 7 months 16 days.

Lucy S., wife of Joseph K. Pendleton, daughter of Simon and Lucy S. Watson, died Apr. 24, 1875, aged 54 years.

Joseph, son of Capt. Joseph K. Pendleton, lost at sea Mar. 31, 1879, aged 21 years 11 months.

Joseph H. Ryder, died Sept. 9, 1882, aged 36 years, 1 months 16 days.

Capt. Eben G. Babbidge, died April 5, 1870, aged 49 years, 7 months 25 days.

Helen, daughter of E. G. Babbidge, died Aug. 27, 1882, aged 17 years, 9 months 5 days.

Hannah Brown, wife of Wm. Brown, died 1892.

Walter S., son of Andrew and Jane Pendleton, died Oct. 25, 1877, aged 21 years 15 days.

Florence A., daughter of Andrew and Jane Pendleton, died Apr. 23, 1880, aged 34 years 8 months.

19

Benjamin Thomas, born in Islesborough, Feb. 22, 1801; died Jan. 24, 1870, aged 69 years, 11 months 18 days.

Jane, wife of Benj. Thomas, died in Camden, 1892.

Myra Warren, died May 5, 1883, aged 18 years, 11 months 18 days.

William H. Brown, died Dec. 4, 1888.

Hannah B. Fields Brown, died Aug. 11, 1892.

Esther, wife of Lewis Hatch, and daughter of Joshua and Betsey Dodge, died Mar. 2, 1873, aged 62.

Elisha K. Pendleton, died Jan. 10, 1875.

Catherine S., wife of Elisha K. Pendleton, died Apr. 9, 1892.

Fuller P., son of Elisha K. and Catherine Pendleton, supposed to have been lost at sea between the 10th and 23d of Feb., 1870.

Justin F., son of Elisha K. and Catherine Pendleton, lost at sea Feb. 21, 1870.

Clara A. Ryder, wife of Joseph Ryder, daughter of Elisha K. and Catherine Pendleton, died Sept. 23, 1886.

Peleg P. Boardman, died Jan. 2, 1892.

Bridget, wife of Stephen Fairfield, daughter of Dea. John Pendleton, died Jan. 9, 1884.

Sarah Blake, wife of Chauncey Davis, died———.

Joanna Fairfield, wife of Andrew Fairfield, daughter of John and Maria Veazie, died ———.

*East side of Gilkey's Harbor, on the land formerly owned
by Joseph Pendleton.*

There are a number of graves, and but a single grave-stone, that of Mr. Josiah Eames, drowned in Camden Harbor, January 11, 1822.

Polly Pendleton, daughter of Joseph and Wealthy Pendleton, was buried here.

These graves are overgrown with woods and neglected.

*Old Burying Ground on the Bonnet on the east side, on
the land of William S. Dodge.*

Joshua Dodge, died Mar. 24, 1858, aged 76 years 2 months.

Elizabeth or Betsey S., wife of Joshua Dodge, aged 73 years; died Nov. 4, 1865, aged 72.

Noah Dodge, Senior, died July 23, 1816, aged 54.

Mrs. Rosanna Dodge, died May 18, 1835, or July 23, 1814, aged 54.

Noah Dodge, Jr., died Mar. 17, 1823, aged 22 years.

Phebe Dodge, died Mar. 26, 1823, aged 15 years.

Christiana (Dodge), wife of John Roberts.

Harriet B., wife of William S. Dodge, aged 32, died Jan. 8, 1860.

Flora R., second wife of William L. Dodge, aged 32, died 1875.

Walter F. Dodge.

Rose, wife of Walter F. Dodge.

*Record of Graves in the Burying Ground on the late Mark
Pendleton's Land.*

Nettie, daughter of Chauncey Davis, wife of Leslie Rollerson, died 1890.

Mark Pendleton, Jr., born Feb. 2, 1811; died Apr. 23, 1888.

M. Louette, daughter of F. C. Pendleton, died July 5, 1886, aged 16 years 2 months.

Mark Pendleton, Sr., died Dec. 25, 1867, aged 83 years.

Lydia, wife of Mark Pendleton, Sr., died June, 1869, aged 83 years.

Lyman Pendleton, died 1891; Sally, first wife, died —; Lucretia second wife, died ——.

Joshua Pendleton, the preacher, died ——. His wife Sally, died ——.

Samuel Pendleton, the first settler, father of Mark Pendleton the first, died 1826.

Bathsheba, wife of Samuel Pendleton, about 1828.

John Richardson, died ——.

Bathsheba, his wife, daughter of Samuel and Bathsheba Pendleton, died ——.

Howard, son of J. B. and Melissa Pendleton, died Oct. 14, 1889, aged 13 years.

Ethel, son of D. A. and Annie Warren, Nov. 1, 1875, March 4, 1890.

Samuel, son of Daniel Warren, died May 14, 1872. Fell from aloft on board his vessel, and was killed.

Bathsheba, wife of Daniel Warren, daughter of Mark Penleton first, died Jan. 15, 1858.

Phineas D. Rollerson, died Mar. 24, 1859, aged 34.

Clara J., daughter of Phineas and Celia Rollerson, aged 14 years.

George W., son of Phineas and Celia Rollerson, died in Fernandina, Fla., Dec. 16, 1877, age 19 years 7 months.

James Michaels, died ——.

Nancy J. Maker, daughter of Daniel and Bathsheba Warren, died in Concord, Mass., Dec. 1880.

Mrs. Turner, Rev. Joshua Pendleton's wife's mother, died ——.

Mary Ellen, wife of Franklin Flanders, died ——.

Lyonaise Pendleton, son of Dodge Pendleton, died ——.

Ellen, wife of Richard P. Pendleton, daughter of Pillsbury Coombs, died Nov. 27, 1883, aged 42 years, 6 months 12 days.

Vincent Pendleton, died ——.

His wife, Eliza Kimball, died ——.

Fannie, wife of Joel Small, died Oct. 3, 1876, aged 34 years.

### Trim Homestead.

Elisha R. Trim, died Feb. 6, 1871, aged 64 years 6 months 24 days.

Phebe W., wife of Elisha R. Trim, died May 28, 1876, aged 74 years 4 months.

Joseph S. Trim, son of Elisha and Phebe Trim, died July 9, 1864, aged 24 years, 10 months 5 days.

Emily, wife of Robert Trim, died Sept. 13, 1866, aged 19 years, 9 months 24 days.

### Williams Homestead.

Capt. Thomas Williams, died May 13, 1866, aged 73 years 7 months.

Lydia S., wife of Thomas Williams, died March 10, 1863, aged 70 years 5 months.

Caroline, daughter of Thomas and Lydia S. Williams, died Apr. 15, 1876, aged 50 years, 5 months 20 days.

### West Side, Upper End.

Godfrey Trim, died Apr. 17, 1808.

His wife, Mary Rose, died Aug. 30, 1825.

Zachariah Marshall, died ——.

Prudence Marshall, died ——.

Sally Dodge, died ——.

*Record of the Graves on the late Henry Boardman's land.*

Henry Boardman, aged 78.

His wife Catherine, daughter of Jonathan and Lydia Sprague, aged 87 years.

Joseph Boardman, born Apr. 10, 1801; died Feb. 19, 1879.

His wife Niobe, born Sept. 9, 1801 ; died Jan. 13, 1879.

George, son of Joseph and Niobe Boardman, died Aug. 12, 1852, aged 22.

Sabra, wife of Edmund D. Boardman, died ——.

Theodore S. Hatch, died in Havana, July 6, 1854, aged 30 years 9 months.

Ann C. Hatch Warren, died Oct. 15, 1876, aged 56 years 10 days.

Henry Boardman, Jr., died Oct. 1, 1857, aged 33 years 4 months.

William Boardman, died Aug. 9, 1865.

His wife Jane, died Dec. 30, 1869, aged 80 years 8 months.

Leonidas O. Boardman, died at Washington, D. C., Feb. 3, 1865.

*Graveyard on the East Side, on the land formerly owned by S. B. Fletcher.*

Sylvester H. Brown, died Feb. 11, 1847, aged 32 years.

Thomas Fletcher, died in Michigan, June 2, 1869 ; born in 1811.

Penelope M. Fletcher, born June 1, 1813 ; died June 2, 1878.

Stephen Oscar Fletcher, died Apr. 30, 1869, aged 29 years, 2 months 20 days.

Sarah L. Fletcher, died 1870.

Iva Ella Dodge, died in Franklin, Mass., 1890.

Grace Tracy, daughter of Sewell B. Fletcher, died——.

George Washington, son of W. J. and G. W. Fletcher, died in Brooklyn, N. Y., Nov., 1890 ; born October 20, 1818 ; aged 72.

Mehitable Fletcher, wife of S. H. Fletcher, died——.

Barbara, wife of Sewell C. Fletcher, died——.

Nora, daughter of S. H. Fletcher, died——, aged about 15 years.

Sewell C. Fletcher, died Oct., 1891.

M. G. Fletcher, daughter of Sewell B. Fletcher, aged 16 years.

John Brown, died———; his wife Peggy died———.

Amelia Huse Brown, died———.

*Grave on Hewes' Point, in the late Mr. Randlett's Orchard.*

Daniel Randlett, died about 1889.

His wife Jane about 1874.

Ann Randlett, died, aged about 90; Daniel Randlett's mother.

Margaret Ann, daughter of Daniel Randlett, aged about 30 years.

Frank Leighton, married Phebe Randlett; he died ———, aged 21.

Joseph Randlett, died ———, age 13 years.

*Graves on the land of late Rathburn Dodge.*

Queen Ann, wife of Joseph J. Brown.

Rathburn Dodge; his wife Eliza (Grover) Dodge.

Mary Dodge, aged about 18 years; Eben M. Dodge, died in New York.

Solomon Dodge, died 1891.

Nancy King Dodge, aged about 80 years.

Elizabeth Jackins, died ———.

Mary Ann, daughter of Simon and Betsey Dodge, wife of Abraham Dodge, died 1891.

On a headland on the north side of Crow Cove there is a burying ground. The land was formerly owned by Benjamin Williams, and was used more than a century for a burying place. The graves are overgrown with bushes and weeds, and many of the gravestones are broken. I am indebted to Mr. Benjamin Ashley Warren for the information obtained.

Shubael Williams, died July 17, 1804, aged 70 years.

Abigail, wife of Shubael Williams, died Apr. 5, 1799.

Samuel Williams, died Sept. 10, 1820, aged 65 years.

Capt. Benjamin Williams, died March 4, 1848, aged 81 years.

Jane, wife of Benjamin Williams, died Aug. 4, 1837, aged 70 years.

Ibre Williams, son of Benjamin and Jane, died March 30, 1834, aged 26 years.

Julia Ann, daughter of Benjamin and Jane, died Oct. 19, 1841, aged 60 years.

James B. Williams, son of Benjamin and Jane, died ——.

Benjamin Williams, son of Benjamin and Jane, died ——.

Capt. Amos Williams, born 1758; died 1840.

Elizabeth, wife of Amos Williams, died Nov. 16, 1864, aged 80 years.

William, son of Amos and Elizabeth Williams, died 1861.

Capt. Joseph Williams, died Apr. 22, 1842, aged 75 years: his wife Sarah died ——.

Joseph Williams, died April 2, 1842, aged 75 years.

Robert Trim Williams, died ——.

Darius Williams, died; wife Lucy died ——

Temperance Merithew, died ——.

Joseph W. Robinson, drowned in Bangor, Oct. 25, 1853, aged 26 years, 6 months 27 days.

Hosea Coombs, died——; Betsey, wife of Hosea Coombs, died July 15, 1804, aged 38 years.

George Coombs, son of Solomon and Abigail Coombs, died ——.

Josiah Farrow, died Aug. 14, 1817; a soldier in the revolution.

Ruth, wife of Josiah Farrow, died May 7, 1838, aged 70 years.

Samuel Farrow, died Jan. 4, 1826, aged 37 years.

Harriet (Farrow) Hervey, died ——.

Elizabeth, wife of Stephen Boardman, daughter of Josiah and Ruth Farrow, died Jan. 1, 1817, aged 28 years.

Elihu Hewes, died 1808, aged 87 years. (Probably father of Paoli Hewes.)

Samuel and Mary Warren, first settlers, died ——.

Benjamin Warren, died Oct., 1862.

His wife Abigail, died 1847.

Isaac, son of Benj. and Abigail, died 1839.

Stephen Warren, died June 7, 1889.

His wife Lydia, died Sept. 10, 1867, aged 52 years, 9 months 10 days.

Hattie Louise Hayes, died June 20, 1872, aged 19 years 3 days, daughter of Stephen and Lydia Warren.

Ephraim Randlett, died Apr. 30, 1885, aged 36 years, 7 months 11 days.

Samuel Herrick, son of Reuben and Mary Herrick, aged 18 years.

*The Record of Gravestones in Greenwood Cemetery.*

Flora A. Burgess, wife of I. M. Burgess, Mar. 10, 1857, June 11, 1882.

Lucy L., wife of Isaac Burgess, died May 21, 1890, aged 74 years 2 days.

Emeline, wife of Thomas H. Parker, died Jan. 4, 1892, aged 77 years, 7 months 19 days.

Adeliza, wife of J. H. Veazie, died May 23, 1886, aged 50 years, 1 month 2 days.

Samuel Haynes, died Aug. 21, 1876, aged 71 years, 11 months 7 days.

Capt. William F. Veazie, Jr., lost at sea, Nov. 17, 1875, aged 25 years, 5 months 1 day.

Nahum H., son of Lincoln and Louisa Coombs, drowned at Gibraltar, Sept. 6, 1875, aged 19 years.

Capt. Lincoln Coombs, died 1892.

Capt. David H. Rose, Oct. 8, 1830, Feb. 21, 1890.

20

Rita E. Rose, born Nov. 6, 1872; died May 21, 1879.

Capt. Henry Rose, Jr., died in East Boston, May 22, 1879, aged 58 years 11 months.

Hattie L., wife of Otis F. Coombs, Jr., daughter of Isaac and Lucy Burgess, died June 10, 1878, aged 31 years, 5 months 22 days.

Capt. Otis F. Coombs, died at sea, Dec. 19, 1877, aged 57 years, 9 months 23 days.

Angelia, wife of Otis F. Coombs, died July 22, 1891, aged 63 years, 4 months 25 days.

Cora L., wife of Frank H. Mayo, daughter of Otis F. and Angelia Coombs, died July 30, 1884, aged 21 years 7 months.

Silas Bunker, born Dec. 1, 1806; died Feb. 14, 1877, aged 70 years, 2 months 14 days.

W. E. Lowell, born Oct. 7, 1828; died Aug. 14, 1888.

Capt. Henry B. Coombs, died Jan. 3, 1884, aged 74 years 10 months and 25 days.

Morilla Marks, wife of William P. Sprague, died Nov. 7, 1880, aged 36 years 4 months.

Morilla B., daughter of William P. Sprague, born Jan. 6, 1871; died Feb. 7, 1881.

Capt. Hosea C. Wyman, lost at sea, Apr. 1, 1879, aged 45 years, 6 months 18 days.

B. Lewis Ryder, died Sept. 14, 1891, aged 38 years, 9 months 25 days.

Benjamin Ryder, died Oct. 8, 1881, aged 67 years 9 months 25 days.

Nancy, wife of Benjamin Ryder, died Aug. 23, 1882, aged 69 years 3 days.

Eben Grover, died Mar. 9, 1876, aged 42 years, 11 months 12 days.

John Veazie, died Jan. 4, 1888, aged 70 years.

Deborah, 2d wife of John Veazie, died Apr. 26, 1888, aged 63 years.

Ethie A. Veazie, died 1871, aged 9 years.

Stevia D., son of Stephen Knowlton, died Nov. 28, 1884, aged 15 years 6 months.

Ethel L., daughter of Stephen Knowlton, died Aug. 8, 1892, aged 27 years, 1 month 12 days.

Effie Jean, wife of H. E. Coombs, 1858——1890.

Eliza Jane, wife of Marion W. Rose, died in the West Indies, March 16, 1857, aged 27 years, 1 month 3 days.

William G. Coombs, lost at sea, Nov. 17, 1875, aged 38 years, 1 month 9 days.

*Record of Gravestones on the East Side of Sabbath-Day Harbor, on the Bluff.*

Abizer Coombs, died Oct. 3, 1861, aged 62 years, 2 months 15 days.

Polly, his wife, died——.

Joseph Knowlton, died March 27, 1882, aged 83 years, 11 months 21 days.

Rhoda, wife of Joseph Knowlton, died June 7, 1864, aged 63 years, 2 months 19 days.

The cemetery on the west side, at the upper end of the island, is enclosed with a stone wall, and has been used for a burying place more than a century. The date on the oldest stone is May 26, 1790.

*A Record of the Gravestones.*

William Lassell, husband of Ruhamah Lassell, died June 10, 1852, aged 58 years, 5 months 17 days.

Lydia Lassell, died May 31, 1826, aged 48 years.

George Lassell, died March 7, 1823, aged 36 years.

Ellison Lassell, born Sept. 5, 1754; died Dec. 16, 1850.

Sarah Lassell, wife of Ellison Lassell, died May 26, 1790.

Gamaliel Pendleton, died July 12, 1892, aged 69 years 11 months.

Lavina J., wife of Joseph Clark, daughter of G. R. and M. T. Pendleton, died Jan. 30, 1872, aged 21 years.

Niobe, wife of John Batchelder, daughter of Samuel and Lucy C. Pendleton, died Oct. 31, 1850, aged 36 years.

Orrington M., son of John and Niobe Batchelder, died Jan. 13, 1851, aged 15 years 9 days.

Cordelia E., wife of Nathaniel Nickels, daughter of Samuel and Lucy Pendleton, died Jan. 2, 1837, aged 25 years, 10 months 13 days.

Lydia, daughter of Rathburn and Lydia Dodge, died Aug. 6, 1842, aged 42 years, 6 months 26 days.

Betsey, wife of George W. Dodge, born in New Shoreham, R. I., Sept. 3, 1808; died Apr. 24, 1851, aged 42 years, 7 months 21 days.

George Dodge, died at sea, July 27, 1855, aged 14 years, 5 months 11 days.

Benjamin J., son of Shubael and Dorothy Pendleton, died Feb. 25, 1870, aged 15 years.

Frederick, son of Shubael and Dorothy Pendleton, died——.

William F. Gates, died Nov. 30, 1879, aged 34 years, 1 month 25 days.

James Dodge, born Apr. 27, 1818, died March 16, 1872, aged 53 years, 10 months 19 days.

David Ladd, died Nov. 2, 1888, aged 61 years.

Solomon Page Coombs, died Nov. 2, 1888, aged 61 years.

Irene, daughter of Mark B. and Abigail Dodge, died Dec. 25, 1844, aged 19 years, 11 months 20 days.

Cora A., daughter of E. J. and Julia Dodge, died Aug. 16, 1863, aged 11 years, 4 months 22 days.

Hattie E., daughter of E. J. and Julia Dodge, died Aug. 26, 1876, aged 19 years, 10 months 25 days.

Irene M., wife of H. M. Welch, born Mar. 31, 1844; died Dec. 26, 1887.

Aaron M. Hill, died March 8, 1886, aged 69.

Nancy, his wife, died 1876.

Rathburn Dodge, 2d, died Oct. 9, 1864, aged 55 years, 2 months 12 days.

Charity, wife of Rathburn Dodge, died March 5, 1878, aged 64 years, 7 months 8 days.

Rathburn Dodge, Sr., died Sept. 18, 1846, aged 79 years.

Andrew Jackson, son of Abraham and Charity Dodge, died Sept. 2, 1848, aged 18 years, 5 months 25 days.

Elbridge B. Sawyer, died Aug. 27, 1873, aged 39 years 12 days.

Thomas Decker, died about 1866.

Ada B. Decker, died 1887; daughter of Thomas and Lydia Decker.

Capt. Samuel Pendleton, died Sept. 21, 1884, aged 53 years, 8 months 7 days.

Lucy C., wife of Samuel Pendleton, died Aug. 4, 1877, aged 87 years, 10 months 5 days.

Jonathan Sprague, died Aug. 2, 1803, aged 48 years, 10 months 22 days.

Lydia, wife of Jonathan Sprague, died June 4, 1848, aged 86 years.

Rathburn D. Sprague, born March 15, 1797, died Nov. 7, 1880, aged 83 years, 7 months 23 days.

Sarah, wife of Rathburn D. Sprague, died 1879.

Lydia, wife of Simon Sprague, died Sept. 1, 1848, aged 63 years, 1 month 27 days.

Joseph Sprague, lost at sea, Mar. 30, 1844, aged 25 years, 5 months 11 days.

Capt. Rodolphus Pendleton, drowned in Penobscot Bay, Oct. 28, 1866, aged 48 years, 7 months 14 days.

William Dix, died Aug. 25, 1876, aged 72 years 5 days.

Ann L., wife of William Dix, died March 26, 1887, aged 76 years, 3 months 1 day.

Sophronia A., daughter of William and Ann Dix, died Dec. 15, 1858, aged 16 years 3 months.

Simon D. Sprague, died Nov. 20, 1877, aged 6- years 2 months.

Emma, wife of Alonzo Coombs, died——.

Alice, daughter of Alonzo and Emma Coombs, died——.

Nathaniel Sawyer, born Nov. 18, 1792 ; died Nov. 16, 1870.

Sarah, wife of Nathaniel Sawyer, born Sept. 16, 1794, died Sept. 14, 1871.

Druzetta, wife of George W. Sawyer, died Apr. 22, 1853, aged 24 years, 7 months 7 days.

Lucy A., wife of William A. Coombs, died Dec. 30, 1879, aged 30 years.

Henry McFarland, died——.

Mary McFarland, died——.

Susan McFarland, died——.

Simon Sprague, Sen., died June 26, 1863.

George W. Knights, died——.

Sophronia, his wife, died——.

Mrs. Prudence Chassa, died 1870.

Solomon Sprague, died——.

Lucretia, his wife, died——.

Edgar E. Coburn, died July 22, 1875, aged 14 years.

Capt. John Coombs, died——.

Jennie Small, his second wife, died about 1872.

John Coombs, Jr., died Feb. 5, 1892.

Adeline, wife of Isaac Pendleton, died——.

Berton Sprague, son of Solomon Sprague, died——.

Robert Marshall, died——.

Nancy, his wife, died——.

Izetta, wife of James Henry Dodge, died Apr. 11, 1892.

Joseph Emerson, Izetta Dodge's father, was buried here.

Mark B. Dodge, born Feb. 20, 1803; died May 23, 1867.

Abigail Dodge, his wife, born 1801; died Dec. 20, 1884.

*Record of Gravestones in the Cemetery on the East Side, Upper End.*

Godfrey Trim, died Feb. 14, 1886, aged 60 years, 3 months and 7 days.

Owen, son of Godfrey Trim, drowned at Delaware City, Aug. 5, 1862, aged 17 years 6 months.

Capt. Pillsbury Coombs, died Jan. 27, 1890, aged 81 years.

Lois W., his wife, died Oct. 29, 1889, aged 78 years 2 months.

Diana, daughter of Pillsbury and Lois W. Coombs, died May 7, 1874, aged 27 years; wife of C. F. Coombs, Jr.

Almeda Coombs, daughter of Pillsbury and Lois W. Coombs, died Dec. 23, 1881, aged 41 years 5 months; wife of Alonzo Wyman.

Jordan Veazie, died Jan. 14, 1839, aged 32 years.

Philena, wife of Andrew P. Gilkey, died April 22, 1879, aged 73 years 21 days.

Andrew P. Gilkey, died Feb. 23, 1890, aged 80 years 10 months.

Azubah, first wife of Andrew P. Gilkey, died November 11, 1839, aged 28 years.

Capt. Andrew J. Gilkey, died March 28, 1873, aged 24 years 1 month.

Andrew J. Gilkey, son of Andrew P. and Azubah Gilkey, drowned July 12, 1849, aged 16 years 9 months.

Philip E., son of Andrew P. and Philena Gilkey, died Dec. 6, 1854, aged 11 years, 3 months 3 days.

Capt. Martin S. Coombs, died Sept. 8, 1886, aged 39 years, 6 months 9 days.

Eliza F. Coombs, daughter of Othniel and Sarah Coombs, died Nov. 25, 1857, aged 20 years 2 days.

Capt. Noah D. Rose, died in 1883, in Boston.

James Skinner, died July 27, 1879, aged 78 years, 5 months 21 days.

Lucy, wife of James Skinner, died Nov. 30, 1859, aged 58 years 3 months.

Mighill Parker, died Feb. 17, 1827, aged 63 years.

Lydia J. Burgess, wife of George A. Coombs, died Feb. 20, 1864, aged 22 years 8 months.

Ethelinda Chestina, wife of Benjamin R. Redman, died Feb. 25, 1878, aged 32 years, 9 months 10 days.

James Trim, died Dec. 9, 1820, aged 49 years.

Mary R., wife of William Ryder, died Dec. 26, 1850, aged 30 years, 5 months 18 days.

Prudence Trim, wife of Israel Dodge, died Dec. 5, 1854, aged 76 years 8 months.   He was drowned in 1807.

Prudence, daughter of Simon and Betsey Dodge, died Jan. 7, 1856, aged 22 years.

Betsey, wife of Fields Coombs, died August 15, 1865, aged 70 years 5 months.

Capt. Fields Coombs, died May 20, 1848, aged 62 years 4 months.

Jane, wife of Samuel Marshall, died Jan. 23, 1851, aged 54 years, 5 months 9 days.

Deacon Jonathan Parker, died April 6, 1841, aged 68 years.

Wealthy, wife of Simon Parker, died Jan. 17, 1847, aged 74 years, 7 months 29 days.

Deacon Joshua Farrow, died March 13, 1879, aged 84 years 5 months.

Eunice, wife of Joshua Farrow, died October 19, 1873, aged 76 years 7 months.

Lucy H. S., wife of Capt. J. L. S. Coombs, died April 1, 1876, aged 29 years 6 months.

John Veazie, died September 15, 1841, aged 55 years 15 days.

Naomi, wife of John Veazie, died March 29, 1872, aged 82 years, 1 month 6 days.

Lauranie, wife of Noah Roberts, died May 29, 1860, aged 28 years, 1 month 9 days.

Betsey, wife of Thomas Ryder, died Nov. 27, 1850, aged 35 years.

Joseph Ryder, died May 16, 1858, aged 83 years.

Sarah, wife of Joseph Ryder, died Jan. 13, 1857, aged 77 years.

*The Record of Gravestones in the Cemetery on the East Side, Upper End.*

Martha A., wife of Freeman S. Keller, died Jan. 5, 1856, aged 20 years, 4 months 7 days.

Phœbe, wife of John Seely, died June 9, 1849, aged 34 years, 6 months 20 days.

Lucinda J., wife of F. C. Pendleton, died June 26, 1866, aged 22 years.

Maria R., wife of John Veazie, died June 19, 1858, aged 36 years 10 months.

Naomi A., wife of Capt. Edwin Coombs, died Aug. 4, 1866, aged 23 years 8 months.

Samuel Warren, died Aug. 5, 1878, aged 74 years 6 months.

William A. Parker, died in Kingston, Jamaica, Mar. 12, 1857, aged 41 years, 8 months 12 days.

Caroline, wife of Wm. A. Parker, died Nov. 30, 1875, aged 57 years, 7 months 16 days.

Henry Rose, died July 10, 1864, aged 79 years 11 months.

Hannah, his wife, died June 9, 1863, aged 80 years 12 days.

Nancy, wife of Capt. A. H. Parker, died July 29, 1875, aged 32 years.

Jordan V., son of Thomas H. and Emeline Parker, died Dec. 4, 1862, aged 23 years.

Jane Parker, died Jan. 23, 1808, aged 62 years.

Bridget, wife of Samuel Veazie, died Apr. 28, 1858, aged 69 years, 11 months 18 days.

Samuel Veazie, died Dec. 2, 1841, aged 62 years.

Elizabeth, wife of William Coombs, died Aug. 11, 1850, aged 35 years 5 months.

Sarah S., the second wife of William Coombs, died Feb. 8, 1884, aged 34 years 3 months.

Capt. J. B. Coombs, died in Havana, July 14, 1873, aged 40 years, 1 month 14 days.

Edward L. Coombs, died Nov. 3, 1875, aged 18 years 5 months.

Cora Coombs, died Jan. 13, 1880, aged 16 years 5 months.

Olive Trim, wife of Capt. David Warren, died Oct. 6, 1842, aged 23 years, 7 months 9 days.

Otis C. Veazie, died July 26, 1848, aged 28 years.

William Wyman, died Nov. 13, 1842, aged 58 years.

James F. Wargent, born Apr. 12, 1851; drowned in Belfast bay, July 7, 1888.

George Warren, born Jan. 12, 1812; died Dec. 2, 1890.

Sally, his wife, born May 31, 1812; died Sept. 6, 1891.

Andrew J. Spinney was lost at sea Nov. 17, 1875, aged 32 years 2 months.

Lydia E., wife of A. J. Spinney, died July 22, 1876, aged 36 years, 8 months 7 days.

Rev. Varnum G. Rose, born Nov. 23, 1810, died Dec. 14, 1865, aged 60 years 21 days.

Capt. Benjamin Grover, born July 21, 1822, died July 19, 1872.

Eliza Farrow Coombs, wife of Philip Coombs, died Feb. 5, 1890.

# CHAPTER X.

## FAMILY GENEALOGIES.

I HAVE been aided in the preparation of these genealogies* by town records, family bibles, and by traditions of the older people. The town records were, a part of the time, kept very poorly, and many of the families had no records; so that errors are unavoidable. Some of the descendants of the early settlers have changed the spelling of their names, and that has increased the difficulty. Of the sixty families who settled here prior to the incorporation of the town, only one descendant has been an inmate of the State prison, and that was without doubt a case of insanity. The descendants of these families in Islesborough were educated in the common schools, and were almost invariably taken from school at the age of ten or twelve years, to go on board of the coasting vessels, which would haul up for the three winter months, when they could go to school from five to eight weeks. Very few, if any, went to the winter school after they were seventeen years old. These men have made sea captains, and sailed and done business all over the world, and I have never known a case where their education was at fault in doing business.

---

* It is assumed that all persons named belonged in Islesborough.

## ADAMS FAMILY.

William Adams married Rosina Pendleton. Children:

i James B., b. February 8, 1844, m. Mary E. Pendleton. He was a soldier in the rebellion.
ii Francis W., b. September 8, 1845, m. first, Susie Keller; second, Rose Sprague.
iii Harlan P., b. August 25, 1848.
iv Nathan G., b. December 4, 1851, m. Angeline E. Keller.
v Ida J., b. May 15, 1858, m. William Coombs.

William C. Adams married Elizabeth A. Hutchins. Children:

i Betsey, b. November 30, 1850.
ii John H., b. August 25, 1854.
iii Hiram T., b. August 7, 1855, d. 1855.
iv Addie A., b. December 7, 1856.
v Lovinia J., b. February 28, 1860.

Harlan P. Adams married——. Moved to New Haven, Conn. Children, born in Islesborough:

i George Alfred, b. February 27, 1870.
ii Rosina Frances, b. May 22, 1872.
iii Lucretia, b. April 7, 1875.

Nathan G. Adams married Angeline E. Keller. He died 1890. Children:

i Josiah L., b. May 14, 1873.
ii Lottie M., b. October 14, 1875.
iii Emma C., b. November 9, 1877.
iv Walter N., b. June 21, 1881.
    Melvin, William, Rosina, Cleveland, Laura E.

## AMES FAMILY.

Thomas Ames was from Marshfield. He married first Rebecca Harnie, in Marshfield, Jan. 9, 1764. She was the mother of all his children, and died June 28, 1807, aged 66. He married second, Mrs. Lucy Comstock.

Published Aug. 13, 1808. He married third, Mrs. Lucy Jordan, of Thomaston, Aug. 28, 1812. He died 1826. Children :

   i   Mercy, b. August 28, 1772, m. Thomas Gilkey, December 6, 1792.
   ii  Jabez, m. Jane, daughter of John Gilkey, Sen.
  iii  Thankful, m. Andrew Phillips. He was from Kittery.
  iv  Sally, m. Joshua Pendleton. Removed to Northport, where he died.
   v  Lydia, m. Seth Farrow, July 5, 1822.
  vi  Rebecca, m. John Farrow. He d. June 26, 1811, aged 62. She d. September 26, 1842.
 vii  Betsey, m. Joseph Jones ; no children.
viii  Luther, died in Boston, unmarried, aged 21 years.


Jabez Ames, son of Elder Thomas Ames. He married Jane, daughter of John Gilkey, Sen. She died March 11, 1851. He died Jan. 21, 1829. Children, all born in Islesborough :

   i   Jane, b. April 15, 1789, m. December 25, 1805, Captain William Boardman. He died August, 1865, aged 86. She died December 30, 1869.
   ii  Grace, b. September 29, 1790, m. Abiezer Veazie. He d. in Camden, about 1840, aged 51 years. Descendants in Rockland.
  iii  Jabez, b. May 19, 1793, m. Lydia S. Mason, of Hope.
  iv  Betsey, b. April 18, 1795, m. Fields Coombs, Jr., December 26, 1814. He d. May 20, 1848, aged 62 years. She died August 15, 1865, aged 70 years.
   v  Lenity, b. March 7, 1797, m. Ralph Wade, of Lincolnville, December 17, 1820.
  vi  John, b. January 23, 1799. He d. in Vineland, N. J., 1886.
 vii  Catherine, b. July 12, 1801, m. Robert Sherman, October 9, 1825.
viii  Susan, b. October 22, 1803, m. Isaac Sherman, May 29, 1825.
  ix  Isaac, b. November 18, 1806, m. Rebecca Tarbell.
   x  Louisiana, b. May 20, 1809, m. ----, of Northport.


John Ames, born Jan. 23, 1799. He was a mariner. Married Delilah, daughter of Noah Dodge, Jan. 28, 1821. She died in Baltimore, 1879. He died in Vineland, New Jersey, 1886. Children :

   i   John J., b. May 18, 1821, m. ---- Balch, of Lubec, d. in California.

ii  Emerson, b. November 19, 1822, in Waynesboro, Penn.
iii  Susan, b. April 13, 1824, m. Charles W. Hammond, of Corinth, d. in Baltimore.
iv  Preston A., b. August 31, 1826; of Hingham, Mass.
v  Hudson H., b. February 20, 1828. Lived in Brighton, Calais and Baltimore. Married and had a family.

## BABBIDGE FAMILY.

Eben Babbidge married Martha Dodge. He died April 5, 1870. Children:

i  Stephen, b. November 15, 1844, m. Laura Veazie. His daughter Laura Bell, b. September 22, 1866, m. — — Keller.
ii  Ebenezer, b. August 27, 1846, m. Caro Hatch.
iii  Esther, b. August 23, 1849, m. A. G. Nelson.
iv  Winfield S., b. February 4, 1853.
v  Thaddeus, b. June 30, 1855, m. Adriana Pendleton.
vi  Lewis H., b. December 8, 1856.
vii  Martha and Margaret, b. January 21, 1859, d. 1859.
viii  Cora A., b. June 8, 1861.
ix  Helen, b. December 28, 1864.
x  Margaret F., b. April 12, 1866.

Eben G. Babbidge married Caro Hatch. Children:

i  Margaret F., b. October 12, 1866, m. Ernest Thomas.
ii  Clarence E., b. April 4, 1869, m. Lena Rackett.
iii  Harry A., b. December 19, 1871.
iv  Caro Ella, b. March 31, 1881.
v  Mary, ——

Thaddeus Babbidge married Adriana Pendleton. Children:

i  Mariel Beulah, b. 1877.
ii  Abbie L., b. June 28, 1878.

Charles D. Bates married Eliza Coombs. Children:

i  Beulah C., b. January 7, 1878.

## BACHELDER FAMILY.

John Bachelder married first Niobe, daughter of Samuel
Pendleton. She was born Jan. 18, 1815; died Oct. 31,
1850. Married second, Lydia Jane, widow of Solomon
Sprague, Oct. 18, 1852. Children :

    i  Orrington M., b. December 25, 1835, d. 1850.
   ii  Alonzo, b. April 10, 1838.
  iii  Cordelia M., b. April 18, 1839.
  iv  Alurum A., b. October 26, 1842.
   v  Vandalure A., b. February 7, 1844.
  vi  Lucy M., b. December 21, 1845.
 vii  Samuel E., b. February 18, 1847, d. 1849.
viii  Francena R., b. December 25, 1848, d. 1849.
  ix  John A., b. August 2, 1850.
   x  Isaac G., b. June 6, 1853.

## BOARDMAN FAMILY.

Joseph Boardman married, October 2, 1774, Mary,
daughter of Thomas Pendleton. She was born 1758.
This was the first wedding in Islesborough, and Mr.
George Pendleton says he has conversed with Mrs. Boardman. She said all the people on the island came to her
wedding. There were but three families then settled on
the island, viz : Thomas Pendleton, Shubael Williams
and William Pendleton. Capt. Thomas gave Mary and
Joseph a farm, and they built their house near Boardman's
Cove. He died Oct. 29, 1831. Wife died July 26, 1827.
Children :

    i  Thomas, b. June 24, 1775.
   ii  Joseph, Jr., b. March 10, 1777.
  iii  William, b. July 28, 1779.
  iv  Stephen, b. May 24, 1782, m. Elizabeth Farrow, 1811. She d.
       January 21, 1817.
   v  Mary, b. February 8, 1785, m. Josiah Farrow.
  vi  John, b. December 20, 1787, d. September 27, 1792.
 vii  Betsey, b. July 16, 1789, d. October 2, 1792.
viii  Isaac Case, b. August 28, 1792.
  ix  Henry, b. May 14, 1794.
   x  Lydia, b. August 28, 1797, m. Martin Stone.
  xi  Margaret, b. February 12, 1800, m. William Stone.
    22

Thomas Boardman was born Jan. 25, 1775. Married Lydia Pendleton. His wife died Oct. 5, 1843. He died Oct. 5, 1845. Children :

   i  Elizabeth, b. April 1, 1800.
  ii  Thomas, Jr., b. January 27, 1802, d. 1823.
 iii  Joseph, b. November 8, 1804, m. Niobe Sprague.

William Boardman married Jane Ames. He was born July 28, 1779. She was born April 15, 1789 ; died Dec. 30, 1869. Capt. Boardman commanded the schooner Rising Sun, about one hundred tons burden, which was the first vessel sailing from here that went to Europe. She had for a cargo a load of timber, bound for Liverpool. Children that were born in Islesborough :

   i  William, Jr., b. June 12, 1809, d. 1815.
  ii  Mary Jane, b. September 13, 1811.
 iii  Durock, b. August 9, 1813.
 iv  Dolly M., b. April 3, 1815, m. Peleg Decrow.
  v  Betsey, b. October 21, 1816, m. G. W. Dunton.

Children that were born in Hope and married in Islesborough :

  vi  Esther, m. Royal Brown.
 vii  Josiah, m. Diana Boardman.
viii  Isaiah, m. Mary H. Boardman.
 ix  Loisky, m. Thomas Boardman.
  x  William 3d, unmarried.

Isaac C. Boardman was born August, 1792. Married Esther Farrow. Published Jan. 11, 1817. Children :

   i  Esther F., b. March 9, 1819, d. in 1827.
  ii  Isaac M., b. May 24, 1821. He is now a prominent citizen of Belfast.
 iii  Ruth, b. August 27, 1823, m. George Dyer.
 iv  Mary P., b. January 18, 1826, d. 1827.
  v  Joseph, b. November 15, 1827, d. young.
 vi  Pamelia, m. Henry P. Came.
 vii  Georgiana, b. in Belfast.

Henry Boardman married Catherine Sprague, daughter of Jonathan, Dec. 4, 1818. He lived on the east side, adjoining the Joshua Dodge estate. The estate still belongs to his heirs. Children:

 i Ann C., m. Theodore Hatch.
 ii Charlotte, b. June 16, 1821.
 iii Susan A., b. August 29, 1823, m. Nathaniel Hatch, Jr., January 4, 1849.
 iv Henry O., b. May 30, 1825, d. October 1, 1857.
 v William P., b. February 16, 1830, m. Hattie Baker.
 vi Mary H., b. November 15, 1832, m. Isaiah Boardman.
 vii Regina J., b. December 15, 1835, m. Peleg Boardman.

Joseph Boardman, son of Thomas Boardman, married Niobe Sprague, June 26, 1824. He died Feb. 18, 1879. She died Jan. 14, 1879. He lived at the lower end of the island. He represented the town in the Legislature, was a Democrat, and always had an influence in his political party, which continued as long as he lived. He belonged to the Masonic fraternity, and was buried with Masonic honors. Children:

 i Lydia P., b. October 14, 1824, m. Oliver Brown.
 ii Diana, b. December 1, 1825, m. Josiah Boardman.
 iii Thomas 2d, b. July 8, 1828, m. Loisky Boardman.
 iv George W., b. May 15, 1830, d. August 12, 1851.
 v Edmund D., b. March 12, 1831, m. Sabra C. Collins.
 vi Peleg P., b. November 23, 1833, m. Regina Boardman, d. February, 1892.
 vii Elizabeth, b. December 24, 1836, m. Lorenzo Pendleton.
 viii Leonidas Oscar, b. July 22, 1841, m. Lydia E. Patterson, of Northport. He d. February 3, 1865. One son, Elder C., b. February 3, 1865.
 ix Lavinia A., b. June 10, 1839, m. Thomas F. Brown.

Isaiah Boardman, son of William, married Mary Boardman. Children:

 i Linda E., b. June 2, 1855.
 ii Ada D., b. October 11, 1858, d. December 8, 1863.
 iii Willard, b. April 8, 1861, d. December 25, 1863.

iv   Millard E., b. June 1, 1865.
v    Edna A., b. May 13, 1867.
vi   Evelyn Adell, b. May 13, 1870, d. October 18, 1872.


Edmund D. Boardman, son of Joseph, married Sabra C.
Collins. She died 1858. Second wife, Mary Heal, of
Lincolnville. Third wife, Angelia Dodge. Children :

i    Flora L., b. April 6, 1853, m. George W. Sargent.
ii   Margie M., b. February 27, 1857, d. 1861.
iii  Loren V., b. October 2, 1869.
iv   Florence L., b. ——, d. 1871.
v    Freeman Eugene, b. February 21, 1871 ; son of Flora.


Peleg P. Boardman, son of Joseph Boardman, died 1892.
He married Regina Boardman. Children :

i    Corydon H., b. February 7, 1860.
ii   Wendell H., b. June 18, 1864.
iii  Leonora B., b. April 16, 1874.
iv   Frank Curtis, b. July 23, 1875.


George W. Boardman married Marintha A. Dodge.
Children :

i    Effie J., b. January 12, 1878.

## BROWN FAMILY.

John Brown married Margaret Hewes, Nov. 22, 1812.
Wife died Oct. 10, 1840. Children :

   i   Pamelia W., b. December 22, 18--.

   ii   Penelope H., b. January 13, 1813, m. Thomas Fletcher.

   iii   Sylvester, b. July 27, 1815, m. Elsie Pendleton.

   iv   Joseph J., b. August 12, 1818, m. Queen Ann Dodge.

   v   William H., b. December 17, 1821, m. Mercy J. Farnsworth.

   vi   Oliver M., b. February 9, 1823, m. Lydia P. Boardman, December
       15, 1844.

   vii   Betsey J., b. June 2, 1826.

   viii   Royal P., b. June 2, 1826, m. Esther Boardman, Sept. 28, 1847.

   ix   Thomas F., b. September 2, 1830, m. Lavinia Boardman, Septem-
       ber 2, 1830.

Joseph J. Brown, died Sept., 1856. He married Queen
Ann Dodge, who died Apr. 16, 1856. Children:

   i   Pamelia, b. December 7, 1843, m. Andrew Allen.

   ii   Alvah A., b. September 28, 1850.

   iii   Martha J., b. December 16, 1855.

   iv   Joseph, d. young.

   v   Clarisada and William.

William H. Brown married Mercy Jane Pendleton, Aug.
26, 1846. She died June 24, 1856. Second wife, Hannah Fields. Children :

   i   Orburn M., b. March, 1847, d. 1849.

   ii   Orianna, b. April 11, 1849, d. 1851.

   iii   Washington, b. June 8, 1851, d. July, 1869.

   iv   Melrose, b. July, 1852, d. 1854.

Royal P. Brown married Esther Boardman, Sept. 28,
1847. Children :

   i   Elvira E., b. November 14, 1848.

  ii   John, b. September 4, 1851, d. 1851.
 iii   Cecilia L., b. November 11, 1852, d. 1854.
  iv   Dorothy Jane, b. August 31, 1856, d. 1857.
   v   Royal E., b. August 30, 1855.
  vi   Lucinda E., b. July 25, 1858.

Oliver M. Brown married Lydia Boardman, Dec. 15, 1844. Children :

   i   Adelia E., b. April 4, 1850, m. Oliver S. Fletcher.
  ii   Francis I., b. August 22, 1852.
 iii   Rose G., b. May 5, 1856.
  iv   Fred L., b. July 10, 1857.
   v   Ada M., b. September 5, 1859, m. Perkins.
  vi   Aldervilla, b. December 17, 1862.
 vii   Hattie I., b. July 4, 1865.

Thomas F. Brown married Lavinia A. Boardman. Children :

   i   Leartus F., b. February, 1858, m. Alice Herrick.
  ii   Ernestine J., b. April, 1860, m. Charles Ayers.
 iii   Abby, m. Pendleton.

### BUNKER FAMILY.

Silas Bunker came from Charleston or Bangor, Me., 1839. He married Eleanor J. Rose, Jan. 10, 1839. He was chairman of the board of selectmen for five years. Went to California in 1849. He also built three churches in Islesborough. Children :

   i   Edgar A., b. December 11, 1840, m. Betsey A. Coombs.
  ii   Emery N., b. January 3, 1843, m. Adrianna A. Coombs.
 iii   Velocia E., b. June 27, 1846, m. James E. Coombs.

Emery N. Bunker married Adrianna A. Coombs. Children.

   i   Newton, b. April, 1875.
  ii   Henry A., b. March 28, 1881.

SILAS BUNKER.
1806—1877.

## BURNS FAMILY.

William Burns, from Bristol. Town officer, 1794.

William H. Burns married Mary J. Knowlton. Children:

  i  Emily Z., b. June 22, 1852.

Dr. S. D. Buzzell. Children, born in Islesborough:

  i  Oscar D., b. September 6, 1855.

## BURGESS FAMILY.

Isaac Burgess was highly esteemed for honesty, uprightness, veracity and virtue. He was born in Vinalhaven, March 16, 1810. He married Lucy, daughter of Joseph Ryder, of Vinalhaven. She was born Mar. 19, 1816. He removed to Islesborough. Wife died in Islesborough. He was a master mariner for many years; an active and zealous Christian from youth to old age. He was regarded with r e s p e c t by all his acquaintances. Children, all born in Islesborough:

  i  Mary A., b. October 8, 1836.
  ii  Reuben H., b. March 11, 1838, died in Darien, 1877, or October 9, 1876.
  iii  Lydia J., b. May 20, 1841, d. February, 1862.
  iv  Harriet I., b. December 11, 1846, d. June, 1872.
  v  Isaac M., b. January 3, 1851.
  vi  Hannah M., b. May 10, 1853.
  vii  Nellie E., b. March 2, 1860.

## COOMBS FAMILY.

Peter Coombs* came here from Brunswick. He was one of the first town officers. He settled at Sabbath-Day Harbor. He sold out to Mighill Parker, Aug. 6, 1791,

---

* He may have been father of Hosea and Fields Coombs.

and returned to Brunswick. Parker sold out to Joseph Ryder.

**Anthony Coombs, Sen.**, came from New Meadows. He was a town officer in 1789. He died in 1815, at the age of 100 years. Ruth, his wife, died 1826. They had seven sons and two daughters.

i   Anthony.
ii  Jesse.
iii Robert.
iv  Ephraim.
v   Benjamin.
vi  Jonathan.

**Anthony Coombs, Jr.** He was a town officer in Islesborough in 1792-6. He lived on the second lot below Sabath-Day Harbor. He married probably Hannah Holbrook. He died Jan. 8, 1835. Children, probably:

i   Abiezer.
ii  Henry B.
iii Ephraim.
iv  Nancy, m. John Rea, of Castine, June 3, 1815.
v   Lois, m. Lewis Murch, of Belfast; published March 5, 1825.
vi  Hannah, m. Roger Mertithew; published June 5, 1820.
vii Daughter, m. John Warren.

**Jesse Coombs**, son of Anthony, Sen. He married Hannah, daughter of William Richards, of Bristol, April 16, 1794. He died Sept. 5, 1823. She died Nov. 16, 1859. Children, all born in Islesborough:

i   Jesse, b. November 19, 1795, m. Wealthy Trim, November 22, 1813. Moved to Bucksport, where he died.
ii  Sally, b. September 29, 1797, m. James Farren; published September 15, 1812. Moved to New Hampshire, where she died.
iii Othniel, b. June 25, 1799, m. Sally Marshall; published April 27, 1816. He died in Islesborough.
iv  Wealthy, b. March 8, 1801, m. Isaac Allard; published September 29, 1819. Moved to Belfast, where she died.

v   Temperance, b. February 8, 1803, m. Thomas Marshall, Jr., July
20, 1820. Moved to Philadelphia, where she died.
vi   Rebecca P., b. April 6, 1805, m. Elder Samuel Macomber, September 12, 1824. Lived and died in Bluehill.
vii   Philip F., b. March 7, 1807, m. Eliza M. Farrow, June 3, 1838;
Eliza died February 5, 1890.
viii   Pillsbury, b. January 25, 1809, m. Lois Trim, July 22, 1832.
ix   Lucinda (or Louisiana) m. William Gulliver. Lived in Searsport, where she died.
x   Hannah, b. April 15, 1815, m. Ira Porter. Lived and died in
Searsport.
xi   Cyrena, b. May 20, 1817, m. Jacob Sargent, of Brewer; published
December 19, 1837. She lives in Bangor.

Robert Coombs, son of Anthony, Sen., lived near Jeremiah Hatch, West Bay. He married Lucy Thomas, July
10, 1790. (?) She died June 20, 1835. Children :

i   Robert, Jr., b. June 25, 1783, m. Jane Gilkey, 1823.
ii   Jacob, b. March 31, 1785, probably m. Prudence Turner; published April 15, 1821.
iii   Lucy, b. February 28, 1787, m. Otho Abbot, of Montville, October
7, 1816.
iv   Jesse, b. April 4, 1789, m. Desire Turner (or Trim), Mar. 2, 1816.
v   Isaac, b. February 9, 1790, m. Betsey Boardman.
vi   Luther, b. June 3, 1805, m. Diana Basford, of Belfast, May 9,
1828.
vii   Catherine, b. May 13, 1809, m. Bagley, of Belfast.
viii   Louisa, b. July 18, 1811, m. Arthur Farnsworth, June 21, 1832.
ix   Isaiah, b. August 16, 1838, by second wife.

Ephraim Coombs, son of Anthony, died Jan. 9, 1812,
aged 36 years. He married――――, of Bristol. Children :

i   William R., b. May 14, 1800, m. Mary H. Sargent, b. 1801 ;
d. 1890.
ii   Anthony, went to Utah.
iii   John, d. in New York.
iv   Isaiah.
v   Moses, d. in Baltimore.
vi   Ephraim, Jr., m. twice.

23

Elder Ephraim Coombs, son of Ephraim, was a minister of the Baptist church for thirty or forty years. He held town offices for a number of years. He died May 10, 1872, aged 75 years. He married first, Hannah Cyphers, of Sidney, Me., published Dec. 15, 1818. Second, Jane Thayer, published June 19, 1830. She died 1871. Children:

   i   Watson, b. January 26, 1820, m. Mary Sargent; d. in Brewer.
   ii  Sarah A., b. June 3, 1827, m. Jonas Page, of Bangor.
   iii Wilson, b. October 30, 1830, m. Lucy A. Marshall.
   iv  Amariah, b. July 3, 1832, m. Mary J. Marshall.
   v   William Richards, b. February 28, 1834, m. Ida I. Adams.
   vi  Mary J., b. October 11, 1836, m. Benjamin Heal.
   vii James S., b. July 3, 1841, m. Sally Hawes. James was a soldier
        in the 2d Maine regiment.
            Child, Zeruiah, b. April 2, 1860.
  viii Laura A., b. January 24, 1843, m. Gershom F. Libby.
   ix  Franklin, d. unmarried.


Wilson Coombs, son of Ephraim, born Oct. 30, 1830. Married Lucy Ann Marshall. Published Jan. 6, 1855. Children:

   i   Lucy E., b. November, 1856, d. December 22, 1875.
   ii  Rose E., b. December 17, 1857, d. 1858.
   iii Frederick W., b. July 18, 1860.
   iv  Wellington P., b. November 3, 1861, drowned 1880.
   v   William L., b. July 14, 1863, m. Calista A. Decker.
   vi  Augustus Perry, b. August 29, 1865.
   vii Elmira M., b. March 1, 1867, m. Charles E. Coombs.
  viii Bertha B., b. March 30, 1870.


Amariah Coombs, son of Ephraim, Jr., born July 3, 1832. Married Mary J. Marshall, daughter of Samuel, July 25, 1852. Children:

   i   Dora E., b. December 7, 1852, m. Matthew Randlett.

ELDER EPHRAIM COOMBS.

ii Ellen J., b. March 7, 1855.
iii Lovina, b. July 5, 1856.
iv Otis Watson, b. January 5, 1858, d. October 30, 1875.
v Estelle, b. September 27, 1859.
vi Walter, b. October 16, 1861.
vii Daughter, b. December 16, 1864.


Benjamin Coombs, son of Anthony, Sen., married Abigail Williams, June 16, 1791. She died July 13, 1842. Children:

    i John, m. Nancy Garner, July 14, 1822. Children:
        1 Lucy, b. July 25, 1829, m. Harvey Decker.
        2 Ruth, b. August 16, 1834, m. Joseph Decker.
    ii William, m. Betsey Williams, September 19, 1833. Children:
        1 Benjamin 2d, b. February 4, 1834, d. 1836.
        2 Samuel W., b. March 10, 1836, d. 1836.
        3 Rosilla, b. September 17, 1837, m. John Clark.
        4 Joseph V. B., b. July 27, 1840, m. Lizzie Small.
        5 William A., b. June 17, 1842, m. Lucy A. Decker.
    iii Rebecca, d. unmarried.
    iv Christian, d. unmarried.


Jonathan Coombs, son of Anthony, Sen., married Martha, daughter of Samuel Warren, Nov. 16 or June, 1790. Moved to Albion, where he died. Children:

    i Jonathan B., m. Abby Redman. Children, b. in Islesborough:
        1 Robert E., b. September 9, 1854, d. 1862.
        2 Abraham L., b. August 29, 1861.
        3 Clara E., b. January 1, 1858, d. 1859.
        4 Abby E., b. March 22, 1873.
        5 Ernest R.
    ii Samuel Warren, b. Islesborough, August 25, 1810. Lived in Mattawamkeag.
    iii George.
    iv Ruth, m. Nicholas Gilman, of Passadumkeag.
    v Thankful, m. Amos Dennis, of Passadumkeag.
    vi Betsey, m. David Scott, of Greenbush.
    vii Walter B. (?)

Abiezer Coombs, son of Anthony, Sen., married Mary Burke, of Ellsworth, Nov. 23, 1823. He died Oct. 3, 1861. She died May 5, 1881. Children:

i   Henry, b. July 18, 1825, d. January 26, 1826.
ii  Abiezer, b. June 20, 1827, d. January 12, 1846.
iii Mary Ann, b. May 29, 1829, m. Micajah Maxey, November 29, 1850.
iv  Hannah B., b. May 29, 1831, m. Stephen Knowlton, Oct. 10, 1852.
v   Nancy E., b. January 6, 1833, m. Robert Marshall, Sept. 16, 1850.
vi  Lois, b. September 20, 1835, m. Alverdo Dodge, Sept. 21, 1856.
vii Joseph Anthony, b. September 16, 1837, m. Ella Haynes. He d. in 1890.
viii Elzina, b. November 27, 1839, m. Stephen Knowlton, August 21, 1860.


Henry B. Coombs, son of Anthony, Junior, lived on the east side of Sabbath-Day Harbor, known as the Bluff. He sold his land on the Bluff, and then bought the estate formerly owned by Jeremiah Dodge, near Sprague's Cove. This was his home for many years, and where he lived and died. He was known as Uncle Henry by the inhabitants, and liked and respected by the whole town. This estate is now owned by the Islesborough Land and Improvement Company. He married Rhoda Grover. He died Jan. 3, 1884, age 74 years, 10 months and 25 days. Children (probably not in order):

i    Eliza J., m. Wellington Rose, February 2, 1850.
ii   Henry, m. Lydia Jane Sprague.
iii  Izetta M., m. Frank Dix, September 6, 1858.
iv   Paulina, b. October 11, 1843, m. William Collins, March, 1861.
v    William G., m. Ella Haynes, May 11, 1865. He was drowned, November 19, 1875.
vi   Stephen B., m. Lydia A. Sawyer, January 14, 1856.
vii  Alonzo, m. first, Emma Van Amburg; second, Lizzie Hatch.
viii Joseph G., m. Mrs. Hannah Martin.
ix   Flora C., b. October 25, 1849, m. Samuel E. Haynes, March 11, 1865.

Alonzo Coombs, son of Henry B., married first, Emma Van Amburg, second, Lizzie Hatch. Children:

i   Ada A., b. October 15, 1854, m. Elvin J. Ryder.
ii  Alice S., b. October 23, 1857.
iii Alonzo M., b. January 11, 1862, d. 1862.

Othniel Coombs, son of Jesse, married Sally Marshall. Published April 27, 1816. He was highly esteemed, and a man of remarkable energy and industry; honest and upright in all his dealings. He was born and died in Islesborough. His youngest son Joseph had the estate, and took care of them in their old age. He had many children, all of whom were highly respected. Children:

i    Sally, b. November 20, 1818, m. William Farrow.
ii   Lois, b. February 6, 1821, m. Henry Rose.
iii  Lydia J., b. April 6, 1823, m. Samuel Coombs, of Bangor.
iv   Arphaxad, b. February 12, 1826, m. Harriet Coombs. Children:
        1  Arphaxad, Jr., b. November 30, 1851.
        2  Angelia E., b. October 4, 1853.
        3  Hattie, b. July 8, 1857.
v    Martin S., b. March 30, 1829, m. Catherine P. Thomas, widow.
     He d. September 8, 1868. Children:
        1  Wellington M. Coombs, b. September 16, 1854, m. Georgiana Gilkey.
        2  Eliza C., b. October 26, 1857, m. Charles Bates.
        3  Robert P., b. May 3, 1860.
vi   Lucena D., b. June 10, 1831, d. about 16 years old.
vii  Mary Ann, b. February 1, 1835, d. April, 1838.
viii Eliza F., b. November 22, 1837, d. November 26, 1857.
ix   George A., b. August 30, 1840, m. Lydia J. Burgess, 1862.
x    Joseph L. S., b. September 24, 1842, m. Lucy Parker. She d.
     April 1, 1876. Son Martin S. b. June 26, 1875.
xi   Adrianna, b. December 15, 1845, m. Emery N. Bunker, 1866.

Philip F. Coombs, son of Jesse Coombs, born March 27, 1807. He married Eliza M., daughter of John Farrow, June 3 (10), 1838. She was born August 24, 1809; died February 5, 1890. He was a farmer. The estate descended to him from his father. While in active life, labor unremitting was his lot, though not a murmur escaped his lips. Honesty and plain dealing were his distinguishing traits. His lot is now divided between his son Watson and daughter Roxana. He now lives with his son Watson. Children :

 i Dexter F. Coombs, b. April 20, 1839, m. Margaret .

 ii Philip C., b. October 31, 1841, m. Caroline V. Warren, July 25, 1867.

 iii Watson H., b. December 26, 1843, m. Sarah E. Knowlton, January 2, 1868.

 iv Othniel B., b. May 20, 1847, m. Philena H. Grover. Children : Anna M., b. November 7, 1875. Bivence (?) and Gertrude.

 v Roxana F., b. February 24, 1854, m. Edward Parker.

 vi Eliza R., b. May 16, 1853, m. William P. Marshall, June 8, 1867.

Pillsbury Coombs, son of Jesse, was a master mariner, a zealous Christian, and an honest man. He won general respect and popularity by his social disposition and kind manners. He was born in Islesborough, Jan. 25, 1809, and died Jan. 27, 1890. He married Lois Trim, July 22, 1832. She was born May 12, 1811, and died October 29, 1889. Children :

 i Mary Jane, b. February 26, 1833, m. Jacob Wyman, June 13, 1853.

 ii Pillsbury P., b. July 1, 1834, m. Mary A. Redman, March, 1859. Son Herbert E., b. May 17, 1860.

 iii Lois E., b. September 30, 1835, d. October 29, 1886; m. R. P. Pendleton.

 iv James E., b. May 1, 1839, m. Angeline Spinney.

 v Almeda, b. July 14, 1840, d. December 23, 1881; m. Alonzo Wyman, 1858.

 vi Lucena D., b. August 15, 1845, m. Joseph A. Sprague.

 vii Diana, b. April 21, 1848, d. May 7, 1873; m. O. F. Coombs, 2d, 1869.

 viii Rosanna, b. November 17, 1847, m. Austin Wyman, July 7, 1868.

 ix Frederick W., b. September 17, 1854, d. ——.

 x Emily E., b. July 29, 1851, m. Millard P. Parker.

James E. Coombs married first, Angeline F. Spinney, 1857, and second, —— Bunker. Children :

   i   Imogene, b. November 12, 1857.
   ii  Jacob L., b. September 21, 1859.
  iii  Charles E., b. December 1, 1861, m. Nellie Coombs.
  iv  Artha A., b. November 12, 1872.
   v  Ervina E., b. November 26, 1877, d. ——.

Luther Coombs, son of Robert, Sen., born June 3, 1805. He married Diana Basford, of Belfast, May 9, 1828. He died, and the widow married second, Reuben Carver, of Vinal Haven, 1858. Children :

   i   Luther, b. May 7, 1829.
   ii  Jacob W., b. August 18, 1831.
  iii  Catherine E., b. August 6, 1834.

Robert Coombs, Jr., born June 25, 1783. Married first, Jane P. Gilkey, of Phillips, Dec. 25, 1823 ; married second, Louisa Dean, of Lincolnville, 1837. Children :

   i   Lucy J., b. September 5, 1824, d. 1827.
   ii  Statira, b. April 13, 1826.
  iii  Robert A., b. July 3, 1828.

Isaac Coombs, son of Robert, born February 9, 1790 ; married first, Betsey Boardman, Jan. 23, 1823. She died May 4, 1835, aged 35. He married second, Althea Palmer. Published June 16, 1836. He died January 27, 1840. Children :

   i   Elizabeth, b. June 30, 1823, m. Mansfield Clark.
   ii  Isaac, b. April 29, 1826, m. Almira Drinkwater. He is a ship-
        master and shipbuilder of Camden.
  iii  Thomas B., b. November 5, 1829, d. September 15, 1830.
  iv  Orzilla, b. October 20, 1831, m. Orris Clark.
   v  Edwin, by second wife, b. April 28, 1837.
  vi  Emily A., by second wife, b. April 28, 1837.

Hosea Coombs, brother of Fields, Sen., from Brunswick, settled the next lot below Sabbath-Day Harbor.

Married first, Elizabeth Page (both of Bath), Sept. 25, 1782 (or Mary Page), daughter or sister of Rev. Solomon Page, minister at Bath about 1762. Married second, Judith Buckmore, of Northport (nee Maddocks), Sept. 11, 1813. Children, probably :

i    Simon, m. Mary McDonald, of Belfast, March 2, 1814.
ii   Fields, m. Betsey Ames.
iii  Hosea, d. at sea, or at Norfolk ; unmarried.
iv   Otis, d. unmarried.
v    Solomon Page, m. Abigail Pendleton, 1824.
vi   Jeremiah, d. in Chelsea hospital, unmarried.
vii  Betsey, m. Robinson Crockett, of Brooksville.
viii Isaac (?) married -    -,
ix   John. (?

Capt. Fields Coombs, son of Hosea Coombs. He married Betsey Ames, Dec. 26, 1814. He died May 2, 1848, aged 62 years and 4 months. She died August 15, 1865, aged 79 years 5 months. Children :

i    Emeline, b. May 14, 1815, d. January, 1892; m. Thomas H. Parker, February 6, 1839.
ii   Eliza J., b. March 23, 1817, m. Mark Pendleton, Jr., 1837.
iii  Otis, b. 1819, d. March, 1820.
iv   Otis F., b. February 22, 1821, m. Angelia Veazie; d. December 19, 1877.
v    Catherine, b. February 23, 1823, d. August 9, 1826.
vi   Deborah, b. April 27, 1825 ; m. first, Otis C. Veazie, January 21, 1844; m. second, John Veazie. Died 1888.
vii  Hannah L., b. November 17, 1827, m. Arphaxad Coombs.
viii Lincoln, b. August 3, 1830, m. Louisa Farnsworth.
ix   Charles A., b. February 22, 1832 ; m. first, ——— Veazie ; second, Ellen Smith.
x    Theresa Rose, b. March 11, 1835, d. January 9, 1838.
xi   Edwin, b. October 29, 1837 ; m. first, Augusta M. Veazie, September 25, 1864 ; second, Lovina Marshall, January 29, 1860.

Otis F. Coombs, son of Fields, married Angelia Veazie, Feb. 4, 1844. She died in 1891. He represented the town in the Legislature, and was the first master of Island Lodge of Free Masons. He was postmaster, town clerk,

OTIS F. COOMBS.
1821—1879.

and a man of honor and esteem. He died on board his
vessel, the brig Caroline Eddy, in the Mediterranean sea,
December 19, 1877, and was buried in Islesborough with
Masonic rites. Children :

   i  Betsey A., b. August 8, 1844. m. Edgar Bunker.
   ii  Otis F., b. May 22, 1847. m. Diana Coombs, January 21, 1869.
       She d. in 1874. His second wife, Hattie, d. June 10, 1878.
   iii  Charles O., b. October 28, 1851, m. Adelma A. Wyman.
   iv  Emerson G., b. July 25, 1855, m. Martha Ryder. Children :
       1  Edith E., b. August 6, 1876.
       2  Isabella and Caro L.
   v  Helen E., b. February 25, 1859, m. B. Lewis Ryder.
   vi  Caro, m. Frank H. Mayo.

Lincoln Coombs, son of Fields, married Louisa Farnsworth, daughter of Arthur. She was born Oct. 3, 1833.
He died April 3, 1892, from apoplexy. He had been for
nearly forty years one of the best known sea captains of
the town. Toward the last of his life he retired from the
sea, owing to ill health. He commanded a vessel at the
time he was twenty, and through his long seafaring career
had charge of many vessels, in nearly all of which he
went on foreign voyages. He was a man much respected
and liked. Capt. Coombs was 61 years of age. Children :

   i  Lincoln O., b. April 16, 1855, d. February 14, 1859.
   ii  Nahum H., b. September 2, 1856, d. September 6, 1875.
   iii  Urania J., b. April 21, 1860.
   iv  Sabrina, m. Charles A. Rose.

Solomon Page Coombs, son of Hosea, married Abigail
Pendleton, Nov. 4, 1824. He lived on the lot next below
the Ryder lot, at Sabbath-Day Harbor. His son, Solomon P. Coombs, Jr., had the old homestead, which has
now upon it several summer cottages. Mr. Coombs died
February 22, 1873. His widow died September 2, 1879.
Children :

   i  John Monroe, b. July 28, 1825, m. first, Lucy Wyman ; second,
      Jane Small.

  24

ii   Solomon P., b. October 8, 1827, m. Lydia P. Warren, February
     26, 1879. He d. 1891.
iii  George H., b. May 3, 1830; unmarried.
iv   Jarandum, b. December 11, 1833, m. John B. Moody.
v    Ruth P., b. December 28, 1835, m. Fred Smith.
vi   Orinda A., b. October 1, 1839, m. Chipman Cobb.

John Monroe Coombs, son of Solomon P. Coombs, born
July 28, 1825; died June 17, 1875. Married first, Lucy
Wyman, March 22, 1851; married second, Jane Small,
June 24, 1866. She died June 15, 1873. Children:

i    John A., b. January 14, 1854, d. July 6, 1861.
ii   Emma, b. April 1, 1856, d. March 27, 1870.
iii  Sewall Swazey, b. April 23, 1861.
iv   John M., b. August 22, 1867, d. 1892.
v    Charles C., b. October 8, 1868.
vi   Ralph A., b. February 5, 1872.

Fields Coombs, brother of Hosea, from Brunswick. He
was the first town clerk, in 1789. He married first, Phebe
Holbrook. She died Jan. 9, 1801. He married second,
Martha Veazie. I suppose this to be the same man.
Children, probably:

i     Isaac, b. November 1, 1785.
ii    Bridget, b. May 10, 1788, m. Samuel Veazie.,
iii   Naomi, b. February 23, 1790, m. John Veazie.
iv    Ruth, b. December 15, 1791, m. David Swett, of Orland, August
      12, 1812.
v     Mighill, b. April 5, 1794, drowned in Penobscot river; unmarried.
vi    Charles, b. November 18, 1796; married.
vii   Charity, b. September 26, 1798, m. William Farrow.
viii  Fields, b. December 24, 1801.
ix    Lucy V., b. April 12, 1803; m. first, William Hewes, 1821; sec-
      ond, William Wyman, 1829.
x     Louisiana, b. June 21, 1805, m. Robert Trim.
xi    Sampson, b. September 27, 1806.
xii   Thatcher, b. March 25, 1808, m. Elnora Philbrook.
xiii  Hosea, b. June 26, 1810; married.
xiv   Jairus, b. February 17, 1815; married.

Sampson Coombs, son of Fields, born Sept. 27, 1806 ; married Experience Whitman, May 16, 1832. He died Jan. 11, 1851. Children :

 i Jairus, b. July 3, 1833.
 ii Martha J., b. May 6, 1835.
 iii Lydia A., b. March 9, 1837.


Thatcher Coombs, son of Fields, born March 25, 1808. Married Elnora Philbrook. Widow died September 16, 1864. Children :

 i Almira F., b. November 6, 1837.
 ii Margaret F., b. September 27, 1839.
 iii Fostina A., b. December 28, 1840, d. 1841.
 iv Fostina A., b. December 4, 1841.
 v Sylvina P., b. July 10, 1843.


Jairus Coombs, son of Fields, born Feb. 17, 1815. Married Statira Lane. He died April 25, 1882. His wife died in 1892. Children :

 i Martha A., b. May 25, 1845, m. Henry Freeman.
 ii Charles E. H., b. April 20, 1847, d. 1849.
 iii Charles, b. November 11, 1849.
 iv Fields, b. April 15, 1851, d. 1856.
 v Jairus C., b. June 10, 1854, m. Abby Smith.
 vi Eben L., b. August 20, 1855, m. Effie Wyman.
 vii Fields S., b. October 6, ——, m. —— Grant.


Isaac Coombs married Mary Johnson. He died Mar. 4, 1858. Children :

 i Helen A., b. March 23, 1856, m. Ambrose F. Hatch.
 ii Isaac E., b. October 2, 1858, d. 1860.


Charles O. Coombs, married Adelma A. Wyman. Born Oct. 28, 1851. He was drowned Mar. 31, 1879. Child:

 Edgar B., b. January 28, 1878.

## CLARK FAMILY.

Mansfield Clark, married Elizabeth Coombs, July 15, 1840. He died Feb. 7, 1879, aged 58 years. Children:

   i   Clarissa, b. August 2, 1843, m. Elisha Trim.
   ii  Cryella, b. July 23, 1853, d. 1856.
   iii Isabella F., b. October, 1855, m. Dow.
   iv  Ernest M., b. March 27, 1857.
   v   Clifford L., b. April 19, 1860, d. 1861.
   vi  Jessie M., b. July 7, 1866.
   vii Lavinia, m. George Coombs.


Orris Clark married Anzilla Coombs. Published June 7, 1856. Children:

   i   Henrietta L., b. December 2, 1857.
   ii  Frank C., b. March 17, 1862.
   iii Avery E., b. April 9, 1868.
   iv  Amasa P., b. April 9, 1868, d. 1868.


Eliphalet Clark married Rosilla Coombs. Children:

   i   Joseph W., b. July 23, 1864.
   ii  Elsie W., b. August 18, 1874, d. ——.
   iii Huldah, b. 1872.


## CLARY FAMILY.

Alfred Clary. Child:

   Eliza A. C., b. December 7, 1850.


## COBB FAMILY.

Chipman Cobb married Orinda Ann Coombs, Sept. 4, 1859. Children:

   i   Ida M., b. November 16, 1859, d. 1860.
   ii  Evabell, b. October 31, 1860, d. 1876.
   iii Solomon H., b. July 16, 1864.
   iv  Helen M., b. ——, m. George Williams.
   v   Annie.
   vi  Eva.

## COBURN FAMILY.

Charles A. Coburn married Mary A. Sawyer, Jan. 14, 1856. He died Aug., 1867. Children :

  i  Frank A., b. December 5, 1856.
  ii  Grace E., b. December 6, 1858.
  iii  Edgar E., b. April 15, 1861, d. 1875.

Alpheus A. Coburn married Rebecca Haynes. He died Aug., 1868. Children :

  i  Edith A., b. July 21, 186-.

## COLLINS FAMILY.

David Collins married Eliza Y. Sawyer. He died 1884. Children :

  i  Joseph W., b. August 8, 1839, m. Paulina Coombs.
  ii  Elizabeth M., b. July 1, 1843, m. Maximilian Pendleton.
  iii  Edward, d. in 1891 ; m. Irene L. Pendleton.
  iv  Hattie.
  v  George.
  vi  Paul.
  vii  Emma.

George N. Collins married Serene F. Gilkey. Children were :

  i  Clara A., b. March 3, 1864.
  ii  Edith Rose, b. July 5, 1866, m. Leon W. Wyman.
  iii  Effie Blanche, b. February 27, 1870.
  iv  John G., b. December 9, 1872.

Davis Collins married Betsey Barker. Children :

  i  Edith R., b. July 5, 1865, m. Edgar Boardman.
  ii  Lydia A., b. ——, m. Loomis Decrow.

## COOKSON FAMILY.

Thomas Cookson married Roxanna Farrow, Dec. 26, 1833. He died in California, 1886. Children :

  i  Tucker F., b. April 5, 1835.
  ii  Vandelia Y., b. November 9, 1836.

iii  Walter S., b. March 26, 1839, m. Philbrook.
iv  James P., b. July 27, 1841, d. young.
v  Eugene P., b. May 11, 1844, d. young.
vi  Caroline, lives in California.

## COTTRELL FAMILY.

Sylvester Cottrell, from Rhode Island, via Portsmouth, N. H. He married Mary, oldest daughter of Thomas Pendleton. His house was built near the Point, southwest from the steamboat wharf, near the brook, at Hewes' Point. He made a deed of land to Samuel Jackson, of Plymouth, July 1, 1790, which was the first deed recorded in Hancock Records. Mr. Cottrell and wife moved to New Brunswick in their old age, where they died. Children, probably:

i  Pamelia, m. Paoli Hewes, Dec. 11, 1787.
ii  Polly, m. Simon Dodge, about 1790.
iii  Joseph, m. Prudence Grinnell, May 3, 1803.
iv  Sylvester Jr.
v  Joshua, m. Olive, daughter of Benjamin Coombs.

## DAVIS FAMILY.

Chauncey C. Davis married first, Sarah M. Blake. She died July 20, 1864. Second, Lydia J. Pendleton. Children were:

i  Jane L., b. December 11, 1855, d. 1856.
ii  Annette M., b. September 26, 1857, m. Phineas L. Rolerson.
iii  Charles M., b. June 13, 1860.
iv  Samuel W., b. October 23, 1870.
v  Sarah M., b. October 21, 1873.
vi  Nancy Ellen, b. October 14, 1875.
vii  Evelyn, b. August 29, 1877.
viii  Rose, m. Otis Dodge.

## DECKER FAMILY.

Thomas Decker died June 28, 1866. Married Lydia Grover. She died June 28, 1866. Children:

i  Andrew J., b. February 24, 1842, d. 1863.

ii  Adoniram, b. September 8, 1844, m. Harriet Coose.
iii Eliza A., b. August 25, 1847.
iv  Thomas J., b. March 25, 1851, m. Rosanna Warren.
v   Adabell, b. June 28, 1861, d. 1886.

### Adoniram Decker married Harriet Coose. Children :

i   Walter, m. Ruth Moody.
ii  Morris, m. —----- Hatch.
iii Calista, m. W. Leighton Coombs.

### Thomas J. Decker married Rosanna Warren. Children were:

i   Lizzie Porter, b. May 31, 1878.
ii  Arthur Alvin, b. September 16, 1875.
iii James Garfield, b. June 26, 1880.

### DECROW FAMILY.

### Loomis B. Decrow married Lydia Collins. Children :

i   Aubern Llewellyn, b. November 16, 1869.

### DIX FAMILY.

William Dix was born at Tremont, Maine, August 20, 1804. He died at Islesborough, August 25, 1876. His wife was Ann L. Grindle. She was born at Mt. Desert, Maine, December 25, 1809, and died at Islesborough, March 26, 1887. Children :

i    Frederick C., b. February 13, 1827, m. Catherine B. Sherman.
ii   Nehemiah, b. March 10, 1829, d. young.
iii  Eunice, b. January 20, 1831, d. in Lincolnville, aged about 18.
iv   Francis G., b. February 11, 1834, m. Izetta Coombs.
v    Judith G., b. February 11, 1834, m. Hosea Wyman.
vi   Adaliza or Adaline T., m. James Harrison Veazie.
vii  Harriet S., m. Wilber Lowell.
viii Sophronia A.
ix   George M., m. Caroline Redman.

### Francis G. Dix married Izetta Coombs, Sept. 6, 1858. Children :

i   James R., b. October 1, 1860.
ii  William H., b. October 17, 1872, d. 1874.
iii Bertha J., b. June 23, 1875.

George M. Dix married Carrie J. Redman.      Children :

i   Almah L., b. August 1, 1874.
ii  Jessie Adell, b. September 4, 1877.
iii Luella M., b. March 7, 1879.


## DODGE FAMILY.

Simon Dodge, Sen., was here early.   His house was near
"The Gully," east side, below Hewes' Point.   He must
have died after 1823, as his grandson, Simon Dodge, was
then called "third."   His estate was divided between his
sons Joshua and Noah; now owned by Alvin Warren.   He
married first Prudence Rose.   He married second Sarah
Nash, widow of Dodge Pendleton.   Children, probably:

i    Noah, of Islesborough, d. July 23, 1816, aged 54.
ii   Israel, of Islesborough.
iii  Solomon, d. unmarried.
iv   Simon, Jr., of Islesborough, d. February 6, 1826.
v    Mark, of Islesborough.
vi   Joshua.
vii  Lydia, m. Simon Sprague.
viii Mary, m. ——— Sargent.
ix   Wealthy, m. Ezekiel Parker.
x    Experience, m. William Grinnell.
xi   Rathburn, d. September 18, 1846, aged 79.
xii  Perhaps a daughter, who m. ——— Billington.


Noah Dodge, son of Simon, married Rosanna Rose.
She died May 18, 1835.   He died July 23, 1816, aged 54.
Children :

i    Hannah, b. May 27, 1786.
ii   Simon, b. May 15, 1788, d. 1798.
iii  James, b. June 13, 1790, d. December 24, 1831.
iv   Rosanna, b. January 24, 1793, m. Henry Rose.
v    Hiram, b. June 24, 1795, m. Betsey Ciphers.
vi   Delilah, b. November 16, 1798, m. John Ames.
vii  Noah, b. March 15, 1801, d. March 17, 1823.
viii Jeremy, b. July 20, 1805, m. Betsey Gilkey.
ix   Phebe, b. November 5, 1807, d. March 26, 1823.

Israel Dodge, son of Simon, married Prudence, daughter of Godfrey Trim, ————. He was drowned February 17, 1807, aged 35. She married second, Thomas Marshall, January 9, 1823. Children:

    i   Abraham, m. Charity Dodge; published March 22, 1829. He was drowned between Islesborough and Boston. She m. second Rathburn Dodge.
    ii   Sally, m. Simon Dodge, Jr., 1823.
    iii   Betsey, m. Simon Dodge, Jr., 1826.

Simon, son of Simon Dodge, was born on Block Island, R. I., November 1, 1768. He married in 1789 Mary, daughter of Sylvester Cottrell. She was born July 5, 1770. He died in his field, Feb. 6, 1826. Children:

    i   Prudence, b. April 17, 1790, in Islesborough.
    ii   Experience, b. October 30, 1796, in Islesborough.
    iii   Simon, Jr., b. July 5, 1799, in Islesborough.
    iv   Solomon, b. September 17, 1800, in Islesborough, m. Lydia Gould; published July 14, 1826. Daughter: Artimisa, born Sept. 26, 1830.
    v   Rathburn, b. August 10, 1806, in New Brunswick.
    vi   Charity, b. July 27, 1811, m. Rathburn Dodge, Jr.
    vii   Queen Ann, b. April 8, 1825, m. Joseph J. Brown.

Mark Dodge, of Block Island, son of Simon, Sen., married in 1798 Wealthy, daughter of Nathaniel Pendleton, and grand-daughter of Thomas Pendleton, Jr. They settled on a farm south of Samuel Pendleton, near the Bonnet Point, where they built their house. It is now owned by Capt. Warren. He died June 21, 1823. Children:

    i   Noah, b. March 10, 1799, m. Elizabeth J. Brown; published December 14, 1829.
    ii   Christiana, b. May 13, 1801, m. Roberts.
    iii   Lydia, b. January 24, 1806, m. Wood, of Belfast.
    iv   Mark Zebulon, b. September 1811, m. Sarah Knowlton, 1832. He died in Rockland, June 21, 1833.
    v   Wealthy, b. July 16, 1813.
    vi   Charles, b. September 11, 1815, m. Rebecca Yeaton.

25

vii  William S., b. November 27, 1817, m. Sarah J. Pendleton, moved
     to Gouldsboro, d. there, Jan. 17, 1889.
viii Joseph, b. September, 1819, m. Rebecca Clough of Blue Hill;
     published December 30, 1844.
 ix  Elbridge, b. November 4, 1822, m. Lucy M. Spaulding, of Rock-
     land, July 4, 1848.

Joshua Dodge, son of Simon, Sen.   He married Betsey,
daughter of Wm. Steward.   She died Nov. 4, 1865, aged
72.   He died March 24, 1858.   Children :

   i  Esther, b. August 8, 1811, m. Lewis Hatch, January, 1831.
  ii  Eliza, b. December 12, 1812, m. Johnson Sargent, Dec. 18, 1835.
 iii  Mary, b. August 14, 1814, m. Varnum Rose.
  iv  Walter Franklin, b. April 11, 1816, m. Rosanna Rose, 1840.
   v  James, b. April 27, 1818, m. Hannah Rose.
  vi  Prudence, b. February 6, 1821, m. James Burns Williams.
 vii  Martha W., b. July 6, 1823, m. Eben S. Babbidge, Dec. 19, 1843.
viii  Solomon, b. March 1, 1825, m. Lydia P. Nash, February 5, 1848.
  ix  William S., b. July 14, 1827, m. Harriet Bunker.
   x  Dorothy H., b. February 25, 1830, m. Joshua Farrow, Jr.

Rathburn Dodge, son of Simon, Sen., married Lydia
Pendleton, daughter of Samuel.   Rathburn Dodge was a
prominent man ; taking an active part in town affairs,
and the wealthiest man in the town.   The frequent allu-
sions to him in the town records show the estimation with
which he was held in the town.   He died September 18,
1846, aged 79.   She died Aug. 6, 1842.   Children :

   i  Lucretia, b. October 4, 1792, m. Solomon Sprague.
  ii  Israel, b. April 7, 1794, d. at sea.
 iii  Lydia, b. January 10, 1800, d. August 6, 1842.
  iv  Mark B., b. February 20, 1803, m. Abigail Dodge.
   v  Rathburn, Jr., b. July 6, 1806, m. Charity Dodge.
  vi  George W., b. March 18, 1809, m. Betsey Dodge.
 vii  Horatio N., b. September 2, 1817, went away.

James R. Dodge, son of Noah, born June 13, 1790,
died Dec. 24, 1831.   Married first Deborah or Rosanna
Rose ; married second, Hannah Sawyer.   Children :

   i  Ann M., b. January 10, 1820.

ii   Sarah W., b. January 29, 1821.

iii   James H., b. April 2, 1822, m. Nancy Dodge, June 21, 1855.

iv   Noah, b. April 15, 1824.

v   Oakes C., b. July 18, 1825. Lived in Rockland, d. in Florida.

vi   Sabra W., b. March 12, 1827.

vii   Melinda A., b. September 3, 1829.


Hiram Dodge, son of Noah, married Betsey Cyphers, June 10, 1821. He lived and died on Seven-Hundred-Acre Island. Children :

i   Hiram, Jr., b. February 5, 1822, d. unmarried, December 27, 1841.

ii   Phebe, b. November 20, 1823, m. Prince Rogers, of New York, April 1, 1844.

iii   Stephen, b. September 16, 1825. Went away and returned in 1884, after forty-five years absence.

iv   Noah, b. March 28, 1827, d. 1827.

v   Crosby, b. April 28, 1828, d. 1828.

vi   Caroline H., b. September 6, 1829, m. —— Hunt.

vii   Elizabeth A., b. December 14, 1831, m. C. Magee, of Brooksville.

viii   James E., b. January 14, 1834, d. unmarried.

ix   Paulina, unmarried.

x   Melissa A., b. May 31, 1837.

xi   Lorenzo, b. April 9, 1840, d. December 27, 1841.


Jeremy Dodge, son of Noah, married Betsey Gilkey, Nov. 21, 1830. She died in Belfast, in 1892. He died there about 1888. Children :

i   Ferdinand, b. October 26, 1832, m. —— Lancaster.

ii   Isabella, b. May 10, 1834, m. W. P. Sprague.

iii   Francis, b. in Belfast.

iv   Alphonso, b. in Belfast.


Mark B. Dodge, son of Rathburn, born Feb. 20, 1803, died Aug. 6, 1855. Married Abigail Dodge, Feb. 27, 1824. Children :

i   Irene, b. Jan. 10, 1825, d. December 25, 1844.

ii   Penelope, b. February 11, 1826, d. February 20, 1826.

iii   Mark Judson, b. March 6, 1829, m. Julia A. M. Thomas. He m. second, Aug. 13, 1871.

iv   Lorenzo Rathburn, b. March 2, 1833, m. Sarah Small, February 13, 1861. He died——.

George W. Dodge, son of Rathburn, born Mar. 18,
1813. Married Betsey Dodge (sister of Mark B. Dodge's
wife), July 24, 1834. She was born at New Shoreham,
R. I., Sept. 3, 1808; died April 24, 1851. Children:

  i  Alverdo, b. June 1, 1837, m. Lois Coombs.
  ii  George E., b. February 16, 1841, d. young.

Capt. Alverdo Dodge, married Lois Coombs, daughter
of Anthony Coombs, Sept. 21, 1856. Children:

  i  Betsey E., b. June 18, 1859, d. 1860, m. Clifford Dodge, and
     second Herbert Coombs.
  ii  Lois, b. March 18, 1865.

Simon Dodge, Jr., born July 5, 1799. Married first
Sally, of Israel Dodge (cousin), Jan. 23, 1823; married
second, Betsey, of Israel Dodge (cousin). Published July
14, 1826. He died April 4, 1854. Children:

  i  Sally, b. January 26, 1827, d. —.
  ii  Betsey L., b. May 3, 1830, m. Amos Smith, September 30, 1855.
  iii  Mary A., b. May 4, 1832, m. Abraham Dodge.
  iv  Prudence J., b. November 4, 1833, d. young.
  v  Simon M., b. February 9, 1835, m. Corilla Atwood.
  vi  Charity, b. 1837, m. Edward Tucker.
  vii  Robert H., b. 18—, d. in Islesborough.
  viii  Samuel C., b. 18—, d. in Islesborough.
  ix  Experience, b. May 26, 1849, m. Tewksbury Dodge.
  x  William, b. 18—, m. Amelia Trim.

Rathburn Dodge, son of Simon, Jr., born Aug. 10,
1806, died July 14, 1879. Married Eliza Grover, of Deer
Isle. Published July 28, 1833. She was born April 4,
1811; died Aug. 14, 1868. Children:

  i  Mary A., b. July 21, 1834.
  ii  Abraham, b. November 15, 1836, m. Mary A. Dodge, May 30, 1869.
  iii  Mary C., b. July 1, 1840, d. April 23, 1860.
  iv  Tewksbury P., b. May 28, 1845.
  v  Solomon, b. March 11, 1848.
  vi  William M., b. May 15, 1851, d. November, 1872.
  vii  Eben M., b. February 23, 1852.

Rathburn Dodge, Jr., born July 6, 1809, died Oct. 9, 1864. Married Charity Dodge, daughter of Simon, and widow of Abraham Dodge, 1837. She died 1878. He died October, 1864. Children, perhaps not in order:

    i   Nelson. (?
   ii   Abraham. (?)
  iii   Edmund, b. April 30, 1842, d. September, 1843.
   iv   Irena A., b. March 31, 1844, m. Irvin T. Small, Feb. 17, 1861.
    v   Lydia A., b. January 14, 1848, m. Aaron Hill.
   vi   Amanda H., b. September 27, 1853, d. September 15, 1855.


Walter Franklin Dodge, son of Joshua Dodge, born April 11, 1816. He was a merchant, and largely interested in commerce. At the age of 35 he was one of the wealthiest men in Islesborough. Towards the last of his life he moved to Boston, but returned to Islesborough, where he died, Aug. 16, 1869. He married Rosanna Rose, Jan. 10, 1840. She was born March 23, 1812, died Feb. 4, 1875. Children:

    i   Franklin A., b. November 25, 1841.
   ii   Laura A., b. August 10, 1844.
  iii   Freeman E., b. December 9, 1852.


James Dodge, son of Joshua Dodge, born April 27, 1818, died Feb. 16, 1872. He married Hannah Rose, July 9, 1844. Children:

    i   James H., b. ---, d. ---.
   ii   James H., b. Aug., 1846, m. Izetta Emerson.
  iii   Arabell, b. Sept. 7, 1847, m. Joseph McFarland.
   iv   Lois E., b. May 14, 1853, m. Llewellyn Gilkey.
    v   Walter C., b. July 5, 1856, drowned Nov. 5, 1878.
   vi   Betsey A., b. March 27, 1864.


William S. Dodge, son of Joshua, born July 14, 1827. Married first, Harriet Bunker, Jan. 1, 1850. She died Dec. 12, 1859. Married second, Mrs. Relief M. Warren, Mar. 18, 1861. She died Mar. 14, 1865. Married third,

Flora M. Bunker, of Charleston, Sept. 13, 1865. She died Jan. 5, 1875. Children:

    i   Silas M., b. June 1, 1853, m. Betsey Pendleton.
    ii  Hobart A., b. May 9, 1858, m. — — Warren.
    iii Mabel, b. November 9, 1866.
    iv  Daughter, b. —.


Charles Dodge, son of Mark, born September 10, 1815. Married Rebecca Yeaton, of Deer Isle. Published April 1, 1837. Children:

    i   Charles H., b. January 27, 1838, m. Mrs. Rebecca Dodge, March 9, 1861.
                Son, Otis E., b. April 14, 1862, m. Rose Davis.
    ii  Yeaton, b. January 11, 1840, m. Elizabeth Robinson.
    iii George, b. February 2, 1843, drowned.
    iv  Mark, b. August 29, 1844.
    v   Witherly, b. April 11, 1846.
    vi  Martha M., b. June 20, 1848, m. Laban Pendleton.
    vii James, b. June 23, 1851, d. December 19, 1851.
    viii Mary, b. June 12, 1855, m. Eben Dodge.
    ix  Joseph S., b. August 29, 1860, m. Meda M. Pendleton.


William Dodge, son of Mark Dodge, born November 22, 1817. Married Sarah, daughter of John Pendleton, April 14, 1838. Died in Gouldsborough, January 17, 1889. He followed the sea, and was for several years a master mariner, but meeting with misfortune he retired from the sea, and in 1862 moved to Gouldsborough, where by judicious management he accumulated a handsome competency. Possessed of a strong physical development, rare vocal powers, and a frank, open manner, he won the confidence and the friendship of all who knew him. By the even tenor of his life and his great zeal in religious works he won the esteem of all. Children, born in Islesborough:

    i   William A., b. December 18, 1839.
    ii  Lorenzo D., b. September 26, 1843.
    iii Mary V., b. February 8, 1849, d. —.
    iv  Sarah E., b. February 14, 1852.

Noah Dodge, son of probably Mark, came from Block Island. He was born March 10, 1799. He died March 1, 1871 or 1872. Married Elizabeth J. Brown, of Belfast; published Dec. 14, 1829. Children:

   i  Noah B., m. Alice Pendleton.
  ii  William F., m. May Emma Bird, of Belfast.
        Son: John B., b. May 28, 1865.
 iii  John H., b. December 22, 1831, drowned April 16, 1846.
 iv  Jacob, m. Josephine Brown.
  v  Joseph, m. Lucinda Parrot.
 vi  Oakley, b. May 12, 1845, drowned.
 vii  Mary Jane, d. when 4 years old.
viii  Sarah, b. April 12, 1847, m. Georgia A. Moor.
 ix  John A., m. Hattie Keller.

Noah B. Dodge, son of Noah, married Alice Pendleton. She died 1867. Children:

   i  Henry M., b. July 11, 1851.
  ii  Frederick H., b. July 19, 1856, d. 1856.

Emery J. Dodge married Julia A. Thomas, May 11, 1851. Children:

   i  Cora A., b. March 22, 1852, d. —.
  ii  Fred E., b. March 25, 1854, m. Sadie C. Patten.
 iii  Hattie E., b. October 6, 1857, d. —.

Jacob D. Dodge married Arabella O. Pendleton, Dec. 28, 1861. She died 1866. Child:

   Jessie A., b. September 23, 1864.

William C. Dodge married Amelia Trim. Published May 16, 1863. Lost on the brig Europa. Sailed for the island of Martinique. Never heard from.

Capt. Jonathan B. Dodge, born in Islesborough about 1795. Master mariner, lived in Rockland.

James R. Dodge, son of James R., married Nancy Dodge, June 21, 1855. He died 1878. Children:

  i  Mirantha A., b. April 10, 1858, m. George Boardman.
  ii  Mary, b. June 15, 1860.
  iii  Menoda, Byron and Ira.

Mark B. Dodge, 2d, son of Rathburn, married Abigail Dodge, Feb. 27, 1824. Children:

  i  Irene, b. January 10, 1825, d. December, 1841.
  ii  Penelope, b. February 11, 1826, d. February, 1826.
  iii  Mark J., b. March 6, 1829, m. Julia A. Thomas.
  iv  Lorenzo R., b. March 2, 1833, m. Sarah Small.

## DOW FAMILY.

Charles H. Dow married Isabella F. Clark. Child:

Charles L., b. September 21, 1876.

## DRINKWATER FAMILY.

William Drinkwater. Child:

Mary E., b. September 20, 1840.

## DURGIN FAMILY.

Rev. William J. Durgin, a Baptist clergyman, came here in 1843. He married first, Hannah N. ———, who died here August 2, 1857, aged 58. He married second, Mrs. Deborah Lord. Published Aug. 28, 1867. He died Dec. 19, 1868. She died January 15, 1890, aged 90. Children:

  i  Susan W., b.    , d. April 3, 1845, aged 20 years 4 months.
  ii  Albion, d. August, 1851.
  iii  Eliza A., d. September, 1851, m. Abner Marshall.
  iv  Hannah, d. January 7, 1858, aged 21 years.
  v  James C., d. August 2, 1864.
  vi  Otis, d. May 21, 1871, m. Orisee J. Sherman.
  vii  Henderson, m. Maria Pendleton; was in the U. S. service in the Rebellion.

Elbridge Henderson Durgin married Maria Pendleton. He died Feb. 15, 1886, aged 46 years.   Children :

   i   Mary Ella, b. March 30, 1871.
  ii  William II., b. October 15, 1873.
 iii  Geneve E., b. October 3, 1875.
 iv  Kate R., b. November 19, 1881.
   v  Charles P., b.——, d. 1881.
 vi  Richmond, b. March 23, 1885.
vii  Etta M., b. September 22, 1883.

## DYER FAMILY.

Elijah Dyer.   Children :

   i   Roscoe S.
  ii  Charles, b. February 12, 1866.
 iii  Mary Ann B., b. ——, d. November 4, 1867.
 iv  Joshua, b. ——, d. November 10, 1867.
   v  George D., b. February 14, 1870.

## EAMES FAMILY.

Elisha Eames was son of Deacon Josiah Eames, of Marshfield and North Bridgewater, Mass.[*]   Elisha came to Islesborough about 1800.   He purchased the Oliver Pendleton farm, near Dark Harbor, and settled on it. Pendleton was the original s e t t l e r , and had a quitclaim deed from General Knox and the Waldo heirs, Nov. 13, 1799, of 100 acres of land near Dark Harbor.   Pendleton moved to Camden and died there.   This beautiful estate has remained in the family until recently, when it was sold by Edwin Eames to Mr. J. D. Winsor, of Philadelphia, and his associates, who have built a wharf, and also an elegant hotel thereon.   Mr. Eames was town clerk

---

[*] Mitchell's History of Bridgewater, Mass., says that Deacon Josiah Eames and his wife, also an Eames, went from Marshfield to North Bridgewater in 1770, and that his family went to Long Island.   Elisha Eames, their son, was in Islesborough shortly after 1800.

26

many years, and also a deacon of the church. He married first, Sarah, daughter of Timothy Packard, of North Bridgewater, Mass. She was born 1767, died 1790. He married second, Anna, daughter of Seth Mann, of Braintree, Randolph part, in 1791. She was born May 18, 1764, died in Islesborough, June 20 (22), 1835 (Gravestone). He died, Dec. 3, 1843, aged 81 years 11 months (Gravestone). Children :

  i  Josiah, b. 1787, m. Rebecca, daughter of Ephraim Noyes, of No. Bridgewater, 1808. Children:
      Sarah, 1812.*
      Luther, 1813.
      Rebecca Noyes, b. in Islesborough, November 28, 1809.
      Ephraim Noyes, b. July 14, 1818.
      Spencer, b. April 20, 1820.
      Dianthe, b. October 7, 1821. The father was drowned on his way to Camden, about 1822, and the family returned to Massachusetts.
  ii  Isaac, b. 1789; m. Abby Haymond, 1811. I do not see that this family came here.
  iii  Calvin, by second wife.


Calvin Eames, son of Elisha. He lived on the old homestead of his father, just below Dark Harbor. He told the writer in 1880 that his father or grandfather was cousin to Elder Thomas Eames, of Islesborough. He married Mary Ann, daughter of Capt. John Harlow, of Bangor. Published in Bangor, Nov. 3, 1833. She was born April 28, 1811; died 1891. He died a few years since. Children, perhaps not all :

  i  Francis W., b. February 27, 1835, d. March 16, 1835.
  ii  Edwin A., b. October 27, 1846, m. Amelia A. Pendleton, May 10, 1868.
  iii  Elisha C., d. June 23, 1859, or 1857.
  iv  George O., d. September 4, 1865.
  v  Lucy A., married W. P. Farnsworth, 1856.

* A Sarah Eames married in Islesborough, March 8, 1840, Thomas Witham, of Danville.

### ELWELL FAMILY.

William Elwell, from St. George, via Burton's Island, arrived with his family at Long Island, July 10, 1789. He married Viane Wadsworth. He had nine children when he came here—Vinson, Alban, Prudence, Salome, Dorcas, George W., Lewis, William and Thomas; after he came here, Silvia, born Aug. 18, 1790, and William, born January 5, 1792. The family moved to Northport. His son Lewis, prior to 1812, commanded a sloop of eighty tons, called "The Harvard," which was owned by Harvard College.

Charles Elwell probably married a daughter of Samuel Pendleton, in 1789. He died in 1795. Children:

i Joseph, b. February 14, 1790.
ii Betsey, b. August 31, 1792.
iii Deborah, b. November 20, 1794.

James O. Elwell married Maria Fletcher. Children:

i Milton F., b. March 8, 1873.
ii Nellie, b. July 9, 1878.

### EMERSON FAMILY.

Seth Emerson. Children:

i Cora I., b. November 15, 1857, (?) d. 1860.
ii Alva, b. October 31, 1861.

### EMERY FAMILY.

Rev. Ephraim W. Emery was a Baptist minister for many years in Islesborough. He was eminently a good Christian. He was earnest in presentation of the truth according to the old theology, and never neglected to inculcate its tenets on all occasions. He was regarded with honor and esteem. He moved away. Children :

  i  Sarah J., b. January 17, 1833.
  ii  Frances M., b. March 27, 1834.

## ENGSTRAM FAMILY.

John Engstram married Angelia C. Wood. Children :

  i  John, b. 1876.
  ii  George, b. March 16, 1878.
  iii  Alma, Louis, Augustus, Carroanna.

## FAIRFIELD FAMILY.

Stephen Fairfield married Bridget Pendleton, April 10, 1838. He married for a second wife Helen Pendleton. Children :

  i  Andrew P., b. March 27, 1840, m. Joan Veazie. Children :
      1  Augusta, m. Simmons Moody.
      2  Llewellyn, and another child, b. July 21, 1879.
  ii  Melissa C., b. October 15, 1843, m. Calvin Hatch.
  iii  Harlan O., b. October 15, 1842, d. 1842.
  iv  John P., b. August 31, 1849, m. Etta Thomas.
  v  Victoria H., m. Gilbert L. Moore.

## FARNSWORTH FAMILY.

Robert Farnsworth, Jr., from Waldoborough, married Jane, daughter of John Gilkey. Published September 14, 1818. Children :

  i  Mercy J., b. July 6, 1819, m. first, Albert Pendleton ; m. second, William Brown.
  ii  Sylvina, b. January 7, 1823, d. April 10, 1835.
  iii  Robert Emery, b. September 2, 1826, d. about 1846.
  iv  Abigail A., b. October 12, 1828, m. ―― Hobbs.
  v  William P., b. March 17, 1831, m. Lucy A. Eames.
  vi  Rozella Bartlett, b. November 13, 1833, m. Lemuel Palmer Hatch.
  vii  Victory, b. March 19, 1839, m. Josiah Hobbs, of Camden or Hope.
  viii  Hollis M., b. May 7, 1843.
  ix  Oliver T., (?) of Camden.

x  Victory, another account says, b. March 20, 1840, m. Isaiah Barbour, of Camden, February 13, 1861.

William P. Farnsworth married Lucy A. Eames. Published April 11, 1855-56. (?) Children:

i  Edward E., b. August 4, 1856, drowned.
ii  Laura M., b. August 23, 1857, m. Nelson Kimball.
iii  Lincoln A., b. August 23, 1859, m. Lilla M. Hatch and Bertha Atwood.
iv  Fred O. and Paulina, b. August 21, 1866.
v  Zavilla M., b. January 19, 1871.

Arthur Farnsworth, brother of Robert, married Louisa Coombs, daughter of Robert, June 21, 1832. Children:

i  Louisa, b. October 31, 1833, m. Lincoln Coombs.
ii  Mary Ann, b. 1840, m. John B. Matthews.
iii  James, b. August 26, 1844, m. ——, died ——.
iv  Luther A., b. August 26, 1844, m. Florence Philbrook.
v  Josephine J., b. ——, d. July 27, 1865.
vi  Arthur Farnsworth, d. July 27, 1865.

Luther C. Farnsworth married Florence Philbrook, June 21, 1869. Children:

i  Arthur Myron, b. May 11, 1870, m. Lelia Haynes.
ii  Melvin J., b. July 29, 1872.
iii  Nahum C., b. October 26, 1874.
iv  Anna L.

### FARROW FAMILY.

Josiah Farrow, son of John Farrow, was born in Windham, February 10, 1754. He was a soldier of the Revolution, and at the taking of Burgoyne. He removed to Bristol with his father, and from thence to Islesborough. He married Ruth Richards, of Bristol, February 21, 1785. She died May 7, 1834, aged 70. He died August 14, 1819, aged 66. Children:

i  Josiah, b. January 26, 1786, d. August 11, 1861.
ii  Betsey, b. February 29, 1787, d. January 2, 1817.

iii   Samuel, b. May 26, 1789, d. January 3, 1826.
iv   William, b. February 21, 1791, d. August 19, 1870.
 v   John, b. February 9, 1793, drowned at sea March 3, 1818.
vi   Joshua, b. October 4, 1794, d. March 13, 1879.
vii   Esther, b. September 21, 1797, m. Isaac C. Boardman.
viii   Philip, b. December 14, 1798, d. young.
 ix   Elsie, b. August 14, 1800, m. Mighill Parker. Published November 20, 1823.
  x   Harriet, b. June 23, 1802, m. ——— Harvey. (?)
 xi   Thomas, b. March 28, 1806, d. in Boston.
xii   Elmira, (?) b. September 23, 1811, married Robert Hichborn, of Stockton.

Josiah Farrow, Jr., born Jan. 2, 1786; died in Belfast, Aug. 11, 1861. He married Mary, daughter of Joseph Boardman. Published April 19, 1815. She was born February 5, 1784, died Oct. 3, 1862. One child :

Mary, b. March 18, 1822, m. Hon. Joseph F. Hall, of Lincolnville. Their son, Bordman Hall, settled in Boston.

William Farrow, son of Josiah, Sen. Born Feb. 21, 1791; died August 19, 1870. Married first, Charity, daughter of Fields Coombs. Published May 9, 1818. Married second, Mrs. Jerusha Blake, of Penobscot. She died in Newport, R. I., Nov. 28, 1892. He moved to Belfast after 1834, where he died. Children were :

  i   William, b. February 10, 1819, d. June 10, 1824.
 ii   Sophronia D., b. December 25, 1820, m. ——— Tibbetts.
iii   Fidelia, b. August 16, 1822, m. ——— .
 iv   Charity, b. July 26, 1824, unmarried.
  v   Prince William, b. October 15, 1826, m. Marcia O. Spear, Rockland.
 vi   Esther B., b. September 12, 1829.
vii   Helen Mar, b. February 10, 1832, m. J. M. Pendleton, Rockland.
viii   William, Jr., b. July 22, 1834.
 ix   Thomas J., b. in Belfast.
  x   Willard Milton, now of Mason, Tenn.
 xi   Alpheus, d. ——— .

Samuel Farrow, son of Joseph Farrow, was born May 26, 1789. He married Phebe Parker, December 5, 1818. He died January 3, 1826. Children :

 i Betsey, b. February 16, 1822, m. Charles Herrick, of Corinth.
 ii Phebe, b. October 7, 1823, m. Erastus Ball, of Corinth.
 iii Elsie, d. in infancy.

Deacon Joshua Farrow married Eunice Trim, Sept. 27, 1821. He died March 13, 1879, aged 84. She died October 17, 1873, aged 76. Child, one son :

 Joshua, Jr., b. March 21, 1826, m. Dorothy H. Dodge. He had six children in Islesborough. Removed to Winchester, Mass. Children in Islesborough :
  1 Fillmore, b. December 3, 1849.
  2 Frederick, b. June 11, 1854.
  3 Isabelle, b. April 28, 1856.
  4 Minnie, b. May 21, 1860.
  5 George, b. July 14, 1861.
  6 Son, b. November 4, 1864.

John Farrow was born in Bristol. He settled in Islesborough, and died there June 26, 1841, aged 62 years. He married Rebecca, daughter of Thomas Ames. She died September 26, 1842. Children :

 i Rebecca, b. October 3, 1800, m. Aaron Pendleton, September 14, 1825.
 ii John, b. August 19, 1802. First of Islesborough, then of Boston. He m. first, Harriet, daughter of John Pendleton, January 31, 1828. She d. in May, 1839, in Boston. He next m. Harriet A. Haywood, of Boston. Died there June, 1843. Children :
  John P., author of this History.
  Joseph O., who d. in Boston in 1837.
 iii James, b. October 23, 1804, m. Judith Grindle, November 12, 1837; d. on board his vessel in Bangor.
 iv Ambrose, b. February 9, 1807, d. in Havana.
 v Eliza M., b. July 19, 1809, m. Philip Coombs.
 vi Roxana, b. July 19, 1811, m. Thomas Cookson, December 26, 1837. He d. in California, in 1886. Children : Tucker, Vandelia, Walter S., James, Caroline. Roxana d. in 1851.

vii  William, b. January 29, 1814, m. Sally, daughter of Othniel
   Coombs. Published February 17, 1840; d. October 9, 1878.
   One child, Emily, b. April 23, 1845.
viii  Dexter, b. October 23, 1816. Removed to Northport. Married
   Lucy Knowlton. Representative in 1845, Senator in 1847.
   One child, Rebecca, who d. young.
 ix  Sarah, b. February 23, 1819, m. Watson Hinds, of Belfast. She
   d. September, 1886. Children: John W. and Ellen.

John Pendleton Farrow, master mariner, author of this
history. Married Elona, daughter of David Philbrook.
Children :

  i  John Oscar, b. October 8, 1852, m. Emma Hatch.
 ii  Herman M., b. March 31, 1865, m. Laura Grindle.
iii  Hattie E., b. May 20, 1872.

James Farrow married Judith Grindle. Published Nov.
12, 1837. Children :

  i  Harriet, b. November 25, 1838, m. ---- Pendleton.
 ii  James, b. March 30, 1841, drowned at sea.
iii  Sarah.

Ambrose Farrow, born Feb. 9, 1807. Married Dolly
Wood Pendleton, Nov. 15, 1834. He died July, 1839,
or 1840. She died Oct. 12, 1892. Children :

  i  Maria, b. October 4, 1835, m. Daniel Hatch.
 ii  George, b. January 2, 1838, m. Delilah Sherman.

George Farrow, son of Ambrose, was killed at the
battle of Fair Oaks. He married Delilah Sherman.
Children :

  i  Fostina A., b. May 20, 1859.
 ii  George M., b. September 29, 1861.

John Oscar Farrow married Emma Hatch. He is a
master mariner. Children :

  i  Cochituate E., b. April 5, 1878.
 ii  William Ellis, b. July 28, 1879.
iii  J. Malcolm.

## FERREN FAMILY.

Joseph Ferren, from Eaton, N. H., married Lois Marshall, December 24, 1812. Children:

i Lois, b. May 18, 1814.
ii Joseph, Jr., b. May 21, 1816.
iii Thomas, b. November 24, 1818.
iv Moses, b. April 16, 1820.
v Sally R., b. October 28, 1822.

## FLANDERS FAMILY.

Franklin Flanders married Maria E. Pendleton. Children were:

i Lydia E., b. August 23, 1860.
ii Frank C., b. October 22, 1871.
iii Melvin, b. October 31, 1875.

## FLETCHER FAMILY.

David Fletcher married Nancy Ray. Children, born in Islesborough, moved away; no descendants here.

i David, Jr., b. May 5, 1832.
ii Joseph, b. January 19, 1834.
iii Maria, b. April 3, 1836.
iv Melissa, b. April 10, 1838.
v William, b. April 5, 1840.
vi Modelia, b. May 2, 1842.
vii Elam, b. August 24, 1844.

Thomas Fletcher married Penelope M. Brown, daughter of John, Dec. 30, 1830. She died 1878. He died 1869. Children:

i Sewall B., b. June 19, 1832, m. first Sarah L. Clough, second Sarah Small Dodge.
ii Joseph W., b. October 7, 1847.
iii Melville E., b. April 16, 1850, d. 1851.
iv Stephen C., b. ——, d. 1869.
v Sylvester, b. ——, m. Philena Michaels.
vi Amelia M., b. ——, m. James Elwell.

27

William J. Fletcher married Georgiana W. Fields, Jan. 7, 1869. Children :

  i  Stephen O., b. April 26, 1870, m. Myra Hatch.
  ii  Eva B., b. September 7, 1873.
  iii  Laforest L., b. December 19, 1876, drowned July 16, 1878.
  iv  Washington B., b. ——, d. in New York.

Oliver F. Fletcher married Addie E. Brown. Children were :

  i  Lo —— Edna, b. May 30, 1868.
  ii  Nathan Clifford, b. December 13, 1869.
  iii  Sophronia L., b. February 6, 1876.

## GARNER FAMILY.

Edmund Garner.  Children :
  i  Solomon P., b. April 20, 1844.

## GILKEY FAMILY.

John Gilkey settled at Islesborough prior to 1775, at Long Island Harbor, now Gilkey's Harbor.  He married Sylvina Thomas, probably of Marshfield, Mass., about 1766.  She died April 23, 1832.  He died Sept. 4, 1814, aged 74.  Children :*

  i  Matilda, m. Gideon Pendleton.

---

* In Col. Gabriel Johonnot's list of marriages at Castine is January 30, 1788. Charles Turner Thomas and Mary Gilkey, both of Islesborough.  I do not see who she was, unless daughter or sister of John, Sen.

ii  Benjamin Thomas, of Islesborough. On arriving at manhood he
     left the Benjamin off from his name.
iii Jane ——, m. Jabez Ames.
iv  Sylvina, m. Thomas Morton.
 v  John, of Islesborough, Lincolnville and Hope.
vi  Philip, b. ——, 1788, of Islesborough and Searsport.
vii Grace, m. Rev. Lemuel Rich, both of Islesborough. Published
     February 16, 1810. He was from East Machias.
viii Rachel.
ix  Isaac, probably of Hingham, Mass.
 x  Jacob, of Hingham, Mass.
xi  Lucinda, (?) m. Benjamin Carver, of Northport.

John Gilkey, Jr., married Olive or Sally Fearing, of
Hingham, Mass.; moved away from Islesborough about
1823.  He and his wife both died in Hope.  Children, all
born in Islesborough :

 i  Sally, b. September 7, 1803, m. Alfred Wade, of Lincolnville,
     December 27, 1824.
 ii Caleb, b. September 24, 1805, moved to Camden and Hope, d. in
     Ca m d e n, September 25, 1886.  Married and had a large
     family.
iii Olive, b. August 28, 1807, m. Alfred Wade, of Lincolnville.
iv  Martha, b. October 28, 1809, m. ——.
 v  Caroline, b. December 19, 1811, m. ——.
vi  Mary, b. January 25, 1814, m. ——.
vii John Fearing, b. April 16, 1816, of Camden; married three times.
viii Jacob, b. November 8, 1818.
ix  Lydia Cushing, b. June 29, 1821, m. Nathan Pendleton, of
     Prospect.
 x  Abigail Bates, b. July 31, 1823, m. ——.

Thomas Gilkey, son of J o h n, Sen., married Mercy,
daughter of Thomas Ames, Dec. 8, 1792.  He died Oct.
10, 1847, aged 78.  His wife died March 1, 1862.  At
her death she had eleven children, seventy grandchildren,
seventy-eight great-grandchildren, two great-great-grandchildren.  His youngest son, Nelson Gilkey, lives on the
old homestead.  Children :                                    •

 i  Sibyl, b. August 25, 1793, m. James Sherman.  Published De-
     cember 6, 1815.

ii   Jane, b. September 17, 1795, m. Robert Farnsworth. Published
     September 14, 1818.
iii  Thomas, Jr., b. September 27, 1797, m. Dorothy Farnsworth,
     June 15, 1820.
iv   Elisha, b. November 27, 1799, m. Martha Pendleton, daughter of
     Capt. Jack or John, December 6, 1827.
v    Betsey, b. April 12, 1802, m. Jeremiah Dodge, November 21, 1830.
vi   John, b. June 8, 1804, m. Lucinda Pendleton, December 23, 1831.
vii  Otis, b. November 24, 1806, m. Lois Elwell, February 23, 1831.
     Moved to Northport; two children born in Islesborough.
viii Andrew P., b. March 25, 1809, m. Azubah Veazie, March 20, 1831.
ix   Avery, b. September 4, 1811, m. Eliza Pendleton, Dec. 4, 1834.
x    Nelson, b. December 13, 1814, m. Angelia Pendleton, March
     25, 1837.

Philip Gilkey, son of John, Sen., born 1788. Married
first, Jane, daughter of Job Pendleton ; married second,
widow Deborah Cushing, of Hingham, Mass. ; married
third, Mrs. Judith Wade, of Lincolnville.  He removed
to Searsport in 1825, where he died, in 1871.   Children,
all born in Islesborough except the last :

i    Jane P., b. April 9, 1807, m. Robert P. Coombs, December 15,
     1823.  She d. August 7, 1884.
ii   Philip, Jr., b. October 14, 1808, m. Artemisa Pendleton, daughter
     of John, November 21, 1830.
iii  Isaac, b. October 3, 1811, of Searsport, m. Martha Blanchard.
iv   Grace, b. November 6, 1813, d. 1825.
v    Lydia, b. April 15, 1815, m. Nathan Pendleton, of Searsport.
vi   Judith P., b. April 29, 1817, m. William Hardy, of Bucksport.
vii  Welcome, b. June 6, 1819, d. November 21, 1821.
viii Royal, by second wife, b. May 24, 1821, m. Hannah Young.
ix   Welcome, b. October 20, 1823, of Searsport, married.
x    Anna, b. October 20, 1823, m. Hugh Ross, Jr., now of Bangor.
xi   Lincoln, b. July 3, 1825, of Searsport, married.

Andrew P. Gilkey, son of Thomas, born March 25,
1809.  Married first Azubah, daughter of Samuel Veazie,
March 20, 1831.  She died Nov. 14, 1839, aged 28.
Married second Philena, widow of Jordan Veazie.  She

Nelson Gilkey

was born April 1, 1806, died April 22, 1879. He was
representative, in 1862. He died 1889. Children :

  i   Ariana, b. June 9, 1830, m. David P. Withee, October 28, 1848.
  ii  Andrew P., b. October 27, 1832, d. March 25, 1873.
  iii Lycurgus P., b. November 14, 1834, m. Josephine Sprague.
  iv  Philip C., b. September 3, 1843, d. December 6, 1854.
  v   Ethelinda E., b. May 15, 1845, m. Benj. R. Redman.  Published
      June 23, 1862.  She d. February 25, 1878.

Avery Gilkey, son of Thomas, born Sept. 4, 1811,
married Eliza Pendleton, daughter of John, Dec. 4, 1834.
Children :

  i    Georgiana, b. October 7, 1835, d. 1841.
  ii   Oscar, b. September 15, 1841, d. 1841.
  iii  Albion, b. October 9, 1840, d. May 31, 1841.
  iv   Eliza, b. April 25, 1842, m. George W. Hatch.
  v    Avery G., b. October 7, 1843, d. 1865.
  vi   Llewellyn, b. December 14, 1845, m. Lois Dodge.
  vii  Delmar? b. October 8, 1847, m. Martha Philbrook.
  viii Georgiana, b. October 12, 1849, m. Wellington Coombs.
  ix   Sarah A., b. June 8, 1852, m. Winsor Williams.

Nelson Gilkey, son of Thomas Gilkey, born Dec. 13,
1814. Married Angeline, daughter of John Pendleton,
March 25, 1837. He was chairman of the board of
selectmen for many years, town clerk, lighthouse keeper,
a member of the Legislature and postmaster, all of which
offices he has filled with ability.   Children :

  i    Florine, b. January 22, 1838, m. William Kimball, 1862.
  ii   Roscoe P., b. August 26, 1839, m. Sally Ames, 1859.
  iii  Paris, b. June 11, 1841, m. Malvina J. Sherman, 1862;
  iv   Lebbeus, b. July 11, 1843, d. February 5, 1851.
  v    Georgiana, b. December 14, 1844, m. Lemuel Hatch.
  vi   Artemisa, b. February 7, 1848, d. February 15, 1854.
  vii  Artemisa L., b. February 15, 1854, m. Ephraim E. Pendleton,
       November 7, 1871.

Thomas Gilkey, Jr., married Dorothy Farnsworth, June
15, 1820. He died in 1882. Children :

  i    Dorothy, b. December 14, 1820, m. Jefferson Pendleton.

ii   Elizabeth, b. January 15, 1821, m. Isaac W. Sherman.
iii  Ana, b June 10, 1824, m. Ephraim Pendleton.
iv   Martha, b. October 15, 1828, m. Charles C. Hatch.
v    Thomas W., b. November 12, 1835.

Thomas W. Gilkey, son of Thomas, born Nov. 12, 1835. He married first, Martha Harlow, of Bangor, 1857. She died Oct. 14, 1868. He married second, widow Wealthy Pendleton.  Children:

i    Rosamond P., b. October 15, 1859.
ii   Elmer, b. January 17, 1862.
iii  Benson G., b. September 21, 1864.
iv   Martha W., b. July 20, 1871.
v    Gracie R., b. April 27, 1878.

Otis Gilkey, son of Thomas, born Nov. 24, 1806, married Lois Elwell, Feb. 23, 1831.  Children:

i    Byron, b. November 15, 1833.
ii   Lois E., b. June 19, 1834.

John Gilkey, 2d, son of Thomas, born June 8, 1804. Married Lucinda Pendleton, daughter of Jonathan, Dec. 23, 1831.  Children:

i    Delia Ann, b. May 17, 1834.
ii   Sibyl S., b. August 4, 1835, d. 1845.
iii  Nathan P., b. November 1, 1837.
iv   Serene, b. ——, m. George Collins.

Llewellyn W. Gilkey, son of Avery, married Lois Dodge, July 13, 1869.  Children:

i    Altamera, b. October 8, 1870, d. 1871.
ii   Ralph Winslow, b. May 6, 1872.
iii  Beulah E., b. October 13, 1877.
iv   Lincoln Cleveland, b. June 10, 1881.

Roscoe P. Gilkey, son of Nelson, born Aug. 26, 1839. Married Sallie M. Ames, 1859.  Children:

i    Jennie M., b. July 7, 1860, m. Sanborn Gould.
ii   Georgie E., b. March 5, 1862.
iii  John Judson, b. May 28, 1868, d. 1884.

Paris Gilkey, son of Nelson, married Malvina J. Sherman. Published Dec. 29, 1862. Children :

i Frank W., b. June 21, 1864, m. Belle Tyler.
ii Fanny Judson, b. July 21, 1867, m. Edward Dodge.
iii Oscar, b. August 12, 1878.

## GRINDLE FAMILY.

Francis Grindle, Esq., came here from Mount Desert (or Bluehill), when he was quite young, and became an active man in the town. He was a deacon of the first Baptist church, was first mail contractor, lighthouse keeper, and was one of the prominent men to build the middle church. In his younger days he followed the sea as a master mariner. In the latter part of his life he was engaged in agriculture. He died Jan. 14, 1857, aged 72 years. He married first, Judith Carter, of Bluehill, Sept. 2, 1801. She was born July 21, 1780; died Sept. 14, 1839, aged 59. He married second, Eliza, widow of Robert Pendleton, and daughter of John Harlow, of Bangor. Published April 20, 1840. She died in 1890. Children, by first wife :

i Judith, m. first, James Farrow; second, Eben Collamore, of Lincolnville.
ii Ann L., b. December 25, 1809, m. William Dix.

By second wife :

iii James F., b. Oct. 20, or 4th, 1842. Lives on the old homestead at Grindle's Point. Shipmaster. He married Theresa P. Rose. Published January 23, 1866. She was of Belfast. Children :
   1 Laura E., b. November 3, 1866, m. Herman M. Farrow.
   2 Hortense, b. September 14, 1868, d. ——.
   3 Mary E., b. May 14, 1875.
   4 Varnum Francis, b. March 27, 1877, d. Feb. 5, 1881.
   5 Walter A., b. December 28, 1878, d. January 27, 1881.
   6 Edith, b. ——.
   7 Frank S., b. ——.

## GRINNELL FAMILY.

William Grinnell came here from Block Island, prior to 1787. He was selectman in 1791. Married Experience, daughter of Simon Dodge, Sen. He moved to Belfast about 1806. He died December 5, 1842, aged 79. His widow died March 23, 1851, aged 87. Children, born in Islesborough:

   i  Sally, m. —— Rogers.
   ii  Priscilla, m. —— Apollos Alden, of Belfast, November 2, 1807.
  *    She d. October 10, 1868, aged 80.
   iii  Phebe, d. February 7, 1807, aged 20.
   iv  Simeon, d. February 14, 1807, aged 14.
   v  Prudence, m. Joshua Cottrell, May 3, 1803.
   vi  Rosanna, m. Moses H. Young, of Belfast. She d. August 20, 1891, aged about 86. One daughter survives her, Mrs. Theodore Cary, of Houlton.

## GROVER FAMILY.

William Grover, born Sept. 20, 1779, in Gloucester, Mass. Married Nov. 29, 1805, at Deer Isle, to Rhoda Stockbridge; died Dec. 29, 1861. She was born Sept. 22, 1788, in Gloucester, Mass.; died Feb. 3, 1867. He served twelve months on board the frigate Constitution, and thirteen months on the sloop-of-war Merrimac. He came to Islesborough in 1839, from Deer Isle. Children, all born in Deer Isle:

   i  Eliza, b. June 7, 1807, d. October 10, 1807, at Deer Isle.
   ii  Rhoda, b. August 9, 1808, m. Henry B. Coombs.
   iii  Eliza, b. April 24, 1811, m. R. Dodge. She d. August 6, 1868.
   iv  Nancy, b. August 20, 1813, m. Benjamin Ryder.
   v  Lydia, b. March 18, 1817, m. Thomas Decker.
   vi  Dorothy R., b. October 17, 1820, m. James Gleason, of Prospect. Published February 28, 1843. She m. second, Shubael H. Pendleton.
  vii  William S., b. July 1, 1823, d. July 15, 1823.
 viii  Joseph Rowe, b. August 29, 1824, m. Olive R. Warren.
   ix  Benjamin, b. July 21, 1822, m. Mary A. Burgess. He died July 19, 1872.
   x  William, b. July 23, 1831, m. Harriet McFarland, 1852; second, Sarah M. Keller.
       Son, Lerotts, (?) b. December 22, 1853.
   xi  Eben, b. March 27, 1833, m. Nancy Jane Ladd. He d. 1876.

Nathan Grover. Children :

i Ebenezer B., b. July 19, 1820.
ii Emily, b. April 1, 1824.

Joseph Rowe Grover, son of William, born August 29, 1824. Came to Islesborough with his father. Married Olive R. Warren, December 19, 1847. Children :

i Viola, b. October 21, 1849.
ii Lubrenda, b. June 8, 1852, d. December 31, 1853.
iii Mary A., b. July 19, 1854, m. John P. Bragg, of Lincolnville, December 4, 1873 ; now of Islesborough. He has been superintendent of schools, collector of taxes, &c.
iv Eliza J., b. ——, m. Nelson P. Hamilton, of Rockland, January 14, 1882.
v Lena H., b. June 14, 1859, m. Otho R. Coombs, December 24, 1874.
vi David W., b. May 1, 1862, m. Ellen Wyman, October 15, 1890.
vii Joseph W., b. September 2, 1864, m. Sadie Benton, April 15, 1890.
viii Chester M., b. May 9, 1867.
ix Olive L., b. November 20, 1873.
x Media M., b. September 6, 1877.

Benjamin Grover, son of William, married Mary Ann Burgess, 1855. Children :

i Frederick M., b. October 15, 1855, m. Ethelinda Parker.
ii Wesley E., b. August 27, 1857.
iii Minnie E., b. July 11, 1859, d. 1875.
iv Lucy E., b. March 3, 1861.
v Lizzie L., d. October 21, 1875.

Eben Grover, son of William Grover, married Nancy J. Ladd, 1855. He died 1876. Children :

i Ella J., b. August 29, 1855, m. James H. Ryder.
ii Davilla E., b. August 3, 1858.
iii Edda E., b. May 19, 1861.
iv Frank, b. ——.

## HATCH FAMILY.

Jeremiah Hatch, Jr., from Marshfield, Mass., came about 1784. He married Lydia, daughter of Nicholas

28

Porter, of Marshfield, Nov. 22, 1778; by Rev. Mr. Wales.
She died Dec. 28, 1834, aged 76. He died May 22, 1839.
Children :

    i  Jeremiah J., b. March 18, 1780, d. young.
    ii  Lydia, b. July 22, 1782, m. George Warren.
    iii  Isaac, b. October 26, 1784, m. Betsey Warren.
    iv  Sarah, b. August 5, 1787, m. Elisha Nash.
    v  Jeremiah 3d, b. December 18, 1789.
    vi  Abigail, b. August 22, 1791, m. Benjamin Warren.

Isaac Hatch, son of Jeremiah, born October 26, 1784;
died July 11, 1825. Married Betsey Warren, July 16,
1808. She died January 7, 1832. Children :

    i  Amasa, b. November 7, 1808, m. three times.
    ii  Sarah A., b. October 11, 1811, m. Johnson Veazie.
    iii  Deborah, b. October 5, 1815, m. Samuel Veazie.
    iv  Philena, b. October 6, 1817, m. Samuel Warren.
    v  Isaac, Jr., b. November 7, 1820, m. Sarah Porter.
    vi  Elizabeth, b. July 24, 1823, m. ———.
    vii  Benjamin Ichabod, b. February 15, 1826, m. Mary Durgin, 1852,
        d. March, 1892. A man of great respect.

Amasa Hatch, son of Isaac, born Nov. 7, 1808. Married first, Sophronia, daughter of Joseph Pendleton, Dec.
22, 1832. She died Oct. 1, 1849. He married second,
Emeline Pendleton. Published Mar. 1, 1851. She died
Jan. 20, 1861. He married third, Mrs. Mary Coombs.
Published March 6, 1862. Captain Hatch was noted for
his benevolence. His humanity extended to all: his
kindness to friends and neighbors, and his tenderness to
the weak and suffering. He was an honest and Christian
man. Children :

    i  Sophronia, b. May 21, 1833.
    ii  William E., b. October 21, 1835, m. Emily A. Farrow.
    iii  Wealthy, b. November 22, 1838, m. William Hatch.
    iv  Amasa, Jr., b. August 17, 1844, m. Sophronia Pendleton.

    Children by second wife :

    v  Sarah A., b. July 12, 1854, m. Henry P. Hatch.
    vi  Emma, b. March 29, 1859, d. 1859.

Children by third wife :

vii Hugh R., b. May 20, 1865. Graduated at Colby University. Baptist clergyman.
viii William E., b. December 13, 1866, m. Lena Farnsworth.
ix Belle M., m. Ambrose Hatch.

Amasa P. Hatch, son of Amasa, born Aug. 17, 1844; married Sophronia Pendleton. He was lost at sea, March 30, 1889. Children :

i Philena, b. February 10, 1872.
ii Fred Avery, b. March 30, 1874.
iii Alton Calvin, b. December 27, 1875.
iv Edwin E., b. July 28, 1879.
v Harry E., b. ———.

William E. Hatch married Emily A. Farrow, in 1858. He died October 10, 1868. She died April 3, 186–. Child :

Emma, m. John O. Farrow.

Benjamin R. Hatch, son of Isaac, born Feb. 15, 1826. Married Mary Durgin, in 1852. He died of heart failure, suddenly, March, 1892. He was a master mariner, principally engaged in coastwise and West India voyages. His honesty and uprightness distinguished him. Few men in our community have died more respected and esteemed, and ill will was a stranger to him. He entertained no unfriendliness towards others, and had no enemies in return. Children :

i Francis L., b. October 23, 1851.
ii Laura R., b. February 21, 1857, d. 1857.
iii Lilla M., b. April 5, 1859, m. Lincoln Farnsworth.

Frank L. Hatch married Sarah S. Pendleton. Children :

i Lulu A., b. May 8, 1874, d. 1877.
ii Edith M., b. November 1, 1875.

Deacon James Hatch was born in Hanover, Mass.,
March 3, 1796. . He was a resident of Islesborough many
years. He was a deacon of the first Baptist church, a soldier in the war of 1812, and a pensioner during the last
part of his life. He was a cabinet-maker by trade, and
many of the old settlers made use of his handiwork in
their last resting place. Very few, if any, commanded
more respect than Deacon Hatch. He married Mary
Townsend, October 26, 1817. He died March 13, 1878.
His youngest son, Pyam, resides on the old homestead.
Children :

   i   James Luther, b. May, 1820 ; twice married.
   ii  Charles Chauncey, b. March 4, 1822, m. Martha P. Gilkey.
   iii David Lewis, b. November 12, 1824, m. Sarah E. Wilson.
   iv  Sarah Kingman, b. April 13, 1826, m. Thomas R. Williams.
   v   Daniel A., b. October 19, 1828, m. Maria Farrow.
   vi  Lemuel Palmer, b. October 19, 1830, m. Rosilla Farnsworth.
   vii Wealthy P., b. March 28, 1832, m. Alfred P. Pendleton.
   viii Calvin, b. May 25, 1835, m. Melissa Fairfield, 1859.
   ix  William Curtis, b. May 4, 1837, m. Wealthy P. Hatch, January
       29, 1862.
   x   George W., b. September 2, 1839, m. Eliza Gilkey, October 31,
       1861.
   xi  Mary H., b. May 15, 1841, m. Roscoe Pendleton.   Published
       September 11, 1866.
   xii Pyam D., b. March 27, 1846, m. Myra E. Pendleton.


James L. Hatch married first, Lydia P. Williams, Dec.
29, 1841 ; second, Lizzie Durgin. He died in 1883.
Children :

   i   Lydia M., b. March 25, 1843, d. 1844.
   ii  James E., b. September 29, 1847.
   iii Marion H., b. September 20, 1848, d. 1848.
   iv  Thomas W., b. July 12, 1852.


Charles C. Hatch, son of James, married Martha Gilkey, June 4, 1846.   Children :

   i   Caro E., b. March 15, 1850, m. Eben Babbidge.
   ii  Alfred Porter, b. November 15, 1851, m. Roxana Pendleton.

DEACON JAMES HATCH.

iii  Charles D., b. October 20, 1853.
iv  David I.., b. September 8, 1855, d. 1856.
v  Frank W., b. May 30, 1858.

Calvin Hatch, son of James, married Melissa Fairfield, Dec. 7, 1859. Children:

i  Ella L., b. July 18, 1861.
ii  Laura F., b. 1864, m. Edward D. Hatch.

George W. Hatch, son of James, married Eliza Gilkey, Oct. 31, 1861. Children:

i  George O., b. March 11, 1863, m. Addie Merrill.
ii  Myra Addemar, b. February 4, 1871, m. Oscar Fletcher.
iii  Westboro B., b. November 23, 1873.
iv  Lula E., b. September 21, 1876.

Pyam D. Hatch, son of James, married Myra E. Pendleton, Jan. 21, 1870. Children:

i  Christine N., b. September 24, 1871, m. Morris Decker.
ii  Dorothy R., b. August 7, 1873.
iii  Edwin, b. May 6, 1879.
iv  Abbie B., b. August 28, 1880.

Alfred Porter Hatch, son of Charles C., born Nov. 15, 1851. He married Roxana Pendleton. She died July 25, 1882. He married second, widow Sarah E. Hatch. Children:

Edna H., b. April 1, 1878; Letitia A., b. January 10, 1881; Calvin C., b. May 10, 1882.

Nathaniel Hatch was born in Hanover, Mass., July 4, 1800. He was brother of Deacon James Hatch. Came here in 1837. Died July 2, 1864, at Belfast. He married Dec. 22, 1822, Jane Elizabeth Valleau. He lived on the

---

* She had children: Leslie, 15, Preston, 10, Robert, 9, James, 5, and Forest, 3 years of age.

west side of Crow Cove. He married second, Mary E. Sargent, of Belfast. Children:

   i  Theodore S., b. October 2, 1823, d. July 6, 1854. Married Ann Boardman, October 20, 1846.
   ii  Nathaniel, b. September 10, 1825. Married Susan Boardman, January 4, 1849.
   iii  Lemuel, b. May 2, 1831, d. in infancy.
   iv  Andrew, b. September 10, 1832, d. September 10, 1847.

Theodore S. Hatch married Ann C. Boardman, October 20, 1846. He died July 6, 1854. Children:

   i  Elizabeth L., b. December 24, 1847, m. —— Wood.
   ii  Zilpha J., b. March 26, 1850, m. Samuel Veazie.
   iii  Theodore, Jr., b. and d. 1852.

Nathaniel Hatch, Jr., married Susan A. Boardman, January 4, 1849. Children:

   i  Henry P., b. August 20, 1849, m. Sarah Hatch.
   ii  Cora L., b. January 24, 1852, d. 1859.
   iii  Estelle F. b. September 18, 1858, m. —— Fields.
   iv  Edith C., b. May 24, 1860, d. 1869.
   v  Rowena L., b. May 23, 1864.

Henry Porter Hatch married Sarah A. Hatch. Children were:

   i  Rose, b. November 19, 1877.
   ii  Cora A., b. October 31, 1878.

Lewis Hatch was born in Hanson, Mass., August 31, 1806. He married Esther, daughter of Joshua and Betsey Dodge, Jan. 26, 1830. Children:

   i  Esther A., b. May, 1832, m. ——.
   ii  Lemuel L., b. November, 1834, m. Georgietta Gilkey.

Daniel A. Hatch married Maria Farrow, 1856. Children were:

   i  Ambrose F., b. December 5, 1856.
   ii  Edward, b. November 13, 1859, m. Laura P. Fairfield.

William Hatch married Sophronia Hatch. Child :

Ambrose L., b. August 28, 1873. Adopted.

Lemuel L. Hatch, married Georgie Gilkey, February 21, 1865. She died July 3, 1868. Children :

i Flora G., b. ——, d. ——.

Ambrose Farrow Hatch, son of Daniel A., married first, Helen A. Coombs. She died April 20, 1881 ; second wife, Bell Merritt Hatch. Child :

Lutner, b. May 7, 1879.

## HAWES FAMILY.

Daniel A. Hawes married Sarah S. Merrithew, January 13, 1850. Child :

Lertna, b. June 19, 1853.

Edmund Hawes married Caroline Roberts, December 25, 1821.

## HAYNES FAMILY.

Samuel Haynes came from Newburyport, September, 1856, with his wife and five young children. Married Rosanna Marshall. He died August 21, 1876. Children :

i  Solomon W., came after his father. He married Abby Van Amburg. Children :
  1  Walter E., b. April 25, 1859, m. Delia Coombs.
  2  Alice, m. E. Pendleton.
  3  Leita, b. October 8, 1872, m. Myron Farnsworth.
ii  Daniel E., m. Isabel King.
iii  John R., m. Annie Knowlton, July 21, 1861.
iv  Mary R., m. Alpheus A. Coburn, of Patten, Aug. 13, 1859. He d. on passage from Granada to Navassa in 1860.

v  Samuel E., m. Flora Coombs.  Children :
    1  Stella M., b. November 15, 1872.
    2  Fred, b. ——.
    3  Velocia, b. ——
vi  Joseph F., m. Attala (?) Ryder.
vii  Ella, m. William Coombs ; he was lost at sea.  Married second,
    Anthony Coombs.

## HEAL FAMILY.

Benjamin F. Heal married Jennie M. Coombs.  Children were :

  i  Frank C., b. July 31, 1873.
  ii  Caro, b. June 8, 1875.
  iii  Nettie May, b. June 7, 1877.

## HEMMENWAY FAMILY.

Luther Hemmenway.  Children :

  i  Leslie B., b. September 2, 1852.
  ii  George L., b. October 5, 1857.

## HERRICK FAMILY.

Reuben Herrick married Mary J. Warren, May 7, 1838.  Children :

  i  John W., b. June 3, 1839.
  ii  Sarah M., b. ——, d. 1841.
  iii  Isaac H., b. October 1, 1843, m. Flavilla Warren.
  iv  Samuel P., b. September 25, 1845, d. 1861.
  v  James, b. March 2, 1848.

Isaac H. Herrick married Mrs. Flavilla Warren, of Belfast, Nov. 21, 1867.  Children :
  i  Bertha Ann, b. September 16, 1869, d. April 30, 1875.
  ii  Mary E., b. June 17, 1877.

## HEWES FAMILY.

Paoli Hewes came to Islesborough prior to 1787.  He married Pamelia, daughter of Sylvester Cottrell, at Castine, December 11, 1787, by Col. Johonnot. He was constable in 1791. He established salt works at Hewes' Point about 1812. Hewes' Point was named for him. He moved to Belfast, where he died June 19, 1848, aged 80. Elihu Hewes died in Islesborough, Jan. 14, 1808, aged 81. Gravestone. I suppose father of Paoli. His children supposed to be:

  i  Paoli, Jr., m. Mercy Barter, of Deer Isle. Published June 23, 1823.

  ii  William, m. Lucy, daughter of Fields Coombs. Published Oct. 27, 1821. Married November 29, 1821. She was born April 12, 1803. William Hewes was drowned in Belfast Harbor, October 1, 1828. Mrs. Hewes married second, William Wyman, of Belfast, afterwards of Islesborough, Nov. 20, 1829. Children:

     1  William Hewes, Jr., b. December 7, 1823, died in Baltimore.

     2  Elbridge, b. ——, m. Sylvina Thomas. He was drowned at sea.

  iii  Thomas, ——.

  iv  Joseph, ——.

  v  Peggy, m. John Brown, November 12, 1812.

Elbridge Hewes married Sylvina Thomas, June, 1850. Children:

  i  George W., b. August 25, 1851.

  ii  Ednor E., b. April 17, 1854.

### HOLBROOK FAMILY.

Jonathan Holbrook, Sen. Children:

  i  Jesse, perhaps lived at Goose Falls, Brooksville, early.

  ii  Prince, went to Ohio after 1816, died there. Son:
      Jesse, lived in Bangor, d. in Rockland.

  iii  Jonathan, Jr., m. Hester Carter, of Northport. Born in Northport. Son:
      John F., d. in Rockland.

  iv  Thomas, m. Nancy Dickey, in Northport. He d. in Knox.

  v  Phebe, m. Fields Coombs, of Islesborough.

  vi  Ruth, m. Mighill Parker, Sen. She d. in East Corinth.

  vii  Hannah, m. Jonathan Parker. She d. in Islesborough.

  viii  Lucy, m. Robie Frye, of Montville and Belfast. He d. January 16, 1867, aged 81 years and 10 months.

20

## HOPKINS FAMILY.

Ebenezer Hopkins married Elizabeth Warren.  Children:

i   Sylvinia E., b. March 12, 1856.
ii  Jacob Quincy, b. July 4, 1860.
iii Warren J., b. October 8, 1863.
iv  Maggie Bell, b. November 20, 1865.
v   Julia G., b. October 24, 1874.
vi  Rufus M., b. March 23, 1874.

## HUNT FAMILY.

John W. Hunt married Caroline Dodge.  Child:

Carrie E., b. January 9, 1867.

## HUTCHINS FAMILY.

John Hutchins came to Islesborough about 1798.  He had four children.  Mr. Hutchins and wife died in Islesborough.  Children:

i   Mercy, b. May 8, 1798.
ii  John, Jr., b. September 7, 1800, in Islesborough.
iii Betsey, b. March 30, 1803, in Islesborough.
iv  Job, b. May 4, 1806, in Islesborough.

John Hutchins, Jr., married Annis M. Merrithew, of Vinalhaven.  They had four daughters.  She died in Islesborough, January, 1881.  Mr. Hutchins died Jan., 1883, in Belfast.  Their home was an island in East Penobscot Bay, adjoining the main island, where they lived many years, and from whence the island derives its name. Children, all born in Islesborough:

i   Mercy Jane, b. February 25, 1831, m. —— Trundy.
ii  Elizabeth A., b June 6, 1835, m. —— Adams.
iii Addie S., b. November 20, 1839, m. —— Condon.
iv  Rhoda A., b. December 12, 1845, m. Jacob Page.

## JONES FAMILY.

Joseph Jones, fence viewer in Islesborough in 1790.

Joseph Jones married first, Betsey Ames, daughter of Thomas Ames; second, Mrs. Hannah Eames, of North Bridgewater, Mass., Nov. 25, 1838.

## KELLER FAMILY.

James Keller married Dorcas Williams, Jan. 1, 1807, or Mar. 10, 1810.

Isaac Keller married Cynthia Ladd. Children :

  i  Sarah M., b. August 17, 1849, m. William Grover.
  ii  David J., b. March 1, 1851.
  iii  Pillsbury E., b. March 1, 1853.
  iv  Alma M., b. June 19, 1856.
  v  Leuphenia E., b. May 22, 1861.

George F. Keller married Emeline Sprague. Published June 15, 1859. Children :

  i  Rose E., b. February 6, 1861, m. Joseph Heald.
  ii  George B., b. December 16, 1864.
  iii  Charles B., b. December 17, 1867, d. 1875.

Freeman S. Keller married Martha A. Merrithew, Mar. 18, 1854.

Samuel Keller. Children :

  i  George W., b. September 23, 1856.
  ii  Susie E., b. August 16, 1859, m. Frank Adams.
  iii  Hiram, b. ——.
  iv  Lizzie, b. ——.

Finley B. Keller married Harriet Libby. Children, not in order :

  i  Mary E., b. November 30, 1849, m. James B. Adams.
  ii  Eunice A., b. April 26, 1852.
  iii  Angelia C., b. June 16, 1854, m. Nathan Adams.
  iv  William F., b. April 20, 1856, m. Edith Carlton.
  v  Charles G., b. August 9, 1859, m. Lucy Higgins.
  vi  Hattie, m. John A. Dodge.
  vii  Cheney F., m. Laura B. Babbidge.

Hiram B. Keller married Elnora Grover. Child :

  Ludella M., b. August 5, 1876.

### KNIGHT FAMILY.

George W. Knight married Sophronia Williams. Children were :

  i   Louisa A., b. August 27, 1852, m. George Forbes, of Belfast.
 ii   Charles H., b. August 19, 1854.
iii   Euphralia Isabel, b. October 12, 1856, m. Martin V. Pendleton.
 iv   George W. M., b. October 7, 1859.

### KNOWLES FAMILY.

Joseph Knowles married Leonora I. Philbrook, Oct. 16, 184—. Children :

  i   Gertrude, b. ——.
 ii   Percy, b. ——.
iii   Bertha, b. ——.
 iv   Edgar, b. ——.
  v   Josephine, b. February 2, 1865.
 vi   Cora D., b. ——, d. 1879.

Joseph P. Knowles married Melvina Rider, Sept. 25, 1867.

### KNOWLTON FAMILY.

Joseph Knowlton married —— Buckmaster. He died March 18, 1882. Children :

  i   Sarah E., b. December 20, 1843, m. Watson F. Coombs.
 ii   Elizabeth, d. November 12, 1861.
      The rest of the family not born in Islesborough.

Stephen Knowlton married first, Hannah Coombs, Oct. 10, 1852; second, Elzina Coombs. Children :

   i   Emma G., b. April 16, 1853, m. William Black.
  ii   Abby L., b. September 9, 1854.
 iii   Walter, b. July 28, 1856, d. 1856.
  iv   Herbert, b. same date.
   v   Minette J. R., b. October 24, 1857.
  vi   Mary H., b. January 18, 1859.
 vii   Ida F. D., b. October 31, 1860, d. 1862.
viii   Ethel, b. ——.
  ix   Agnes L., b. ——.
   x   Stephen, b. ——.
  xi   Rose E., b. ——.

### LADD FAMILY.

David Ladd married Cynthia Smith. He was frozen to death Jan. 20, 1853, aged 66. Children, probably :

  i   Cynthia, ——.

OLD AMES HOUSE, REMODELLED, AS SEEN FROM GILKEY'S HARBOR.

ii William, b. June 24, 1839.
iii Israel, ——.
iv Oliver, ——, d. August 7, 1859.
v James Lewis ——.
vi Jeremiah, ——. Married. Children :
    1 Gershom L., b. June 28, 1858.
    2 Jeremiah H., b. September 16, 1860.
vii David, ——.

## LASELLE FAMILY.

Ellison Laselle was born Sept. 7, 1754. Lived first on Laselle Island, then at Turtle Head. Estate settled 1802. Owned the eastern part of Mark Island. Married first, Sarah ——. She died May 26, 1790, aged 33 ; married second, (?) Mary ——. Children :

i Lydia, b. August 11, 1778.
ii Ellison, b. August 29, 1780. He or his father or both moved to north part of the island, where his lot was laid out, October 12, 1799, including Turtle Head. He d. December 16, 1850, or December 11, 1851, unmarried.
iii John, b. December 15, 1782.
iv William, b. December 23, 1784, m. Rhuhama Philbrook, March 23, 1850 (?); she was born March 17, 1786. He died June 10, 1852, aged 68.
v George, b. December 30, 1786, d. March, 1823, unmarried.
vi Joshua, b. on Laselle Island, probably m. Molly Philbrook. Lived in Searsmont. He was over 92 in 1891, and his wife over 90. Soldier in the war of 1812.

## LAWRY FAMILY.

Zenas Lawry was from Friendship. Married Wealthy, probably daughter of Simon Dodge, Sen. She married second, Jonathan Parker. Child :

David P., (?) m. Thirza B. Powers, of Eddington. Published July 26, 1880.

## LIBBY FAMILY.

Addison Libby. He died Oct. 23, 1864. Married Eliza Pendleton, Sept. 25, 1859. Children :

i Walter S., b. June 14, 1861, d. ——.
ii Walter A., b. January 25, 1865.

Josiah A. Libby married Eunice Bradshaw. She died Sept. 5, 1858. Son:

    Leslie, b.    , d. June, 1852.

## MARSHALL FAMILY.

Benjamin Marshall. "July 5, 1783. Old Mr. Ben Marshall was at town meeting." He sold land near Godfrey Trim's, Apr. 24, 1793. Children, probably:

  i  Thomas, ——.
  ii  Zachariah, ——.
  iii  Joshua, ——.

Joshua Marshall, probably son of Benjamin, married Rachel Chaples, both of Islesborough, Jan. 22, 1799, in Belfast; by James Nesmith, Esq.

Thomas Marshall, probably son of Benjamin, from Block Island about 1793. He married first, Lois, daughter of Godfrey Trim, Sept. 10, 1791. He married second, Mrs. Prudence Trim Dodge, widow of Israel Dodge, Jan. 9, 1823. Children:

  i  Betsey, m. Benjamin Boardman.
  ii  Lois, m. Joseph Farren, 1812.
  iii  Thomas, m. Temperance Coombs, July 20, 1820.
  iv  Robert, m. Prudence Dodge, January 21, 1824.
  v  Sarah, m. Othniel Coombs.
  vi  Mary, probably, who m. William Wright, of Middletown, Conn., April 11, 1819.

Thomas Marshall, Jr., married Temperance Coombs, July 20, 1820. Children:

  i  Othniel, b. ——.
  ii  Thesia J., b. ——.
  iii  Isaac M., b. ——.
  iv  James M., b. March 8, 1833.
  v  Betsey B., b. June 9, 1835.
  vi  Hannah J., b. December 5, 1837.

Robert Marshall, son of Thomas. He married first, Prudence Dodge, Jan. 21, 1824. She died, and he mar-

ried second, Nancy Allen, of Bangor. Published Aug.
5, 1843. He moved to Orrington, after 1844. Children,
all born in Islesborough :

   i  Elizabeth, b. October 17, 1824, d. Jan. 31, 1842.
   ii  Robert, Jr., b. August 1, 1826, m. Nancy E. Coombs, September 16,
      1850. Moved to Hampden, where he died. Children, all b. in
      Islesborough :
         1  Robert H., b. June 29, 1852.
         2  Florence A., b. August 3, 1853, d. 1860.
         3  Elzina R., b. March 9, 1855.
         4  Flora A., b. March 10, 1857.
   iii  Prudence, b. February 28, 1828, d. January 31, 1842.
   iv  George W., b. December 30, 1830.
   v  Lois Trim, b. April 28, 1833, probably m. Elisha Snare, of Or-
      rington.
   vi  Clarinda A., b. April 14, 1835, d. about 1840.
   vii  Thomas A., b. February 20, 1837.
   viii  Joshua S., b. January 26, 1844.

Samuel Marshall, son of Zachariah, married Jane,
daughter of Benj. Williams, Jan. 9, 1830. He died in
1874. She died in 1851. Children, all born in Islesborough :

   i  Mary J., b. March 2, 1832, m. Amaziah Coombs.
   ii  Lucy A., b. October 16, 1833, m. Wilson Coombs.
   iii  Samuel, b. April 3, 1835, m. Climena McFarland.
   iv  Fostina, b. July 4, 1836, m. Nason F. Reynolds.
   v  James O., b. September 15, 1837, unmarried, perhaps the "Oscar"
      who died in 1884.
   vi  Lavinia, b. June 30, 1840, m. Edward Coombs.
   vii  William, b. ——, m. Eliza Coombs. Children :
         1  Lavinia P., b. November 17, 1869, m. George Francis.
         2  Alfred A., b. November 6, 1871.
         3  William W., b. April 9, 1875.

Abner Marshall married Eliza A. Durgin. She died
Sept. 11, 1851. One child :

   Eudora, b. August 7, 1845, m. Nathan Pendleton.

Zachariah Marshall, son of Benjamin. Said to have had a first wife, whom I do not find. He married Rebecca Williams. Children, probably :

i   Prudence, m. John Welch, 1817.
ii   Emily.
iii   Hannah.
iv   Abigail.
v   Thomas.
vi   Andrew, m. Fannie Williams.
vii   Samuel, m. Jane Williams.
viii   John, probably m. Phebe, daughter of Benjamin Coombs. Children were :
　　　1   Phebe A., b. August 9, 1826, m. Isaac Warren, Jr.
　　　2   Drusilla, b. July 28, 1828, d. in Islesborough.

Andrew Marshall married Fannie Williams. Children :

i   Frances J., b. January 25, 1837, m. Frank Hook.
ii   Andrew F., b. April 20, 1838. Lost at sea.
iii   Julia M., b. Feb. 6, 1845, d. 1888.

## MERRITHEW FAMILY.

Roger Merrithew, from Vinalhaven, married first, Polly Coombs; married second, Hannah Coombs, Jan. 5, 1820. Children :

i   Abram, b. September, 1816.
ii   Mary, b. May 3, 1818, m. Daniel Dow.
iii   Rhoda, b. December 10, 1823, m. Joseph Adams.
iv   Margaret, b. December 4, 1825, m. Levi Merrithew.
v   Elzara, b. February 23, 1830.
vi   Moses, b. July 1, 1833.
vii   Lucena, b. July 23, 1836.

Reuben Merrithew married Betsey Ryder. Children :

i   Martha A., b. August 29, 1835, m. Freeman Keller.
ii   Thomas R., b. June 22, 1837, m. Angeline Redman.
iii   James T., b. August 21, 1839, d. 1841.
iv   Christopher C., b. October 14, 1841.
v   Lucy A., b. August 26, 1844, m. Frank Rhodes.
vi   Ephraim L., b. May 5, 1846, m. Lillian Pendleton.
vii   Reuben T., b. December 13, 1847, dead.

Benaiah Merrithew married Temperance Williams, Apr. 6, 1826. Children:

i    Amanda M. F., b. September 29, 1829, d. 1834.
ii   Rozilla, b. October 23, 1835, d. 1837.
iii  Sarah S., b. May 23, 1838, m. Daniel Hawes.

## McFarland Family.

George McFarland married Susan N. ——. She died Oct. 20, 1850, aged 48. Children:

i     Benjamin, b. April 9, 1823, d. July 18, 1847, aged 24.
ii    Thomas, b. September 30, 1825.
iii   Margaret, b. September 22, 1827, m. Benjamin Prescott.
iv    David, b. September 16, 1829.
v     William, b. May 6, 1831, d. May 22, 1853.
vi    George, b. October 4, 1832, d. 1852.
vii   Harriet, b. November 16, 1834, m. William Grover.
viii  Olive, b. January 2, 1837, m. Isaac J. Merritt, 1854.
          One child, Ludivellin, b. May 26, 1856.

Henry McFarland died July 6, 1865. Married Mary, daughter of Joseph Ryder. Children:

i    John, b. June 2, 1840, m. Prudence A. Dodge.
ii   Susan, b. June 2, 1840, m. Anthony Coombs.
iii  Joseph H., b. February 18, 1843, m. Belle Dodge.
iv   Mary, b. July 2, 1865, d. 1878.
v    Martha, b. July 2, 1865.

## Merritt Family.

Isaac J. Merritt married Olive McFarland, 1855. One child.

## Michaels Family.

James F. Michaels married Philena Pendleton. Published Feb. 11, 1847. He died Nov. 30, 1867. Children:

i   Philena M., b. February 21, 1849, m. John Pendleton.
ii  Abba A., b. January 23, 1852, d. 1854.

30

## MOODY FAMILY.

Jacob Moody, from Haverhill or Searsmont, bought a lot of William Grinnell, west side, below Sprague's Cove. Married Betsey Prescott. He died Sept. 13, 1860, aged 91, or April 16, 1855. Wife died October 12, 1881, aged 87, or September 12, 1859. Children, not born in Islesborough :

i Stephen.
ii John B.
iii Thomas T., m. Margaret Knowlton, December 15, 1850. Children were :
    1 Joseph J., b. April 30, 1851, m. Silvia Heal.
    2 L. P. Moody, b. July 27, 1852.
    3 Luella E., b. September 19, 1853, d. 1857.
    4 Mary J., b. April 1, 1855, m. John Bird.
    5 Polly L., d. 1855.
    6 Ann A., b. October 23, 1856.
    7 Luella, b. March 24, 1859.
    8 Louisa E., b. March 24, 1859.
    9 Ellen, d. 1877.
iv Isaac.
v Jacob, Jr., m. Polly ——. He d. September 12, 1859. She d. April 16, 1855.

John Bricket Moody married Jarandum Coombs. She was born December 11, 1833. Felba was drowned in Searsmont pond.

## MOORE FAMILY.

Gilbert L. Moore married Victorine H. Fairfield, Nov. 16, 1860. Children :

i Charles W., b. September 22, 1861.
ii Martha J., b. September 4, 1865.

George A. Moore married Sarah J. Dodge, Oct. 1, 1869. Children :

i George B., b. November 29, 1870, d. 1871.

## NASH FAMILY.

Elisha Nash, from Weymouth or Scituate, Mass. He bought a lot of land of Simon Dodge, Jr., Aug. 18, 1791, bounded by Paoli Hewes and Samuel Pendleton. He married Sally Hatch, Oct. 6, 1814. She was born 1787, died Nov. 3, 1842. He died February, 1852, aged 87. Children :

  i  Charles, b. May 28, 1816, married.
 ii  Sarah, b. January 14, 1819, m. Godfrey Trim, 1841.
iii  Mercy A., b. July 31, 1821, m. Isaac C. Pendleton, 1845.
 iv  Lydia Porter, b. July 31, 1821, m. Solomon Dodge, 1848.
  v  Abigail W., b. September 14, 1823, m. Isaac C. Pendleton, 1851.

Charles Nash, son of Elisha, born May 28, 1816. He was a justice of the peace and selectman for many years. He was social, friendly and respected, and a good citizen. He lived on the old homestead of his father, and had the care of his aged parents. He married Hannah Robinson. Published May 27, 1853. He died February 23, 1880. Children :

  i  Elisha, b. September 12, 1857, d. July 4, 1859.
 ii  Sarah J., b. June 20, 1859, m. Frank Collins.
iii  Ida May, b. December 20, 1860.
 iv  Elisha L., b. March 4, 1863, m. Celia Warren.

## NICHOLS FAMILY.

Bela Nichols, from Prospect, married Dorcas, daughter of Dolge Pendleton, in 1800. He was a quarter-master in the American army. His house stood where the Masonic hall now stands. He moved to Eastport in 1814, and died there. Children, born in Islesborough :

  i  Dodge, b. April 8, 1803.
 ii  Nathaniel, b. April 12, 1805.
iii  Jarum, b. July 17, 1808. Lived in Prospect.
 iv  Lucretia, b. April 17, 1812.

## PAYNE FAMILY.

Doctor John Payne was born in Gorham, October 16, 1801; was a graduate of the Medical School of Maine in 1841, and practiced in Islesborough. His practice was large, and he had a full amount of success. He moved to Northport, and afterwards to Belfast. He had a social disposition, and a good share of energy and activity. He died in Belfast, October 8, 1857. Children:

  i  Lycurgus, b. August 28, 1824, d. 1863. He was a graduate of Maine Medical School in 1857.

  ii  Nelson Miller, b. September 8, 1826. He died at Dover, N. H., in 1871. Graduated at the Philadelphia Homœopathic College at the head of his class in surgery. He was a surgeon in the army, at one time attached to headquarters of Fifth Army Corps.

## PARKER FAMILY.

Deacon Jonathan Parker, from Groton, Mass., married first, Hannah, daughter of Jonathan Holbrook; married second, Wealthy Dodge. The latter married first, Ezekiel Parker, brother of Jonathan; second, Jonathan Parker; and third, Zenas Lawry. Jonathan Parker, Sen., died April 5, 1841, aged 68. Children:

  i  Jonathan, b. May 25, 1796. Lived in Lincolnville, m. Margaret Jones, May 31, 1818. He died June 10, 1823. Their daughter Deborah J. C., b. March 14, 1823, m. William F. Veazie, December 16, 1848.

  ii  Silas, b. May 30, 1799, m. Sibyl Drinkwater, 1821, went to Boston.

  iii  Lucy, b. August 11, 1801, m. James Skinner.

  iv  Jane, b. December 5, 1803, born blind, d. January 23, 1868.

  v  Philena, b. April 1, 1806, m. Jordan Veazie, and A. P. Gilkey.

  vi  Lovisa C., b. September 22, 1808, d. young. I have it that she married Ferdinand Skinner, of Searsmont, December 5, 1841.

  vii  Ellison, b. November 30, 1810, m. in Lincolnville.

  viii  Thomas H., b. April 26, 1813, m. Emeline Coombs.

  ix  William Avery, b. July 1, 1815, m. Caroline Veazie.

  x  Sabrina, b. May 22, 1818, m. James Warren.

THOMAS H. PARKER.
1813.

William A. Parker, born July 1, 1815, married Caroline
Veazie. He died in Kingston, Jamaica, Mar. 10, 1857.
She died Nov. 30, 1875. Children :

  i   Bridget E., b. September 19, 1843, m. Samuel Johnson.
  ii  William A., b. May 25, 1845, m. Georgiana Spinney.
  iii Millard P., b. June 6, 1850, m. Emily Coombs.  He died in Ha-
      vana in 1892.
  iv  Lizzie, b. May 9, 1857, m. Godfrey Pettingill.

Thomas H. Parker, son of Jonathan, was born April
26, 1813.  He had the old homestead of his father.  Was
representative in 1868; selectman, and justice of the
peace; for fifty years a merchant; member of the Free-
Will Baptist church for sixty years.  He married Emeline, daughter of Fields Coombs, Feb. 6, 1838.  She was
born May 15, 1815; died Jan. 4, 1892.  Children :

  i   Jordan V., b. October 6, 1839, d. December 4, 1862.
  ii  Marilla, b. July 6, 1842, m. William P. Sprague, 1860, d. 1880.
  iii Augustine Harrison, b. March 9, 1844, m. 1861.
  iv  Luinda, b. March 11, 1851, m. George A. Warren.
  v   Artha A., b. October 16, 1853, m. John Warren.

Augustine Harrison Parker, born March 9, 1844, married Nancy W. Harriman.  Published May 11, 1861.
She died July 29, 1875, aged 32.  Children, not in order :

  i    Elma A.
  ii   Jessie.
  iii  Rosalind C., b. July 5, 1864, m. Chester Thomas.
  iv   Flora C., b. July 5, 1864, d. ——.
  v    Ernestine, m. Alanson Yeaton.
  vi   May Belle J., b. May 2, 1869.
  vii  Cora, m. John Yeaton.

Mighill Parker, Esq., bought land of Peter Coombs,
Aug. 6, 1791, where the hotel now stands at Sabbath-
Day Harbor.  He married, probably, Ruth Holbrook
(or Harriet).  He died in Islesborough, Feb. 17, 1826.
He was the first justice of the peace, and the first repre-
sentative for the town, in 1822 ; also one of the selectmen

in 1797, and held town offices until 1826, the year of his
death.  Children :

   i   Sally, b. May 23, 1793, m. John Williams.
  ii   Phebe, b. June 7, 1796, m. Samuel Farrow.
 iii   Mighill, Jr., b. November 3, 1798, m. Elsie Farrow.  He died in
       Bangor, December 18, 1871.  She d. in Bangor, December 17,
       1839, aged 39.  Children :
       1  David S., d. in Mattawamkeag, 1889.
       2  Joseph Mighill, d. in California.
       3  Josiah Farrow, twin, d. in California.
 iv   David S., b. September 12, 1801, d. May 20, 1821.
  v   Elisha, b. May 19, 1806, m. Christiana Thomas, of Northport.
       Moved to Islesborough, then to Corinth, where he died.  Chil-
       dren were :
       1  Ruth A., b. in Islesborough, September 7, 1832.
       2  Phebe E., b. in Islesborough, June 30, 1834.
       3  Judson, b. in Corinth.
 vi   Alden, b. July 27, 1808.  Moved to Winterport, then to Bangor.
       Returned to Winterport after 1812, and d. there.
vii   Anderson, b. September 4, 1811, m. Sophronia Horn, of Ripley,
       settled in Bangor, and d. there.
viii   Diana, b. April 22, 1814, m. Joshua Hawes, of East Corinth,
       March 22, 1836.

Eben Parker married Alva A. Boardman.


Ezekiel Parker, brother of Jonathan, married Wealthy,
daughter of Simon Dodge, Sen.  He died, and she married second, Zenas Lawry.


Simon Parker, of Islesborough, bought land of Rathburn Dodge, June 6, 1791, for one hundred and twenty-
five cords of wood, near Benjamin Coombs and Job
Sprague.

## PENDLETON FAMILY.

The name of Pendleton is the most common one in
town, as is shown by the census of 1880 and 1890.  Capt.

William Pendleton, Jr.,[*] born in Westerly, R. I., Feb. 11, 1727, came here in 1767-8, and brought his family in 1769. He settled on the lower end of the island, and his sons settled near him. He married first, Judith Carr or Judith Burdick, and also a second wife, Priscilla Cheesbro. May 18, 1794, he sold to his son Jonathan the Ensign Islands, and one-half of Seven-Hundred-Acre Island. The deed was signed by his wife Priscilla, and witnessed by Peggy and Sally Pendleton. May 15, 1794, he sold his homestead to his son Harry for two hundred pounds. They were both then of Islesborough. His wife did not sign this deed. He moved to Northport in 1795 or 1796, and lived with his son Harry, where he died, August 28, 1820, aged 93 years. Children :

   i  Job, of Islesborough.
  ii  Henry, b. about 1760.
 iii  Oliver, of Islesborough.
 iv  John, b. 1751, of Islesborough.
  v  Peggy, (?) witnessed deed, May 18, 1794.
 vi  Sally, (?) witnessed deed, May 18, 1794.
vii  Nancy, (?) m. William Pendleton, son of Peleg Pendleton, of Searsport. Published January 9, 1795. They lived in Islesborough and Searsport.

Job Pendleton, son of William Pendleton, born about 1747, came with his father and settled on the island now known as Billy Job's Island, about 1769, near to Long Island, and included in the town of Islesborough. He was a mariner and farmer, and bought one hundred acres of land near Cape Jellison, in 1790, of Joseph Clary, of Frankfort, for sixty pounds. He died on his own island, Jan. 25, 1794, aged 47. His grave is in the old burying ground at the lower end of Long Island. His will, dated Dec. 27, 1793, proved April 17, 1794, Hancock County

---

[*] C. H. Pendleton, Esq., of Westerly, R. I., United States Inspector, Post Office Department, has given much attention to the Pendleton family history.

Records, appoints his brother John executor. It gives
"Miss Lydia one hundred acres of land near Cape Jellison, and one-eighth of schooner William; to son William
one hundred and thirty-seven acres, north part of my
island; to Priscilla eighty acres, west part of my island;
to Amos eighty acres of same; to daughter Lydia fifteen
shillings; to Lucy, Joanna, Job, Peleg, and the one my
wife is now pregnant with," other bequests.   His estate
was appraised at one thousand and fifty-three pounds, one
shilling, and two pence.   He married first, Sally Crandall.
She died in Islesborough, Aug. 16, 1786, aged 34.   He
married second, Lydia ——, Sept. 20, 1791.   She died in
Lincolnville, 1855-1860.   Children :

   i  Lucy, named in her father's will.
  ii  Joanna, named in her father's will.
 iii  Peleg, lived in Lincolnville, and d. there, February 11, 1874,
       aged 84.   His son Job was living there in 1885.
 iv  Sarah.
  v  William, b. February 26, 1774, of Islesborough.
 vi  Lydia, b. 1776, m. Thomas Boardman.
vii  Priscilla, named in father's will.
viii  Amos.
 ix  Job, Jr.
  x  Posthumous child, named in father's will.


Henry Pendleton, or Harry, son of William, born about
1760.   Settled on the lot above his father, which was
occupied by William Brown in 1885.   He was one of the
first town officers, and often afterward.   He bought one
hundred acres of land of his brother Jonathan in 1795.
Married Rebecca, daughter of David Alden, of Northport,
in 1781.   He moved to Northport prior to 1818, and
died about 1844, aged about 84.   His wife was born Sep-

tember 17, 1762. When nearly one hundred years old
she walked nearly two miles to attend the funeral of a
daughter, aged about 80. She died in Northport, March
5, 1864, aged 101 years. They had thirteen children, five
of whom died in infancy.

   i  Judith, b. in Islesborough, 1782, m. Thomas Witherly, of Northport. She died at the age of 80. Large family.

  ii  David, of Northport. He m. Rebecca Cates, of Harrington. He
died aged over 90. Large family, among whom were Erastus
O. and Benjamin, of Bangor.

 iii  Betsey, m. Henry Sherman; she died aged over 80. Large family.

 iv  Henry, d. unmarried, aged 30.

  v  William, m. Mary Ackley. He died at the age of 50. Large
family.

 vi  Rebecca, m. William Howard. Four children.

vii  James A., m. Clara Ackley. He died at the age of 77. Large
family.

viii  Amos, b. in Northport, February 22, 1818. He wrote July 24,
1885, that he was the youngest of thirteen children. He m.
Martha Ann Hall. Seven children, some of whom live in
Bangor.

 ix  Five children, d. in infancy.

Jonathan Pendleton, son of William, was appointed
Ensign to do military duty in Islesborough, and took possession by squatter's claim of the islands at the south-
western entrance of Gilkey's Harbor, and from him they
derive the name of Ensign Islands. Married first, Jane,
daughter of John McIntire, of Warren. She died February 25, 1802, aged 47. Married second, Lucinda Hatch.
She died January 17, 1850. He died Sept. 25, 1841.
Children, all born in Islesborough :

   i  John M., b. July 4, 1774, d. October 25, 1780.

  ii  Judith, b. August 30, 1776, d. April 25, 1781.

 iii  William, b. January 4, 1778.

 iv  Job, b. September 26, 1779, d. March 4, 1780.

  v  Isaac, b. March 31, 1781.

 vi  Jonathan, Jr., b. January 9, 1783.

vii  Jane, b. February 26, 1785, d. July 17, 1792.

viii  Polly, b. October 18, 1787, m. Simeon M. ——, September 3, 1806.

 ix  John, b. September 27, 1789.

31

x   Catherine, b. October 4, 1791, d. July 23, 1792.
xi   Prudence, b. November 13, 1793.
xii   Robert, b. January 18, 1796.
xiii   Agnes, b. November 18, 1797, m. James Tolman, of Hope.   Published June 10, 1821.
xiv   Nathan, b. January 12, 1800, of Madison.
xv   Esther, b. March 31, 1803, m. Daniel Gould, of Camden.   Published May 23, 1823.
xvi   Jane, second, b. August 14, 1804, m. Benjamin Thomas, July 13, 1823, d. in Camden, January, 1885.
xvii   Lucinda, b. June 29, 1806, m. John Gilkey.

Oliver Pendleton, son of William, lived on the lot where the hotel Islesborough Inn now stands, below Dark Harbor. He sold out to Elisha Eames, and moved to Camden, and from there to Hope, where he died a very aged man.   Children, probably :

i   William, of Camden, m. Nancy Pendleton, of Islesborough, January 9, 1795.
ii   Alexander, lived in Northport.   He went away from home and was gone sixty years, when he returned, and died November 19, 1886, aged 100 years.
iii   Ambrose.
iv   James.
v   Sally, m. Nathaniel Palmer, of Belfast.   Published April 16, 1805. (?)
vi   Sukey, m. Joseph Palmer, of Belfast, in Islesborough, October 29, 1806.

John Pendleton was the fifth son of William, and probably came here about the same time as his father. Married first, Peggy Young. She died February 21, 1784. He married second, Betsey Rogers, of Marshfield, Mass.; married third, Mrs. Jane Henderson, sister of his first wife; married fourth, Mrs. Sarah D. Clough, of Warren. Her daughter, H. Antoinette Clough, married Rev. Jonathan Adams, of Woolwich and Deer Isle, July 16, 1821. They were parents of Rev. Jonathan E. Adams, D. D., of Bangor. John Pendleton was the first town treasurer of the town, 1789. He moved to Camden; was captain

of militia in 1813. Died December, 1830; buried Dec.
26, a very old man. Children :

  i  Margaret, m. William, son of Job Pendleton.
 ii  Mary.
iii  Arthur.
 iv  Jack, of Islesborough, on old homestead.
     By second wife.
  v  Adam, d. unmarried.
 vi  Eliza, m. Frye Hall, of Belfast.
vii  Henry, settled in Virginia.
viii Elisha, settled in Virginia.
 ix  Jane, m. Archibald Buchanan, of Camden.
  x  George, lived in Camden, m. ——— Johnson, of Belfast.
 xi  Dyer. (?)
xii  Dolly, (?) m. ——— Wood, of Camden.


William Pendleton, son of Job, born Feb. 26, 1774,
died Aug. 26, 1837, aged 63. Married Peggy, daughter
of John Pendleton (cousins). She was born May 19,
1782, died August 6, 1841, aged 59. Children (births and
deaths copied from family Bible):

  i  Margaret, b. April 24, 1798, (?) m. Elbridge Hopkins, of Orland,
     November 18, 1833.
 ii  William, b. June 1, 1800, d. December 28, 1820.
iii  Charles, b. August 5, 1802, m. Elizabeth Eaton.
 iv  Aaron, b. March 30, 1805, m. Rebecca Farrow. He d. in Brewer,
     July 21, 1887.
  v  Sarah E., b. September 23, 1807, m. Rathburn D. Sprague, d. De-
     cember, 1879.
 vi  Emeline, b. April 12, 1810, d. March 20, 1811.
vii  Albert, b. April 17, 1812, m. Mercy J. Farnsworth.
viii Reuben, b. March 12, 1815, m. ——— Simons. Lived in Camden.
 ix  Mary A., b. September 12, 1817, m. James Seward, of Camden,
     December 11, 1836.
  x  Jefferson, b. March 6, 1820, m. Dorothy Gilkey, February 7, 1843.
     Lived in Camden.
 xi  William E., b. January 27, 1823, married. Is a pilot in New
     Orleans.
xii  Joseph A., b. November 28, 1824, went to New York.


John Pendleton, son of John, born Sept. 17, 1778, who
was always known as Jack Pendleton. He inherited the

old homestead and house, which was built by his father
when he was three years old. He married first, Martha
McGlathery, of Pemaquid or Camden. She died in 1809.
He married second, Betsey Farnsworth, a native of Waldoborough, in 1810. He was a deacon of the church
for many years, and died July 18, 1863, respected and
regretted by all who knew him. His widow died July 18,
1881, aged 88 years. His estate was divided somewhat
during his lifetime. The lots of Benjamin Thomas, Stephen Fairfield, John Gilkey, Thomas Gilkey, and William
Adams, all came from his lot. Stephen Fairfield, his son-
in-law, had the balance, and after his death it was sold to
the Islesborough Land and Improvement Company. The
house was taken down in 1892. Children:

   i  Martha, b. January 5, 1804, m. Elisha Gilkey, of Camden, De-
      cember 6, 1827.
  ii  Harriet, b. May 22, 1805, m. John Farrow, Jr., January 31, 1828.
 iii  John, Jr., 3d, b. October 1, 1807, m. Jane Chapin, of Boston.
 iv  Artimisa, b. April 31, 1809, m. Philip Gilkey, Jr., of Belfast,
      November 21, 1830.

  By second wife:

   v  Eliza, b. September 2, 1811, m. Avery Gilkey, December 4, 1834.
  vi  Andrew, b. June 3, 1813, m. Jane Thomas.
 vii  Dolly Wood, b. December 25, 1814, m. Ambrose Farrow, Nov.
      15, 1834.
viii  Angeline, b. December 14, 1816, m. Nelson Gilkey, March
      25, 1838.
 ix  Bridget F., b. January 27, 1818, m. Stephen B. Fairfield, April 10,
      1838.
  x  Julia Ann, b. February 5, 1820, m. Joseph W. Trim, September
      1, 1842.
 xi  Sarah C., b. October 31, 1821, m. Augustine Tobey.
 xii  Oliver, b. June 18, 1823, d. April 16, 1825.
xiii  Rosina, b. May 31, 1824, m. William Adams. First child born
      1843. He d. October 15, 1890, aged 72. She d. December 4,
      1862, aged 38.
xiv  Jane, b. January 10, 1826, m. Judson Philbrook, January 13, 1847.
 xv  Alfred P., b. June 5, 1830, m. Wealthy Hatch, December 26,
      1854. He was a soldier in the civil war, and d. in the battle
      at Fair Oaks. His widow m. second.
xvi  Judson, (?) b. December 11, 1831, died January 12, 1832.

CAPT. JOHN PENDLETON.

Andrew Pendleton, son of Capt. Jack, born June 3, 1813; married Jane, daughter of Benjamin Thomas, Dec. 19, 1842. Children :

   i   Adelia F., b. May 22, 1845.
   ii  Francis F., b. October 30, 1846.
  iii  Orando A., b. November 21, 1847, d. 1847.
  iv  Lillian R., b. April 4, 1849, m. E. L. Merrithew.
   v  Adrianna J., b. October 4, 1853, m. Thaddeus Babbidge.
  vi  Walter S., b. October 10, 1856, d. October 26, 1877.
 vii  Niran S., b. May 5, 1859.
viii  Morris A., b. September 9, 1861.
  ix  Hugh R., b. December 31, 1865.

Jonathan Pendleton, Jr., married Lydia J. Knowles. Sons died in Islesborough. Children :

   i   Richmond H., b. November 29, 1811, m. Nancy Watson.
   ii  Elisha K., b. May 16, 1813, m. Catherine Knowles.
  iii  Lydia J., b. May 14, 1816, m. Daniel Philbrook.
  iv  Joseph K., b. June 6, 1818, m. Lucy G. Watson.

Richmond Hatch Pendleton, son of Jonathan, married Nancy Watson. He died 1891. Wife Lucy was born in Thomaston, 1817; died 1886. Children :

   i   Christiana, b. September 15, 1840.
   ii  Nathan, b. August 29, 1845, m. Eudora A. Marshall.
  iii  Dorothy F., b. August 29, 1845, d. 1860.
  iv  Myra E., b. March 12, 1847, m. Pyam D. Hatch.
   v  George F., b. January 21, 1849, m. Mercy A. Pendleton.
  vi  Lydia Jane, b. April 3, 1852, m. Chauncey Davis.
 vii  Sarah, b. August 21, 1854.
viii  Eveline, b. August 21, 1854.
  ix  Maria, b. December 15, 1858, m. Henderson Durgin.
   x  Watson, not on Islesborough records. Married Maria Lear.

George F. Pendleton married Mercy A. Pendleton. Children :

   i   Ada G., b. June 1, 1877.
   ii  Mabell, b. September 14, 1878.

Nathan Pendleton married Eudora A. Marshall. Children were :

   i   Clifford E., b. July 17, 1867, m. Jennie Annis.
   ii   Lila Imogene, b. October 18, 1872.

Robert Pendleton, son of Jonathan, born Jan. 18, 1796; died in Islesborough, August 30, 1839, aged 43 years. Married Eliza C. Harlow, of Bangor. She married second, Francis Grindle. Published April 20, 1840. She died May 16, 1891. Children :

   i   Charles A., b. January 10, 1824, m. Susan Sherman, d. September 20, 1879.
   ii   Catherine M., b. October 27, 1825. Married first, Joel Thomas, second, Martin S. Coombs.
   iii   Lorenzo, b. September 8, 1827, m. Elizabeth Boardman. He was in the legislature in 1877.
   iv   Mary A., b. October 18, 1829, d. May 17, 1886. Married Calvin W. Sherman.
   v   Charlotte A., b. August 10, 1831, m. Emery Williams.
   vi   Horatio B., b. June 11, 1830, m. two sisters, —— Baker.
   vii   Eliza J., b. August 8, 1834, m. Humphrey Ayers.

Charles A. Pendleton, born Jan. 10, 1824. Married Susan E. Sherman, Dec. 4, 1847. He died September 21, 1879. Children :

   i   Fostina A., b. October 15, 1848, d. March 17, 1852.
   ii   Charles R., b. April 6, 1852, m. Cora S. Higgins.
   iii   Eliza S., b. April 6, 1856, d. August 9, 1878.
   iv   Thomas H., b. June 17, 1858, d. June 3, 1878.

Charles R. Pendleton married Cora S. Higgins. Children were :

   i   Florence, b. September 19, 1876.
   ii   Thomas Chester, b. August 26, 1878.

Lorenzo Pendleton, son of Robert, born Sept. 8, 1827. Married Elizabeth Boardman, 1860. She was born Dec.

24, 1838. He was a representative from Islesborough in
1877. Ten children, of whom four died young:

  i   Elroy G., b. April 12, 1861.
  ii  Frederick D., b. November 29, 1862.
  iii Lorenzo R., b. June 24, 1867.
  iv Evelyn A., b. July 13, 1873.
  v  Grace A., b. July 1, 1877.
  vi Ermina F., b. November 17, 1882.

Aaron Pendleton married Rebecca Farrow, November
14, 1825. He moved to Northport, then to Brewer, where
he died. Children :

  i   Caroline, b. in Islesborough, July 13, 1826, m. Lewis A. Knowl-
      ton. She d. in Belfast.
  ii  Henderson, b. in Islesborough, October 10, 1828, m. Aurilla
      Drinkwater.
  iii Jerrard, b. in Northport.
  iv Ambrose, b. in Northport.

Joseph K. Pendleton, son of Jonathan, Jr., married
Lucy S. Watson, Jan. 8, 1842. She died April 24, 1867.
He died January 22, 1890, aged 71 years and 7 months.
Children :

  i   Joseph A., b. October 26, 1842, d. August, 1857.
  ii  Roscoe C., b. July 2, 1844, married.
  iii Joseph K., b. October 11, 1847.
  iv Lucy J., b. November 11, 1849.
  v  Roxana, b. August 4, 1852, m. Alfred Hatch.
  vi Elisha W., b. October 7, 1854.
  vii Calvin W., b. April 12, 1857.
 viii Loranius T., b. June 31, 1863.

Lyman B. Pendleton married Sally Herrick, who died
in 1868. He died in 1890. Children :

  i   Sarah, b. October 12, 1829.
  ii  Lyman G., b. January 20, 1834, m. Lydia J. Flanders.
  iii John, b. January 23, 1843, m. Melissa Michaels.

Lyman G. Pendleton married Lydia J. Flanders. Published Jan. 3, 1852. Children:

i Sarah L., b. November, 1855.
ii Betsey E., b. May 8, 1859, m. Silas Dodge.
iii Georgietta, b. January 22, 1872.

Benjamin Pendleton died in 1892. Children:

i Clarinda, d. December 24, 1854.
ii Nason E., b. November 27, 1855, m. Abbie Rolerson.
iii Jacob G., b. April 22, 1861, m. ——.
iv Atlanta, or Abbie E., b. March 20, 1861, m. Philip Pendleton.
v Isaac J., b. – –, d. June 14, 1875.

John Pendleton married Melissa Michaels, May 28, 1864. Children:

i John B., b. August 8, 1865.
ii James L., b. November 22, 1867.
iii Lyman L., b. May 10, 1869.

Albert Pendleton, son of William, married Mercy J. Farnsworth, 1837. He died June 29, 1845. Children:

i Arabella O., b. October 8, 1838, m. Jacob Dodge.
ii Maria L., b. October 8, 1838, m. —— Hoxie.
iii William W., b. June 13, 1841.
iv Ellen J., b. October 27, 1843, m. Jerrard Pendleton.

Roscoe C. Pendleton, son of Joseph K., married Mary H. Hatch. Published Sept. 11, 1866. Children:

i William P., b. April 2, 1868.
ii Sarah H., b. August 10, 1870, m. Morrill Law.
iii Frank Lewis, b. February 5, 1874.

Richard P. Pendleton married first, Lois E. Coombs, 1864, and second, Carrie Losee. Children:

i Meda May, b. December 3, 1865, m. Joseph Dodge.
ii Emma Jane, b. January 12, 1871, m. Fred Losee.

Elisha K. Pendleton married Catherine S. Knowles, of Belfast. Published Jan. 11, 1841. He died January 10,· 1875. Children :

i Fuller H., b. February 4, 1842.
ii Justin H., b. August 1, 1845, drowned February 21, 1870.
iii Clara A., b. November 16, 1847, m. Joseph Ryder.

George W. Pendleton married Lucy J. Pendleton. He was drowned in 1882. Children :

i Joseph A., b. March 28, 1871.
ii Lucy E., b. October 10, 1874.
iii Marion F.

Thomas Pendleton, son of James, and grandson of Caleb Pendleton, was born in Westerly, R. I., January 3, 1719. Married Dorcas, daughter of Tristram Dodge, of Block Island, in 1741. He was a master mariner, engaged in the whale fishery to Greenland, and on one of his voyages put in to Castine, where, excited by the beauty of Penobscot bay, he determined to settle. In 1753 he sold his estate in Westerly for eleven hundred and thirty pounds, and in 1766 moved to Long Island, where he took up nine hundred acres. His whole family soon followed, and he settled them on his land on the island. His house was a few rods to the north-east of Dark Harbor. He took an active part in town affairs, and his name often occurs in the first town records. In person he was tall, with red hair and blue eyes. He died in 1809. His wife died in 1796. Children, all of Islesborough :

i Mark, d. aged 19 years.
ii Stephen, d. young.

———
* This sketch of Thomas Pendleton, Sen., and family, was compiled and contributed by George Pendleton.

  iii  Samuel, b. 1745.
  iv  Margaret, b. 1747.
   v  Thomas, Jr., b. 1749. Town officer in 1790. Bought land of Benjamin Thomas, March 28, 1793, for twelve pounds, one hundred acres at Saunders Harbor. Deed witnessed by Nathaniel and Cynthia Pendleton.
  vi  Gideon, b. 1751.
 vii  Joshua, b. 1755.
viii  Nathaniel, b. 1757, m. Cynthia West.
  ix  Mary, b. 1758, m. Joseph Boardman, October 2, 1774.
   x  Stephen, 2d, b. February 9, 1763.


Samuel, third son of Thomas Pendleton, was born in Westerly, R. I., in 1745. Married on Block Island, in 1766, to Bathsheba, daughter of John Dodge, sister of Simon. He settled on land of his father's on the island. His house was built at Pendleton Cove, in 1772. Samuel bought all the islands which lie west of a south course from Cape Rosier, including seven small islands. He was Deacon of the first church, and was highly respected. His will dated March 2, 1822. His wife died March, 1828. Children, all born in Islesborough :

    i  Dorcas, b. December 2, 1767. Said to have been the first child born on the island. Probably married second, —— Ewell, about 1789.
   ii  Niobe, b. 1771, m. Vincent Elwell, of Northport, December 14, 1792. She d. June 2, 1812. No children.
  iii  Lydia, b. January 7, 1773, m. Rathburn Dodge. (?)
  iv  Dodge, b. 1776.
   v  Bathsheba, b. 1778, d. young.
  vi  Joshua, b. October 17, 1781.
 vii  Mark, b. 1784.
viii  Bathsheba, 2d, b. 1786.
  ix  Prudence, b. March 10, 1788, m. Jacob George, of Prospect. She d. February 18, 1876.
   x  Samuel, Jr., b. January 14, 1791.
  xi  Simon D., b. December 22, 1792.


Nathaniel Pendleton, son of Thomas, was in Islesborough in 1793, and July 19th bought a lot of land at

Little Harbor, of George Ulmer, for sixty pounds, bounded on land of Jonathan Pendleton and Thomas Brazier. He and his wife Cynthia, of Duck Trap, sold land in Islesborough to William Pendleton, January 1, 1795, for one hundred and eighty pounds. This lot was in the southwest corner of the island, near Saunders Harbor, against Seven-Hundred-Acre Island. He was drowned crossing the bay. Married Cynthia West. (?) Children probably :

   i  Cynthia, m. ——— Drinkwater, of Duck Trap, November 13, 1789.
   ii  Nabby, m. David Thomas, of Islesborough. She d. January 17, 1867, aged 99.
   iii  Wealthy, m. Mark Dodge.

Gideon, son of Thomas Pendleton, Sen., married Matilda, daughter of Captain John Gilkey, and settled on Acre Island. His house was on the same spot where Hiram Dodge lived. He was the first man from Islesborough to command a vessel sailing to the West Indies, and on his return had his vessel seized by the Collector, Joseph Hook, of Castine, for smuggling two pounds of tea. He sold land in Islesborough, May 4, 1794. In 1814 he moved to New Brunswick, where he bought a large island near St. Andrews, now called Pendleton Island. He died there at the age of nearly 90. Children, born in Islesborough :

   i  James G., b. 1781, m. Elizabeth, daughter of Jabez Philbrook, 1806. Removed to Ohio, in 1818. He d. August 8, 1867, aged 84. She d. January 4, 1865, aged 81. They had twelve children.
   ii  John.
   iii  Isaac.
   iv  Charles.
   v  Matilda.
   vi  Lenity.
   vii  Gideon, Jr. (?)
   viii  Stephen. (?)

Joshua, son of Thomas Pendleton, married and settled
where the late Jonathan Pendleton lived. Planted an
orchard and cleared a large farm.    Town officer 1789.
Moved to Northport about 1814.    Married first, Sally
Nutter; second, Sally, daughter of Jabez Ames.    Children:

 i Sally.
 ii Lois.
 iii Nancy.
 iv Abigail.
 v Joshua, by second wife.
 vi Mercy.
 vii Luther.
 viii Joseph.
 ix Andrew.
 x Thomas.
 xi Benjamin.
 xii Lydia.
 xiii Thankful. (?)

Stephen Pendleton was the youngest son of Thomas.
He was born in Westerly, R. I., February 9, 1763.  He
married in Islesborough, September 25, 1786, to Prudence,
daughter of Simon Dodge.  She was born on Block Island
May 23, 1763.  They settled in Islesborough on land
bought of Joshua Pendleton.  His house was where the
house of the late Captain Elisha K. Pendleton now stands.
When the war of the revolution commenced, Stephen was
serving in the British navy, under Capt. Hendy, and was
retained three years.  He got his discharge by taking oath
of parole, and then returned to Islesborough, where he
found employment shipping wood to Cape Cod from Pendleton's Cove.  He was six feet one inch high, and
weighed two hundred pounds; was noted for his great
muscular ability.  After the war he was employed by the
British to assist Capt. Hendy in surveying the line between Maine and New Brunswick.  He purchased eight
hundred acres near St. Andrews.  He was living in New
Brunswick when the war of 1812 commenced.  He then
returned to his home in Islesborough, joined an American

privateer, and was in several engagements; taken prisoner, paroled, and returned to Islesborough, where he lived until 1827. He took an active part in all that helped to build up the town, more especially in building the roads. He was a member of the Baptist church. His pew in the meeting-house was No. 22. He died in Lubec, September 6, 1845. His wife Prudence died in Northport in 1827. Children, born in Islesborough :

   i   Hiram, b. May 20, 1787, went west.
   ii  Dorcas, b. January 13, 1789.
  iii  Prudence, b. February 6, 1791.
  iv  Stephen, Jr., b. August 23, 1792.
   v  Mary, b. November 6, 1794, m. John Trim, 1815.
  vi  Simon. (?)
 vii  John Brooks. (?)


Dodge Pendleton, oldest son of Samuel Pendleton, Jr., was born in 1776. Married Sally Nash, of Hingham, Mass. Settled below Bounty Cove, to the westward of Pendleton Mountain, on land given him by his father in 1796. He held several town offices. He was drowned in the bay, October, 1806 (or December 11, 1811). The widow married second, Simon Dodge, Sen. Children :

   i   Sally, b. April 7, 1798, m. Isaac Warren.
   ii  Abigail, b. February 10, 1796, m. Solomon P. Coombs, 1824.
  iii  Elisha, b. January 19, 1801, m. Mary Lindsey.


Elisha Pendleton, son of Dodge, was born January 19, 1801 ; married Mary Lindsey, Jan. 11, 1831. He died Dec. 17, 1877. Children :

   i   Isaac, b. September 12, 1838.
   ii  Elizabeth, b. September 12, 1838.
  iii  Charles W., b. January 1, 1841.
  iv  Sibyl L., b. December 6, 1843, m. —— Weed.
   v  Napoleon B., b. January 8, 1846.
  vi  Asenath, b. May 8, 1848.
 vii  Eliza M., b. July 5, 1850.
viii  Lydia, b. September 8, 1858.
  ix  Abigail, b. September 8, 1858.

Joshua Pendleton, second son of Samuel Pendleton, Jr., was born in Islesborough, Oct. 17, 1781. In his early life he was a mariner. He was a volunteer in the war of 1812; a member of the Baptist church in 1820; entered the ministry in 1824, and was a minister for thirty-six years. His mission was on the islands along the coast of Maine. Joshua married July 4, 1800, Sally Randall, of Lincolnville. He first settled on Mark Island, which he purchased of his father. Children :

   i  Nathaniel, b. April 7, 1803, m. Eunice Grover.
  ii  Joseph Jones, b. January 29, 1806, m. Mary Collins.
 iii  Samuel, b. May 29, 1808, m. Mary Grover, of Deer Isle, July 3, 1828. He removed to Winter Harbor, Gouldsboro, and died there June, 1890.
 iv  Adam T., b. June 2, 1813, m. Eliza J. Bracy, of Mount Desert. Published April 29, 1837.
  v  Shubael H., b. July 5, 1817.
 vi  Sarah Jane, b. March 6, 1822, m. William Dodge, April 14, 1838. Removed to Gouldsboro in 1862. He settled south-west from the mountain, on land willed him by his father, Rev. Joshua Pendleton. He died in Islesborough, December 12, 1859. His widow died April 3, 1863.

Samuel Pendleton, 2d, married Polly Grover. Children :

   i  Eunice, b. January 8, 1828.
  ii  Samuel Caleb, b. March 27, 1831.

Mark Pendleton, Sen., son of Samuel, was born in 1784. He died Dec. 25, 1867, aged 83. Married Lydia, daughter of John Ball, of Block Island, in 1806. Children were :

   i  Vincent, b. January 25, 1807.
  ii  Simon, b. September 4, 1809.
 iii  Mark, Jr., b. February 2, 1811.
 iv  Dodge, b. March 12, 1813, d. 1893.
  v  Lydia, b. June 15, 1815.
 vi  Bathsheba, b. May 16, 1817, m. Daniel Warren, Dec. 21, 1837.
 vii  Isaac Case, b. January 19, 1822, m. Mercy Nash.
viii  Samuel R., b. September 27, 1820, m. Elsie Brown, Oct. 21, 1848. Son, Samuel A., b. October 9, 1853.

ix  Charlotte, b. July 8, 1824, m. John Sears.
x  Philena, b. April 24, 1826, m. James Michaels, and then Sylvester
    Fletcher.
xi  Lyman, m. Sally Herrick.
xii  Jane.

Samuel Pendleton, Jr., born January 14, 1791, married
Lucy B. Sprague, January 15, 1810, daughter of Jonathan
Sprague. She was born September 29, 1789, and died
August 4, 1877. He died Sept. 21, 1844. He bought
the estate of Godfrey Trim, Sen., near the upper end of
the island. Children :

i  Cordelia O., b. February 18, 1812, d. January 2, 1837, m. Nathaniel
    Nichols, October 11, 1835. They had one child.
ii  Phebe, b. July 21, 1813, d. January 6, 1867, unmarried.
iii  Niobe, b. January 15, 1815, d. October 31, 1850. She m. John
    Bachelder. They had eight children.
iv  Albert, b. May 6, 1816, d. May 29, 1877 or 1879.
v  Rodolphus, b. March 14, 1818, d. October 8, 1866. He was
    drowned in Penobscot Bay.
vi  Gamaliel R., b. August 12, 1822, m. Matilda T. Sawyer. They
    had three children.
vii  Maximilian, b. December 19, 1833, m. Elizabeth Collins. One
    child went to Lawrence, Mass.
viii  Deborah, b. October 1, 1820, d. ——, m. —— Valais, of Bucksport.

Simon D. Pendleton, son of Samuel, born December 22,
1792. He married Dec. 22, 1816, Mary S. Fowler, of
Prospect. They lived on the homestead of Samuel, and
had the care of his parents in their old age. In 1836 he
sold his land in Islesborough and moved to Prospect. He
died Dec. 28, 1870. His wife, Mary S., died January 31,
1885, aged 90 years. Children, born in Islesborough :

i  Elsie, b. December 9, 1819.
ii  Prudence, b. March 25, 1821.
iii  Mary Ann, b. September 26, 1823.
iv  Rosetta, b. January 17, 1827.

v   Simon A., b. September 29, 1829.
vi  Nancy Jane, b. October, 1830.
vii Levi A., b. April 29, 1833.


Nathaniel Pendleton, the oldest son of Joshua, married
April 7, 1823, Eunice, daughter of Capt. George Grover,
of Deer Isle. He settled first on Mark Island, where he
built a house; then moved to Acre Island, where he
lived until 1828. He then removed to Hancock county,
where he became a man of distinction. He was a physician of note. He died in Gouldsboro, where a monument is erected to his memory. He was wealthy at the
time of his death. Children, all born in Islesborough:

i   Solomon, b. November 8, 1826.
ii  Francina A., b. September 3, 1828.
iii George W., b. September 24, 1831.
iv  Martha A., b. September 26, 1833.
v   Martin V., b. November 6, 1824.


Joseph Jones Pendleton, son of Joshua (the preacher),
was born January 29, 1806. He married March 7, 1822,
Mary Collins, daughter of John Collins, of Frankfort.
He followed the sea, and at the age of twenty-two was
master, and owned an estate in Islesborough, where he
built the first brick house. He was a member of the first
Baptist church in 1826, and took an active part in church
and school affairs. In 1862 he sold his homestead in
Islesborough and moved to Belfast. Children, all born in
Islesborough except the first:

i   Joseph T., b. on Mark Island, Penobscot Bay, in 1824. He m.
    Sarah F. Tracy, of Gouldsboro. They live at Belfast.
ii  Mary Jane, b. September 8, 1827, m. Capt. Elias Seavey, of
    Saco, Maine. He d. in St. Thomas, December 20, 1858.
iii Ephraim Emery, b. September 4, 1831, m. Ann Maria Thomas.
    Second, married Artemisa L. Gilkey. He served in the
    navy in the rebellion. He was the first man in Islesborough
    to have command of a naval vessel.

iv Joshua A., b. October 17, 1836. He m. Eunice Hammond, of Gouldsboro. He was master of a Danish steamship of St. Thomas. He d. in St. Thomas, January 12, 1859.

v George W., b. February 25, 1838, m. May 3, 1870, to Martha Durgin. He was a master mariner, Professor of Nautical Science, an extensive traveler, and quite a historian.

vi Nathaniel S., b. February 4, 1846, m. Emily Wood, of Northport. He lives in Belfast.

vii Eleanora C., b. April 5, 1840, d. July 31, 1846.

Shubael Pendleton, son of Joshua, married first, Eunice Bickford, and second, Dorothy Closson, March 9, 1844. Children :

i Edward F., b. April 3, 1845, m. Amy Keller.

ii Frederick P., b. August 17, 1848, d. 1875, m. Mary E. Keller.

iii Rhoda M., b. February 16, 1849, m. Jason R. Ryder.

iv Martin V., b. January 21, 1852, m. Isabel Knight.

v Benjamin F., b. November 19, 1854, d. 1870.

vi Solomon, b. October 25, 1857, d. 1857.

vii Lenora, b. April 25, 1859, d. 1859.

Dodge Pendleton, son of Mark Pendleton, was born March 12, 1813. He married Mary J. Whalen, of Vinalhaven, Jan. 16, 1843. Children :

i Sibyl F., b. August 6, 1845, m. Franklin Flanders.

ii Lydia J., b. March 8, 1848, m. Arnold Annis.

iii Lyonnais, b. November 28, 1850, m. Sarah Rolerson.

iv Dodge T., b. April 29, 1854, d. 1876.

v Dennis M., b. November 23, 1855, m. Mary E. Haynes.

vi Hannah E., b. May 13, 1858, d. 1858.

vii Rose, b. May 13, 1858, d. 1858.

viii Roderick N., b. ——, m. Mabel Haynes.

Vincent Pendleton, son of Mark, Sen., born January 25, 1807. Married Eliza Kimball, of Swanville. She died in 1872. Children :

i Elizabeth, b. October 5, 1830, m. Simon Sprague, Jr.

ii Alice B., b. September 15, 1832, m. Noah B. Dodge.

iii Mary A., b. March 10, 1834.

iv Celia Ann, b. January 27, 1836.

v Philip G., b. December 5, 1837, m. Abbie Pendleton.

33

vi Caleb F., b. October 3, 1839.
vii Fanny D., b. October 23, 1842, m. Joel Small.
viii James O., b. October 22, 1843, m. Junietta Pendleton.
ix William B., b. July 27, 1845, m. Lawrence.
x Victoria, b. March 1, 1850, m. —— Tripp.


Philip G. Pendleton, son of Vincent, married Sarah A. Pendleton, in 1869. Children:

i Abbie Eugenie, b. February 15, 1870.
ii Frank Rufus, b. August 14, 1872.
iii Eliza H., b. January 12, 1877.
iv Caro, Edwin P., Rita, Ralph, Harold.


Caleb F. Pendleton, son of Vincent, married Mary Kimball. Children:

i Hannah E., b. March 25, 1865, m. Andrew Garland.
ii Alma Alice, b. December 25, 1873, d. 1874.
iii Nahum E., m. Ethel Coombs.
iv Hattie.


James O. Pendleton, son of Vincent, married Junietta Pendleton. Children:

i Leila A., b. July 28, 1874, d. 1876.
ii Edna Mildred, b. 1876.


Capt. Mark Pendleton, Jr., born February 2, 1811. He was a master mariner and gentleman of the old school. He was enterprising and ambitious, and his labors were crowned with success. He took an active interest in town affairs, and was an active participator in everything that related to the town. His sons are also enterprising and successful shipmasters and shipowners, and are well and favorably known as such all over the United States. He married Eliza J., daughter of Fields Coombs, March 10, 1837. He lived and died on the estate of his father, below

CAPT. MARK PENDLETON.
1811—1888.

MRS. ELIZA J. PENDLETON,
1817—Living.

Bounty Cove, and to the westward of Pendleton Mountain. He died April 23, 1888. Mrs. Pendleton resides on the old homestead. Children:

  i   Richard P., b. July 28, 1839, married.
  ii  Fields C., b. March 6, 1842, married.
  iii Guilford D., b. March 4, 1845, married.
  iv  Winfield S., b. September 2, 1847, married.
  v   Eliza L., b. November 18, 1850, m. Lester A. Lewis.
  vi  Mark, b. September 16, 1852, d. 1854.
  vii Emma J., b. July 8, 1855, d. 1863.
  viii Mark Pierce, b. Jan. 11, 1860. He represented Islesborough in the Legislature in 1889. He is editor and proprietor of the Belfast Age. He married in Bangor, September 10, 1889, Inez L. Matthews, of Bangor.


Fields C. Pendleton, son of Mark, born March 6, 1842. Shipmaster and owner. Married first, Lucinda J. Seely, March 27, 1863. She died June 25, 1865. He married second, Mrs. Sabrina P. Brown. Published October 3, 1866. Children:

  i   Nellie L., b. April 29, 1868, d. July 6, 1886.
  ii  Fields S., b. March 21, 1870.
  iii Alice L., b. April 3, 1872.
  iv  Sabrina C., b. August 30, 1874.
  v   Grace N., b. January 20, 1876.
  vi  Edwin S., b. December 4, 1877.
  vii Effie, b. April 13, 1880.
  viii Phebe E., b. January 26, 1884.


Guilford D. Pendleton, son of Mark, born March 4, 1845. Shipmaster and owner. Married Mrs. Orissa P. Durgin, December 30, 1869. Children:

  i   Eva, b. August 6, 1874, d. December 5, 1874.
  ii  R. Dudley, b. April 2, 1876.
  iii Kate L., b. April 3, 1878.
  iv  Annie L., b. July 19, 1885.

Winfield S. Pendleton, son of Mark, born September 2, 1847. Shipmaster and owner. Married Lucy A., daughter of Judson Philbrook, January 15, 1871. Representative in 1880. Children:

i   Winfield S., b. April 15, 1872.
ii  Judson P., b. September 25, 1873.
iii Lewis N., b. February 15, 1875.
iv  Ethel L., b. May 11, 1878.
v   Mark, b. February 12, 1883, d. November 27, 1887.
vi  Bowdoin Neally, b. June 27, 1885.

Isaac Case Pendleton, son of Mark, Sen., married first Mercy A. Nash, December 17, 1845. She died June 17, 1849. Married second, Abigail Nash. Published April 2, 1851. Children:

i    Laban K., b. September 30, 1847, m. Martha M. Dodge.
ii   Isaac E., b. April 20, 1849, m. Nettie Veaton.
iii  Charles N., b. August 2, 1852.
iv   Mercy A., b. June 26, 1854, m. George Pendleton.
v    Junietta, b. November 25, 1855, m. James O. Pendleton.
vi   Emily, b. October 19, 1858, d. 1858.
vii  Solomon D., b. December 2, 1859.
viii Lydia A., b. May 14, 1865, m. Frederick D. Pendleton.

Laban K. Pendleton, son of Isaac C., married Martha M. Dodge, August 8, 1870. Children:

i   Caro M., b. June 27, 1872.
ii  Freeman K., b. October 30, 1874.
iii George Lewis, b. November 27, 1877.

Isaac C. Pendleton, son of Isaac C., married Antoinette Veaton. Child:

i  Nellie R., b. May 25, 1875, m. John H. Bentson.

Rodolphus Pendleton, son of Samuel, Jr., born March 14, 1818. Married Margaret Sawyer, January 16, 1851. He was drowned between Turtle Head and Fort Point, October 26, 1866. Children:

i  Samuel, b. April 18, 1852.
ii Charles E., b. July 2, 1854.

iii  Herbert L., b. July 6, 1856.
iv  Camilla L., b. December 5, 1857.
v   Flora B., b. April 17, 1860.

Gamaliel R. Pendleton, son of Samuel, Jr., married Matilda Sawyer, February 3, 1847. He died in 1892. Children were :

i  Irene L., b. July 24, 1848, m. Edward Collins. Published June 6, 1867.
ii  Lovina J., b. August 31, 1851, m. Joseph Clark. She d. in 1872.
iii  Alpheus A., b. January 8, 1855, m. Maggie Whitcomb.

Peleg Pendleton, son of William Pendleton, was born in Westerly, R. I., February 12, 1732. He was a mariner, and was at the eastward often prior to the Revolutionary war. He came to Maine about 1782, and tradition says lived for a while on this island, and in 1783 removed to that part of Prospect now Searsport. He has now many descendants here. It is safe to say that his sons who came here, and his grandsons, have all been master mariners, and the sails of their ships have whitened every sea known to commerce. Capt. Peleg Pendleton died July 12, 1810. He married in Stonington, Ann Park, September 7, 1758. She was a woman fit to be the wife of an emigrant to a new country. She died March 20, 1817. Children, all born in Stonington :*

i  Peleg, Jr., b. June 22, 1760; lost at sea about 1781.
ii  Ann, b. June 4, 1762. Did not come to Maine.
iii  Abigail, b. December 2, 1764, d. December 7, 1764.
iv  Thomas, b. June 4, 1767. No record of marriage. Died June 8, 1801.
v  William, b. July, 1769. Lived in Islesborough and Searsport. Mar. Nancy Pendleton, of Islesborough. Published January 9, 1795. He died in Searsport, March, 1824. His children born in Islesborough were Nancy, b. April 27, 1797, probably married Timothy Porter, of Prospect. Lois, b. April 12, 1799;

----

* C. H. Pendleton, of Westerly, R. I., June 2, 1890, says that Peleg and all his children were born in Westerly.

Peleg, b. May 8, 1801, m. Betsey Brown, of Lincolnville; Joseph, b. April 11, 1803, and other children, born in Searsport.

vi Joseph, twin of William. Lived and died in Islesborough.

vii Abigail, b. August 11, 1771, m. Eben Griffin, of Searsport. She died 1815. Had a large family.

viii Lydia, twin sister of Abigail, m. —— Wilcox, of Stonington. Did not come to Maine.

ix Greene, b. June 21, 1774. Lived in Prospect (Searsport). Married Nancy Park. He died April 24, 1863. They had nine children, all deceased except one son, Capt. James G. Pendleton.

x Prudence, b. October 5, 1777, m. Alexander Nichols, of Searsport. He died March 6, 1824; she died November 24, 1854. They had many children, all now deceased; but many grandchildren living.

xi Phineas, b. September 26, 1780, of Searsport. Twelve children there.

Joseph Pendleton, son of Peleg, born July, 1769. He settled on the east side of the island, above Dark Harbor. He was a prominent man in the town for many years; a man of remarkable energy and industry, and a gentleman of the old school. He married Wealthy, daughter of Benjamin Thomas, Nov. 16, 1794. She died August 21, 1843, aged 67. He died August 21, 1858, aged 89. Children :

i Nancy, b. August 8, 1796, m. Ephraim Gould. She d. August, 1844.

ii Wealthy, b. January 19, 1798, d. unmarried, 1868.

iii Mary, b. November 22, 1801, d. 182-.

iv Susanna, b. January 29, 1803, m. Willis Fish, of Hope.

vi Joseph, b. November 20, 1805, married.

vii Sophronia, b. September 12, 1808, m. Amasa Hatch.

viii Peleg, b. February 12, 1811, m. Sibyl Sherman, 1837. He died September 30, 1838.

Son, Peleg, Jr., b. July 29, 1838, died.

ix Lydia Jane, b. January 29, 1814; m. first, Solomon Sprague, and second, John Bachelder.

x Nelson, b. November 28, 1816, m. Ann Fish. He died 1862.

xi  Ephraim, b. March 28. 1818, m. Ann Gilkey, February 10, 1846. He moved to Stockton, being there in 1885.
xii  Emeline, b. June 21, 1821, m. Amasa Hatch.  She d. 1861.

Joseph Pendleton, Jr., born Nov. 20, 1805.  Married Emily Richards.  Published April 11, 1836.  He died July 30, 1852, or 1853.  Children :

i  Amasa, b. May 15, 1837, d. December 23, 1838.
ii  Emily, b. September 17, 1840, d. March 22, 1842.
iii  Amelia, b. August 4, 1843, m. Edwin Eames.
iv  Ellen, b. October 9, 184-, m. Stephen Fairfield.
v  Ann, b. July 21, 1846.
vi  George, b. August 23, 1849.
vii  Sophronia E., b. December 7, 1853, m. Amasa Hatch.

## PHILBROOK FAMILY.

Jonathan Philbrook, with his wife and nine children, came from Greenland, N. H., to the second parish in Georgetown, now Bath, in 1742.  He built a house on the Point, near where the mansion of Governor King stood.  He was the principal inhabitant of the town, and in May, 1753, Jonathan Philbrook and forty-six others petitioned that they might be set off into a separate or second parish.  The petition was granted, and the second parish was organized April 2, 1754, at the house of Philbrook.  He and his son, Lieutenant Jonathan, were two of the committee to procure a minister.  In 1755 he and his sons built two coasting vessels, and I think they may be called the pioneers of shipbuilding in Bath.  Jonathan Philbrook, Jonathan Philbrook, Jr., and Job Philbrook, were petitioners for the new county (of Lincoln), in 1752.

William Philbrook, Joshua Philbrook, and Job Philbrook, were soldiers in the first company of the second parish in Georgetown (now Bath), in 1757.  In May, 1766, Job Philbrook was taken prisoner by the Indians, and carried to Canada, but was exchanged, and returned in October following.

Of the sons of Jonathan, William and Job came here. Tradition has it that Joseph also came, but I do not find him.

William Philbrook was born in 1718. One account says he married Charity Grant, but I find that he was published to Mary Grant, in Georgetown, Sept. 18, 1844. He settled on Seven-Hundred-Acre Island. Jonathan Stone, who surveyed Seven-Hundred-Acre Island in 1785, says he found "William Philbrook there," and that he came before the war. He was a petitioner from the island to the General Court in 1787. He was drowned about 1789, or just prior to that time. Children, as far as I see:

  i  James, was in Hampden 1777; had lot 78 there.
  ii  David, settled in Gardiner.
  iii  Jonathan, came here and lived in several places. Was in Hampden, in 1786. He was drowned prior to 1800. He had wife Mary, and son John, of Hampden, and Mercy, who m. John Bullock, of Camden.
  iv  William, Jr., settled in Islesborough.
  v  Joseph, settled in Islesborough.
  vi  Abigail, m. Mark Perry or John Perry, of Camden.
  vii  Molly, m. Joshua Lassell, of Lassell Island. Nine children.

William Philbrook, Jr., of Thomaston, and Diodama Lassell, of Warren, were published in Thomaston, May 6, 1780. He probably moved on to Seven-Hundred-Acre Island soon after. He was selectman in 1795. He was a large, powerful man, and his brother Joseph, though not equal to him in size, was a man of great muscular strength. During the war of 1812 their vessel was captured and they were taken prisoners by the British and sent to Castine. While on their way the prize crew went below to rest. The Philbrooks had a fight with the crew, took them prisoners, recaptured their vessel, and delivered the British as prisoners to the proper authorities. Children, probably :

  i   Elisha, m. Polly or Dolly Williams.
  ii  William, m. Lucy Drinkwater, of Northport. Published July 3, 1824.
  iii  Joseph.
  iv  Daniel.
  v   Oliver, m. Anna Stover, October 22, 1825.
  vi  Jabez.
  vii  Ambrose.

Jabez Philbrook, son of William Philbrook, Jr., married Judith Thayer, of Vinalhaven, Dec. 23, 1820. He died in 1884. Children, born in Islesborough :

  i   Jane, b. March 8, 1822.
  ii  Barbara A., b. November 18, 1824.
  iii  Lusetta, b. September 1, 1827.
  iv  Jabez A., b. October 6, 1831, m. Eliza J. McKenney, 1854.
  v   Joseph H., b. April 24, 1833, m. Elizabeth Flanders, March 1, 1853.
  vi  William, b. November 5, 1837.

Ambrose Philbrook, son of William, Jr., married Lydia Warren, Jan. 22, 1833. Children :

  i   Lydia D., b. October 16, 1833, m. James Jackson.
  ii  Ambrose B., b. July 1, 1835, m. Maria L. Philbrook, 1857.
  iii  George W., b. December 8, 1836.

Jonathan Philbrook married Phebe Holbrook, October 26, 1806.

Job Philbrook, son of Jonathan, born in Greenland, N. H.; baptized 1729. Settled in Georgetown. In 1744, when he was about fifteen years of age, he was taken prisoner by the Indians and carried to Canada, where he remained several years. He married first Mary, probably daughter of David Trufant, of Georgetown. Published there Nov. 12, 1750. She died about 1774. He married second, Dolly Hinckley, at Castine ; married third, widow

34

Hannah Coombs. He went to Vinalhaven, then to Castine, then to Seven-Hundred-Acre Island, Islesborough, then to Vinalhaven again, where he died about 1802. Children :

i   Jeremiah, b. in Georgetown, December 8, 1753, m. Sarah Leadbetter, of Fox Island. He died September 16, 1819. She died February 2, 1847, aged 88.

ii  Mary, b. ——, m. William Rackliff, Sen., of Rackliff Island, South Thomaston.

iii Lydia, m. John Smith, of Vinalhaven. Six children.

iv  Joel, b. August 14, 1759, m. in South Fox Island, and moved to Ohio.

v   Jane, b. ——, m. Isaiah Tolman, Matinicus, about 1780; his third wife. He was ancestor to all the Tolmans in Knox County.

vi  Job, by second wife, b. in Castine, November 8, 1775, of Islesborough.

vii Jonathan, lived in Prospect, when his son John was born, December 10, 1796, probably moved to Sedgwick. The late Hon. Luther G. Philbrook, of Castine, was grandson of Jonathan.

viii Hannah, by third wife.


Job Philbrook, Jr., born in Castine, November 8, 1775. Settled at Islesborough. Married Sylvina, daughter of Gideon Pendleton, Dec. 2, 1802. She died 1877, aged 89. He died Oct. 12, 1845. Children :

i    Job, Jr., b. September 26, 1803, of Islesborough and Frankfort.

ii   Sylvina, b. September 17, 1805, m. Elisha Grant, of Otis, Maine, 1821.

iii  Harriet, b. September, 1807, m. William Drinkwater, October, 1827.

iv   Henrietta, b. January 7, 1810, m. Capt. James Drinkwater, October, 1827, of Rockland.

v    Matilda, b. February 21, 1813, m. Albert Hutchins, of Penobscot.

vi   Daniel, b. April 30, 1815, m. Lydia Pendleton.

vii  Almira, b. May 24, 1817, m. Thatcher Coombs, October, 1836.

viii Elbridge G., b. May 11, 1819, m. Angelia Philbrook, August 30, 1844.

ix   Isaac, b. April 2, 1821. Lost at sea on a voyage to Savannah.

x Cordelia, b. September 13, 1823, m. William Ryder, January 1, 1851.

xi Lenora J., b. June 10, 1825, m. Joseph Knowles, of Belfast, October, 1842.

xii Grace A., b. September 18, 1828, m. Robert Knowles, of Islesborough, July 5, 1852.

xiii James J., b. October 10, 1831, m. Lydia D. Philbrook. Children were :

    1 George F., b. September 2, 1853.
    2 Laura P., b. January 28, 1856.
    3 Ellen F., b. October 11, 1859.
    4 Frank A., b. May 28, 1866.
    5 Chester J., b. August 30, 1870.

Job Philbrook, Jr., born Sept. 26, 1803. Married Alice Tyler, of Frankfort. He moved there, and was living in 1892. "Capt. Job Philbrook was born in Islesborough, Sept. 26, 1803. He quit going to sea about sixteen years ago, after following the business for forty years, and has resided in Winterport for the past eleven years. He has six children living, and three grandchildren. Mr. Philbrook is smart and stirring, and bids fair to live as long as his grandfather, for whom he is named, Mr. Job Philbrook, who settled in Vinalhaven, and was 104 years old when he died. Mr. Philbrook's grandfather on his mother's side, Mr. Gideon Pendleton, of Deer Island, New Brunswick, was 90 when he died." Children, all born in Islesborough :

i John Tyler, b. September 21, 1831, d. ——.
ii Betsey M., b. May 5, 1833, d. 1842.
iii Martin V., b. June 21, 1836.
iv Isaac, b. April 16, 1838.
v Rinaldo, b. November 14, 1841.

Daniel Philbrook, son of Job, was born April 30, 1815. Married Lydia Pendleton, daughter of Jonathan, Jr., June, 1831. Children :

i Lavinia M., b. November 22, 1837.
ii Almira E., (?) b. March 31, 1840.

iii   Flora E., b. ——, d. March 14, 1865.
iv   Daniel E., b. ——, d. Feb. 1, 1886.
v    Charles H., b. ——, d. October 9, 1870.

Joseph Philbrook was probably son of Jonathan, and brother of William, Sen., and Job, Sen., or the son of William, Sen.   He lived on Seven-Hundred-Acre Island, and was highway surveyor in 1794 ; petitioner to General Court in 1787.   He married Polly Lassell ; died June 13, 1841.   Children :

i    Submit, b. February 14, 1784, d. unmarried, February 26, 1859.
ii   Ruhama, b. May 17, 1786, m. William Lassell.
iii  Diodama, b. April 13, 1788, d. unmarried, August, 1819.
iv   David, b. November 30, 1789, married.
v    Lois, b. April 26, 1792, m. Ruel Philbrook, of Vinalhaven, July 12, 1812. She died in Northport, 1844.
vi   Rachel, b. March 15, 1800, m. Rev. Simon Cox, of Searsmont and Rockland.  He died January 28, 1851.  She d. January 8, 1872.
vii  Ambrose, b. December 20, 1804, m. Mary Woodbury.  He was drowned at Northport, September, 1824.  His son, Benjamin, b. March 4, 1821. (?)

David Philbrook, son of Joseph, born Nov. 30, 1789. Published Sept. 14, 1814.   Married Margaret Perry, of Vinalhaven.   He died Dec. 3, 1857.   Children :

i    Judson, b. April 8, 1821, m. Jane Pendleton.
ii   Angelia, b. March 16, 1824, m. Elbridge Philbrook.
iii  Orinda, b. March 1, 1826, married first, Captain Samuel or David Haskell, May 26, 1846, and second, David Williams, published January 28, 1851.
iv   Peleg, b. August 28, 1828, d. young.
v    Elona, b. 1830, m. John P. Farrow.
vi   David, Jr., b. 1832, m. Sarah Warren.  He was a soldier in the rebellion, and was killed at the battle of Fair Oaks, January 13, 1862.  She died February 24, 1859.  One child, Alfred, b. June 10, 1856, d. 1859.

Judson Philbrook, son of David, born April 18, 1821 ; married Jane, youngest daughter of John Pendleton, Jan.

13, 1847. He was drowned at sea, Jan. 30, 1868. She died Jan. 18, 1888. Children :

i Martha J., b. January 13, 1849, m. Delmar Gilkey. ·
ii Lucy A., b. March 1, 1852, m. Winfield S. Pendleton.
iii Judson A., b. September 10, 1855. Lost at sea April 23, 1875.

## PRESCOTT FAMILY.

Benjamin Prescott married Margaret McFarland. Children were :

i Susan M., b. February 25, 1852, d. 1853.
ii Julietta J., b. May 25, 1859.

## PRUDEN FAMILY.

Stephen Pruden married Temperance Williams, Sept. 11, 1823. He died. She married second, Rev. Ephraim W. Emery, Mar. 10, 1832. Children :

i Stephen H., b. January 16, 1825.
ii Temperance W., b. May 18, 1826.

## RANLETT FAMILY.

Matthew Ranlett married Dora E. Coombs. He was drowned Dec. 10, 1878. Children :

i Charles O., b. June 23, 1872, d. 1875.
ii William E., b. October 30, 1873.
iii Lottie Blanche, b. June 6, 1876.

Ephraim Ranlett married Mary E. Warren. Children :

i Jerry Herman, b. March 10, 1874.
ii Hattie E., b. May 17, 1875, d. 1878.
iii Lauraine E., b. October 20, 1878.

## REDMAN FAMILY.

Benjamin R. Redman married Ethelinda C. Gilkey. She died Feb. 25, 1878. Children :

i Walter H., b. September 22, 1864.
ii Chestina B., b. 1876, d. 1879.
iii Elnora, m. Charles Williams, of Emery.

Varnum R. Redman married Dora Trim.  Mr. Redman
was drowned at sea.  Child :

    i  Ethel L., b. September 19, 1877.

## RICH FAMILY.

Rev. Lemuel Rich was son of Samuel Rich, of East
Machias ; born there Jan. 10, 1780.   Baptist minister ;
came here in 1809.   Married Grace, daughter of John
Gilkey.   Published Feb. 16, 1810.   He moved to Union
in 1819, and preached there and in Hope for several years.
He was afterward a missionary, and is said to have
preached in every coast town from Kittery to Eastport,
and in the British provinces.   He was imprisoned at St.
Andrews, N. B., for preaching there without the permis-
sion of the parish priest of the church of England.*   He
died at Hope Corner, in 1864.   Children, some of whom
were born in Islesborough :

    i  Mary Ann, m. —— Sherman.
   ii  Lemuel F.
  iii  Statira, m. —— Pendleton.
  iv  Elizabeth, m. Albert Dunbar.
   v  Leonora, m. —— Elder.
  vi  John.
 vii  Joseph.

## RICHARDS FAMILY.

James Richards married Sarah J. Warren.   Children :

    i  Addie A., b. July 26, 1859, m. Benjamin Barry.
   ii  Nora E., b. May 16, 1867.
  iii  Grace C., b. March 12, 1881.

## RICHARDSON FAMILY.

John Richardson married Bathsheba, daughter of Samuel Pendleton, July 12, 1804.   It is said he was a French
naval officer under Napoleon.   They settled on French-

———

*Rev. W. H. Shailer's Historical Discourse, 1874, page 56.

man's Island. The wife died Oct. 10, 1843. He died
December, 1848. One child, who died young.

## ROBERTS FAMILY.

John Roberts was born on the island of Guernsey, in
the English Channel, in 1788. He was a cooper by
trade, and came to Islesborough in 1833, where he died,
Dec. 23, 1862. He married Christiana Dodge, daughter
of Mark Dodge. She was born April 13, 1803, and died
July 12, 1874. Children :

i Noah, b. June 22, 1826. He died in Honduras, September 21,
1852.
ii George W., b. November 23, 1829, m. Lydia E. Wood. There are
no children living.
iii Phebe C., b. May 15, 1834, m. Daniel Warren.
iv Zebulon M., b. June 1, 1836, d. February 3, 1863, m. Arvilla
Warren.

## ROBINSON FAMILY.

Joseph Robinson, from Lincolnville, married Sarah E.
Coombs, June 1, 1851. He died Oct. 24, 1853. Child :

i George H., b. December 5, 1852.

## ROLERSON FAMILY.

Phineas Rolerson married Celia A. Pendleton. He died
March 26, 1860. Children :

i Clara J., b. March 30, 1851, d. May 14, 1857.
ii Sarah I., b. August 25, 1855, m. Lyonais Pendleton.
iii Phineas L., b. September 5, 1856.
iv George W., b. June 14, 1858, d. December 16, 1877.
v Abbie F., b. January 30, 1860, m. Nason Pendleton.

## ROOKS FAMILY.

Henry Rooks married ————, daughter of Francis

Grindle. Removed to Northport or Lincolnville. Children, born in Islesborough :

  i   Louisa, b. May 15, 1831.
  ii  Emily A., b. December 1, 1832.
  iii Sarah A., b. April 7, 1835.


## ROSE FAMILY.

Henry Hancock Rose came from Block Island about 1785. Poundkeeper in 1808. Said to have changed his name to Henry. Wife Deborah. Children :

  i   Deborah, m. James Dodge.
  ii  Mercy.
  iii Daniel.
  iv  Huldah.
  v   Henry.


Henry Rose, son of Henry Hancock Rose, was born in New Shoreham, R. I., Aug. 9, 1784. Came here with his father. Married Hannah, daughter of Noah Dodge, Dec. 25, 1808. She was born May 27, 1786; died June 9, 1866. He died July 10, 1864. Children :

  i   Varnum G. Rose, b. November 23, 1810. He m. Mary, daughter
     of Joshua Dodge, January 1, 1834. Children :
     1   James F., b. October 18, 1839, d. 1891.
     2   Theresa, b. May 26, 1841, m. James F. Grindle.
     3   Julia A., b. June 26, 1842.
  ii  Rosannah, b. March 23, 1812, m. Franklin Dodge.
  iii Eleanor, b. June 10, 1814, m. Silas Bunker.
  iv  Theresa, b. June 12, 1816, d. aged 17.
  v   Henry H., b. January 23, 1822, m. Lois M. Coombs, February 7,
     1844. He d. East Boston, May 22, 1879.
  vi  Hannah, b. ——, m. James Dodge.
  vii Noah D., b. March 23, 1824, m. Nancy Thomas. Published
     August 2, 1851. He d. at sea. Children : /.        1863-
     1   Edward E., b. April 26, 1852.
     2   Edith E., b. July 3, 1854.
     3   Phineas P., b. August 28, 1857.
     4   Hugh M., b. April 27, 1861, died at sea.
  viii David H., b. ——, m. Julia Knowlton.

DAVID H. ROSE.
1830—1890

ix Marion W., b. December 31, 1827, m. Eliza J., daughter of
  Henry Coombs. She d. March 15, 1857. He d. December
  19, 1857. One child.
    1 Hannah M., b. June 25, 1852.

David Henderson Rose, born in Islesborough, Oct. 8,
1830; married Julia A. Knowlton, of Northport. Few
men had a more active life, and few men in Islesborough
have met with more success commanding a vessel at a very
young age. His voyages were foreign and coastwise,
always giving satisfaction to his owners. Pleasant, agreeable and sociable, he had many friends and no enemies.
For forty years he followed the sea, and during that time
he never met with a serious accident, never losing a
vessel, and always making money for his owners. During his last sickness he was patient, suffering without
complaint. All that kind hands could do was done for
him, to smooth the way from whence no traveler returns.
He was a member of the Masonic fraternity, and was
buried with Masonic rites. He died at his home, Feb. 21,
1890. Children :

  i Charles Albert, b. May 7, 1863, m. Sabrina E. Coombs.
  ii Eugene Henderson, b. November 18, 1864, m. Leola L. Fuller.
  iii Lena Mabel, b. April 10, 1867.
  iv Rita Evelyn, b. November 6, 1872, d. May 21, 1879.

## RYDER FAMILY.

Joseph Ryder was son of Lot Ryder, of Provincetown
and Vinalhaven, born 1775. He married Mary Lewis, sister of Benjamin Lewis, of Vinalhaven. She was born
——, 1780. He came to Islesborough about 1836, with
his family, and settled at Sabbath-Day Harbor. He
bought one hundred acres of land of Elisha Parker, on
the western side of Saturday Harbor, where his grandson
now lives. There was a grist mill on his land, at the head
of the harbor, where the old gentleman found employ-
35

ment. His sons were employed in fishing, and brought their fish to him, and he dried them for market. Mrs. Ryder died Jan. 13, 1857. He died May 16, 1858, aged 83. His estate was divided between his sons, Thomas, Benjamin and William. The children all came here and settled.

   i   Benjamin.
   ii  William.
  iii  Thomas.
  iv  Susan, m. Thomas Trim.
   v  Lucy, m. Isaac Burgess.
  vi  Betsey, m. Reuben Merrithew.
 vii  Mary, m. Henry McFarland, of Montville, February 14, 1841.

Benjamin Ryder, son of Joseph Ryder, born in Vinalhaven. Came here with his father, and settled at Sabbath-Day Harbor, on a part of his father's estate. In early life he was a fisherman. After his father's death he went into trade, and remained a trader until his death. He also kept a public house for many years—the "Seaside House"—upon the site of which now stands "The Islesborough" hotel. He was chosen by the town to hold offices of trust, which he faithfully and honestly performed. He was noted for his sociability, and was a man of piety, and honest in his convictions. He was prudent and industrious, a man with a kind heart and obliging disposition, a good neighbor, and a valuable townsman. He married Nancy Grover, of Deer Isle, Dec. 8, 1836. She was born Aug. 9, 1808, died August —, 1882. Mrs. Ryder was a good housewife and an excellent mother, and his family of three boys were well brought up and fitted for the responsibilities of life. He died Oct. 8, 1881, aged 67 years 9 months. They were buried in the Greenwood cemetery, where a monument is erected to their memory. Children:

  i  Joseph H., b. 1837, d. 1838.
 ii  Sarah H., b. December 28, 1838, d. 1838.
iii  Dorothy A., b. May 19, 1841, d. 1848.

BENJAMIN RYDER.
1813—1881.

MRS. NANCY RYDER.
1808—1882.

iv James, b. September 9, 1843, d. 1848.
v Isaac F., b. September 18, 1845, d. 1848.
vi Jason Roscoe, b. July 18, 1847, m. Rhoda M. Pendleton, December 24, 1870. Children :
    1 Bertha A., b. 1871.
    2 Blanche E., b. December 5, 1873.
    3 Lettie C., b. July 25, 1876.
    4 Fred C., b. 1879.
    5 Josie L., b. 1881, d. 1881.
    6 Mart L., b. 1884.
    7 Gertrude L., b. 1886.
vii Benjamin Lewis, b. August 8, 1848, m. Helen C. Coombs. He d. September 14, 1891.
viii James Henry, b. June 3, 1851, m. Ella Jane Grover.

William Ryder, son of Joseph Ryder, married first, Mary R. Trim, daughter of James, February 6, 1842. She died December 26, 1850, aged 30 years, 3 months, 18 days. He married second, Mrs. Cordelia Philbrook, January 19, 1854. Children :

i Melvina, b. October 24, 1843, d. ——.
ii Joseph L., b. October 24, 1845, m. Clara A. Pendleton.
iii Mary C., b. November 5, 1846, d. 1860.
iv Elvin J., b. June 5, 1849, m. Ada A. Coombs.
v Martha F., b. October 11, 1855, m. Emerson Coombs.
vi Mary, b. ——, m. Marion Coombs.

Joseph L. Ryder died 1882. Married Clara A. Pendleton, December 25, 1869. She died 1884. Children :

*i Kate Winifred, b. November 25, 1870, d. ——.
ii Herbert Elvin, b. October 7, 1872.
iii Luella M., b. October 3, 1875.
iv Clara J., b. May 17, 1877.

Elvin J. Ryder married Ada A. Coombs. He died July 22, 1877. Child :

i Ralph M., b. November 14, 1872.

Thomas Ryder, son of Joseph Ryder, married first, Betsey Hardy, of Camden, Feb. 22, 1838. She died Nov. 5,

1850. He married second, Vienna Richards, of Lincolnville, February 19, 1852. She died May 31, 1859. Married third, Sarah Wilson. Married fourth, Mrs. Maria Frye. Published August 1, 1862. Married fifth, Mrs. Lizzie Briggs, of Lincolnville, February 15, 1864. After his last marriage he moved to Lincolnville. Children:

i   William H., b. December 25, 1838.
ii  Georgiana, b. May 16, 1842, d. ——.
iii Morris M., b. November 9, 1840, d. May 2, 1841.
iv  Silvia A., b. August 10, 1850, d. 1850.
v   Georgiana, b. May 16, 1843.
vi  Harriet C., b. September 5, 1847, m. Elick Z. Henderson.
vii Betsey J., b. October 11, 1852, m. Robert Harvey.
viii Joseph H., b. June 18, 1845, married ——, d. ——.
ix  Sylvanus M., b. June 18, 1845, d. ——.
x   Franklin F., b. October 1, 1856.

### SARGENT FAMILY.

Jacob Sargent married Syrena Coombs, 1837. Children were:

i   Mary H., b. September 26, 1838.
ii  Hannah R., b. November 17, 1840.
iii Charles H., b. October 8, 1842.
iv  Jacob O., b. August 27, 1844.

### SAUNDERS FAMILY.

Cornelius Saunders, from Gloucester. He and his wife both died in Islesborough. Children:

i   Sally, m. Joseph Williams, November, 1804.
ii  Edward, m. Betsey Marshall.
iii Hannah, m. Samuel Hastings, of Sedgwick, August 1, 1804.
iv  Eliza, m. Fessington Chase. Published October 27, 1821.

Edward Saunders and son Edward, Sarah and Hannah, warned out of town, Nov. 2, 1802.

Jonathan Saunders married Elizabeth Orne, of Friendship, March 8, 1853. Child :

  i  Nathan Hobbs, b. May 11, 1834.

## SAWYER FAMILY.

Nathaniel Sawyer married Sarah Grover. He moved here from Isle au Haut. He was a ship carpenter. Born Nov. 18, 1792, died Nov. 26, 1870. She was born Sept. 16, 1794, and died February 14, 1871. Children :

  i  William, b. March 24, 1817, d. April 22, 1817.
  ii  Eliza B., b. August 28, 1818, d. January 19, 1888, m. David Collins. They had eight children.
  iii  Paul, b. August 24, 1820, d. January 30, 1888, m. Lovina E. Ray. They had four children.
  iv  Amelia, b. January 14, 1823, m. William Collins. They had ten children.
  v  Nathan, b. September 1, 1826, d. July 22, 1826.
  vi  Matilda T., b. September 1, 1826, m. Gamaliel R. Pendleton. They had three children.
  vii  George W., b. October 30, 1828, d. January 10, 1880, m. first Druzetta Sprague, second Arvilla Davis. They had three children.
  viii  Elbridge B., b. July 10, 1832, d. August 27, 1878. He married Hope Clark. They had four children.
  ix  Lydia A., b. March 3, 1837, m. Stephen B. Coombs. One child.
  x  Mary A., twin to Lydia A., m. Charles A. Coburn. They had four children.

Paul Sawyer married Lovina E. Ray. Children :

  i  Druzetta C., b. November 24, 1849, d. 1859.
  ii  Nathaniel W., b. March 28, 1852.
  iii  Arvilla E., b. May 16, 1857.
  iv  Florence S., b. February 3, 1861.

## SEELY FAMILY.

John Seely married Phebe, daughter of John Veazie, October 26, 1834. She died June 9, 1849, aged 39.

  i  Robert N., b. May 17, 1835.
  ii  Charles N., b. May 24, 1838.
  iii  Sabrina P., b. May 24, 1840, m. first, Wesley Brown; second, Fields C. Pendleton.

iv  Mighill E., b. August 10, 1842.
v  Lucinda J., b. July 16, 1844, m. Fields C. Pendleton, d. June
   26, 1866.

## SHERMAN FAMILY.

Valentine Sherman was one of the first Selectmen in
1789. He sold land to Robert Sherman, August 1, 1791,
for sixty pounds. Deed witnessed by Samuel Boyd and
William Pendleton. His children* I suppose were:

i  Robert, of Islesborough.
ii  James, of Islesborough.
iii  Susan.
iv  Sally.
v  Jane.
vi  Henry, m. Betsey, daughter of Harry Pendleton. She d. at the
    age of over 80. Probably removed to Camden. Large family.
vii  Ruth.
viii  Stephen, bought land of Thomas Pendleton, Jr., here, —100
     acres,— May 17, 1793, for 160 cords wood. Deed witnessed
     by William Elwell and Jonathan Parker.

Robert Sherman, son of Valentine Sherman, married
first ———; married second, Eunice Turner, April 8,
1792. He died April 29, 1835. Children:

i  James, b. February 8, 1788.
ii  Susannah, b. February 13, 1793, m. Abner Farrow, of Bristol,
   February 12, 1812.
iii  Sarah, b. November 20, 1795, m. William Kidder, of Lincoln-
    ville, January 29, 1825.
iv  Robert, Jr., b. March 6, 1798, of Islesborough.
v  Lydia, b. May 4, 1800, m. ———.
vi  Isaac, b. July 4, 1802, of Islesborough.
vii  Jane, b. October 31, 1804, m. Ebenezer Collamore, "both of
    Northport," June 21, 1829.

James Sherman, son of Robert, married Sibyl Gilkey,
daughter of Thomas Gilkey, sen., 1815. Children:

i  James Sherman, Jr., b. December 8, 1816, m. Lucy H. Parker,
   January 1, 1838. Lost at sea.

* It is possible that these were his brothers and sisters.

MRS. CATHERINE SHERMAN.
1801—Living.

ii Sibyl, b. September 25, 1818, m. first, Peleg Pendleton ; second, James Perry.
iii Thomas G., b. November 26, 1819, d. December 1, 1841.
iv Betsey, b. August 12, 1821, m. John F. Gilkey.
v Isaac W., b. September 17, 1823, m. Elizabeth Gilkey, December 7, 1843. He moved to Camden, and became a noted ship-master.
vi Winslow, b. July 22, 1825 ; unmarried.
vii Franklin, b. November 8, 1827 ; unmarried.
viii Rufus Benson, b. July 17, 1830. Lived in Lincolnville.
ix Maria F., b. January 26, 1833, d. June 9, 1834.
x Fostina J., b. October 27, 1835, d. September 25, 1836.
xi Caroline, b. January 12, 1837, d. unmarried.

Robert Sherman, Jr., born March 6, 1798, died April 29, 1835. He married Catherine Ames, Oct. 9, 1825, who was born July 12, 1801, and is the oldest person living in Islesborough. Nine children :

i Robert P., b. January 25, 1827, d. April 13, 1849.
ii Catherine B., b. 1828, m. Frederick G. Dix. Published May 9, 1853.
iii Royal Gilkey, b. September 27, 1830, m. Louise McCobb, of Lincolnville, and moved there.
iv Sabrina, b. November 30, 1832, d. January 11, 1839.
v Clementine, b. December 4, 1834. (?) m. Daniel Thomas.
vi Hudson, b. 1837, m. Jennie Berry.
vii Orisee A., b. April 4, 1843, m. first Otis Durgin, second Guilford D. Pendleton.
viii Justina J., b. February 4, 1846, m. Onslow Thomas.
ix Statira R., d. May 2, 1841.

Isaac Sherman, son of Robert, born July 4, 1802. Married Susan Ames, daughter of Thomas Ames, May 29, 1825. He died April 22, 1844. Children :

i Susan, b. December 12, 1825, m. Charles A. Pendleton.
ii Calvin W., b. July 30, 1828, m. Mary A. Pendleton.
iii Edson, b. October 30, 1830, m. Helen, daughter of Thomas Gilkey.
iv Relief Moody, b. March 3, 1833, m. Benjamin Warren.
v Lydia Phillips, b. June 17, 1835, m. Olney Scott.
vi Stephen V., b. January 2, 1838, d. September, 1860.
vii Delila A., b. December 22, 1840, m. George Farrow.
viii Melvina J., b. December 19, 1843, d. in Islesborough.

Capt. Calvin W. Sherman, son of Isaac, born July 30, 1828. Married Mary A., daughter of Robert Pendleton. Published Sept. 16, 1852. He was a Senator in 1882; Representative twice. Children :

   i   Llewellyn.
   ii  Frank W., unmarried.
  iii  Nora, m. Loranus Pendleton, son of Joseph.
  iv  Fred Bliss, unmarried.

Edson Sherman, son of Isaac, born October 30, 1830. Married Helen Gilkey. Children :

   i   Thomas E., b. September 27, 1856, d. 1891.
   ii  Edward L., b. April 14, 1860, d. 1861.
  iii  Willard R., b. January 31, 1868.
  iv  Flora M., b. May 3, 1862, m. Jerry Hayes.
   v  Charles E., b. May 20, 1877.

Hudson Sherman, son of Robert, Jr., born 1837. Married Jennie Berry. Capt. Hudson Sherman moved to Portland. He was a successful shipmaster for many years. He was noted for his successful treatment of yellow fever, and many captains are indebted to him. The dread disease lost half its terror when it was known Capt. Sherman was in port. He was always willing, by day or night, to render his services, as many captains and sailors can testify. Children :

   i  Armenia N., b. July 27, 1863, m. —— Varney.
   ii  Ulysses G., b. May 5, 1868.

## SKINNER FAMILY.

James Skinner married Lucy Parker, daughter of Jonathan. She died November 30, 1859. He died July 27, 1879. They had no children.

## SMALL FAMILY.

Joel Small married Frances D. Pendleton. Published January 18, 1862. She died September 29, 1876. Children were:

i Walter J., b. February 22, 1863, m. Rose Pendleton.
ii James I., b. September 27, 1865, m. Carrie R. Lawrence.
iii Flora E., b. March 6, 1873, m. Leslie Rolerson.
iv Sarah B., b. January 11, 1875, d. August 23, 1876.

## SMITH FAMILY.

Amos Smith married Elizabeth L. Dodge, September 30, 1855. Children:

i Erastus C., b. February 14, 1857.
ii Eliza A., b. August 26, 1859, m. Joseph Silver.
iii Ida M., b. January 25, 1862.

Frederick W. Smith. Children:

i Abby D., b. December 20, 1859.

## SPRAGUE FAMILY.

Widow Lydia Dodge Sprague came here with her children. In the north-west burying ground is a gravestone with the following inscription: "Jonathan Sprague died in New Shoreham, Aug. 2, 1803, aged 43. Wife Lydia died in Islesborough, June 4, 1848, aged 86. Both natives of New Shoreham, R. I. Erected by son, Simon Sprague." Children, all born in New Shoreham:

i Simon, b. May 27, 1784, of Islesborough.
ii Solomon, b. ——, of Islesborough.
iii Sally, m. Daniel McCurdy, January 21, 1804.
iv Lucy, m. Samuel Pendleton, Jr., 1810.
v Catherine, m. Henry Boardman, December 4, 1818.
vi Niobe, m. Joseph Boardman, July 20, 1824.
vii Lydia S., m. Thomas Williams. Published August 23, 1817.
viii Rathburn Dodge, m. Sarah C. Pendleton.

36

Simon Sprague, Sen., married Lydia Dodge.   He died
June 26, 1868.   Children :

  i  Simon, Jr., b. September 2, 1811, m. Elizabeth Pendleton.
  ii  Elzada, b. April 13, 1815, m. Noah Sargent.
  iii  Joshua, b. September 19, 1819, d. March 29, 1844.
  iv  Druzetta, b. March 15, 1818, m. George M. Sawyer.


Solomon Sprague, Sen., married first, Lucretia, daughter of Rathburn Dodge, February 12, 1812.   Married
second, Lydia J., daughter of Joseph Pendleton, October
5, 1834.   She was born January 29, 1814.   She married
second, John Batchelder.   He lived and died on his estate
at Sprague's Cove, which derived its name from him.
Children, all born in Islesborough.   Perhaps not in order:

  i  Lucretia, b. 1812.
  ii  Barbour B., b. June 9, 1815.
  iii  Maria, b. August 29, 1821, m. John Veazie, Jr.
  iv  Angeline, b. April 24, 1825, d. November 27, 1832.
  v  Elvira, b. August 22, 1827, d. August 11, 1843, or July 10, 1845.
  vi  Angeline, b. October 1, 1832, d. June, 1847.
  vii  Emeline P., b May 4, 1839, m. George E. Keller, 1859.
  viii  Solomon, b. December 25, 1842, d. January 9, 1845.
  ix  Lydia Jane, m. Henry Coombs, 2d.
  x  Rose E., b. October 3, 1849, d. September 22, 1862.
  xi  Herbert J., m. Mary Pendleton.
  xii  Joshua D., b. April 25, 1845.


Rathburn D. Sprague was born on Block Island, the son
of Jonathan and Lydia Sprague.   He was a mariner until
he was 35 years of age, always sailing in ships on foreign
voyages.   He held offices of trust in the town for a number of years.   Was a justice of the peace, notary public,
deacon of the First Baptist church, and an insurance agent
for over forty years.   He married Sarah C., daughter of
William and Peggy Pendleton, Feb. 7, 1833.   She was
born Sept. 23, 1807.   He died Nov. 9, 1880, aged 84.
Children :

  i  Leonidas Bray, b. December 26, 1833, d. October 12, 1836.

RATHBURN D. SPRAGUE.

ii  William Pendleton, b. October 1, 1835, m. Marilla Parker.
iii  Sarah J., b. October 6, 1837, m. L. P. Gilkey.
iv  Laurinda A., b. October 25, 1840, m. George T. Wyman, who
    died on board the steamship Saxon, February 4, 1886, on a
    reef in the Bahama Islands, where the ship went to pieces.
    Capt. Wyman's son, Frank E., who was with him, was
    drowned at the same time.
v  Joseph A., b. August 9, 1845, m. Lucena Coombs.
vi  Ophelia A., b October 11, 1851.

William P. Sprague, born Oct. 1, 1835. Merchant and
postmaster, North Islesborough. Married first, Marilla
Parker, June 16, 1860. She died Nov. 7, 1880, aged 38
years 4 months. He married second, Isabella Dodge.
Children :

i  Willie W., b. December 4, 1861, m. Mildred Veazie.
ii  Eugene Hale, b. May 23, 1864, m. ――――.
iii  Marilla B., b. June 6, 1871, d. 1881.
iv  Thomas R., b. April 7, 1878.
v  Lelia.
vi  Nettie.

Simon D. Sprague, Esq., born September 2, 1811,
married Elizabeth Pendleton, June 14, 1853. He died
November 20, 1877. Children :

i  Lydia E., b. August 13, 1854, m. Frank Adams.
ii  Joshua S., b. January 30, 1856, d. 1879.
iii  Druzetta F., b. July 4, 1858.
iv  Elzada R., b. July 13, 1860.
v  Frederick A. L., b. November 5, 1863, m. Flora Ladd.
vi  Etta A., b. March 15, 1866.
vii  Clara J., b. July 13, 1868.
viii  Cora A., b. June 22, 1870, d. 1879.
ix  Lottie M., m. Jason Ladd.

John Sprague (probably Jr.), was a juryman in 1791.
Rathburn D. Sprague used to call him "Uncle."
Tradition says that he used to swim to the main
land and back quite frequently. He was one of the
commissioners appointed by the General Court, March 9,

1797, to settle and quiet settlers on the island. I find no family.

## STONE FAMILY.

Martin Stone married Lydia Boardman. Published 1823. Removed to Belfast. His widow married second, Timothy Warren. Child, born in Islesborough :

 i  Nancy, b. November 7, 1823, died June 8, 1835.

William Stone married Margaret Boardman. Published June 14, 1823. He died in Belfast. Children, born in Islesborough :

 i  Margaret, b. November 30, 1824.
 ii  Mary P., b. July 21, 1828.

## THOMAS FAMILY.

Benjamin Thomas, from Cape Elizabeth ; one of the first settlers. The Jordan Genealogy says : "Benjamin Thomas, of Long Island, Penobscot Bay, married Mary, daughter of Robert Jordan, of Cape Elizabeth. She was born in 1747. He died about 1821. She died about 1828." Children, probably :

 i  Benjamin, Jr.
 ii  Mary, b. June 3, 1774, m. James Trim, December, 1792.
 iii  Wealthy, m. Joseph Pendleton.
 iv  Lucy, m. Robert Coombs.

David Thomas, Jr., from Marshfield, about 1784. Lived on Seven-Hundred-Acre Island. Seemed to have been of a different family from Benjamin. Deacon of Baptist church ; married Nabby, daughter of Nathaniel Pendleton. "Mrs. Abigail, mother of Jacob Thomas, died January 17, 1867, aged 99 years." Children :

 i  Tilden, b. February 22, 1786, d. January 15, 1827.
 ii  John, b. May 16, 1788, d. young.
 iii  Elisha, b. November 14, 1790.

iv John, 2d, b. June 2, 1793.
v Daniel, b. April 30, 1796.
vi Mercy, b. November 22, 1798.
vii Abigail, b. June 17, 1802.
viii David, Jr., b. April 20, 1804.
ix Lydia, b. August 18, 1805.
x Isaac, b. December 15, 1807.
xi Rhoda, b. February 27, 1810.
xii Jacob, b. June 6, 1812, m. Julia A. Hopkins. Published December 9, 1836. Isaac and Jacob lived and died on the estate of their father.

Daniel Thomas, probably son of David, married Rebecca Perry. Published 1821. Children:

i Rebecca, b. October 14, 1821.
ii Abigail, b. June 20, 1823.
iii Daniel W., b. February 14, 1828.
iv Iddo, b. October 23, 1833, d. unmarried.

Daniel W. Thomas married Clementine Sherman. Children:

i Charles Chester, b. May 25, 1858, m. Rosalind Parker.
ii Caro Anna, b. September 9, 1860, m. Preston Merrill.
iii Ernest, b. January 27, 1864, m. Maggie Babbidge.

Isaac Thomas, son of David, born December 15, 1807. Married first Angelica Warren, October 26, 1839. She was born December 10, 1808; died July 9, 1841. Married second, Betsey J. Farrow, March 7, 1843. Married third, Mrs. Mary, widow of Daniel Thomas. Published December 6, 1859. He died May 27, 1881, aged 75 years 6 months. Children:

i Ann M., b. May 11, 1841.
ii Roseltha, b. December 20, 1843.
iii Isaac A., b. October 7, 1845, d. October 10, 1845.
iv Sarah J., b. February 5, 1850.

Benjamin Thomas, brother of Charles, married Jane Pendleton September 4, 1823. She died in Camden, 1891. He died January 26, 1870. Children:

i Benjamin, Jr., b. February 16, 1823, d. 1823.

ii   Jane, b. August 8, 1824, m. Andrew Pendleton.
iii  Isaac, b. February 16, 1826, m. Augusta Porter, of Camden.
iv   Avery G., b. Feb. 16, 1826, d. May 13, 1828.
v    Julia M., b. June 30, 1829, m. Judson Dodge.
vi   Sylvina, b. September 28, 1831, m. Elbridge Hewes.
vii  Nancy G., b. April 20, 1835, m. Noah Rose.
viii Hannah L., b. March 18, 1840, m. W. E. Currier, of Camden.
ix   William H., b. February 23, 1842; was a soldier in the Rebellion.
x    Amanda, b. May 26, 1843, m. Adelbert Hooper.
xi   Edward E., b. October 11, 1844, was drowned off the coast of
     North Carolina. Captain Hewes, his brother-in-law, was
     drowned at the same time.
xii  Onslow, b. November 10, 1846, m. Justina J. Sherman. He was
     lost at sea.

Eno A. Thomas married Emma A. Heal, October 7, 1865. Children:

i    Eunice F., b. September 2, 1868.
ii   Walter H., b. May 27, 1870.

Castanus M. Thomas married Adelia F. Pendleton, October 3, 1862. Children, not in order:

i    William M., b. August 30, 1865.
ii   Jennie D., b. August 30, 1865.
iii  Benjamin.
         Jason H., Eunice, Cassie, Bert or Herbert.

John Fred Thomas died February 2, 1873. Married Sarah Thomas. Child:

i    Isaac Fred, b. October 3, 1872, d. of small pox.

Joel Thomas married Catherine M., daughter of Robert Pendleton. She was born September 8, 1827. No children by Thomas. He died on Seven-Hundred-Acre Island. She married second, Martin S. Coombs. Published December 26, 1852.

Rev. Charles Turner Thomas married Rachel or Mary Gilkey, of Islesborough, in Castine, January 30, 1788, by Colonel Johonnot. They seem to have had four sons :

i Benjamin.
ii Isaac.
iii Caleb.
iv Charles.

## TILDEN FAMILY.

Elihu Tilden or Elisha Tilden. Children from Islesborough Records :

i Rufus, b. September 23, 1808, d. January 9, 1809.
ii Mary A., b. January 8, 1810.
iii Polly, b. September 1, 1812.
iv Josiah, b. January 31, 1815.
v Elisha, b. July 28, 1817.
vi Isaac, b. April 18, 1819.
vii Caroline, b. June 3, 1821.
viii Emily, b. August 11, 1823.
ix Priscilla, b. September 24, 1826.
x Roxanna, b. May 19, 1829.
xi Thomas Orcutt, b. May 11, 1832, d. November 3, 1832.

## TOOTHAKER FAMILY.

Nathaniel Toothaker lived in West Bay Cove. He and children moved out of town, Nov. 2, 1802. Two of his daughters :

i Mary or Mercy, m. William Howard of Northport, Mar. 23, 1807.
ii Thyer or Bethiah, m. Luther Simmons, same date.

## TRIM FAMILY.

Godfrey Trim was here in 1793 ; selectman in 1798. Children :

i James, b. September 5, 1771.
ii Godfrey, b. ——, moved to Corinth ; his descendants there and in the vicinity.
ii Robert, m. Lucy Marshall.
iii Lois, m. Thomas Marshall, September 10, 1791.

iv   Prudence, m. Israel Dodge.  He was drowned in 1807 (?)  She
    d. December 5, 1854, aged 76 years, 8 months.
v    Desire, (?) m. Isaac Turner.
vi   John (?)


James Trim, son of Godfrey, born Sept. 5, 1771.  He
married Mary, daughter of Benjamin Thomas, December
13, 1792.  She was born June 3, 1774, died August 3,
1860.  He died December 9, 1820, aged 49.  Children :

i     Wealthy, b. January 10, 1794, m. Jesse Coombs, 1813.
ii    Eunice, b. February 26, 1797, m. Joshua Farrow, 1821.
iii   James, Jr., b. December 23, 1800, went to New York.
iv    Robert, 2d, b. June 22, 1803, m. Lucena P. Coombs.
v     Godfrey, b. November 7, 1805, m. Sarah Nash, October 21, 1841.
vi    Olive, b. February 26, 1808, m. David Warren.
vii   Lois, b. August 12, 1811, m. Pillsbury Coombs, 1832.
viii  Thomas, b. March 7, 1815, m. Susan L. Ryder, June 22, 1839 ;
    moved to Bucksport.
ix    Mary, b. July, 1818, m. William Ryder.
x     Desire, m. Jesse Coombs.


Robert Trim, son of Godfrey, married Lucy Marshall.
She died March 6, 1863.  He died May 22, 1854.  He
and his sons were master mariners, noted for their ability.  Children :      •

i     Elisha R., b. July 13, 1806, m. Phebe, daughter of Amos Wil-
    liams, January 23, 1834.  She died May 28, 1876, aged 74 years
    4 months.  He died February 6, 1871.  Children :
    1   Elisha Moore, b. September 22, 1837.  He as "of
        Stockton," m. Clarissa Clark, January 31, 1865.  He
        moved to Stockton, then to Bangor, where he now
        resides.  He is a master mariner.
    2   Robert, b. July 20, 1843, m. Emily —— ; she died
        September 13, 1866, aged 19 years, 9 months 24 days ;
        m. second, Mary Titus.
    3   Joseph S., b. September 4, 1839, unmarried, d. July 9,
        1864.
ii    Lucy, b. January 20, 1808, d. March 5, 1808.
iii   Cornelia, b. December 12, 1809, m. Samuel Duncan, of Lincoln-
    ville.  Had children.

iv Robert J., b. December 12, 1816, d. in New Orleans, October 1, 1843.
v Joseph W., b. December 28, 1818, m. Julia A. Pendleton, September 1, 1842. Children:
    1 Joseph O., b. August 15, 1843.
    2 Robert O., b. October 11, 1844.
    3 Daughter, b. ——.
    4 Son, b. ——.

Godfrey Trim, son of James, born November 7, 1805, married Sarah Nash, October 24, 1841. He died Feb. 14, 1866. Children:

i Amelia, b. January 5, 1843, m. William Dodge.
ii Owen, b. January 16, 1845, drowned at Delaware City, August 15, 1876.
iii Amariah, b. June 17, 1853, m. Anna Warren.
iv Medora, b. November 1, 1856, m. Varnum R. Redman. He was lost at sea in bark Europa.
v Austin, b. ——, m. Adeline Bunker. Children: Amariah, aged 17, Arthur 15, Melvin 13, Austin 11 and William 9, in 1892.

John Trim, son of Godfrey, Sen., married Mary, daughter of Stephen Pendleton. Published June 13, 1815. Probably moved to Eastport or St. Andrews, N. B.

### TUCKER FAMILY.

Thomas E. Tucker married Charity Dodge. Children were:

i Mary E., b. February 2, 1859.
ii Hattie J., b. November 6, 1861.

### TURNER FAMILY.

Adam Turner was in Islesborough early. Mary Turner, daughter of "Long Island," was married from Thomaston, February 11, 1788.

Samuel Turner, of Islesborough, sold David Thomas, Jr., of Marshfield, Mass., one hundred acres of land on the north end of Seven-Hundred-Acre Island, bounded west by Penobscot Bay, east by Nathaniel Pendleton, Pendleton Island, and adjoining William Philbrook's farm, for 500 pounds, Sept. 7, 1783. Samuel Turner sold lots 12, 13, 14, Chadwick's plan, to Thomas Ames, July 13, 1784, for 400 pounds. I think he moved to Lincolnville, where I find a Samuel Turner, in 1797. Children :

   i  Isaac, m. Desire Trim.
  ii  Eunice, m. Robert Sherman, April 8, 1792.

Isaac Turner, probably son of Samuel Turner, by some said to have been first child born on the island. He lived on the northerly end of the island. He married Desire, daughter of Godfrey Trim, prior to 1800. He and his brother-in-law were drowned between Islesborough and Castine, February 17, 1807. Children :

   i  Levi, m. Louisiana, daughter of Jabez Ames. He died at the house of his son-in-law, in Bangor, April 27, 1877, aged 78 years, 2 months 23 days. Children :
       1  Arvilla J., m. Charles W. Gould, in Bangor, July 13, 1851.
       2  Daughter, m.     Workman.
  ii  Desire, m. Jesse Coombs, " both of Islesborough." Published March 2, 1816. He was born April 4, 1789.
 iii  Prudence, m. Jacob Coombs. Published April 15, 1821.
 iv  Eunice, m. when past middle age, ——Maddocks, of Lincolnville.

### VEAZIE FAMILY.

Samuel Veazie, Jr., son of Rev. Samuel Veazie, of Hull and Harpswell, came here about 1785. He was born in Hull, 1750. Settled on the north-east side of the island, near Coombs' Cove. He was a mariner and a town officer. He married Phebe Holbrook, of Harpswell, about 1775. He died in 1828. She died in 1832. Children, probably not in order :

   i  Samuel, Jr., of Islesborough.
  ii  John, of Islesborough.
 iii  Rachel, m. Lemuel Drinkwater, of Northport ; both lived and died there.

iv  Lucy, m. Timothy Harding.
 v  Martha, m. Fields Coombs, about 1801 — his second wife.
vi  Stephen, school committee in 1808, m. Martha Hardy; moved to
      Corinth.
vii Abiezer, of Islesborough and Camden, where he died about
      1840, aged 51 years, 9 months, 21 days. His descendants are in
      Camden and Rockland. He married Grace, daughter of Jabez
      Ames, of Islesborough. She died in Camden. Abraham Ogier,
      of Camden, was appointed administrator on his estate, May 4,
      1841.


Samuel Veazie, Jr., born about 1779. Came here with
his father. He married Bridget Coombs. She died April
12, 1854, aged 69 years, 11 months 18 days. He died
Dec. 2, 1841, aged 62 years, according to his gravestone.
Children :

  i  Johnson, b. August 6, 1804, m. Sarah A. Hatch.
 ii  Jordan, b. October 15, 1806, m. Philena Parker, February 11, 1836.
      He died January 14, 1839, and the widow married second,
      Andrew P. Gilkey, in 1841.
iii  Samuel, b. April 7, 1808, m. Deborah M. Hatch. Moved to Dix-
      mont, then Brewer, and died there. One son, Samuel Merritt.
 iv  Wales, b. January 10, 1810 ; unmarried ; died in Hingham, Mass.,
      October 7, 1864.
  v  Azubah, b. November 12, 1812, m. Andrew P. Gilkey, March 20,
      1835.
 vi  Charles, b. July 3, 1815, d. i- 1835.
vii  Sally, b. May 13, 1817, m. George Warren, December 20, 1835.
viii Caroline, b. April 15, 1819, m. William Avery Parker, December
      30, 1841. She d. November 30, 1875.
 ix  Otis C., b. July 11, 1820, married Deborah Coombs.
  x  Albion K. P., b. March 12, 1824, m. Mary Withee, of Hermon.
      Published September 28, 1848. She died and he married again.
      Commission merchant ; resides in Bangor.
 xi  Angelia, b. February 17, 1828, m. Otis F. Coombs.
xii  William F., b. April 1, 1829, m. Deborah Parker.


Johnson Veazie, son of Samuel, born Aug. 6, 1804,
married first Sarah A., daughter of Isaac Hatch, Feb. 11,
1834. He married second, Ann C. Otis. Published in
Bangor, Feb. 23, 1851. He moved to Dixmont, then to

Monroe, then to Bangor. He died on the way to Bucksport, in the stage. Mrs. Veazie died Oct. 7, 1864, aged
54. Children:

 i Wales, d. November 26, 1865, aged 30 years, 10 months.
 ii Charles.
 iii Azubah, m. —— Dunbar.
 iv Flavilla, m. first, —— Lane; second, —— Atwood, and resides in
  Brewer.


Otis C. Veazie, son of Samuel, born July 11, 1820,
married Deborah Coombs, January 21, 1844. He died
July 4, 1848. She married second, John Veazie. Children were:

 i Samuel, b. October 30, 1844, m. Zilpha Hatch. Children:
  1 Waldema, b. September 2, 1872.
  2 Azubah, b. March 30, 1877.
 ii Otis C., b. October 29, 1846, m. Lizzie Wood.
 iii Marcellus, b. September 8, 1848, m. Sabrina Warren, daughter
  of James, of Brewer.


William F. Veazie, born April 1, 1829, married Deborah
Parker. Published November 25, 1848. Children:

 i William F., Jr., b. June 16, 1850. Lost at sea on the brig Zavilla
  Williams, November 17, 1875, aged 25 years, 5 months 1 day.
 ii Ada E., b. September 30, 1854, d. January 12, 1857.
 iii Zoa J., b. November 28, 1858, m. William Sawyer.
 iv Mildred, m. William W. Sprague.


John Veazie, son of Samuel, born 1786, married Naomi,
daughter of Fields Coombs, 1814. He died September
15, 1841, aged 55 years 15 days. She died March 9,
1872, aged 82 years, 1 month 9 days. Children:

 i Phebe, b. November 20, 1814, m. John Seely. She d. June 9,
  1819.
 ii Rachel, b. April 21, 1815, m. Isaac Rooks, of Appleton, 1839.
 iii John, b. February 3, 1818, m. Maria R. Sprague.
 iv Rufus, b. June 24, 1821, m. Lucinda E. Trim. Published June
  18, 1858. He d. in Rockland.
 v Jane, b. May 27, 1824, m. Michael Felker, of Searsport, 1846.

vi Clarinda, b. April 15, 1825, m. Nathan F. Fuller, of Searsport, October 18, 1856.
vii James Harrison, b. May 18, 1829, m. Adeliza Dix, Nov. 20, 1854.
viii Lorana, b. April 19, 1832, m. Noah Roberts, July 2, 1848.

John Veazie, Jr., b. Feb. 3, 1818, married first, Maria R. Sprague, Jan. 11, 1841. She died June 20, 1854. He married second, Mrs. Deborah Veazie, Dec. 28, 1859. She died April 26, 1888, aged 63 years. Children : *

i Joanna P., b. July 5, 1841, m. Andrew Fairfield.
ii Naomi A., b. November 26, 1842, m. Edwin Coombs.
iii Laura A., b. April 10, 1846, m. Stephen Babbidge.
iv Lucretia S., b. June 6, 1850, m. Edwin Coombs.
v Eva E., b. April 7, 1852; unmarried; died.

James Harrison Veazie, son of John, b. May 18, 1829, married Adeliza, daughter of William Dix, Nov. 20, 1854. She died July 23, 1886, aged 50 years, 1 month 2 days. Children:

i Sardell, (?) b. 1855, m. William P. Norton.
ii Ann A., b. June 1, 1864. Teacher in Bangor; married.
iii Urania, m. Edward Preble.

## WARREN FAMILY.

Samuel Warren seems to have come from Bristol. Lived near Jonathan Holbrook. Selectman in 1791. Tradition says his wife's name was Porter. Children, not in order.

i John, a Quaker minister, visited England at one time.
ii George, m. Lydia Hatch, 1803.
iii Benjamin, m. Abigail Hatch, 1810.
iv Samuel, m. Ruth Sherman, 1800.
v Betsey, m. Isaac Hatch, July 16, 1808.
vi Patty, m. Jonathan Coombs, 1790.

Samuel Warren, Jr., married Ruth Sherman. He died May 3, 1859, aged 82. Wife died Aug. 30, 1835. Children were :

i David, b. October 6, 1799, m. Olive Trim.

ii   Lydia, b. December 7, 1801 ; unmarried.
iii  Samuel, b. February 18, 1804, m. Philena Hatch, July 1, 1840.
     He d. August 5, 1870.  No children.
iv   Michael, b. February 16, 1806, m. Belona Woodward, January 4,
     1829.
v    James, b. July 4, 1808.
vi   George 2d, b. June 12, 1812, m. Sally Veazie, December 20,
     1835.  She was b. May 3, 1812, d. September 6, 1891.  He
     d. December 2, 1890.


George Warren, son of Samuel, Sen.  George Warren,
"of Warren's Island," married Lydia, daughter of Jeremiah Hatch, 1803.  She was born July 22, 1782.  Children were :

i     Isaac, b. April 17, 1804, m. Sally Pendleton, 1826.
ii    Jeremiah, b. August 4, 1806, m. Abigail Thomas, 1827.
iii   Lydia Porter, b. October 16, 1808, m. Ambrose Philbrick.
iv    Timothy, b. September 7, 1810, m. Lydia Stone, 1835.
v     Elmira, b. March 2, 1813.
vi    Thomas, b. May 12, 1815, m. Hannah Bullock, 1838.
vii   Angelia, b. December 10, 1818, m. Isaac Thomas, October 26,
      1839.
viii  George Winslow, b. December 16, 1824, m. Martha Flanders,
      1849.  He was drowned, October 17, 1875.


Benjamin Warren, son of Samuel, married Abigail,
daughter of Jeremiah Hatch, Jr., 1811.  She died March
25, 1847.  He died Oct., 1862.  Children :

i     Stephen, b. December 12, 1811, d. June 7, 1889.
ii    Nicholas Porter, b. August 25, 1813, m. Harriet Thompson.  He
      was master of ship Northern Chief, and d. on the passage from
      New York to Liverpool, April 26, 1857.  His widow m. second,
      A. D. Bean, of Belfast.
iii   Daniel, b. November 4, 1815, m. Bathsheba Pendleton.
iv    Mary J., b. September 12, 1818, m. Reuben Herrick, of North-
      port, May 7, 1838.
v     Elizabeth, b. November 26, 1820, d. June, 1822.
vi    Samuel, b. April 28, 1823; unmarried.  He was drowned from
      brig Gazelle.
vii   Isaac W., b. September 16, 1825.  Shot in Bangor, while gunning,
      in 1839.

viii   Benjamin A., b. September 7, 1828, m. Relief Sherman, November, 1850.   He died.   She m. second William S. Dodge, February 13, 1861.
  ix   Abigail, b. September 7, 1828, d. January 27, 1847.

David Warren, son of Samuel, Jr., born October 6, 1799.   David Warren was an honest man, and an honor to the town.   He died June 1, 1879.   Married first, Olive, daughter of James Trim, January 31, 1830.   She was born February 26, 1808, died October 6, 1842.   Married second, Mrs. Wealthy Lawry, February 3, 1844.   Married third, Mrs. Lucretia Spinney, of Georgetown, December 29, 1854.   She died December 3, 1867.   Children :

  i   David, b. December 17, 1832.   Moved away.
 ii   Olive Relief, b. August 3, 1838, m. Joseph R Grover.

George Warren, son of Samuel, Jr., born June 12, 1812. Married Sarah Veazie, December 20, 1835.   He died Dec. 2, 1890.   She died Sept. 6, 1891.   Children :

  i   Sarah J., b. September 11, 1837, m. James Richards.
 ii   George Alden, b. January 27, 1840, m. Lucinda Parker.
iii   Caroline, b. September 15, 1841, m. Philip O. Coombs.
 iv   Lydia Ellen, b. October 12, 1843, m. Andrew W. Spinney.
       He was drowned November 19, 1875.
  v   Ann, b. July 16, 1853, m. Amariah Trim.
 vi   Ruth E., b. October 14, 1856.
vii   Addie E., b. February 14, 1859.
viii   Edna, m. James Wargent.   He was drowned in Belfast bay.
 ix   Cyril.
  x   John, m. ——— Parker.

James Warren, was son of Samuel, Jr., b. July 4, 1808. He married first, Sabrina Parker, Oct. 10, 1840.   He moved to Brewer, and married second, there, Mrs. Laura A. Burr.   He was master of brig Annandale, which was wrecked on the coast of New Jersey, in December, 1869, and the master was drowned.   Children by first wife :

  i   Sabrina, m. Marcellus Veazie.
 ii   David, m. Nettie Wyman, and now resides in Foxborough, Mass.

Daniel Warren, son of Benjamin, born November 4, 1815, married first, Bathsheba, daughter of Mark Pendleton, December 21, 1837. She was born May 16, 1817. He married second, Mrs. Caroline Wood, January 5, 1863. Children, perhaps not in order :

   i   Lydia Porter, m. Solomon P. Coombs.
   ii  Nancy J., b. August 30, 1839, m. Moses J. Nelson, June 10, 1858.
  iii  Adeline V., b. February 16, 1841.
  iv  Daniel A., b. August 12, 1843.
   v  Arvilla, m. Zebulon M. Roberts, 1857.
  vi  Samuel, b. January 2, 1845.
 vii  Abigail, b. September 18, 1848.
viii  Rosanna D., b. September 28, 1850.
  ix  Mary A., b. December 12, 1852.
   x  Relief M., b. September 23, 1854.
  xi  Zebulon R., b. October 30, 1864.
 xii  Benjamin A., b. September 14, 1866.
xiii  Celia F., b. September 14, 1870.
xiv  Bertha J., b. September 7, 1875.

Stephen Warren, son of Benjamin, born December 11, 1811, died June 7, 1889. Married Lydia Pendleton, daughter of Joseph, February 23, 1832. She died Sept. 10, 1861, aged 62 years, 9 months, 10 days. Children :

   i   William S., b. December 3, 1836, m. Clementina Pendleton, September 15, 1857.  One son :
        i  Albert W., b. July 23, 1858.
  ii  Sarah J., b. September 19, 1838.
 iii  Ophelia P., b. May 14, 1842.
 iv  Stephen H., b. February 25, 1844.
  v  Benjamin A., b. October 17, 1845.
 vi  Mary E., b. June 26, 1849.
 vii  Harriet L., b. June 28, 1854, d. June 20, 1872.
viii  Noyes, (?) d. June 26, 1873.

Timothy Warren, son of Geo. Warren, Sen., born Sept. 7, 1810. Married first, Sarah, daughter of Dodge Pendleton ; married second, Mrs. Lydia (Boardman) Stone, Jan. 19, 1835. Children :

   i  Maria, b. May 17, 1837.
  ii  Napoleon B., b. September 17, 1838.

Isaac Warren, son of George Warren, born April 7, 1804. Died March 15, 1858. Married Sally, daughter of Dodge Pendleton. Published April 12, 1826. Children:

  i  Isaac, b. August 4, 1828, m. Phebe A. Marshall, June, 1850; m. second, Mrs. Mary J., widow of Capt. Jacob W. Wyman.
  ii  Alfred Porter, b. February 14, 1830, m. Marinda French.
  iii  Sarah Pendleton, b. April 23, 1834, m. David Philbrook.

Jeremiah Warren, son of George, born August 4, 1806. Married Abigail Thomas, in 1827. She died October 14, 1875, aged 73. Children:

  i  Jeremiah, b. November 15, 1827, m. first, Caroline H. Dodge. Published December 26, 1851. M. second, Mrs. Marinda C. Warren. Published November 25, 1857.
  ii  Elizabeth, b. April 12, 1828, m. Eben L. Hopkins, July 6, 1855.
  iii  Franklin, b. October 3, 1836, died unmarried.
  iv  Martin V. B., b. November 14, 1838, m. —— Staples, of Rockland. Children:
      1  Eva B. and Agnes B., b. January 27, 1868. Eva B. d. 1878.
      3  Byron S. P., b. March 2, 1871.
      4  Nellie W., b. September 22, 1874.
      5  ——, March 24, 1878.

Daniel A. Warren, Jr., b. Aug. 12, 1843, married Anna Nickerson. Children:

  i  Kate, b. March 18, 1872.
  ii  Ethan Alvin, b. November 1, 1875, d. 1889.
  iii  Lizzie A., b. December 1, 1881.

John S. Warren married Artha M. Parker. Children:

  i  Arthur Erdine, b. January 4, 1875.
  ii  Estelle, b. November 27, 1876.
  iii  Gertrude L., b. October 4, 1878.
  iv  John Sanborn, b. August 17, 1883.
  v  Genevieve Leah, b. June 2, 1885.
  vi  Emeline Parker, b. March 19, 1892.

38

## WELCH FAMILY.

Bartholomew Welch married Polly Woodward. Published March 23, 1819. He probably died in Searsport. Children, born in Islesborough :

i  Mary B., b. May 11, 1820.
ii  Benjamin, b. July 15, 1821.
iii  Betsey, b. October 2, 1823.
iv  Adeline, b. March 12, 1827.
v  Abbie, b. November 16, 1830.

## WHITE FAMILY.

Samuel White married Betsey Howard.  Child :

i  Mary Augusta, b. April 22, 1877.

## WHITMORE FAMILY.

George Whitmore.  Child :

i  George, Jr., b. August 14, 1855.

## WILLIAMS FAMILY.

Shubael Williams, from New London, Conn., born about 1730. He came to Islesborough and settled between Crow Cove and Bounty Cove. He married first, Abigail Turner. She died April 5, 1798, aged 71 or 79. He married second, Mrs. Temperance Easton, of Northport. He died July 17, 1804, aged 74, according to his gravestone. Children, not in order :

i  Samuel, d. September 10, 1820, aged 65 years.
ii  Amos, b. March 3, 1758.
iii  Joseph.
iv  Benjamin.
v  Abigail, m. Benjamin Coombs, June 16, 1791.
vi  Lucy, (?) m. —— Marshall.
vii  Rebecca. (?)
viii & ix  Two oldest sons are said never to have come here—Charles and another.

Amos Williams, son of Shubael Williams, born March 3, 1758. Married Betsey Burns, of Bristol. He lived on the west side, below Crow Cove. He died March 15, 1840. She died Nov. 16, 1844, aged 80. Children, not in order:

 i John, b. December 24, 1785, m. Sally Parker.
 ii William, b. February 14, 1789, unmarried, d. February 14, 1861.
 iii Thomas Ames, b. October 13, 1792; married.
 iv Betsey, b. May 7, 1798, m. Nathaniel Pruden, of Castine. Published May 8, 1815.
 v Judith P., b. February 17, 1800, m. Michael Heal, of Lincolnville, August 26, 1824.
 vi Phebe, b. January 25, 1802, m. Elisha R. Trim, January 23, 1834.
 vii Rebecca, (?) m. Zachariah Marshall.
 viii Dorcas, (?) m. James Keller, March 10, 1810.
 ix Polly or Dolly, (?) m. Elisha Philbrook, December 25, 1805.

John Williams, son of Amos, born December 24, 1785. Married Sally, daughter of Mighill Parker, Sept. 1, 1814. He died in Belfast, March 1, 1831. His son, Mighill Parker Williams, has been for many years publisher of a newspaper in Hudson, N. Y. Son John, Jr., drowned in Orland.

Benjamin Williams, son of Shubael, married Jenny Burns, from Bristol, December 26, 1791. She died Aug. 4, 1837, aged 70. He died March 4, 1848, aged 81. Children:

 i Elizabeth, b. December 19, 1792, m. James Gilpatrick.
 ii Abigail, b. December 2, 1794, m. Charles Allen, of Northport. Published July 30, 1820.
 iii Jane, b. August 14, 1796, m. Samuel Marshall, 1830.
 iv Shubael, b. June 29, 1798, d. 1798.
 v Benjamin J., b. October 7, 1799; unmarried, d. 186-.
 vi Temperance, b. April 21, 1801, m. Stephen Pruden, September 11, 1823 first, and second, Rev. Ephraim Emery. Published March 10, 1832.
 vii Fanny Young, b. December 17, 1802, m. Andrew Marshall.
 viii James Burns, b. June 18, 1804, m. Prudence Dodge, Jan. 4, 1849.

ix  William, b. March 16, 1806, unmarried; d. about 1838.
x  Ibri, b. November 5, 1808, d. March 30, 1834.
xi  Julia Ann, b. April 2, 1812, d. October 19, 1841.


James B. Williams, son of Benjamin, born June 18, 1804, married Prudence Dodge, January 4, 1849. He died August 22, 1872. Children:

i  Zilpha J., b. January 29, 1850.
ii  James B., b. October 29, 1852, m. Lavinia Williams.


Joseph Williams, son of Shubael, married Sally, daughter of Cornelius Saunders, March 14, 1804. He lived just below the middle meeting-house. He died April 2, 1842, aged 72. His estate went to his sons, Joseph and Darius, and is now owned by Stephen Babbidge. Children:

i  Judith G., b. December 3, 1805, m. Samuel Gilchrist. He was in the ship Ben Rust, and was lost at sea in 1837, in the South Pacific ocean.
ii  Samuel, b. July 22, 1808, d. young.
iii  Betsey, b. March 7, 1810, m. William Coombs, September 19, 1833.
iv  Sally, b. December 2, 1811, m. Robert Penney, of Knox, December 11, 1833.
v  Robert Trim, b. November 8, 1813; unmarried; d. 1890.
vi  Joseph, b. November 5, 1815; unmarried; d. March, 1864. (?)
vii  Lucy, b. April 14, 1817, m. —— Penney.
viii  Darius, b. April 2, 1819, m. Lucy A. Richards, of Camden. She died. He d. in 1880.


George W. Williams married Martha G. Brown, of Dracut. Published October 26, 1841.


Thomas Ames Williams, son of Amos, born Oct. 13, 1792. He married Lydia, daughter of Jonathan Sprague. Published Aug. 13, 1817. He died May 13, 1866. Wife died March 10, 1863, aged 70 years 5 months. Children:

i  George W., b. April 2, 1818, m. Martha G. Brown; removed to Saco.

ii  Thomas R., b. December 7, 1819, m. Sarah K. Hatch, January 9,
1845. His son Winsor, d. November 24, 1892.

iii  Lydia S., b. March 23, 1821, m. James L. Hatch, December 29,
1841.

iv  Caroline, b. October 25, 1825, unmarried.

v  Emery F., b. July 8, 1828 ; married.

vi  Charlotte, b. October 26. 1830, d. April 15, 1831.

vii  Ellison Newton, b. February 18, 1832, d. October 4, 1833.

viii  David, b. July 21, 1835, d. same day.

ix  Shubael, drowned in Kenduskeag Stream, 1830-2-3, about 12 or
14 years of age.

Emery F. Williams, son of Thomas A., married Charlotte A. Pendleton, December 25, 1850. Children :

i  Lavinia, b. April 21, 1852, m. James B. Williams.

ii  Charles E., b. January 14, 1854, m. Nora Redman.

iii  George, m. Nellie Cobb.

David Williams, from Kennebec, of another family than Shubael Williams. Came here when a young man, and built a camp on Lime Island. He lived there, employed in fishing and gunning, until he was passed middle age, when he married Mrs. Orinda P. Haskell, March 27, 1851. She was the widow of Samuel M. Haskell, and daughter of David Philbrook. Soon after marriage he quitclaimed his interest to Lime Island. He then built a house on Warren's Island, where his children were born. He died in Lincolnville, where he had a brother in 1891. Children :

i  Morris.

ii  Willis.

iii  Edward.

iv  Lucy, m. —— Drinkwater, of Northport.

v  Margaret.

vi  Inez.

## WOODWARD FAMILY.

Peter Woodward, town officer in 1790. Probably from Brunswick.

Joseph Woodward, probably brother of Peter. Hog-reeve in 1790. Drowned in Western Bay.

## WOODWARD MARRIAGES IN ISLESBOROUGH.

Polly, married B. Welch. Published March 23, 1819.

Eunice, married Enos Burr, of Castine. Published June 24, 1822.

Belona, married Michael Warren. Published Nov. 9, 1828.

## WYMAN FAMILY.

William Wyman, from Halifax, Nova Scotia, came to Belfast about 1829, then to Islesborough, 1829-30. He married first in Nova Scotia. He had five children by first wife, who died there. He married second, as "of Belfast," November 20, 1829, Mrs. Lucy Coombs Hewes. He died November 13, 1842, aged 58. She died March 10, 1878. Children by first wife :

    i   Joseph, b. in Halifax.
    ii  John C., b. in Halifax.
    iii William, b. in Halifax.
    iv  Ellen, b. in Halifax.
    v   Albert B., b. in Halifax. Was in Orrington, and married there
        Susan B. Brooks, January 6, 1848. She was b. December 1,
        1823. Moved to Brooklyn, N. Y., where he died, August,
        1877, and his wife January, 1882. Children, born in Orrington :
            1   Ross, b. July 26, 1850, m. and lives in Brooklyn, N. Y.
            2   Brooks, b. April 6, 1853, m. and lives in Brooklyn, N. Y.

Children, not in order, by second wife, born in Isles-borough :

    vi  Jacob W., b. about 1830-31. He married Mary J. Coombs, in
        1853. He and his brothers, Rufus and Jairus, were lost
        at sea, bound from Portland to Tortugas, in the brig Winyaw,
        in 1862. Widow Mary was published to Thomas Williams,
        May 8, 1866. Mr. Williams died on what was to be his

wedding-day, and she subsequently married Isaac Warren. Mrs. Wyman's children were :

    1  William A., b. October, 1853, m. Edith Coburn.
    2  Adelma, (?) b. June 29, 1856, m. first, Charles Coombs, and second, W. Haynes.
    3  Freddie, b. June 5, 1858.

vii  Hosea C., m. Judith Dix. He died. Widow resides in Foxborough, Mass. Children :

    1  Sophronia, b. September 22, 1858, m. David Warren, now of Foxborough, Mass.
    2  Caro, b. October 26, 1860, d. 1877.
    3  Clifford, drowned at sea.

viii  Alonzo Everett, b. ——, married first, Almeda Coombs, July 29, 1858. She d. December 25, 1881. He m. second, Lizzie Veazie. Children :

    1  Effie M., b. January 16, 1860, m. Eben I. Coombs.
    2  Mary C., b. May 27, 1861, m. David Grover.
    3  Hugh M., b. October 19, 1873, d. 1875.
    4  Rose M., b. August 21, 187-.
    5  Bessie.
    6  Almeda, b. ——, d. December 23, 1881.
    7  Alberta, b. June 8, 1876, d. 1879.

ix  Jairus, b. April 29, 1841. Lost at sea with his brother Jacob, 1862.
x  Lucy, b. ——, m. John M. Coombs.
xi  George T., b. ——, m. Laurinda A. Sprague, February 7, 1859. He died. She m. second.
xii  Edward Austin, b. March 23, 1847, m. Rosanna, daughter of Pillsbury Coombs, July 7, 1868.
xiii  Rufus, b. November 23, 1843, lost at sea, 1862.

## YATES FAMILY.

William S. Yates.  Children, born in Islesborough :

i  Ruby A., b. February 22, 1857.
ii  Lucy B., b. July 24, 1858.
iii  Sarah W., b. July 18, 1861.
iv  Warren, Thomas, and Alexina, not born in Islesborough.

Thomas W. Yates married Addie Andrews.  He died in 1879.  Child :

i  Reuben E., b. October 29, 1875, d. in 1879.

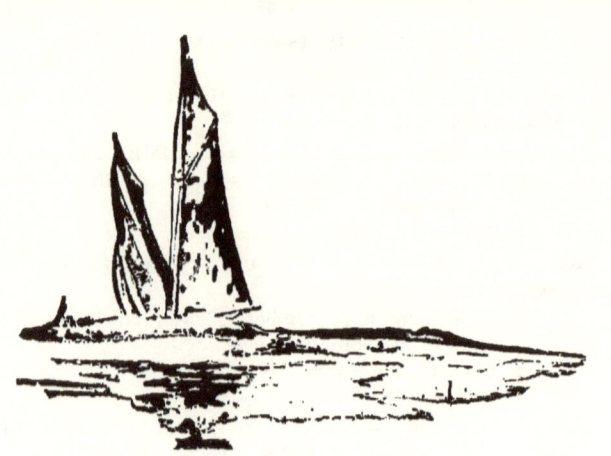

VIEW SOUTHWARD FROM ISLESBOROUGH INN.

# ISLESBOROUGH AS A SUMMER RESORT.*

THE gem of Penobscot Bay, like all of greatest value, best shows its worth in a plain setting; though the ever-changing heavens and their faithful mirror beneath can scarcely be termed a plain, but a perfect setting for the scintillations and the shadows of this treasure. From the bold cliffs on the upper point to the sloping, shelving beach at the southern extremity, each shore is cut and grooved into entrancing irregularity of inlet, bay, beach, bluff, until there are no duplicates of picture the length and breadth of this charming isle. More beautiful in its ever-changing moods than can be reproduced by art.

When it first became known to the outside world, as a pleasure ground, health resort, or blessed retreat from the busy, bustling crowd, there are no exact dates, but a generation ago many names of note are found as habitues of this spot, and doubtless, could we read the soul's record, much of the inspiration which photographs the wild flower or landscape, the summer sea or rolling wave of more than one poet's pictured verse, is due to his love of this spot.

---

* This chapter was contributed to this history by a lady who has spent twelve summers on the island, and who is abundantly qualified to write.

39

On which of the headlands of this island lay our Maine
poet * when he sang :

"I lay upon the headland height and listened
To the incessant sobbing of the sea
In caverns under me,
And watched the waves that tossed and
Fled and glistened,
Until the rolling meadows of amethyst
Melted away in mist."

Those who have feasted their eyes on the beauties of
Turtle Head and its surroundings, need only the name to
recall the spot, beautiful for situation ; its rounded outline
jutting into the upper bay, and so densely covered with
the fragrant pine that avenues have been cut through the
groves to allow frequent views of the ever-changing waters
below and beyond. Across the bay eastward stands the
bold promontory of Castine Head, with its "street lamp of
the ocean" prominent on the rugged cliff, a grateful point
to the eyes of artist as well as mariner.   Beyond the water
at the north the view is made picturesque by the bold shore
of Fort Point, its rounded top crowned with the summer
home "Woodcliff," and its horse-shoe beach lined with
cottages, owned by devotees at the shrine of beauty spread
before them here.   Westward, over the gleaming bay, lie
the irregular shores of the pretty city of Belfast, and the
curves and beaches of the old towns of Northport and
Lincolnville ; while the horizon line discovers ranges of
undulating hills and mountains, sloping to the sea in green
field or groves of evergreen, or pastures fringed with the
cone-shaped cedar.

The rides to Turtle Head, both on the eastern and
western shores, are justly designated two of the most

* His brother, A. W. Longfellow, of the U. S. Coast Survey, spent
one summer at Sabbath-Day Harbor, and Rev. Samuel Longfellow,
another brother, was a visitor often to Penobscot Bay ; and I believe the poet himself was occasionally here, many years ago.

beautiful on the island. The place is of interest to all. Its natural attractiveness is increased by the artistic taste and hospitality of the dwellers by the sea.

On the east coast of Long Island, "Sabbath-Day Harbor" has long been a place of resort, and to those who have loitered here the long summer days through, year after year, every spot has its associations and interest, from the beach, dotted with the first summer cottages built on the island, to the Bluff which protects the harbor, with its bold sides and front. Coombs' Bluff stands boldly out into the bay, raising itself one hundred and forty feet above tide water; the highest land excepting Warren's Mountain, at the south end, on the fourteen miles of undulating surface of the island. This bluff forms a natural breakwater for the harbor, which curves in on the western side of the bluff and up into the land till it forms a firmly-sheltered harbor, for a fleet of small vessels. Here the ancient fishermen came to lie at anchor and keep the quiet rest of the Lord's day, naming it in their quaint style "Sabbath-Day Harbor." Here came the first summer visitors, for a day or a week, to watch the sunrise over the bluff. Wearied with the bustle of towns, their first sweet sleep is broken by the very stillness, then a bird's sleepy note recalls a sense of life, next a consciousness of listening for other sounds; a gleam of twilight through the open window; the dip of an oar at a long distance, but coming nearer with such rhythm that it is just the even pulse of nature, which with each beat brings more of the day; rosy light breaks the eastern sky and spreads low and high over Cape Rosier's long outline till the heavens are glowing and the water spreads out from the shores of Castine and the cape to the corresponding ones of bluff and beach, a mass of moulten color. The stillness; the shadows in the harbor; the gorgeous sunrising above the headland, into the glowing day, filled with the life-tonic of salt sea air, no words can picture.

The day is done, the sun has gone down behind the western mountains of Camden, leaving billows of gorgeous crimson and silver and blue above, and a repetition of all this color in the sea. As the "curtain from unseen hands" falls down, all turn to send their eyes across the bay for the beacon light of Eagle Island. The stars come out, one and another, and another, until never were the heavens . so luminous; never the stars so numerous. The moon comes up out of the sea beyond the Cape and sends her beams, a widening way of shimmering light, to shore.

To those who have dwelt here, while the June blossoms faded, and the fragrant wild rose budded, bloomed and brightened every wayside, covered every heap of rocks, or appropriated all neglected field corners and decaying stumps, born to bloom and blush unseen by the thousands and then fall to give place to the golden harvest of September; there are no sights more beautiful, no associations more heartful. Here they have truly lived, the fathers and mothers older and happier, with the wax and wane of these summer moons, the children grown to youths, then lovers, and still returning to spend their honeymoons, renewed each year in this dear spot.

Here is the comfortable house named "The Islesborough," built in 1885, as an extension to the original house, which was built in 1868 for a dwelling house, and to accommodate a few lovers of this harbor, who each year returned to refresh themselves with its beautiful views, sailing and healthful breezes. These friends returned bringing others so numerous that the proprietor was obliged to build this addition, which grew to be much larger than the original. At the present time it will accommodate about one hundred guests, and is a house much frequented by visitors at this charming resort.

VIEW FROM COOMBS' BLUFF, SABBATH-DAY HARBOR.

SHORE AT COOMBS' BLUFF, SABBATH-DAY HARBOR.

THE ISLESBOROUGH, SABBATH-DAY HARBOR.

VIEW AT BOUNTY COVE.

Two miles below Sabbath-Day Harbor lies "Bounty Cove." Perhaps the great gift of beauty suggested its name. This harbor, protected by a rugged wooded cliff, which extends far into the bay, forms one of the most placid seas. The sloping fields beyond with their crescent-shaped beach, suggest a paradise for the salt sea bathers.

Hewes' Point, which forms the barrier to the Atlantic waves, was the second spot appropriated by summer cottagers. About the shore of this point have clustered a number of picturesque cottages, with a background of groves and hills which charm all eyes. Nowhere on the island are there more lovely bits of landscape than at and from this point with its beautiful groves and bold shore. This land rises one hundred and thirty feet above the water, and on the highest part there is an observatory, than from which no more charming view of Penobscot Bay can be obtained. The wonderfully-diversified outline of the island first attracts, then the sea and land lie before one. Island and bay, mountain and sea, make up such completeness of beauty that one must take them as a whole before a single "bit" can be designated. A clear morning or evening light enjoyed from this spot will mark that day with a white stone. Every season, with the springing grass, comes the householder to his own, to which he adds artistic contributions of shrubs and flowers, to glow and brighten after the wild sweet briars have faded.

The western coast, with its broad bay dotted with islands varying in contour and extent, has its summer dwellers and lovers. On one of its points stands a white lighthouse, which adds interest to the scene from every view. So great a proportion of the inhabitants are those who go down to the sea in ships, all that pertains to their safety must be of special interest. The western bay is seldom without its fleet of sailing craft, than which

nothing fashioned by man's hand is more beautiful.
Through this western bay come the larger steamers to
their ports on the opposite shores of Camden and Belfast.
These all add much to the panorama of sea and shore.
A morning drive down the west coast of the island, when
the sun is behind and eyes can stretch over islands and
sea to the opposite shores and the long slopes and sharp
peaks of Camden mountains, is an event to be remembered; a picture from which no line of beauty can be
missed.          .

If there is one spot more perfect than all others, it is
Gilkey's Harbor, from the old farm-house known as the
"Ames place." The house stands alone, and elevated
about a hundred feet above the water, and a thousand feet
from it, with the rolling greensward stretching down to
the quiet sea below. The upper part of the harbor is
protected by the long arm of Grindle's Point, on which
stands the lighthouse, and the lower part by an archi-
pelago of islands, thus securing a safe harbor for ships of
any size. *Across the western bay the Camden mountains,
flooded by sunlight, define the horizon line, and hem in
this pacific sea and set the perfect picture.

This farm, with much adjoining territory, has been purchased by the Islesborough Land and Improvement Company, which has opened new roads for driving to different
points of interest and beauty through the southern half of
the island. The larger part of the land of this section is
high and sightly, with groves of evergreen trees, both
along the indented shores and covering a large part of the
interior.

From the "Narrows," about midway of the island,
where it is nearly bisected at high water, the land is
narrower and cut deeply by bays and inlets on either side.
The most picturesque of these is Dark Harbor, on the
east side. Here the Land and Improvement Company

ISLESBOROUGH INN—EASTERLY VIEW.

ISLESBOROUGH INN—WESTERLY VIEW.

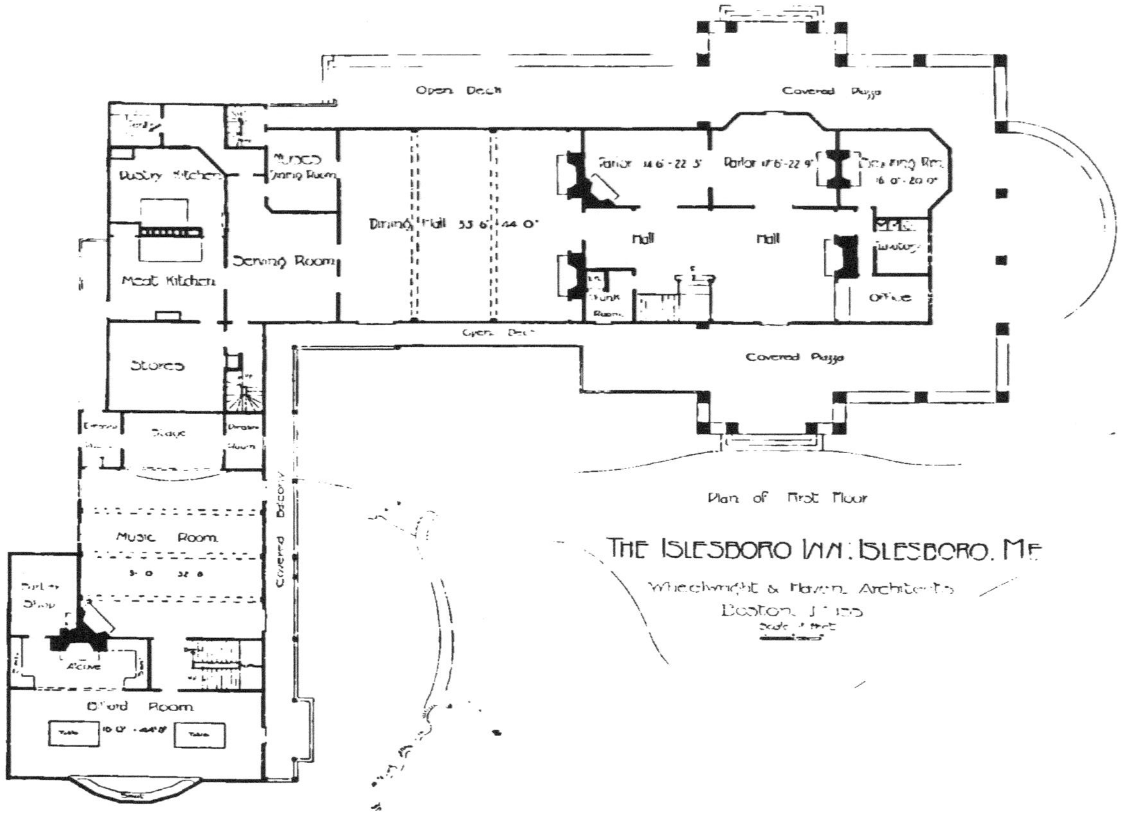
Open Deck
Covered Piazza
Dining Room
Pastry Kitchen
Serving Room
Meat Kitchen
Dining Hall 33 6" 44 0"
Parlor 14 6" 22 5"
Parlor 17 6" 22 9"
Drawing Rm. 16 0" 20 0"
Hall
Hall
Lavatory
Trunk Room
Office
Open Deck
Covered Piazza
Stores
Stage
Covered Balcony
Music Room
Barber Shop
Alcove
Billiard Room
Table
Table

Plan of First Floor

THE ISLESBORO INN: ISLESBORO, ME

Wheelwright & Haven, Architects

Boston

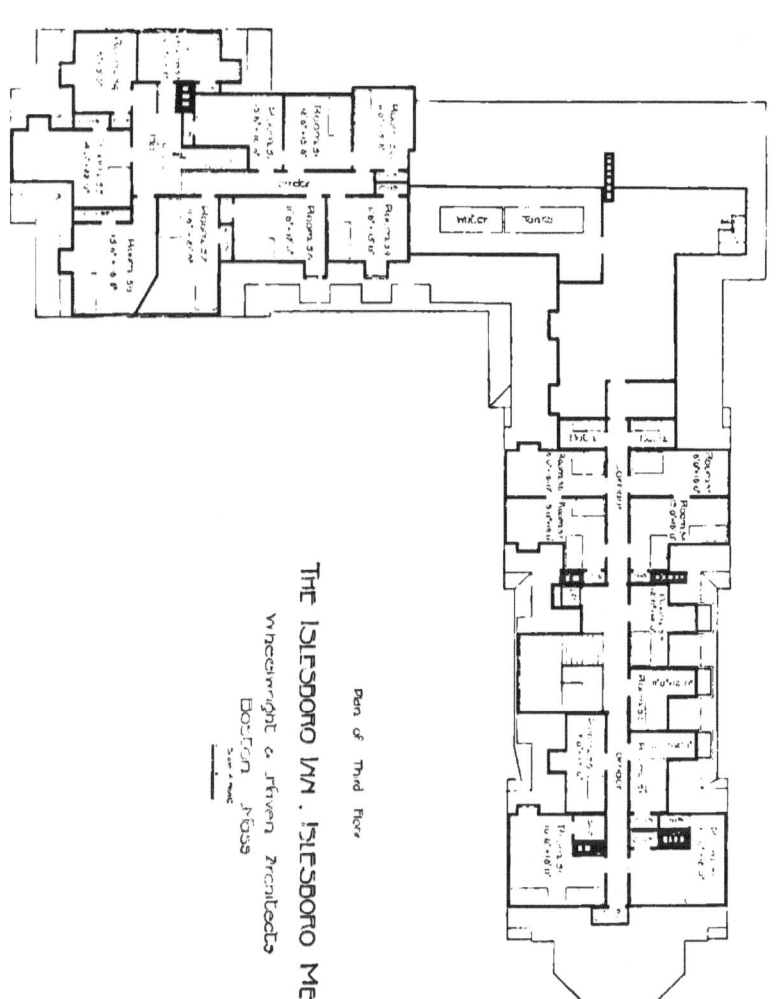

Plan of Third Floor

THE ISLESBORO INN . ISLESBORO ME.

Wheelwright & Haven Architects

Boston Mass

have erected "The Islesborough Inn," on a charming height, which overlooks on the west Gilkey's Harbor, the slumbering islands, and the western bay with its passing fleet of sailing craft and steamers. The views from the east are over the numerous islands of the lower Penobscot Bay, including the justly-famed Isle au Haut,— whose shores are washed by the unbroken waves of the Atlantic—the larger and smaller Deer Isles, and many smaller and more neighborly islands. More easterly, only four miles across the bay, stretches Cape Rosier, and over it the mountains of South-West and Bar Harbors are prominent landmarks.

This fine house, in its situation and appointments, is not surpassed in New England, and its guests only depart with the breath of autumn to return with the summer sun. Already there are fine residences erected in many directions, on most desirable locations, but where all is so complete, it is only the individual taste which determines the location. Not only is the scenery beautiful, but by healthful sanitary arrangements made by the Land Company the sewerage and water supply are perfected. It is quite as impossible to represent perfectly this desirable house, the improvements made on the lands, while nature still is kept in charming simplicity, as it is to faithfully present the whole beauty of Long Island.

# ADDITIONS AND CORRECTIONS.

Page 114.—Schooner Sea (or May) Flower sailed on a voyage to the West Indies. She foundered at sea, having on board William Williams, Josiah Farrow, George Warren and James Sherman, who were picked up and carried to the East Indies, and returned home after an absence of twenty-two months.

Page 257—Dodge Pendleton died Feb. 22, 1893.

Page 298—Shubael Williams married second, Mrs. Temperance Eastes.

Page 239—Capt. William Pendleton Jr.'s family corrected. Children, probably not in order :

  i  Job, b. 1747, d. in Islesborough, January 25, 1794, aged 47.
  ii  Lydia, m. Jacob Crandall, January 24, 1768 ; did not come here.
  iii  John, b. 1751, of Islesborough. He died in Camden, December, 1830.
  iv  Oliver, of Islesborough, died in Hope, a very old man.
  v  Jonathan, of Islesborough, d. September 25, 1841, an aged man.
  vi  Henry, of Islesborough, d. in Northport about 1844, aged 84.
  vii  Mary, b. November 14, 1766, m. Isaiah Wilcox and settled in New York State.
  viii  Bridget, b. 1769, twin with Dorothy or Judith, m. Robert Farnsworth, of Bristol and Islesborough.
  ix  Dorothy.
  x  Judith.

The Belfast, Islesborough and Northport Telegraph and Telephone Company was incorporated in 1891, and organized the same year. Capt. W. S. Pendleton, of Islesborough, was elected President. The Company propose to build their line this year.

Page 6—Chapter 6—Abstract of Contents should be Shubael Williams instead of Shubael Pendleton.

Page 81—Engraving should be Thomas Ames' house instead of Benjamin.

Page 84—For Mrs. Boardman read Miss Boardman.

Page 156—For William F. Gates read William F. Yates.

Page 178—Elder Ephraim Coombs' portrait.

Page 220—Deacon James Hatch's portrait.

Page 234—John B. Moody's father, Caleb, drowned in Searsmont Pond. John B. Moody's children :
i  Ina — died at age of 12 years.
ii  Lizzie Jane and Betsey Ana died.
iii  Caleb Simmons, married Nora Fairfield.
iv  Adin Stanley married Bertha I. Warren.
v  Ruth Edna married Walter Decker.

Page 237—For Flora C. read Elma.

Page 244—Second line for three years read three months.

Page 252—For Elisha K. Pendleton read Joseph K. Pendleton.

Page 254—Last two lines for Samuel read Lemuel and for Samuel A. read Lemuel A. Pendleton.

Page 259—Mark Pierce Pendleton appointed Consul to Picton, N. S., 1893.

Page 216—Priscilla Grinnell m. Appollos Alden of Belfast, November 2, 1807. Mrs. Priscilla Alden m. Captain Joshua Cottrell, July 3, 1836, both of Belfast. Mrs. Priscilla Alden, widow of Appollos Alden, died October 10, 1868, aged 80. I cannot reconcile these. The Alden children were :
i  Darius Alden, b. March 5, 1809, d. in Augusta, November 21, 1889. Man of wealth.
ii  William O. Alden, b. April 3, 1810, of Belfast, d. May 1890. Left his mother Priscilla Cottrell $300 a year. She died before him.
iii  Sarah Jane Alden.

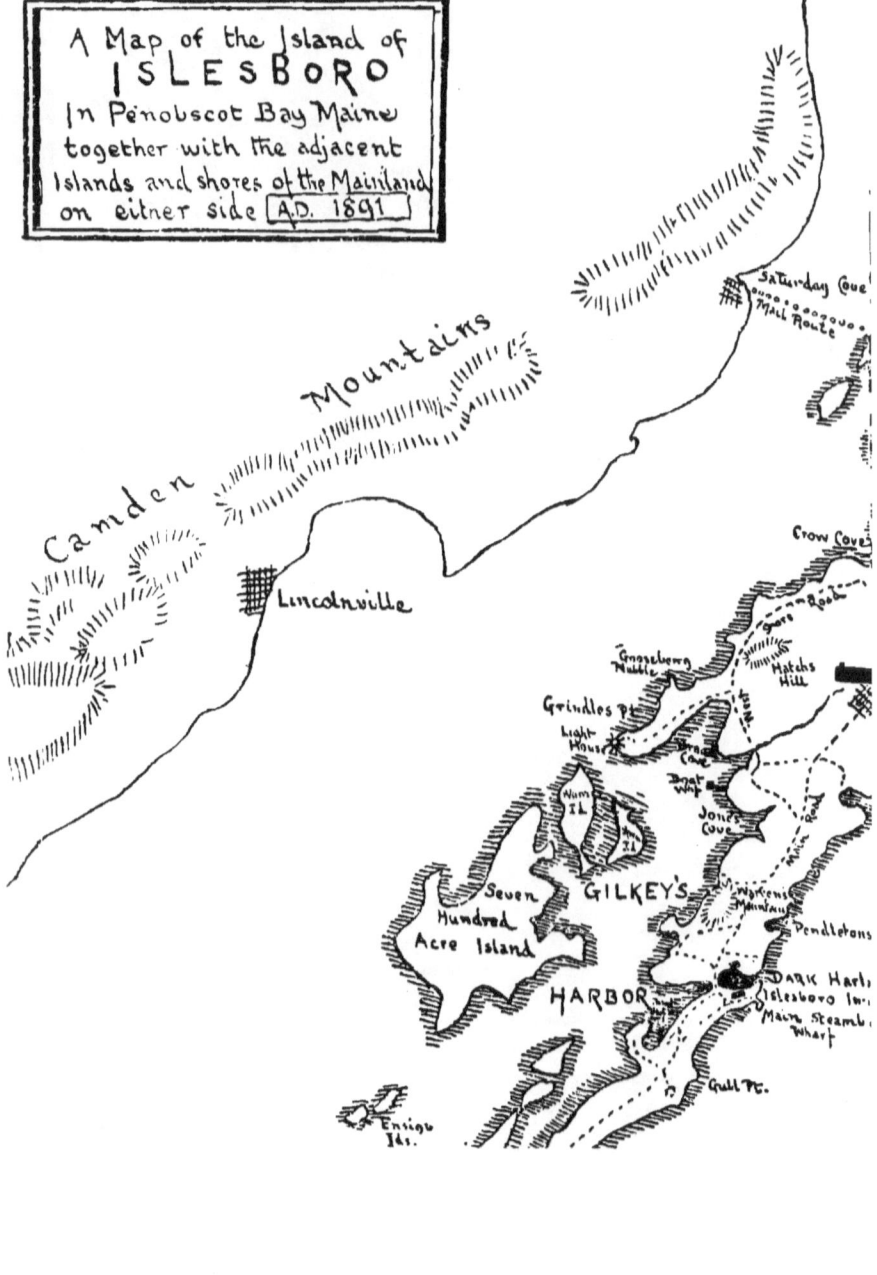

A Map of the Island of
**ISLESBORO**
In Penobscot Bay Maine
together with the adjacent
Islands and shores of the Mainland
on either side A.D. 1891

Camden Mountains

Saturday Cove
Mail Route

Lincolnville

Crow Cove

Gooseberry Nubble

Hatch's Hill

Grindles Pt

Light House

Jones Cove

Num 1A

Num 2A

Warren's Mountain

Pendletons

Seven Hundred Acre Island

GILKEY'S

HARBOR

Dark Harb.
Islesboro Inn
Main Steamb.
Wharf

Gull Pt.

Ensign Ids.

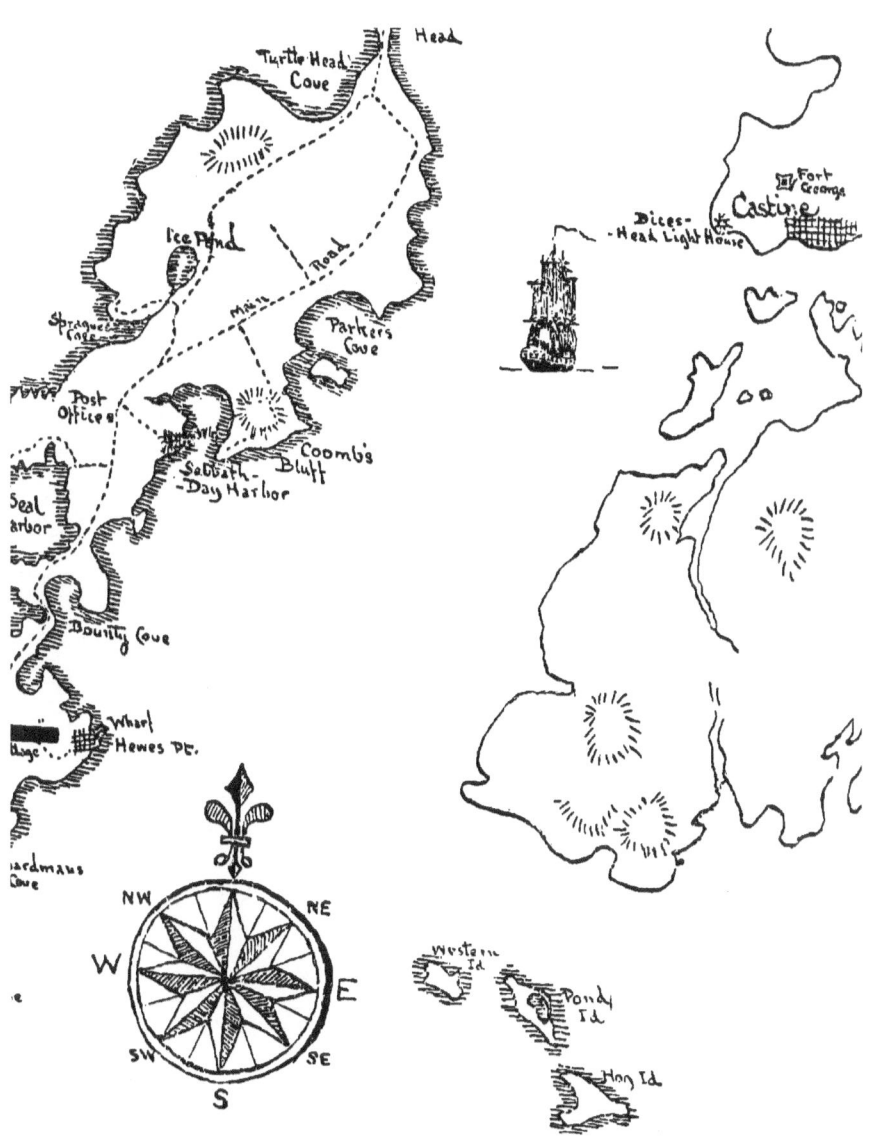